# Mister Memory

*Marcus Sedgwick*

# Mister Memory

MULHOLLAND
BOOKS
HODDER

First published in Great Britain in 2016 by Mulholland Books
An imprint of Hodder & Stoughton
An Hachette UK company

1

Copyright © Marcus Sedgwick 2016

The right of Marcus Sedgwick to be identified as the Author of the Work has been
asserted by him in accordance with the Copyright, Designs and Patents Act 1988.

A CIP catalogue record for this title is available from the British Library

Hardback ISBN 978 1 444 75198 7
Trade Paperback ISBN 978 1 444 75199 4
eBook ISBN 978 1 444 75200 7

Typeset by Hewer Text UK Ltd, Edinburgh
Printed and bound by Clays Ltd, St Ives plc

Hodder & Stoughton policy is to use papers that are natural, renewable and recyclable
products and made from wood grown in sustainable forests. The logging and manufacturing
processes are expected to conform to the environmental regulations of the country of origin.

Hodder & Stoughton Ltd
Carmelite House
50 Victoria Embankment
London EC4Y 0DZ

www.hodder.co.uk

For Ruth, with thanks

# MEMORY

# THE FACTS

The facts of the matter were these:

At a little before ten o'clock in the evening of the first Saturday in July 1899, Marcel Després returned home to his studio apartment in the Cour du Commerce, the narrow passage that connects the Rue Saint-André-des-Arts and the Boulevard Saint-Germain.

Reaching his rooms on the sixth floor, he discovered his young wife, Ondine, *in flagrante delicto* with an American man not unknown to the couple. Després shot his wife dead, then, at the urging of her lover, fled down into the passage, where he suddenly stopped, falling to his knees.

He was arrested by two g*ardiens de la paix* and held in the local Commissariat de Police for two days, when he was declared insane by the Préfecture, and committed to the asylum of Salpêtrière, under the care of Dr Lucien Morel.

Such were the facts of the matter. In Paris, in the years before the century ended, such events were commonplace. The story might have won a few inches of newspaper column, perhaps even merited a portrait of victim and culprit, but only until the next bloody crime displaced it from public view. And so Marcel Després may have rotted out the rest of his days in the Asile de Salpêtrière, were it not for the remarkable finding that Dr Morel made about his new patient some days after his incarceration. For while Morel had various cases of amnesia in his ward, he soon learned that his newcomer had the very opposite relationship with memory.

The memory of Marcel Després was, for want of any other word, perfect. It was total. Complete. He forgot nothing.

*Absolutely* nothing. As the days went by and the doctor tested and tested again, creating ever more elaborate systems by which to measure his patient's skill, he started to draw the only conclusion possible: that Marcel's memory was without limit. It was infinite in scale, if scale is a word that can be applied correctly in the presence of infinity.

For every experience, sight, sound, smell, moment, event, thought, emotion, feeling, the assimilation of every mundane circumstance and outrageous deed that passed into the mind of Marcel Després, once there, could not be forgotten. To Marcel Després, *everything* was not to be forgotten, but to those who met him, it was Marcel himself who was unforgettable.

# FAIRY TALES

Paris at that time can be described as a fairy tale; assuming it's understood that fairy tales are brutish, dark and violent.

Of course, there is beauty in the old stories, a great deal of beauty: there are princesses, who are as simple and pure as they are pretty; there are roses; there are castles. There are slippers of glass and ball gowns. There are other kinds of beauty too: handsome heroes; young men with rare gifts such as courage and honesty. There is both good and bad, and the chances of survival of our hero often depend upon how well he, or she, sees which is which, for what can seem beautiful can hide the greatest evil. A beautiful glass goblet of deep red wine, an apple fresh from the tree: yet both are laden with poison. The young woman who helps you in the forest is, underneath her enchanted appearance, an evil old crone. The stepmother who is meant to protect you throws you to the mercy of the wolves in the forest; the forest itself, so beautiful from a distance, up close is rotting trunks, crawling beetles, nests of ants and the infecting spores of obscene fungi.

This is how it was with the city of light. The place had a claim not only to be the capital city of France, but the world's capital too, at the forefront of developments in all fields of human activity. In art, in music, in literature and theatre. In the sciences and in technology. In medicine, and in policing, and in architecture too; in a generation Haussmann's rebuilding of the city had transformed it from something essentially medieval, a beast of putrefaction, into a modern city with nobler aspirations. The World's Fair of 1889 had seen the construction of Eiffel's tower:

5

initially derided and intended to be merely temporary, in no time at all it became the beloved iconic landmark of the city, which no one would ever dream of tearing down. And across the river to the north, on the far side of the city on the hill of Montmartre, stood another great escapade in construction, half built: the basilica of the sacred heart, Le Sacré-Coeur.

It's facile but nonetheless true to say that we can only be aware of light with the existence of darkness, and both of them were alive and well in Paris. Yet both the beauty and the darkness of the city could be found symbolised in this work in progress. In 1899 it was not yet thirty years since the city had last convulsed in revolution and blood-letting, during the two months of the Commune, until the army had brutally restored order to the city with a week of summary executions in which ten, some said twenty, thousand were killed, turning the waters of the Seine red. So: Sacré-Coeur, designed as both a memorial to the dead and a penance for the crimes of the Communards. But where did the authorities of the status quo decide it should be built than on the hill of Montmartre, right in the heart of the revolutionary camp, and a clearer symbol of implied power it is therefore harder to imagine. And yet, where else should it be built than on Montmartre? *Montmartre*, the hill of the martyrs, so called because it is said that Saint Denis, Bishop of Paris, was decapitated here by pagan priests, fearful of the great number of his conversions. Then again, it is also said that after his head was removed with a sword he picked it up and walked six miles, preaching a sermon as he went, so perhaps we should not take all old stories too seriously.

Paris, like those old stories, was full of both darkness and light. For the forces of light we may count among many others the following: Maurice Ravel, Henri de Toulouse-Lautrec and Pablo Picasso, Guy de Maupassant and Émile Zola, art nouveau, champagne, the cinematograph, telephony, the electric light itself. These and their friends represent the movement upward towards the light, the striving for better and higher things, and to look once at the surface of the city is to see these things and smile. But, appropriately enough, it is a French word that truly captures the nature of La Belle Époque, and the word is *façades*.

For just behind the door, behind the red velvet curtain, beyond the imposing front of that elegant house, are the forces of the underworld: Les Apaches, the gangs of Montmartre; the shanty towns on the ruins of the old fortifications, where the *zoniers* picked through the scraps of the rich and barely survived; the *maisons closes*, brothels only distinguishable by the over-sized numbers above their doors; and, everywhere, crime. Crimes of violence, crimes of greed, crimes of passion; crimes of all three combined. As the century wound up, the Paris police were in danger of being overwhelmed by the sheer quantity of daily acts of law-breaking, and though they had grown again and again in size and sophistication, there were always more criminals than police, and not just ordinary everyday burglars and robbers, fraudsters and cheats, but darker forces at work within the city too, organised networks.

And there is one more ingredient to be found in fairy tales. It is in fact the very thing that truly defines the form: magic. Without magic, a fairy tale is only a folk tale, and that, after all, is no more than a mundane story told between friends and neighbours.

Of genuine magic in Paris, there was probably none to be found. Of *illusion*, there was plenty. That was what the entire city was about: that the truth of what was really happening lay behind the pretty façades. It was as if the whole city was saying, *Don't look at that, look at this! I will show you what I want you to see, and you will be so dazzled by its beauty and its brightness that you won't look any further, you won't want to look any further. You know the darkness is there, but why look at that? When I can give you what you want . . . pleasure.*

If there was one centre of illusion in Belle Époque Paris, if there was one place where light and dark sat in the open, hand in hand and unashamed, it was the cabarets. And this is the right moment to return to Marcel Després, because Marcel was not usually known by his real surname, but by the name he wore on stage: Monsieur Mémoire, Mister Memory.

He'd come to the city ten years before. He'd come, as his name suggests, 'from the meadows', from the village of Étoges, a place that would have been utterly unremarkable were it not for its location in the heart of champagne country. That alone turned what would otherwise have been a sleepy hamlet of eight horses and a dozen cockerels into an industrious community that turned sweat into sparkling glory, most of it crated up and trundled away to the capital.

Marcel was the late and only child of a couple who'd spent their lives breaking their backs in the vineyards around the village. He never knew it but he'd been conceived one late summer day between two rows of vines on a curving hillside. His father, Nicolas, had travelled a little but, failing to make his mark on the world, had returned to the village of his birth, still unwed in his forties. His mother, Celeste, had never been away. She had been married before but her first husband had never given her children. To add insult to injury, he'd been killed in an accident, having fallen drunk into a slurry pit from which he never surfaced, at least not until they dragged his body out the following day.

Nicolas and Celeste made eyes at each other across the rows of vines all that summer of '66, until finally the warmth of the sun and the sweat trickling down their necks and the luscious eroticism of the hanging clusters of grapes had proved too much for them to delay any longer. They'd barely spoken a word to each other before they found themselves mostly naked and powerfully swept up by the utter physical joy, the urging, of their act. But this was no casual fling: once the ice had been broken and the desire had subsided, they found a good and genuine friend in each other. They lay between the vines all that night, talking, scampering away only at dawn when the first *vignerons* returned to the harvest.

Nicolas moved in with Celeste, and it was there, in a little terraced house on the amusingly named Grande Rue, that Marcel was born.

From the beginning, it was clear that Marcel was not like the other children of the village. They did what they were supposed to do: namely, go to school but hate it, run riot around the pond in the evenings, get a clip on the ear when they deserved it, drag their feet to church on Sundays, and grow up to be a sturdy and loyal worker of the vineyards. Marcel did none of these things. Even as a young child, he showed no intention to venture into the world. He did not run and play, he sat and watched. He was well behaved, he did not lie. He did not complain, whine, fight and brawl with the other kids, nor did he climb trees or sneak over the wall to swim in the moat of the local chateau, as the other children claimed they wanted to but never actually did. He went to school obediently, and he did what was required of him. He studied and he took tests, but he did not shine. It seemed he was no great academic either, something Celeste had been secretly hoping for him given his lack of physicality. It is remarkable, given what was to come later, that his extraordinary memory remained unde- tected throughout not only his childhood, but his early adulthood too. Perhaps this can only be explained by his unwillingness, or even refusal, to engage with the world around him. Marcel did not *do*. He sat, and he watched, and, we can only assume, he waited, though what he was waiting for, his parents never knew.

And Marcel did not work. Not properly. They put him in the rows of vines, along with almost everyone else in the village. The work required no thought, none whatsoever, but it needed stamina, and that was something Marcel seemed to lack. Celeste was a short woman, Nicolas a slightly taller man, but from somewhere Marcel had grown to be one metre eighty at the age of fifteen.

The village doctor knew exactly what was wrong with him.

'He grew too fast!' he declared, often and at volume, as if exasperated by the feeble body before him. Marcel would stand quietly, without speaking, as the doctor would throw his hands in the air and walk round in a tiny circle before appearing in front of Marcel again. 'He grew too fast!' Then the hands. As if it were Marcel's fault, or Celeste's.

Marcel became a man. He had no friends. There were no girls, save one. Ginette, the doctor's daughter, had seen Marcel on his frequent visits to the surgery and quite rightly found him handsome. How Celeste encouraged her son to respond to Ginette's interest in him! It would be a good match, this little romance; the doctor's daughter, well off, and a little quieter, a little more respectable, than the other young people. But it was not to be. Ginette tried and tried to have Marcel notice her, interact with her, respond to her, and though Marcel was never rude, and always enjoyed her company, Celeste's 'little romance' dwindled to nothing like an unkept fire.

So Marcel worked a little when he was able, and otherwise pottered around at home, cooking and cleaning so his mother wouldn't have to do it when she and Nicolas got home from the vines.

Then, early in 1889, both his parents died. The influenza that year was a bad one; it struck many in the village over the winter. Marcel became ill too, and of the three you would have laid good money that he would be the one to expire, but it seems that finally his feeble body decided to fight, to kick into life and begin to work. He survived, while his parents, their bodies prematurely aged and weakened from the endless toil in the vineyards, did not. Nicolas and Celeste were put in a grave together in the small cemetery on the edge of the village, within sight of the rows of vines where they found each other.

Marcel was lost. His parents had been loving and good to him; they seemed to understand and forgive his peculiarities where others in the village did not. They had been his whole world. He had the house, which had been his mother's, but he had no income. He fell into debt, and finally he came to a drastic solution. The idea was put into his head by Ginette's father.

'Go to Paris!' he said to Marcel one day. 'Sell the house, clear your debts, and set yourself up in Paris. They are building the World's Fair. They need many, many men. I read about it in the papers. All hands required, all kinds of work. They're still building that metal tower, high into the sky! There must be work to be had there, or at the exhibition grounds. Perhaps Paris will suit you better than our little village has so far.'

Marcel thought about the doctor's idea. He thought about it for a long week, during which, had anyone been present to see him, they would have found him sitting on an old chair in the kitchen, staring into space, or standing at his parents' bedroom window, gazing out across the vineyards. No one could have known what was going through his mind. Nevertheless, at the end of the week, he somehow decided to act. The house was sold with all the furniture, debts were cleared, a trunk was packed, train timetables consulted. And sooner than he could have imagined, it was time to go.

Marcel arrived in Paris, as the expression has it, like a flower. Naïve and trusting, open and guileless, the city might have destroyed him. He arrived in the spring of '89, too late to help construct anything, and yet there was still plenty of work to be had. He found an apartment in the Latin Quarter, the cheapest he could find, on the sixth floor in the little passage known as the Cour du Commerce, and he started his life over again.

He worked!

He worked as a kitchen hand, a porter, a ticket collector, a doorman. He cleaned tables in cafés, dug ditches, swept the streets, and in all these jobs, the same result: the sack. No matter how simple the task he was given, it seemed he could not focus. He would be found staring into space as if deep in thought. He would stare at a chair, or a poster on the wall, and once it had happened often enough in each occupation, he was told to leave.

Still his memory remained undetected, but not for much longer, because his fortunes were to improve. Somehow, he got a junior position in a newspaper office. His job was another simple one, involving the adjustment of two small screws mounted into the frame on the top of the printing cylinder, to control the blackness of the type. Too little pressure and the type would be illegible, too much and it would be blotched. He seemed able to do this delicate but extremely boring task with great skill, and for once his employer, the perpetually bewildered Monsieur LeChat, seemed happy enough with him.

On 12 February 1894, however, history intervened in the life of Marcel Després, and set him on the road to becoming Marcel Mémoire.

There was an explosion at the Café Terminus, Gare Saint-Lazare. It was the work of an anarchist named Émile Henry, but though it was not the first such event, all of Paris was in uproar over this one; it was the most despicable to date. The perpetrator was French! And educated and formerly respectable to boot. Monsieur LeChat made to dispatch his reporters but, the attack occurring in the evening, they were not to hand. He sent errand boys to find them, and learned that his best two were already in their cups in one of the seedier cafés along the Boulevard Saint-Germain. LeChat, in his usual frantic manner, was dismayed that this major event would go unreported by his paper. It was around half past ten when an urchin knocked on Marcel's door up on the sixth floor in the Cour du Commerce; in his desperation, the newspaperman had sent after every able-bodied man he had, even that rather quiet and odd man who watched the ink for him.

Marcel excelled himself.

On returning to the print offices he produced voluminous, detailed and wide-ranging accounts of his interviews with seven different witnesses to the affair. He was focused and fast.

'Excellent! Good!' cried LeChat as Marcel gave his story. 'Fascinating detail. Excellent!'

Then, LeChat himself hastily prepared a report from this verbal account of Marcel's, ordering the presses to be set for immediate printing. They would have the story on every street corner and on every café countertop by dawn, and it was only when LeChat had dispatched the typesetters to do their work that he stopped short, his whirlwind stilling for once. The colour drained from his face, as if frozen by the discovery of a terrible act, and he turned a glare of suppressed fury upon innocent Marcel.

'What game are you pulling on me, boy?' he said.

Marcel shook his head blankly.

LeChat waved a hand at him. 'You think it's funny? Making that stuff up?'

'Sir?' said Marcel.

'No notes, boy. You took no notes.'

It was true. In his haste to take down the story, LeChat had scribbled and scribbled, barely looking up, not realising until now that Marcel had not been reading from a notebook, but merely recounted from memory what he had learned.

'I didn't need notes, sir,' Marcel explained, but that was enough to propel the incendiary nature of Monsieur LeChat into hyperactivity.

'Didn't need notes!' he roared. 'You gave me the names not only of the café owner but all the staff! You gave me the names of all the policemen present, all of them! You gave me the names of the inspectors from the Sûreté. You gave me not just the names, but the addresses too, of all the victims. And you expect me to believe you did that without notes?'

Marcel did expect him to believe that.

He stood there silently. He was wondering what the problem was, but he was not stupid, and it was starting to dawn on him.

'I don't need notes, sir,' he said, and he said it with such innocence and honesty that it took the wind right from LeChat.

'Don't need notes?' he said. 'Don't need . . . You remembered all that? Everything you just told me?'

Marcel nodded. 'Yes, sir.'

LeChat's temper rose one final time before dying for good. 'You're not having me on, are you, boy? I'll wring your neck!'

'No, sir.'

Marcel's open face, his utter honesty, won through. LeChat peered closely at his young apprentice.

'Well, I . . . That's . . . That's remarkable. How do you do it, boy? Some trick?'

'No,' said Marcel. 'No trick. I just remember.'

So the paper ran the story of the Gare Saint-Lazare bombing, and in the days that followed was revered by the other papers for its achievement that night.

No trick. He just remembered.

It seemed that a life as a journalist beckoned for Marcel, but that was not to be the case either. For while his phenomenal memory meant he could dispense with a notebook, he utterly lacked the skills required to be a reporter; above all, he could not write. He did not know how to structure a story, did not understand what needed to be said and what was irrelevant. He got bogged down in details and lost in cul-de-sacs of false logic.

And while his memory never let him down, nor did the sturdy pencils and trusty notebooks of his colleagues, and *they* knew how to write.

Despite all this, he held down the job for two years, until finally LeChat decided he had to let his underperforming reporter go.

Unhappy with this failure, unwilling to return to his life on the inking screws, all might have been lost. He took a job in a factory producing machine parts, working as an 'efficiency expert' because it required someone with a good memory to oversee the production line and try to work out how things could be improved. He lasted no longer there than he had as a reporter.

He drifted for a while, mostly out of work, living off the balance of the sale of his mother's house, until one day the idea was put to him that he ought to try his luck up in Pigalle in the cabarets. In the studio apartment across the passage from his own was a pair of newly arrived art students: a Frenchman from Marseille and a Scot. It was they who told Marcel about the cabarets, for they industriously spent much of their free time up there.

'There are all sorts of acts,' said Fraser the Scot, in his rapidly improving French. 'It's not just the singers, the dancers. Musicians. There are other acts too: magicians, illusionists. There was a memory act we saw once, but it wasn't good. Now you, you could do it well . . .'

Marcel thought about it for another long week, at the end of which he devised a flat little routine that involved perfectly recounting strings of numbers written by a third party at random on a chalkboard. The next day he took his act to Pigalle, where he secured an audition, and a job, in a squalid venue called the Cabaret of Insults. He was next to the bottom of the bill, above a fat old chanteuse whose only job was to make the rest of the acts seem half decent.

Despite that, having worked five evenings that first week, he came home on Sunday night with more money than he'd ever earned in any seven days of his life.

It was Fraser who thought up the name.

Marcel Mémoire. Mister Memory.

# ANOTHER FAÇADE

The front of the asylum of Salpêtrière could easily mislead the visitor to the city of light. What is this grand building? A palace, surely. No? Not a palace. Then it's a court of law. Or a lesser known possession of the university, the Sorbonne. Or the grandest library in the world. No, no and no. What the visitor to the city gazes upon is in fact the imposing, regal, elegant face of a hospital. Once a rough ex-gunpowder factory housing the insane of Paris, the old building was demolished and this magnificent structure erected in its place, though on bad days Dr Morel, to whom Marcel's case has been assigned, swears he can still sense a sniff of the saltpetre from which the site took its name. Perhaps that's just his fancy.

Dr Lucien Morel, the Assistant Chief Alienist of the hospital, met Marcel the morning after his transferral from the commissariat of the 6th. At first he paid little interest to this newcomer, there being more than enough work in the asylum for the elderly doctor, but as the days went by, he began to take a keener look at the patient.

These days, Morel walks a little more slowly on his rounds than he used to. His gait is a strange one, walking with his feet turned out, and never lifting his shoes more than an inch or two above the ground, giving the impression of clearing invisible snow before him as he goes. This action gives his hips a funny little shuffling thrust with every step.

Today his work is interesting him greatly, and he moves a little faster, a little more like he used to.

If the front of the hospital is a grand building, the equal of many better known sites in the capital, what lies behind is a little different. The site occupies almost a square kilometre, and is very much a small town in its own right, composed of many buildings, small avenues, even a chapel. There are the administrative offices, the infirmaries, the dispensary, the *blanchisseries* or laundry rooms, the morgue, the lecture theatres and so on, but Dr Morel is headed to see Marcel in his little cell. This cell is like a tiny terraced house, save that it consists of only one room. The terraces stand in rows of twenty-four *Petites Loges*, with a pavement running along in front of all of them, protected slightly from the elements by a colonnade. The columns are painted an elegant light grey, as are the front doors of the cells. Outside each cell, in the colonnade, a small semicircular wooden bench is set into the wall and supported on twin spirals of iron, again painted in the calm grey that is the hospital's uniform.

Though he would never admit it, the reason Dr Morel hurries through his other calls this morning is that he has begun to suspect there is more to Marcel than had first shown itself. Initially, Morel had him marked down as a hysterical catatonic. From the moment Marcel stopped running, it appeared that his mind and body had shut down. Witnesses described how Marcel, who was well known to his neighbours, burst from the street door, took no more than another six steps, and then just stopped.

One of the pretty *blanchisseuses* who lived and worked in the cour said it was as if he froze, like a statue. The awful horror of what he'd done must have suddenly struck him, she said, and he'd fallen to his knees.

'Was he crying?' her friends asked her the next morning, as they got busy over their linens. 'Was he struck with remorse?'

The girl shook her head firmly. 'That, I don't know. I suppose he must have been. He just knelt there. We all stood around and watched him. He was shaking, ever so slightly. No one went near him.'

She was enjoying this attention, having been fortunate enough to be just returning home as Marcel sprang into the passage.

Never had anyone taken so much interest in her in one stretch, despite her looks. She grew to meet her audience.

'Yes,' she decided. 'It was the remorse that did it. Stopped him in his tracks. He knelt there while old Monsieur Bonvoisin fetched the *gardiens*. And then they came, and even then he didn't move. He didn't try to fight, or get away, or anything. He'd done what he'd done and it was remorse that got him. Fancy!'

Dr Morel had been told that since that moment, Marcel had neither moved without being urged to, nor spoken a word. He stared into space, nodding in a distracted way as they confirmed his name and address in the commissariat. Even a spell in the 'kitchen', the room at the back where arrested parties were 'cooked' for information, was not enough to bring Marcel to speak. After he had been cooked, he took to rocking backward and forward, on his heels if standing, on his haunches if sitting. It didn't seem as if he had even noticed the blows thrown at him, mostly into his stomach to avoid undue questioning from the examining magistrate, and there he sat until he was moved to the asylum.

Still he did not speak.

Hysteria was the speciality of the hospital. Once, the Salpêtrière had been no more than a dumping ground for the mad, as well as a prison for prostitutes. But the purpose of the asylum had grown and changed over the years. Until very recently, it had admitted only female patients and the great Charcot had established not only his own reputation, but also that of the hospital, with his work on the hysterical woman. The last few years had seen the admission of a few men too, and though Charcot was now gone, hysteria was still very much the order of the day.

On their first meeting, Dr Morel walked around Marcel and looked. He had him stripped and measured and weighed. He made notes. He shook his head and he came away. Hysterics, as Morel well knew, could manifest their illness in many different ways; they might scream and rail, of course, but those were obvious and boring symptoms that did not interest him greatly. Much more fascinating were cases of divided personalities, of altered states of consciousness and physicality. Why, some of Charcot's greatest subjects had displayed such wonderful symptoms! The young women whose skin would rise in pronounced lines after a stroke with a blunt needle – Charcot had even been able to spell out one particular girl's name and have the letters rise red and bumpy on her back. That girl was also a great one for *attitudes passionelles*, during which her body and face would contort into strange positions, which she could not be got out of, even by the strongest of the warders.

Catatonia was not unheard of, but it was rare enough. And though hysteria is known to the public as a female affliction, Charcot had proved beyond doubt that there were enough hysterical male patients in the city's hospitals for it to be more than a curiosity.

It seemed that Marcel had entered a catatonic state and that he was, potentially, stuck there. Morel sought to rush in before the disease had a chance to secure itself in Marcel's body. The obvious thing was ice baths, so these were tried, without result. Marcel barely seemed aware that he had been lowered into the icy water, and despite frequent immersions of increasing duration, he rose from the water with his eyes still staring, his body not even shivering.

Morel shook his head, and wondered what to try next to shock Marcel's body into breaking its grip upon his mind. That was the theory of what he was attempting, but everything he tried had the same negative outcome. If only he were a woman, Morel thought, I would try the ovarian clamps. They usually brought rapid if not permanent results, and he had discussed the concept of a male equivalent with Dr Charcot in the year before he left. It would be a simple enough matter, easier than with the female version, for the equivalent structures in the male lay handily placed, of course, outside the body. For some reason that was never spoken aloud they had not developed the apparatus.

Things continued thus, until finally, one day, Morel asks Marcel a simple question that no one has asked him yet.

'What did you do?'

No one has asked that question because everyone knows what he's done. Ondine's lover, Bishop, the American, another of the performers in the cabaret, was there after all; was lucky that Marcel didn't plug him too. Crowds of onlookers had gawped as Ondine's bloody body had been taken away.

But Morel asked the right question. His mind is burdened, he said to himself, and he needs to unburden it. Let us see what happens if we give him that chance.

'Monsieur, what did you do?'

And after all the days of silence, Marcel speaks. His rocking ceases temporarily.

'I killed her,' he says.

'And?' Morel prompts, uncaringly. 'Tell me all of it.'

Marcel stares at the wall of his cell, as if it is a cinematograph screen upon which he's reviewing the whole business. Morel notes this, mentally, unaware how close this is to the truth.

Then, Marcel speaks some more.

'I left work. I took my bicycle and I came home. I left the bicycle in the passage, and came up. The concierge grumbled that I was late. She always grumbles when she has to let anyone in late. I came up to the studio. I heard them before I even opened the door. I heard them.'

He pauses. Morel shuffles a little on his feet.

'Go on,' he says, his voice chipped and flat.

Marcel blinks at the wall.

'I opened the door, I saw them. They were . . .'

He stops again.

'Who are we speaking of?' asks Morel. He's growing impatient, but he has no idea how much his patience will be tested yet.

'Ondine. My wife. And the American.'

'I see. And you were saying . . . ? They were . . . what?'

'They were having . . .' Marcel whispers. His voice is low, and that is the only clue to his state of mind. He is otherwise apparently emotionless, and he speaks as if these things are not of very great interest.

'What, Monsieur?'

Marcel does not seem to feel that the doctor is provoking him. He keeps watching the wall ahead of him.

'Sex.'

'Describe the act, if you please.'

There is a considerable silence, into which Marcel appears to be pouring pain.

'He was standing behind her. They were both standing. She was leaning over the back of the armchair. They were making a lot of noise. Then they saw me, and they stopped. Bishop stepped back, his trousers round his ankles. He had a stupid look on his face. He looked down at himself. Ondine laughed at me. Bishop shouted. I took up the gun and I shot her. Bishop shouted at me again, and then I ran. I ran into the street and then I stopped.'

He falls silent, and still he stares at the wall ahead of him.

'Why did you stop?' asks Morel. 'Why did you not run?'

For the first time, Marcel turns and looks at Morel. He almost makes eye contact, though not quite. The look on his face suggests his answer plainly enough: where would I have run to? And why? She was dead. What does it help to run?

Dr Morel considers the man in front of him. From his notes he believes him to be around thirty-two years of age, but there's something about Marcel that feels younger. Of course, he's only met him since the moment in which he lost his wife, and became a murderer. That would be enough to change anyone's demeanour. Now Marcel is staring at the wall, or not even at it, but through it, and has become unresponsive again. He has resumed his gentle rocking, hugging his knees to his chest.

The doctor is unsure whether to break off for the day, or to continue. In the end, Morel allows that he has done something positive, for a major breakthrough has been achieved – he has got the subject to speak.

But Marcel does not speak the next day, or the next, and Morel grows frustrated with his lack of progress. He wonders whether the man is worth the trouble, for the doctor is fully aware that his years are passing, and he requires a great success before his days are up. A success with which to make his name as great as Charcot's, from whose shadow he still cannot seem to emerge. And if this recalcitrant will not provide it, he will move on to the next.

When Morel returns the following morning, however, he brings another thought with him: perhaps the way to break through is to try to connect with a time when Marcel was not hysterical.

'Monsieur,' says the doctor, 'I have heard that you were a performer of some kind. You worked in the cabarets. Would you tell me about that?'

Marcel is silent. He stares at the wall, he stares at the wall. His heart barely beats, his lungs barely breathe. There is such a stillness about him that were you not to know better you would say he was dead. As if he were dead though alive; airless, though breathing; bloodless, though his heart still beats faintly.

'What did you do?' Morel asks. 'Were you a singer perhaps? An actor? What was it?'

Without looking up, sitting on his bed, staring at nothing, Marcel answers, 'I remembered things.'

Morel is not sure he can have heard correctly.

'You . . . ?'

'I remembered things. That's why they call me Mémoire. Marcel Mémoire.'

'You mean, you helped in the offices in some way?'

Dr Morel has never been to the cabarets. These things are all quite alien to him. He has no idea what passes for entertainment in the Boulevard de Clichy and the surrounding streets. The cabarets of Heaven and Hell. The Cabaret of Nothingness. The Cabaret of Insults. The Theatre of Grand-Guignol.

'I remembered things. I remembered everything. I still remember everything.'

After that remark, it takes Morel a very long time to get Marcel to speak again, and when he does, the doctor remains confused.

'It's my act,' Marcel says, 'to remember things. I remember things, and people find that amazing, and they pay good money to see it.'

'What things?'

'Anything. Numbers, for example. Mostly numbers. On a chalkboard. Someone writes the numbers on the board, and I am given a minute to look at them, and then they turn the board so that only the audience can see it. I stand behind it. Then I call out the numbers, and everyone claps.'

'It's some sort of trick, then?' asks Morel.

Marcel looks at him, as if he is confused. 'No,' he says. 'It's no trick.'

'Then how do you do it?'

'I just . . . remember,' Marcel says. 'I remember everything.'

'Don't be ridiculous,' snaps the doctor, 'no one remembers everything.'

But Marcel doesn't answer, as if there is no need to bother arguing the point. That irritates Morel.

The following day, he returns, somewhat pugnaciously, with a chalkboard and chalk. He sits himself on the far end of the bed from Marcel, and props the board on his knee. He says not a word. He begins to scribble on the board, and a minute later, he turns it round to show Marcel.

Marcel does not seem to have seen it. He does not seem interested, but Morel is patient, and waits, and waits, until finally Marcel turns to look at what Morel has written.

On the chalkboard, in ten rows of ten, are one hundred numbers.

Morel stares at Marcel as he in turn stares at the board. There is a tightness in Morel's chest, and a quickening. He wants to speak, to ask, to demand: how long should I hold the board for? How long do you need? Must I say anything? When will you start? But Morel says nothing because he does not know which of these to say and can see no reason to be arbitrary. Dr Morel abhors whimsy.

Then, Marcel closes his eyes, and starts speaking.

'Nine, four, three, three, six, two, nine . . .'

Morel spins the board round to face himself.

'. . . eight, six, eight, one, three, one, seven . . .'

The quickening intensifies, both of Morel's heartbeat and the speed with which Marcel rattles out the numbers on the board, in order, left to right, and then down, line by line, so that in far less time than it took Morel to write them, Marcel has repeated them all back to him.

'. . . nine, nine, two, five, six.'

Morel has gone cold. He turns and checks for reflections in the cell, some way that Marcel might have been able to see the numbers, but there is none. Patients do not have mirrors, the one small window is high and in the wrong place to have been of use. And he has already noted that Marcel's eyes were shut as he recited. Morel practically breaks the board as he thumps his sleeve across it to wipe the numbers out, heedless of the white smear he makes on the black sleeve of his frock coat.

'Again!' he says, and starts to scribble. A minute later, he shows the board to Marcel, who, in even less time than it took before, closes his eyes and then begins to report.

'Seven, three, four, one, four, nine, zero, four, five . . .'

Again Morel turns the board back and cowers over it to be absolutely sure that only he can see it. Marcel pays the doctor no attention whatsoever as he checks each digit on the board, the numbers spilling from his patient's mouth.

'. . . six, two, five, three, eight, one.'

The magic is over just as fast as last time, but before Morel can start to erase them and try once more, Marcel is speaking again.

'One, eight, three, five, two, six . . .'

It takes Morel a moment or two of bafflement to realise what Marcel is doing. Marcel is saying the numbers backwards. Speechless, his eyebrows walking a little further up his forehead, Morel verifies the reverse sequence. Once again, perfect, not a single mistake, not even a hesitation.

Before Marcel can speak again, Morel tries something else.

'Diagonal: top left, bottom right.'

'Seven, four, nine, eight, seven, three, four, five, two, one.'

'Top right, bottom left,' snaps Morel, and again Marcel relays the numbers faultlessly.

The game continues. Morel scribbles, shows, listens, erases. He expands the quantity of numbers until he cannot fit any more on the board. He tries it with letters instead of numbers, he uses a mixture of both. It does not matter, Marcel cannot be beaten. Finally Morel slumps back, exhausted. He is amazed, both by what he has seen, and also by the showpeople of Montmartre, the people of the cabaret. Dr Morel cannot conceive that they in turn cannot have understood the quite simply extraordinary nature of what Marcel is able to do.

But that is showpeople; they don't care how a thing occurs, as long as it does, and as long as it earns them some money.

# OF LOVE

Oh, Marcel. What must we think of him? It's easy to form the wrong impression of him; this strange wanderer. He is not *only* of the mind, but of the body too, and the soul, and there *were* women in his life, before he married Ondine. It was impossible in Paris not to encounter females of the most alluring kind on a daily basis.

There were the three young seamstresses in the studio across the cour from him, their shoulders and faces right at the window so as to be near the light, so close as to be almost able to lip-read their conversation. It was impossible not to catch their eye when raising a blind, or investigating a noise from below. There were the *blanchisseuses* down in the passage, always singing, their skirts often rucked up as they scrubbed, exposing their sleek calves. There were the ladies of the picture card factory, twenty of them, hammering away all day with little hammers and steel dies to beat images into cards. There was the bookbinder's daughter, there was the girl who sold Marcel his milk and coffee every morning, there were the shapely models who sat, frequently disrobed, for Fraser, the Scottish artist in the studio next door. And all this within the cour itself. Beyond lay Paris, and Marcel found the sophistication of Parisian women to be far beyond the females he had known in Étoges, as if they were a new species.

If it sounds as if Marcel viewed women as distant objects, that may be because there is some truth in it. And yet he was not cold or callous. He was no chauvinist. He had a heart in him, and he admired and respected the many women, young or old, pretty or not, who came his way. And they came his way rather

27

often, because, though he was extraordinarily unaware of the fact, he was a very handsome young man. So there had been romances, though none had lasted any time at all, days usually, weeks at most. Something always went wrong, something that left Marcel puzzled, and each time his confusion grew. It may be that he was not aware of what was happening, or what was expected of him. To paint that picture, it is only necessary to relate the first sexual encounter he had, even though Marcel didn't realise that that was what it was. That alone should make the point, but in case of doubt, consider the day, long ago in Étoges, when Ginette the doctor's daughter suddenly burst into his house one still, summer afternoon.

It was harvest time; the whole village was in the rows, every able man and woman bending themselves to the most important moment of the year. Marcel was not working; he had been particularly distracted of late and was spending more and more time indoors.

Ginette came in through the kitchen door, which stood open.

'Marcel? It's me! Ginette!' she called, and Marcel came down from his room to find the young woman in a state of distress.

'I've been stung!' she declared, and Marcel immediately sought to help. He sat her down at the kitchen table, and never once wondered why she hadn't gone to find her father instead. He was a doctor, after all.

Ginette seemed to hesitate. Marcel noticed that her hands were shaking, and wondered if she was suffering an allergic reaction, as some people were known to.

'It's in a . . .' She faltered. Then seemed to collect herself. 'My leg. I was stung on my leg. Will you look at it for me?'

Marcel nodded. Poor Ginette.

'Show me,' he said.

Ginette wore the long white cotton dress that she always wore as befitting a doctor's daughter, tied in at the waist with a wide black belt, and with a close-fitting bodice. The skirts were looser,

though, and as Marcel knelt before her, he could already see her
ankles above her smart black boots.

'Oh, Marcel,' Ginette said, 'it's high up. It hurts. I'm worried
the sting is still in.'

Marcel nodded. 'I'll see,' he said. 'I know how to take them
out. You must use your fingernails.'

Ginette faltered again, losing her nerve. How she'd steeled
herself in her room to go through with this. They had walked
out on many occasions, as many as she could engineer with
Celeste's help. She had spoken to Marcel of many things often
of love, and of dreams and futures, but nothing she'd done or
said had ever moved Marcel to do anything, to want anything
or take anything, not even a single kiss.

It was a hot afternoon, the hottest of a summer that had been
building steadily. The sort of still heat that made Ginette want
to heave her clothes off, stand in front of Marcel and make him
finally notice her, and she'd thought of a way to do it. Only now,
in the moment, her nerve began to fail.

'Let me see,' Marcel said, comforting her, and with that
Ginette showed him. She'd had to force herself to leave the
house. Before that, as she'd removed her drawers, her fingers had
trembled at what she was planning. Now, at Marcel's gentle
reassurance, she slowly pulled up the long white skirts.

'It's high,' she tried to say, but the words caught in her throat.
Marcel noticed that, as he noticed the shaking of her hands and
the rapid rising and falling of her chest, and understood that the
poor girl was very frightened.

'It's all right,' he said. 'Let me see.'

She let him see.

She pulled the skirt higher still, her legs apart, so that it slid
over her knees, and up her thighs, until finally, she pointed a
shaking finger at the spot where she'd pinched herself a dozen
times till it stood up sore and pink, no more than a sigh from the
place where her inner thigh met dark hair.

There was a silence. Ginette could not bring herself to remember to breathe. Marcel peered at the spot.

'Does it hurt?' he said.

Ginette nodded rapidly.

'I can't see the sting. It must have come out.'

He reached a fingertip towards the pink mark. Of course he saw the other pinkness, right there, a finger's length away. She was only young, really barely a woman; there was a little hair above her lips, which Marcel noted, fascinated, but which he then ignored.

He touched the spot.

'Does it hurt?' he said, and it was all Ginette could do to stop herself fainting. She began to breathe, hard and rapidly.

'I think I should get your father,' he said, concerned that she was having an attack of some kind. 'Let me—'

'No!' Ginette blurted out. 'No. I'm fine.'

'But you seem—'

'I'm fine. Really, I'm fine,' she said, and hurriedly pulled her skirts down, standing and leaving in almost a single motion.

'I'm fine,' she added. 'Thank you, Marcel.'

She left, cursing herself, not really cursing Marcel so much, for it was her own clumsy idea, not his. She really must be utterly unattractive for him not to have leapt all over her in the instant that she showed him her—

Oh God! What had she done? She burned with shame and only then realised she should have asked him to keep what had happened to himself, a thought that would keep her awake for the next several nights.

She need not have worried. Marcel mentioned to Celeste that evening that Ginette had been stung by a bee, but he didn't say where because it didn't seem important. Poor girl, he thought. What on earth was a bee doing up there, anyway?

It would be years before Marcel made the connection, understood what had really been happening. Some of the older men at

LeChat's print shop seemed to take a passing interest in him, and after an especially ribald conversation in a bar one day after work, had correctly deduced that Marcel was not yet familiar with the physical act of love. This didn't concern Marcel half as much as it seemed to concern the other men. That time would come and did it matter at what point in his life it started? He was still Marcel.

He tried to explain this to the men, but such rambling and somewhat incomprehensible philosophy made three of them frown and two of them laugh. So they concluded to settle the matter and having poured a half-bottle of wine into Marcel, and taken a few *bocks* themselves, they dragged him across the river to a *maison close*, their favourite, number 2 in the Petit Place Mars. The madame was well used to such initiatory ventures, and since she was a kindly individual, she selected a girl called Rosa, because she knew she would be easy on the boy.

Upstairs, Marcel found himself reliving his past.

'I've got something that aches,' Rosa said, sitting on the edge of the bed. Despite being kind, subtlety was not her long suit. 'Won't you take a look at it?'

He knelt before her, as she pulled up her skirts. She was naked underneath. Marcel took a good look. She had more hair than Ginette, and more flesh, but otherwise things were pretty much the same. Marcel remembered that hot August afternoon, and he remembered Ginette. He thought about her, and the time they'd spent together. They'd walked around the pond, and up to the church. Sometimes they would walk as far as Montmort-Lucy and admire the chateau and its parkland. There were peacocks on the lawn of the chateau, great strutting birds with miasmic rages of colours to show when they wished to. The chateau was only a small one, Marcel later found out, but being much larger than theirs in Étoges, it remained the grandest thing he knew until he came to Paris. He remembered the first time he'd seen the Panthéon, the Hôtel des Invalides, Notre Dame, and then he knew what real splendour was. He wondered if Ginette would ever come to Paris. She'd always been so kind to him; other people became impatient with him, though he was not always sure why. But not Ginette. Ginette always had time and a kind word. She was interesting too, and pretty, Marcel remembered. Much prettier than this Rosa. This girl who the men—

He was suddenly aware that the woman was still in front of him, waiting.

He looked up at her. He remembered Ginette again, and the day she had been stung by a bee, and finally he understood. He was so surprised he said it out loud, his voice dreaming, his gaze far away, far back in time.

'She wasn't stung by a bee.'

'I beg your pardon?' asked Rosa, though she kept her legs happily apart.

Marcel took another look, and remembered when he'd touched Ginette's phantom sting. How she'd breathed heavily. And given a little moan.

Then fled.

'Well?' asked Rosa, leaning down and unceremoniously feeling around in Marcel's trousers. Nothing.

Marcel looked back up at Rosa, her face no more than a few centimetres from his.

'It's very nice,' he said, feeling that something was expected of him. 'Thank you very much.'

'There are places you can get boys,' Rosa said, leaning back and pulling her skirts down again.

'Oh,' said Marcel, 'I see,' though he didn't see at all.

As fate was to dictate, the very next evening Marcel found himself taking one of the seamstresses who worked across the way into his rooms. Or maybe she took him. Either way, for sure, they were both a little drunk, but this time, as the seamstress felt in his trousers, there was not *nothing*.

Marcel found himself thinking of Ginette, as the seamstress rolled him back on to the bed, and unbuttoned her chemise. She smiled, while Paris smiled too, and got a little older.

She didn't stay the night. When it was over, the effect of the drink seemed to have worn off too.

'Listen, Marcel,' she said, pulling her skirts over her boots which she'd not found a need to remove. 'You're a great guy. Really. But I think that's enough for us. I'll see you.'

Marcel sat up, nodding.

'Right,' he said. He felt he ought to say something. 'Thank you.' And he wanted to add her name but he realised he didn't know it, though he knew the girl so well by sight.

There were the three of them across the passage, just two sheets of glass away, chatting happily again the next morning. They caught Marcel's eye as he rolled up the blind, blinked, and bent to their sewing again. Marcel wanted to wave at the one who'd taken him, but couldn't.

There were a few other women after that, but really, there was no one until Ondine.

They met the very first time Marcel went to the Cabaret of Insults. Fraser, the Scot, and his roommate Fossard, the Marseillais, were now old hands on the cabaret scene, and their usual routine was to work their way through all the favourite haunts: starting out the night in Heaven or Hell (which could be found right next door to each other on the Boulevard de Clichy), they would then move on, depending on their mood – to the Cabaret of Nothingness if they wanted an amusing frisson with death, or, if they felt thoughtful, to a café known as L'Âne Rouge from the red donkey peering down above an otherwise unmarked door, where someone might be reciting their poetry or singing a song or two.

That night, however, Fraser and Fossard knew exactly where to take Marcel and his act: one of the most extremely peculiar cabarets of all, the Cabaret of Insults. Being regular customers, they knew the proprietor well, Monsieur Maurice Chardon, and they assured Marcel they would be able to introduce him. The introduction took some time to obtain, however. Chardon waved at the two young artists and their new friend as cheerily as ever, always happy to see money being spent in his establishment, but he had no time to stop and chat.

'The sword-swallower has toothache,' he explained as he breezed past, 'which means a hole in the second act. Gentlemen, a hole. I have to fill it, would you excuse me?'

Fraser slapped Marcel on the back, and laughed, something he rarely stopped doing.

'Don't look like that! We'll wait him out. We'll have a drink and see the show.'

Fossard, as far as Marcel could make out, was Fraser's opposite. He rarely smiled, let alone laughed, and when he spoke to almost anyone at all his manner was gruff, to say the least. And yet somehow these two were firm friends. Fossard went off in search of a waitress to bark an order at, while Fraser pulled Marcel to a table with three empty chairs, laughing.

'No patience at all,' he said, jabbing a thumb towards his friend. 'Fossard. We could sit here and let a pretty thing come and serve us, but he can't wait for five minutes. Look!'

Fraser pointed to where Fossard was grumpily giving an order of drinks to a fierce little girl who didn't like the way the Marseillais spoke to her.

Fraser was beside himself. 'His accent. Worse than mine. They can't understand him half the time. Or at least they do, but pretend not to.'

Fossard returned, grumbling, which made Fraser laugh even more, throw his arms across his friend's shoulders, and then direct his and Marcel's attention to the stage. A dowdy, and it cannot be avoided, ageing lady was beginning to warble a tune of welcome to the soirée.

'Don't worry,' said Fraser, mugging at Marcel. 'It's not all this bad.'

'No,' announced Fossard, apparently without irony, 'some of it's worse.'

The remark left Fraser unable to breathe adequately for several minutes, by which time the warbler had left the stage, to be replaced by a number of girls (eight, Marcel counted), who danced a frantic quadrille of sorts with speed and some enthusiasm, to the rapturous reception of the largely male crowd. Marcel had not seen so much female skin since his encounter with Rosa in the Petit Place Mars, and though the skin on display was not as intimate, there was much more of it. He found himself thinking of kneeling, and felt the floorboards under his knees. He saw Ginette's dark hair, and he remembered that there had been a subtle scent, something he had not smelled before, and yet which reminded him of something when he was young, very, very young.

Fraser nudged Fossard, winking at him as he nodded at Marcel, trying to suppress his mirth, and largely failing.

'It's like that for everyone, their first time,' he said to his surly friend, mistaking Marcel's absent gaze for rapture.

The girls were, in their way, remarkable. Like the best troupes of the Moulin Rouge, nearby, and the Follies, down the hill a way, the girls had been chosen for their physical similarity, so that when they formed a kicking line, the uniformity of their steps was enhanced in a most impressive way. Such a refinement was unheard of in a cabaret the size of Chardon's, and it was something he was rightly proud of.

As soon as they'd come, they were gone, though they reappeared at frequent intervals throughout the night between the various other turns, which were, as Fraser had explained, very diverse. There were singers, male and female, there was an illusionist, the highlight of whose act was the production of a live chick from an egg that he found underneath a volunteer's hat. There was a man who contorted himself into the smallest conceivable spaces, and ended by passing his entire body through a tennis racket.

'Now if it still had the strings on,' Fraser remarked, already unable to suppress giggles at his own joke, 'that would be impressive.'

Fossard remained unmoved, while Marcel barely heard, so intent was he on finding Chardon and showing him his skill.

The acts came and went, the girls came and went, and Marcel fretted and worried and grew more and more nervous, until finally the evening wore to a close, by which time he had drunk enough to be free of nerves, and was a little tired too.

Eventually, after one last rousing dance number, came the final act, the famous event that gave the cabaret its name – the insults. Monsieur Juron came out, a short man with a fine curling moustache, dressed in evening wear, sporting a top hat. People were on the edge of their seats in anticipation before he even opened his mouth, and then his tirade began.

The variety and extremity of the names he called the customers was breathtakingly inventive. Every conceivable term of abuse, and very many that could not have previously been conceived of, were hurled at this gentleman or that lady, until they either dissolved into laughter or grew red with rage and stormed from the cabaret, to the even greater amusement of their companions. For such was Monsieur Juron's act: to insult each and every patron of the venue not only in double-quick time, but in the most elaborate and imaginative fashion. Simple and bald rude adjectives were mixed with abhorrent things of a sexual nature, and frequently the imagery of farm animals, overlaid with venerable derogatory terms, and bundled up into wondrous portmanteaux of offence the like of which had never been heard since the world began to revolve. Finally, satisfied with having seen the back of at least twelve customers in righteous indignation, Monsieur Juron took a bow to the wild applause of those who knew how to take a joke, and an insult, on the chin.

Marcel blinked, quite unable to work out what he had just witnessed. Fraser was under the table in hysterics. Fossard kicked him. And smiled.

As the lights were raised and the customers began to leave, heading for spots where the entertainment ran even further into the night, and as waiters began to wipe tables and turn chairs over, Chardon came over to see his good customers.

'So? You have something to tell me, gentlemen?'

'No, we have something to show you,' said Fraser, who had pulled himself together from his spell under the table, though it would nevertheless be fair to say he was drunk. He was speaking slow, careful and highly inaccurate French. 'Marcel? Marcel . . .'

Fraser waved an imaginary handkerchief in a flourish in front of his new friend, and drunkenly mouthed the word 'ta-daa'.

Marcel tried to speak to Chardon about what it was that he did, which only caused all three of them, Fraser, Fossard and Chardon himself to shut him up rapidly.

'Don't tell me! Show me!' Chardon said, looking at the clock on the wall.

So Marcel showed him.

There was a chalkboard hanging above the table, with wines listed on it. He pulled a piece of chalk from his pocket, wiped the board clean with the edge of his palm, and handed both board and chalk to Chardon.

He gave his instructions. Bemused, Chardon did as he was bid, showing the board to Marcel for a few moments, who then began his recitation.

Fraser nudged Fossard all through this, who finally moved his chair out of reach. All the while, all three men kept an eye on the numbers on the board, as did two of the dancing girls who'd stopped to watch on their way out.

When it was over, Chardon's eyebrow moved half a centimetre up his forehead.

'Very impressive,' he said, 'but rather dull. A trick of some kind?'

Marcel smiled. 'No,' he said, 'no trick.'

'Have it your way,' said Chardon, unblinking, because in his time in the cabarets of Montmartre, he really had seen it all. 'I'll put you on after Madame Gignot. We'll try a week. You need ten minutes of that stuff. The pay's eight francs a night plus anything anyone throws at you. Don't be late. Ever.'

So that was that, and Fraser cheered and clapped Fossard on the back heartily, and suggested a trip to L'Âne Rouge.

'Coming?' Fraser asked Marcel, who shook his head.

'I have no more money. And I'm tired.'

The Scot and the Marseillais departed, arms around each other for support of various kinds, and disappeared into the night.

Chardon had disappeared too, and when Marcel turned round, he found himself face to face with an attractive young woman.

'I saw you,' she said.

'That?' Marcel said, his eyes falling on the chalkboard, still holding Chardon's numbers.

'No, I meant I saw you earlier. When I was on stage.'

'You're one of the dancers.'

'I'm one of the dancers,' she said. 'But I have a name.'

She waited. Marcel had the feeling something was expected of him.

'What is it? Your name?'

'Ondine. I can make it better.'

Marcel was tired. He'd also been drinking.

From the edge of the stage, the other girl who'd been watching called to Ondine.

'Leave him alone,' she called. 'It's time to go home.'

'That's Lucie,' Ondine said, ignoring her. 'I mean, I can make your act better. It's interesting, but you do it so badly. You have to make it more exciting, more mysterious.'

'I do?' said Marcel.

'Trust me, I've worked in a lot of these places, seen lots of acts. The trick isn't the thing, it's the way you do it.'

'It isn't a trick,' Marcel said.

Ondine shrugged. 'Maybe. Maybe not. But if you want it to work, you need to dress it up. I can do that for you.'

'Ondine!' cried Lucie. 'I'm leaving if you—'

'Coming!' said Ondine over her shoulder. 'I've got to go. But I could help you. If you like.'

'Yes, please,' said Marcel. 'That would be good. Only . . .'

'Only what?'

'Why would you do that?'

Ondine shrugged. 'Because I like you already,' she said, and then vanished into the night with Lucie.

So that was how Ondine and Marcel met.

She came to his studio two days later, and they created a neat little act, ten minutes of baffling mnemonic skill. Ondine begged Marcel to let her in on the trick, and, as the days went by and Marcel stuck to his story that there was no trick, Ondine grew frustrated and then angry. And finally, one day when Marcel recounted exactly every step she and the other dancers had made that first night, and then rattled off every bottle of spirit standing behind the bar, as well as what Monsieur Chardon was wearing, she came to believe him.

Marcel's act was a hit, for a while. He moved rapidly up the bill into the dizzy heights of the middle of the second half of the evening at the Cabaret of Insults, and for that time he was the toast of the show. People came just to see him, and Ondine set her sights on her handsome and oh-so-clever new friend. She ignored Lucie's chiding remarks as Ondine declared they were in love, and then, at the announcement that they were going to get married, things cooled between Lucie and Ondine considerably, though not so much that Lucie didn't attend the little ceremony at the Church of Saint-Valentin.

Ondine moved in to Marcel's apartment in the Cour du Commerce, and for a while they were very happy. But the good times were not to last long, and things fell apart almost as quickly as they had come together. Within six months, Ondine was dead.

# A VISIT TO THE COUR
# DU COMMERCE

Here is the murder room. Marcel's studio apartment, on the sixth floor of the Cour du Commerce, directly above the kitchens of Le Procope, from which the most wonderful aromas ascended to tease the senses, for no one who lived in the cour could afford to eat at the marvellous establishment.

Upon entering, the visitor stands in the larger of the two spaces of which the studio consists, roughly two-thirds of the total area being this combined entrance, kitchen and living room. There was a plumbed-in sink – that is to say, a large stone sink with a drain, but no running water. They'd have to haul all their water up six flights, every day, and Laurent Petit, who has come to view the scene, feels tired at the thought. At least he has a cold water tap in his flat, and a toilet. This place has nothing. But then he guesses Després paid half of what he does in rent.

A moth-eaten sofa and an upturned wine crate comprise the living area. Beyond that, a wall of wooden panelling below and frosted glass above separates the larger space from the bedroom, where a small brass double bed sits under glass skylights, so that on clear nights the stars will drape the room in soft silver. There is little else in the bedroom save a small bedside cabinet upon which stands an oil lamp and some candle stubs. There is a photograph in a second-hand frame. The photograph is of Ondine.

It is here, on the threshold to the bedroom, that young Inspector Petit stands, and considers what happened. The crime being a serious one, the wheels of justice had been set into their fastest motion. It was a mere two days after the crime that Petit was assigned to the case, and sent to interview witnesses at the scene.

True, Laurent Petit was young, but this was something that he did not take to be a disadvantage in life, and perhaps we should not do so either. He was new to the Sûreté too, but didn't waste the few years of adulthood he'd had before joining the detective branch of the Paris police. Until eighteen months before he served in the army, five years in all, during which he saw action in the wars against the Mandingo, and then in Algeria, where he rose to the rank of second lieutenant. He'd come to think, however, that the army was not for him. Well, that was what he told himself at least. And fate advanced.

Fate advanced in two ways. The first was an occurrence he tries daily to suppress or, better yet, erase from his mind. The second was the arrival in Algiers of the former Prefect of Paris Police, Louis Lépine. It was the presence of Lépine, who'd been sent to quell unrest in the same way he had so masterfully ruled Paris for four years, that turned Laurent Petit's mind to the thought that he might make something of himself as a police-man. He joined the Sûreté easily enough; most of his fellow inspectors had been in the army too, and while he has not yet excelled himself, he has a record that cannot be argued with. He's not seen quite as much blood as he did during his time in the army, but it's fair to say that he has been very much surprised at quite how much he *has* seen in his eighteen months.

His boss, the Principal Inspector, a pale man in his early fifties called Boissenot, had a theory about this.

'It's the end of the world,' he would announce across his desk to anyone who would listen. Petit, being new, listened, at least to start with.

'What we are dealing with is nothing less than the terror of the abyss,' Boissenot asserted frequently. 'When I was a young inspector like you, well, I remember the days of the Commune.

Those were bloody times, but after that, everyone seemed to take a breath. I'm not saying there wasn't crime, my boy, of course there was crime, but these days . . . ah!'

He made a small circling motion with a finger that pointed straight up at the flaking plaster of the ceiling.

'These days! It's not enough for a robber to steal an old lady's meagre savings, he has to throttle her too. That Madame Dellard, for instance, we found her denture halfway down her throat. Or that tailor in the Rue Chevalier. What was his name? Seventy-five, beaten to death with brass knuckles for a few francs. Everywhere, such extreme violence! It's as if the criminal mind has become the norm; everyone wants everything and will do anything to get it! Why, that porter dismissed from the Hôtel Poulin de La Dreux for fiddling with the maids, takes a Browning and shoots the whole La Dreux family in revenge. All of them! Three daughters, dead. He even put a bullet in their spaniel. And shall I tell you what's behind this, my boy?'

Here Boissenot paused, finger still pointing at the ceiling and Petit found unwelcome thoughts arising in his mind. He tried to count the hairs on Boissenot's head, he tried to listen to the still air in the room. Anything rather than listen to more descriptions of horror. And yet, as a policeman, it is his job to confront such things. So he nodded to Boissenot, and forced a smile displaying an interest in the gruesome subject matter.

Boissenot barely noticed.

'It's the end of the world. That's what it is. At least, it's the end of the century. Here we are, months away from a new era, and what do we find? We have been cheated. Weren't we promised everything? That fancy exhibition ten years ago, and now they will have another one, and what do we see? The electric light, the wonders of machinery, the wonders of science, technology and medicine, where are these things for the likes of you and me? When I retire I will be lucky to make ends meet. No motor cars for me, no luxuries. And here we are, the end of the century coming, and we have been cheated. That is what under-lies this angst, my boy; it is anger and fear. Anger at what we do not have and fear that when the clock strikes twelve on the 31st of December, we will find that, lo and behold, we are no better off than we were in the previous century. Anger and fear, my boy. Anger and fear.'

Petit was careful not to dally too long in or near Boissenot's office after the first few times he was caught, but he did often think about the old man's theory. Sometimes, he found himself taking it rather seriously, particularly on those days when he is unable to suppress the memory of the first way that fate erupted into his life.

Now, as he stands in the doorway to the bedroom of the man they called Marcel Mémoire, is one of those days.

Petit backs out of the doorway and does something he often does, namely knocks something over. As soon as he feels his rear nudge something, he spins, and manages to catch the vase he's backed into, though in doing so he puts his elbow through the flimsy glass of the door, shattering one of the six panels into a thousand crystalline pieces.

He sighs, and looks furtively at the open door, and the stair-well beyond. He's already had to suffer half an hour of the concierge, and only her laziness prevented her from accompany-ing him up to, as she put it with melodrama, *the scene of the crime*. What she wanted to know was how soon she could rent the place out again, assuming that Després was headed to the guillotine, and anyway, his rent was due on Friday, and who would be paying that?

Petit eventually managed to escape her without learning anything useful. He'd already managed to interview some women from the picture card factory, as well as a Scotsman and a Marseillais, and they had all confirmed the story: Marcel had arrived home, found his wife and an American from the cabaret where they all worked hard at it, and shot Ondine there and then. The *gardiens* had found Marcel in the passage, kneeling on the cobbles, frozen to the spot. From the remorse, a dim-witted *blanchisseuse* had told him, with a knowing look. There were some discrepancies in people's accounts of the murder, however. Some said there had only been one shot, while others said three or four, and Fraser maintained it had been five, definitely five. Petit had already learned in his short time as a detective that people's recollection of events could often be open to question. Memories, even of something so notable as the sound of gunshots very close by, could not always be relied upon. And the interesting thing was that, very often, these people who contradicted one another did not seem to be lying. Each of them could be absolutely convinced of the truth of their own story, sometimes even when presented with facts that meant their memory had to be false. It drives him mad, this inability to be able to rely on witnesses.

Petit looks at the broken glass and then creeps to the head of the stairwell, fearful of the sound of the concierge's footsteps coming to see what the breakage was. Nothing.

He sighs a second time and tells himself to examine the scene of the crime again, then curses himself for using the concierge's expression. That is something else that drives him crazy: the way every simpleton thinks they know all about police matters. Everyone has an opinion, everyone knows the truth. He wishes very much that they would all shut up and let him do what he was employed to do.

So, Marcel had come in the front door, and was probably standing more or less where Petit is now when he'd seen them through in the bedroom. He'd taken up a gun (and Petit would need to find out why they had a gun and what it was doing there) and shot his wife. Then he'd run. Then almost as quickly he'd stopped running. And then he'd been arrested, and, furthermore, Petit gathered that he had not denied the murder. So much was indisputable. Petit hadn't bothered to tell the concierge that even though all this was indisputable, one further thing was certain: Marcel would not be going to the guillotine. The very worst he might get would be transportation; very probably he would get a term of hard labour on French soil, five to ten years, depending on how the judge saw the matter. For Marcel had been lucky. Or clever. Petit was not alone in finding some aspects of the penal code outdated, but there it was: the law remained the law, even when that law stated that the murder by a husband of his wife, finding her in the adulterous act of sexual congress *in the marital home*, was an *excusable* crime. And excusable meant that the punishment for the crime was reduced from capital punishment to a lesser sentence. So Marcel would not have his head removed. There was an outside chance of transportation, which was not called the dry guillotine for nothing – twenty years of hard labour on a starvation diet on the disease-ridden islands off the coast of Cayenne saw very few prisoners return; many didn't even survive the journey there on the prison hulk.

Petit conjures up the moment in his mind: the jealous, angry husband; the experience of seeing his wife with another man. There would have been shouts, perhaps, a moment of unbelievable rage and frustration. Then the gunshot, or shots, depending on whose story you believed. The gun had been recovered by the *gardiens* and was now at the commissariat waiting to be examined.

Petit goes to inspect the bedroom wall, looking for holes made by bullets. There are many holes in the wall, the apartment being, like much of Paris, somewhat dilapidated, and Petit cannot be certain that any of them were made by bullets. That is not necessarily a surprise; he has been told the gun was a St Etienne 8mm, the very one he carried in his time as a second lieutenant; a neat weapon but with poor striking power. Any bullets that hit Ondine very likely stayed in her body. He'd have to read the post-mortem reports.

There's not much more to do. Petit has a notebook full of corroboration from a variety of witnesses; the case is, as the concierge would no doubt have said, one that could be open and shut. And Petit only wants to make sure there is no way in which some shifty lawyer could find a reason for Després to be exculpated, and that he gets the justice he deserves.

Petit is startled from his reverie by a voice from the outer door. 'This the place?'

Petit turns to see Drouot, a fellow inspector from the Quai des Orfèvres, who'd been dispatched by the examining magistrate to go and interview Marcel before the police could beat him to death.

Petit likes Drouot well enough, but unfortunately they are not often assigned to the same cases.

Drouot strolls into the apartment, hands in his pockets.

'That concierge, eh?' he says, shaking his head. He looks at the glass on the floor. 'He shot her through the door?'

'No,' says Petit, without thinking.

'No? So why the broken window? A struggle?'

'No, no struggle.'

Petit dies inside.

'Or perhaps, yes,' he adds hurriedly. 'I don't know. We need to interview the American. The lover.'

'Forget it,' says Drouot, poking the broken glass with his toe.

'Forget it?'

'Forget it. The whole thing's done. They've said he's crazy. Moved him to Salpêtrière.'

'They did what? Who did?'

'The Préfecture. They've declared him to be criminally insane and now he's in a cell in Salpêtrière.'

'They can't do that. Can they?'

'They very much can. And they did. So the job's over and because I'm so nice to you I came to tell you on my way home so you can buy me a beer instead.'

'The Salpêtrière? I thought that was for women only.'

'So did I. Apparently they take crazy men now too. It's nice to see such emancipation, no? So we're done, and you can buy me a beer.'

Drouot is already halfway outside, but turns to find Petit still staring into the bedroom. He's looking over at the portrait of Ondine, dressed in what was presumably her finest dress, her hair done up. Petit finds that he is provoked by this image of her; she was not the most beautiful woman ever, but maybe close. And there was clearly something indisputably sexual about her. There was also, he thinks, a hardness about her face. If one can be sure of such things from a photograph.

'Coming?'

'Hmm? Yes,' says Petit, and, turning, hits his head on the lintel of the doorway to the bedroom.

'What's the matter?' Drouot asks. 'One less problem for us to worry about, yes?'

'It's not right,' says Petit. 'We have a simple case of murder, an easy one to please the chef, and it's taken out of our hands because they say he's mental. That's not right.'

'What's right got to do with it?' asks Drouot, who finally manages to get Petit to leave the studio, and also gets him to buy beer for the two of them. Drouot's beer lowers rapidly, while Petit's grows warm in the glass, until his friend offers to drink it for him.

The next day, however, Petit finds himself determined to act. He goes to complain to Boissenot, who looks extremely troubled at having to think about something other than the end of the world. He passes Petit up the line to the Chef de la Sûreté himself, Cavard.

Cavard is no fool. At forty-eight he is one of the youngest chefs in the history of the Sûreté. He takes one look at Petit and though they have not met before, decides he seems ready to learn a lesson. So he listens to the young inspector's complaint, and promises he will take it up with the examining magistrate at their next meeting. Which he duly does, summoning Petit back to his office two days later.

Petit arrives without great expectation, but nevertheless with at least a little hope of success.

Cavard waves him in.

'I spoke with Peletier, the examining magistrate in this case. I put to him your request that the matter be reconsidered, and he put to me a very pertinent question, which is why you think you have any right to question the decisions of your superiors, and to which he added another question, namely why I thought I should waste his time in bringing your request to him. So, does that give you all you need to know? It does, I think.'

Petit swallows hard and nods, and is about to leave when Cavard calls him back.

'I need keen inspectors like you, however,' he says. 'So I have some work for you. How does that sound?'

Petit nods and says it sounds good, and that is how he finds himself dispatched to the archives department for four weeks, in a mostly fruitless attempt to restore the material that was lost to fire of the days of the Commune. In that time he develops a particular skill in dropping box files so that their contents scatter and shuffle across the parquet of the Sûreté library.

And yet, despite this deliberate humiliation, Petit finds that he has not entirely lost his will to question his superiors, nor has he entirely lost his interest in the case of the murderer Marcel Després, the man they called Monsieur Mémoire. Something in him will not let it drop. Or rather, *someone* in him, someone still living in him, insists that he sees it through.

# MONSIEUR MÉMOIRE

In his cell-cum-room at the Salpêtrière, Marcel has fallen back into a near catatonic state. After the breakthrough, and Morel's discovery of Marcel's incredible memory, it appears that the patient has had some kind of relapse, and now will not speak, will not move unless forced to, will barely eat or drink. The situation becomes so bad that one day Morel orders the warders to bring the force-feeding equipment. The process is so unpleasant that it alone is often enough to bring the indolent out of their torpor and remind them that eating is no bad thing. Yet as the tube is passed down Marcel's gullet, and the funnel held high and the little brass handle wound and wound, Marcel barely reacts, never mind struggles. When it's done, he collapses on his thin pallet and sleeps, his eyes staring into nothingness.

The food does seem to do him some good, however, for the next day, when Morel probes around, there is a little more life on Marcel's face. What Morel would like to do is continue the investigation into the limits of Marcel's mnemonic powers. He curses himself that he wasted so much time on those numbers, but then again, he did not expect Marcel to relapse so soon and so profoundly. He knows that he is hoarding Marcel, and that, in time, he will have to share the case with Dr Raymond, the Chief Physician of the hospital. And he wants to do that; it's the right thing to do. It's just that Raymond has swept aside much of Charcot's work since he replaced the great master, something that irritates Morel. So that's one thing. And then there's the fact that if Morel is ever to make a name for himself, he must produce a masterpiece in his own right.

Over the last few years, the hospital has moved rapidly to shift its position on matters such as hysteria, for example, something that old Morel finds troubling. Just because the new regime chooses not to recognise something, does that mean that it stops existing? Is all Charcot's work now to be ignored or refuted? And the assistance that he, Morel, gave to Charcot? Morel knows that Marcel's is a most interesting case, one perhaps without precedent in the literature, and therefore he wants to be absolutely sure that he knows what he is dealing with before he consults Raymond.

So Morel tries speaking directly to Marcel again, and he tries speaking obliquely, looking for a key to unlock the door, as he found previously when he got Marcel to tell him how he'd killed his wife. Morel cannot help but think about his memory; this unbelievable memory. The doctor finds himself frustrated, like a child given a new toy but forbidden from playing with it. He wants to explore, he wants to test and challenge, he wants to set Marcel impossible tasks but be beaten, and yet all the while Marcel sits staring through the grey walls of his cell, Morel is thwarted.

'Describe your act for me,' he says.

Nothing.

'Would you always perform the same routine?'

Nothing.

'Did you use members of the audience as part of the act?'

Nothing. Or perhaps there is something, but it does not emerge for Morel to witness. Yet in Marcel's mind's eye, the memories come thick and fast.

The night that Marcel is thinking about is no different from many of the others, yet to Marcel there is always something different about each night. The one he has in mind is about six months ago, or, as Marcel knows, five months, three weeks and two nights ago. It was a Thursday evening, and the club was not quite as full as it was on weekends. As Marcel took the stage he noted that there were fifty-one people in the crowd, watching him; thirty-eight men and thirteen women. There were eight waiting staff working, in addition to the two barmen, and Chardon himself, of course.

His routine had gone well for some weeks, very well. But things had started to sour. Many of the cabaret's customers were regulars, who came a couple of times a month, and they had seen enough of Monsieur Mémoire. Now they could remember his act almost as well as he could, it had diminishing charms for them. Ondine had told him he needed to add variety, try new things, become more daring, and he was trying to do just that on that particular Thursday night. He had invited a lady on to the stage, a lady who seemed unable to prevent herself from giggling continuously, but who had managed to play along with Marcel's directions. He'd instructed the room to attain perfect stillness, so that no one got up, or sat down, or moved, and then he'd asked her to blindfold him. Checking that he could not see, she'd then pointed to an object in the room; any object. It might be someone's hat, or a cane. Or it might be a bottle on a table, or a picture on the wall, or even an old gentleman's bow tie. When she'd pointed to it, and while Marcel was still blindfolded, someone in the crowd was silently to hide the indicated object, removing it from view.

He would then, as he'd done on the preceding eight nights of this new trick, announce which of the thousand possible objects in the room had vanished, to rapturous applause. If the applause did not come with the first object, he would proceed to the fifth, eighth, eleventh object, until the applause did come.

But that night, Marcel remembers that it went differently. Deep in his mind he searches for the cause; he knows the cause is there, he only has to find it, the thing among the thousand things that happen every second, the one that started him thinking. He was on. Halfway through his routine. The lady he selected made her way to the front, and up the two little steps on to what was charitably called the stage at the Cabaret of Insults. He produced a blindfold from his pocket, and then the lady announced that she would prefer to use a handkerchief of her own, so there could be no thought of deception, no danger that Marcel's blindfold was in some way compromised, and perhaps allowed some vision. Laughing, Marcel took up the challenge, and he declared in return that, if the lady so liked, she could place both his blindfold and her own handkerchief on top of it, so that he was doubly blind.

That was what she did, tying her own handkerchief across his eyes first, before placing Marcel's black blindfold on top. Even as he gave his final instructions, the touch of the fine cotton on his eyes began a chain of associations in his thoughts. The cotton felt exactly like a scarf that his mother wore tightly around her neck on evenings when summer was starting to fail but before autumn had properly come. That scarf had been black, but with his eyes shut, he could only feel the cloth, rather different from the cotton of the shirt he wore constantly as a boy, day after day without change unless it was in the wash, until finally Celeste had torn it into strips to use as rags, and bought him a new one. That new one had never felt the same, not even when it too was showing signs of wear, and Marcel supposed that each and every thing in the world had its own nature; that no two shirts were the same, just as no two trees were the same, as no two stones were exactly the same, as no two faces were the same, not even from moment to moment. Then he thinks that this lady's handkerchief is closest to the feel of Celeste's scarf, and he remembers that Celeste's scarf got lost one day after church, but it was he, Marcel, who found it; he was nine years and fourteen days old at the time and the church was colder than usual and he found the scarf between the pews and there was dust there, because the woman who swept the church was ill with a fever; the doctor had said it was one hundred and four and that she might not survive, but she did survive, well, for another four nights at least when finally God released her, and she was buried next to her husband, who'd lived from 1804 to 1873, or so it said on his grave, but . . .

Then, Marcel stopped remembering.

He opened his eyes, and saw a man standing next to him on stage, holding both blindfolds in his hands. The man wore Chinese costume and then he realised that it was Bishop, the illusionist, who sometimes dressed as a Chinese coolie for part of his act for some ridiculous reason, although Marcel had no idea what that might be. And standing on the other side of him was a lady with a puzzled look on her face. She giggled.

'What the fuck are you doing?' hissed Bishop, who then turned to the audience with the widest of false smiles. 'Lost in reverie, no doubt.'

He got a laugh, of sorts, then hissed in Marcel's direction. 'You've been standing there for five minutes. Finish your damn act.'

Marcel took a look at Bishop, then at the lady next to him, and remembered what he was supposed to be doing.

He took one look at the audience, then mumbled, 'The third champagne glass from the left on the table by the alcove.'

He walked off stage, followed by uncertain laughter and some genuine applause, for that was indeed the object that the lady had indicated.

Ondine tore him to pieces later that night.

'You looked like an idiot!' she said. 'You are an idiot! What the hell were you thinking?'

Thinking? thought Marcel. What was I thinking? I was thinking that the husband of the lady who swept the church in Étoges was sixty-nine years old when he died, which made him the eighth oldest man to be buried in that graveyard though there were many women there who were much older, that—

But Ondine was not done shouting at him.

'I felt like such a fool. When they told me what you'd done. If Bishop hadn't come to rescue you, you'd probably still be standing there. What were you doing? What goes on in that head of yours when you stare into space?'

And so on, and so on, and Marcel listened to it all.

He remembers it all now again as he sits in his cell with Dr Morel who is getting tired sitting on a small wooden stool, asking questions that provoke no response. Marcel, meanwhile, remembers the cabaret. He remembers it in intricate detail, in perfection, in fact, watching it all in the cinematograph that is his mind, playing things this way, that way, forward and backward, left to right and back again and each and every time feeling everything he felt at the time, as if it were happening to him over again, for real.

He worked many nights, Ondine worked almost every night, and very often he would go to the cabaret even if he was not working, to see the show. He watched the girls dance, and felt proud that one of them was his wife, though he found them all attractive, and they were all very pleasing to look at, for a time, until things began to change. He remembers when he started to feel less than comfortable about the attractiveness of the dancers. He arrived in the club one afternoon, looking for Ondine, and found the girls in rehearsal. Normally this would have aroused no great interest from the waiting staff, but Marcel found them standing around, the men anyway, not even pretending to work, but gazing happily at the dancers. Of the eight of them, every other girl was topless, save for a string of fake jewels dangling between their breasts. They finished a number and the piano player crunched to a halt. Chardon shouted a few insulting remarks at the girls; mostly encouraging them to smile.

'If you're going to show us, then look happy about it. That's what they want. They want to think you want to show them your attributes. It's quite simple, ladies, really, it's very simple.'

One of the girls whined back, 'It might help if that lot weren't ogling us.' Covering herself with an arm, she jabbed a finger at the staff, who cheered in return.

'Nonsense,' cried Chardon. 'You have to get used to it, and so do they. By tonight I want them selling beer, not gazing at what God gave you.'

And he here turned and scowled at his staff, who nodded, sheepishly.

Then the pianist struck up again, and the girls went through the number one final time, in which half of them started with thin black blouses of which they somehow became divested, and Marcel watched with mounting unease as the dancing finished and one of the topless girls, his wife Ondine, made her way over to him, half-heartedly covering her breasts as she did so.

She kissed him on the cheek.

'Hello, husband,' she said.

Marcel didn't know what to say.

'Something the matter?' asked Ondine.

'You . . .' he began, then stopped. 'You were . . . I mean, you shouldn't . . .'

'That?'

Ondine waved her hand back at the stage.

'It's nothing. Relax. It's just what we have to do. Chardon's right. All the other cabarets have nudes. Some way or other. We're behind the times, he says. He says we're losing customers. We have to do something.'

'But you don't,' said Marcel. 'Half of you are still covered up. You could be one of those.'

'I could be,' shrugged Ondine. 'But I don't care, and some of the other girls really do. Mind you, Chardon says we'll all have to do it in the end, just to keep up with the Moulin Rouge. '

'This place is nothing like the Moulin Rouge. Why do we have to—'

'Listen, just forget it, will you? I'm doing it and that's all there is to it. We have to make ends meet, right? So get used to it.'

But Marcel did not get used to it, and with each successive night, there were more memories about which he could feel uneasy: the allure of the dancers' breasts, the jingling jewels, the thump of the piano, the eager faces, the leering gaze, the wide eyes of the hungry men in the crowd of the cabaret, night after night after night.

# PUNISHMENT

One day towards the end of the month finds Inspector Petit leaving the archive room a little earlier than he should. He's been cataloguing and collating for two weeks now and has barely managed to reassemble a couple of files on the activities of the subversives before 1870. These were files that were lost in the fires set by the Communards themselves, which was more than they could have hoped for, or even probably intended, in those fervent days of 1871. The only respite for Petit is when, under the pretext of interviewing some witness who is most likely now long since dead, he can excuse himself from his near-Sisyphean task and waste his time on the streets instead.

It being summertime, Paris is well dressed, the trees in the avenues provide pleasant shade from the sun, and cafés spill out across the pavements in every street.

Around five o'clock, Petit strolls down the Rue Poliveau, heading towards the hospital of Salpêtrière. He has been unable to let go of what he was told to let go of, and finds himself in an awkward position. He is young, and he has principles and, above all else, he has a strong sense of justice. He also knows that advancement in the Sûreté is procured not merely by merit, but by favour too. If he upsets the wrong people . . . Well, that goes without saying. But something, *someone*, has not let him rest, not accept the thought that a freely confessed murderer should be let off. And especially not just because he claims to have lost his sanity.

Petit isn't even sure why he's decided to visit Després, but dimly he's aware that perhaps he could indeed let the whole thing go if he saw this so-called insanity for himself. He might

58

even be able to convince that voice inside him that it would be acceptable to let it go too, though of that he is less sure. The only way to know is to try it, and so that is what he does.

On arrival at Salpêtrière, he's immediately impressed with the hospital, with its physical splendour, but he doesn't realise the impact of that upon him. Were he a touch more self-aware, he might have noticed that he stood a little straighter as he approached the entrance gate, and that he is already taking the concept of madness a little more seriously than he was five minutes previously.

He's also impressed with the efficiency of the place. At first, there seems a little hesitance when he asks to see a . . . what's the word? He struggles for a moment until the gentleman in the kiosk at the massive stone entrance suggests one for him: patient.

'Yes, a patient. Marcel Després.'

The upright gentleman in the kiosk starts to mention matters of visiting times and appointments, but once Petit produces his Sûreté identification card, there is a change of attitude.

The man picks up a telephone at his right hand, something that impresses Petit even more, for despite the continued efforts of the last two chefs of the Sûreté, even they do not have a telephone system as yet. Former Chef Macé even resigned over the issue, but the Préfecture had been unmoved by this protest; a budget was a budget, and the police budget was an especially burdensome one already.

The gentleman in the kiosk speaks to unseen parties, and in no time at all a warder arrives and conducts Petit across the grounds of the hospital a distance of a few hundred metres, unlocks the door of a cell, and invites Petit to enter. All this has deeply impressed Petit on an unconscious level. Unbeknown to him as we have said, he is already reappraising his thoughts and beliefs about the hospital, its function and its inmates.

He has heard some wild stories about the place, but the elegance and opulence of the architecture alone has started a line of reasoning in his head. For important people to think it worthwhile to spend vast sums of money building such a place, and to employ the country's best doctors in the search of cures for illnesses that defy easy classification, can surely only mean that these illnesses are real and present, despite his previous thoughts to the contrary. Like some Arcadian stables of stone in the grounds of a pleasure palace, the cells in which these prisoners, or patients, rest bring to Petit's mind such words as vital, solid, commendable.

The warder indicates that he will wait outside, and bids Petit to enter, which he does, but not before appraising his surroundings one more time. He can hear some shouts and wails from a distance that certainly speak of loosened minds and plunging souls, but the warder doesn't bat an eyelid, so Petit decides that neither should he.

He ducks through the doorway of the cell, mindful of the lintel for once, and it takes a moment for his eyes to adjust from the summer brightness to the crepuscular gloom in the cell. Then he sees him, his murderer, sitting on the narrow bed, staring straight ahead of him.

Now that he is here, he realises he doesn't know where to begin, in fact, he is not sure he has anything to say at all. But the warder is just outside, and presumably within earshot, so it won't do to stand and be dumb. He pulls out a notebook from his pocket, and a pencil. It might be good to take notes, he thinks.

'Monsieur Després? Marcel Després?'

The man on the bed does not seem to have heard. Petit is struck by a sudden sensation that it is as if he is not there, that he is invisible and inaudible, because this is no mere act of ignoring. Després's utter lack of reaction to his name makes it hard to feel they are existing in the same time or space.

He shifts his voice up a notch or two.

'Marcel Després?'

'He can't hear you,' says a voice at the door that makes Petit start and spin around, during which he manages to kick a small wooden stool across the length of the cell.

Petit sees a doctor staring at him.

'May I ask what you're doing here?' Behind him stands the warder, with unblinking gaze as ever, and a short man carrying the hefty paraphernalia of photography equipment, which he sets down just outside the cell door.

Petit hesitates.

'I'm . . . Yes, I . . . My name is Petit, I am an inspector with the Sûreté. This man is . . . I mean to say, I have been assigned to the case of Marcel Després in respect to the murder of—'

'Yes. I know who you are. I just received word of your visit. But as for your case, I would say that the case of Marcel Després is my concern now, and no longer that of anyone at the Sûreté, since his incarceration within the walls of my hospital.'

'*Your* hospital?'

'I perhaps overstate my case. I am Dr Morel, *Assistant* Chief Alienist of Salpêtrière. Monsieur Després is in my charge.'

'A pleasure,' says the young inspector, from well-formed habit, and old Morel responds in kind. They shake hands, without pleasure.

Dr Morel studies Marcel for a moment.

'Much the same . . .'

He turns back to Petit.

'We still have not satisfied ourselves with a conclusion to the question of what you're doing here. Inspector.'

Petit knows he is already on shaky ground, and decides he needs to repair the damage if he is to get anywhere.

'Doctor, forgive the intrusion. While this matter is of course now primarily—'

'Entirely.'

'Certainly one of your concerns here at the hospital, neverthe-less my duties as the officer assigned by the examining magistrate require me to have conducted an interview with the accused for the purposes of—'

'Look here, my boy,' begins Morel, and Petit wishes fervently that his elders would stop referring to him in this way. 'You are speaking nonsense. Don't think for one minute that you can bamboozle me with police jargon. I am probably more aware of the protocol in this case than you are, given that I have been assistant chief physician of this hospital for fifteen years, and you appear to me to be no more than sixteen years old. No doubt you will assure me that you have seen at least five more birthdays than that, but from where I'm standing I would think you should know better than to attempt to pull the wool over my eyes. The examining magistrate can have said no such thing to you because the moment a prisoner of *yours* becomes a patient of *ours*, a decision made by the Préfecture, you or he have absolutely no jurisdiction over his or her person. You have no need, and, I firmly add, no right to interview our patient, and what he may or may not have done ceased to be any concern of the police the moment he stepped foot in our little establishment. I trust I am making myself clear?'

Petit assures the doctor that he is making himself very clear, yet the doctor is not done.

'So, I say again. What is it that you want here?'

Petit throws his arms to the side, narrowly avoiding bashing his knuckles on the doorframe.

'I just wanted to see him.'

Morel stares at him for a decently long time.

'Good answer,' he says. 'I want to see him myself. Here he sits, and yet he may as well be a stone in the street for all the life that's in him.'

Morel waves at the man outside with the camera.

'Shall we do him now? We may as well. Inspector, would you care to see his photograph being made? You know, you've surely heard, that is, about his memory?'

'Some trick of his, I gather. Some club in Pigalle.'

'No!' says Morel with the zealousness of the convert. 'No trick.'

Petit raises an eyebrow. The warder, meanwhile, with the help of Morel, pulls Marcel to his feet and then shuffles him out of the cell to the little wooden seat that protrudes from the wall outside the door. Moving him on to the bench, Marcel sits in the dappled sunlight, while the photographer, a rather stained-looking man in his fifties, fusses about with his stuff.

'You mean,' says Petit, 'he really can remember lots of things?'

That appears to be the most insulting thing that Petit has said or done since he arrived in the hospital.

'Lots of things?' cries Morel. 'No, he cannot just remember lots of things! He can remember everything! Or so I believe. At least, that is what I would like to prove. But it's been hard going. This state you see before you now is his usual condition. I have had a few hours, here and there, where he becomes responsive, and then I have begun my work! And so far, I find that there are . . .'

And here Morel pauses dramatically.

'. . . no limits to his memory, whatsoever.'

Petit looks at Marcel, who's squinting slightly but otherwise shows no sign of life.

'Is that unusual?' Petit says, searching for something to say in return to the doctor.

Morel seems almost to pass out.

'Unusual? Do you have any idea what you're saying? Unusual? Just think of it, for a moment, if you would. How good is your memory? You are a policeman – no doubt you think your memory is rather good. You must use it a lot in the course of your work. And you probably can remember a few other things too, like your parents' birthdays and the address where you grew up. And you probably have wondered from time to time how it is that you can be walking along the boulevard one day and for no particular reason into your head arrives a clear and complete memory from one day when you were eleven and went to the beach and you can remember exactly what your mother said when you splashed water on her dress and what you had for lunch and so on and so on.

'Everyone has moments of recollection like that. But let me ask you, would it be unusual to be able to remember every single moment of your *entire life* in such clarity and detail? Unusual? In all my days of working with the many aspects of memory I have never seen, nor even heard of such a case as this, of our Marcel, Le Mémoire.'

Petit nods, showing penance, though by now he really hates this old goat. He also discovers that voice inside him is starting to speak more loudly again, demanding justice. Demanding that Petit, for God's sake, *does something*.

The photographer announces that he is ready, and asks the other gentlemen to step aside as he ducks under a black hood behind the wooden box that will capture Marcel's likeness. There is a sudden energetic puff from the flash powder, held out towards Marcel at arm's length by the photographer. Petit jumps, Morel wrinkles his nose at the smell of the burning powder, and Marcel remains motionless.

'You make photographs of all your patients?' asks Petit.

'Not all of them, no,' says Morel. 'The more interesting ones. In Charcot's day we used to make many more – particularly the hysterics – some of the things that occurred could not have been believed were they not witnessed by the human eye, or, failing that, captured on the photographic plate. It has become an important part of our work to catalogue the aspects of the insane. We are creating a photographic library of insanity here. Yes, I grant you, Marcel's portrait will not display his mind to anyone else, but he is handsome enough to stand it, don't you think? And I would like to record his being here in every way possible.'

Morel turns to the photographer.

'One more, perhaps, Monsieur Buguet?'

Buguet, the photographer, nods and ducks under his hood again.

Petit watches the tiny brass lever on the front of the box suddenly duck as Buguet depresses a lever, the flash burns with its messy puff, and the photograph is made.

Marcel stares across the yard, he blinks.

'I would have liked to have spoken to him,' says Petit.

'So would I,' says Morel, 'but it seems I will have to go on waiting for his next lucid moment. Can I escort you to the gate, Inspector?'

Petit realises it is not really a gesture of politeness, and that he is being asked to leave. Suddenly, he grows angry.

'Look, I don't see why we should just let this man go free. He murdered someone! He killed his wife! There are dozens of witnesses. He himself admits to it! It's not right, it does not represent French justice. It should not be allowed to stand.'

Morel takes the young man gently by the elbow, nodding to the warder, who starts to help Marcel back into his cell.

'Go free, you say,' says Morel, not rudely, but with great gravity considering Petit's choice of words. 'Let me walk you to the gate. No, perhaps we'll take a longer route; there are one or two things I would like to show you as we go.'

So they walk, and the doctor points out this facility to the inspector, and that building, and chats away amiably about the running of the hospital and how things were in Charcot's day, which Petit can already sense is, to Morel, a golden era, already long gone.

They turn a corner into a small street of cobbles where more rows of cells await them, not quite as elegant as the row where Marcel is being kept.

'Free, you said, I think,' says Morel. 'Go free? Do you think the man is free? I would argue the opposite is true – rarely have I seen a man more *bound*. Yes, he is locked in his cell and if he were to walk the grounds he would be unable to exit through the prison gate, but that is not the true way in which he is bound. I mean he is locked inside his mind. You saw him yourself – in what sense would you say he is free? Is he free to do anything he wishes? Is he free to be anything he wants to be?'

Petit has calmed down a little since his outburst, and yet he wants to argue his case, and has seen a way to do it.

'That may be so,' he says, 'but freedom is not the only question here. There is also the matter of punishment.'

'Punishment? You think that is important?'

'Of course punishment is important,' snaps Petit, feeling nettled once more. 'It is the contract that the criminal makes with society – he commits an act against the individual, which is the same as to commit an act against society, and in return he knows he must receive punishment. That is clear, and it is the reason that we have a clearly stated penal code, so that every malfeasant knows what he will be liable for if caught. We must teach him a lesson.'

The doctor looks at Petit for a moment before answering.

'Perhaps I might find some grounds on which to agree with you there,' he says, after this pause, and just as Petit begins to smile, Morel adds, 'but not for the reasons you imagine.'

The smile drifts off Petit's face.

Morel steps forward again, and invites Petit to join him by the door of a cell. The number 34 is painted in dark grey upon its surface. A small glass window, so small that even a monkey could not have climbed through it, allows a dim view of the cell inside.

'Please,' says Morel, and waves his hand at the window.

Bending down a little to the window, Petit peers inside, misjudging the distance and bumping his nose on the glass as he does so.

He cups his hands over his brow to shield the light, and steps back suddenly as he sees a face three inches away on the other side of the glass.

'Oh, he's awake, is he? Let's say hello.'

Morel pulls out a large bunch of keys from his inside pocket, and fumbles one into the lock, pulling the door open, and allowing the patient inside to step out.

'Good afternoon, Henri,' he says, and the patient smiles, benignly yet uncertainly. 'I am Dr Morel.'

'Good afternoon, Dr Morel,' he says. He wears the same drab garb as Marcel, like coarse pyjamas in grey. He seems a little bemused, but otherwise happy enough, and calm.

'Henri, this is Inspector Petit. Why don't you say hello?'

'Hello, Inspector,' says Henri, and holds out his hand.

The two men shake.

'Very good,' says Morel. 'Well, come along, Petit. We must be going. Henri, if you please . . .'

Shutting Henri back in his cell, Petit wants to ask what had been the purpose of that introduction, but Morel is in full flow as they walk across the cobbles, turning the corner into an identical row. Petit has noted the way that Morel walks, with his out-turned feet and feeble hip-thrust. He is trying not to find it distracting, and focuses on what the doctor is telling him.

'That man you just met, Henri, was a shoemaker. Some eight years ago, on his wedding day, in an insensible rage, he stabbed his father-in-law-to-be to death using a bradawl. He has been confined here ever since, which you would approve of no doubt though perhaps you would consider that things should be taken further.'

Here Morel chops the edge of one hand on to the palm of the other and Petit winces at the obvious reference.

'And yet in the eight years of his confinement, in fact, ever since he emerged from whatever came over him that day, he has shown not a single moment of violence, or even anger.

'There are interesting matters to consider when we talk about crime and punishment. We might perhaps agree on some things, but I would challenge you on some points that you seem to hold very dear, especially when one is considering *maladies de la mémoire*, which is, I might add, the area I have applied myself to over the last ten years.'

They turn another corner and still Petit finds no way to interrupt.

'What is memory, Inspector? This is a question I have asked myself a thousand times over the years, so perhaps it is unfair to spring it upon you, cold, as it were. Let me give you the opinion of our philosophers. Memory is a series of moments, captured by the mind in rather the same way as Buguet just captured Marcel's likeness. A crude analogy perhaps but the principle is good – the mind captures each moment of experience and records them in a vast archive, somewhere in the brain. In fact, from various brain-damaged cases, we suspect that the storage is more complex than that, but for the sake of argument, imagine if you will a vast library of moments, all catalogued and filed and stamped and waiting.'

Petit has no need to imagine that, having just left such a place this very afternoon in the basement of the Quai des Orfèvres. It comes to his mind now, and he's aware enough to realise that he is performing the act of memory, there and then, just as the doctor is describing.

'So, you recall something, and your mind draws it out from the thousands, no, we must surely at least say millions, of files in the archive. It is no wonder that for most of us, even those of us with good memories, this is an imperfect process. But lest you should say that perhaps not all incidents are stored as memories in this great filing cabinet of the mind in the first place, and that that is why our memories are imperfect, let me tell you about the work we have done with hypnotism here. Under hypnosis, all sorts of memories that the conscious patient had forgotten ever existed may be accessed once more. So it is fair to assume that everything is in there somewhere.'

Here, Morel playfully taps Petit on the forehead, and Petit finds himself really detesting the old doctor again. But Morel still isn't finished. He takes a quick glance at his pocket watch as they turn another corner and he draws to his conclusion.

'This makes what our Marcel can do even more extraordinary, if you think about it. He can go to any file, any memory at all, and recall it. A perfect memory, or so I hope to prove. So if memory consists of a series of moments, then where, in all that, is the self?'

There is a pause, during which Petit manages to notice that they have returned back to the original street of cobbles, and says, 'The self?'

'Yes, the self. Who you are, my boy. Who you are. Let's play a quick game – let's ask what you would be if you had no memory. No memory at all. None whatsoever. Go on, think about it.'

And Petit finds, much to his dislike, that he is. *Without memory*, he thinks, *without memory . . .*

'Without memory, one could not do simple things,' he begins, feeling his way into the argument.

'Very good, go on.'

'One could not find one's way home. Or remember how to work. Or who your friends were. Or what your name was. Or—'

'Yes!' says Morel, his eyes sparkling. 'Take it further!'

Petit does. He quickly sees all the mundane things that could not be, and then, before he knows it, he has the sensation of tumbling down an abyss, into nothingness, for he understands that without memory . . .

'We would be nothing. We could not learn, we could not do. We would be unable to function, to think, to reason. We would not know who our friends were, what we did five minutes previously. All higher functions would have to cease, we would merely breathe, perhaps eat, drink, but . . . no more than that. We would just be some sort of living machine. We would truly be nothing.'

Morel stands and admires his pupil.

'Very, very good,' he says slowly. Then he turns. He pulls a key from his pocket, and while Petit is still wondering with horror at what he's just been given to understand, Morel opens the door of a cell.

A man steps out, and Petit suddenly realises they are standing at the door of the same cell, 34, of five minutes before.

'Good morning, Henri,' says Morel. 'I am Dr Morel. This is Inspector Petit. Won't you say hello?'

Henri steps forward, smiling, and shakes Petit's hand.

'A pleasure to meet you,' he says, and as Petit looks into the man's eyes, he can see Henri has no recollection whatsoever of having already met him. Or for that matter, the doctor.

'Thank you, Henri,' says Morel. 'If you please . . .'

Henri smiles and retreats into his cell.

Petit stands, staring.

'That wasn't an act,' he mumbles. He holds an arm out towards the door. 'He had no idea who I was.'

'Indeed. Henri suffers from a special kind of amnesia – he can remember everything up to his wedding day in a normal fashion. But since that awful event he has been unable to create new memories. He can remember for approximately two to three minutes. I allowed five minutes to pass as we walked, by which time I knew you would be a stranger to Henri, as indeed I am too. He seems barely to understand why he is here, or, at least, he has no reason to question it, but has no memory of the wedding day, or what he did. So I bring you again to your question of punishment. What point is there in punishing Henri? He has no consciousness of what he did. Therefore he can have no *conscience* about what he did. Therefore to punish him teaches him nothing. He has no responsibility for his actions. The only reason we might punish him, I agree with you, is for ourselves, for our own satisfaction, for our own sense of right and wrong. For our own pleasure. But it is, I assure you, meaningless, utterly meaningless, to Henri. To keep him amused we gave him a child's puzzle. It takes him around three minutes to solve it each time. His entire waking life now consists of making and remaking that puzzle.'

Petit does not know what to say.

'Such is the case of the amnesiac. But amnesiacs are, to be honest, common enough. I have had to create a new term for Després – the *hyper*mnesiac; he suffers, and I truly believe the word suffers is appropriate, from *too much memory*. That is why he is ill. And as for punishing him, I would ask you to consider the view of our philosophers, namely this: all that we are is an assembly of a sequence of memories. And if they are merely a sequence of individual, discrete events, then how can we create a single continuous self from them? And if there is no continuity of the self, then how can we be held responsible for our actions of five years ago, or six months ago, or even, for that matter, this morning?'

Morel has brought Petit to the gate, and shakes him warmly by the hand.

'Thank you for visiting us today. I take it to be a great honour in speaking with you about such matters.'

Still somewhat in a daze, his head full of glimpses of ideas, and therefore of worlds, that have never occurred to him before, Petit returns the handshake.

But Morel is not finished.

'I trust that you remember that the police have no jurisdiction within the walls of the hospital. As it happens, I can have you prevented from returning here. I hope you would be so good as not to put me to that trouble?'

Petit nods, opens his mouth, but before he knows what he wants to say, he finds himself in the boulevard again, his feet carrying him home, and a voice nagging in his ear, telling him he has failed.

# IN THE RUE
# SAINT-ANDRÉ-DES-ARTS

The days go by. Petit completes his third week of his own particular punishment in the archives in the basement of the Quai des Orfèvres, a cold and damp place even in the height of the summer, where the sight of rats is not uncommon. The old archivist, Gilbert, has actually managed to allocate some petty cash to feed the local stray cats to encourage their loyalty, a poor attempt to keep the rats at bay, but easier on the budget of the Sûreté than calling the rat catcher.

One more week, Petit tells himself, and he can be free of these pointless attempts to recover information lost nearly thirty years ago, before he was born, ancient history. Just so many forgotten memories.

One day, after work, he's walking home down the Rue Saint-André-des-Arts, and finds that he has put himself in a café opposite the fine archway that leads into the Cour du Commerce, the place where Marcel shot Ondine.

His conversation with that crazy doctor from Salpêtrière has not left him. He finds, annoyingly, that his mind keeps returning to it, whether he wants it to or not, and actually, come to mention it, he would prefer it not to. Before his visit to the hospital, he understood things very well. Criminals are bad and should be punished. Cops are, well, perhaps not always good, he knows that already, but as a collective force they are there to restore order, to solve crimes, to bring the guilty before the judges for punishment. But more than once,

Petit discovers that he is thinking about Morel's philosophers, the ones who claim that there can be no self if all we are is merely a sequence of fragmentary moments held by memory. He knows that this is poppycock, or, at least, he very much wants it to be, but time and again in the last week he has been troubled by the disturbing notion that he understands nothing at all. He feels as if he has grown up in a small and simple house, and has now been shown a glimpse through a door to entire rooms that he never knew existed, rooms that are strange, challenging and infinitely more complex than the rooms of his childhood. He feels somewhat bewildered and he doesn't enjoy the sensation in the least.

He orders a *bock* and while he waits for the cool beer to arrive, decides that the philosophers can go to hell. Whether they're right or not is unimportant – they don't have to wrestle with crimes and criminals and judges, and these are simply practical matters with practical solutions. And murderers go to the guillotine. Or at least, they *should*.

It's as the waitress brings his beer and he takes a first sip that he finds he's looking down the Cour du Commerce, and remembers the visit he made to Després's studio, and into his head, for no apparent reason at all, comes a memory, something that was tucked away in everything Morel said about Marcel.

Morel said it was the Préfecture's decision to have Marcel moved to the hospital. Petit had assumed the decision was down to the examining magistrate, this being the first case of insanity that he'd come across in his eighteen months' service.

The next day, he hunts down Drouot and asks him, and Drouot confirms that the decision is taken by the Préfecture.

'In the case of the insane, confinement to an asylum is by request of the family; where the party has no family, then confinement is at the discretion of the Préfecture.'

'Not the examining magistrate?'

'No, it would have been taken out of his hands.'

73

'Even if the insane party is accused of a crime? Of murder?'

Drouot looks at Petit carefully.

'Laurent, you're not doing something you shouldn't be doing, are you?'

Petit has the honesty to look guilty, even if he denies it.

'No, no. No, I was just wondering. About that case we had, yes, that's true, but I'm not doing anything I shouldn't be.'

Not yet, he thinks to himself later, but . . .

He only had one more question for Drouot anyway, sensing it was time to let the subject drop, which was about who at the Préfecture would have made that decision, but that, Drouot didn't know.

Something is not right. He cannot put his mind on exactly what is wrong, but there is definitely something wrong about the whole matter. For one thing, he can't work out how someone at the Préfecture made a decision about Després after only two days when he himself was assigned to the case in the same space of time. Two days was a fast response for the examining magistrate, such speed as the crime of murder demands. For anything lesser it would have been a week, most likely. And yet in that short space of time the decision was made that Després was criminally insane and to move him to Salpêtrière.

For another two days he tries to forget all about the case, with a little success, but then the matter is taken out of his hands.

As he leaves work one day, he finds a shadow at his shoulder, and looking down to his left sees someone he has met before.

He hunts for his name.

'Monsieur Buguet? Yes? We met at the hospital.'

'I've been looking for you for days. Took me over a week to find out where you work. You're some kind of librarian, are you? For the police?'

Petit opens his mouth to refute that, then ignores the matter.

'Can I help you, Monsieur Buguet?'

74

Buguet still has an unwashed air about him; the whiff of photographic chemicals seems to have pervaded his clothes, if not his actual body. He puts a hand on Petit's forearm, bringing him to a standstill.

'I read about your case,' he says.

'I have no case at present,' Petit assures Buguet, but the photographer isn't really listening.

'I think I know who the girl is. The wife. I saw her picture in the paper, days ago, but then you know how the engravings are – they must get apes to make them.'

'Monsieur Buguet, we know who the victim is. Her name was Ondine Després, née Badiou, and she was the wife of Marcel Després until her untimely death.'

'Perhaps I should have said, I know who she *was*. *Before*.'

Petit sees that there is an earnest look on Buguet's face.

'Go on.'

'I'm not sure. Like I said, those engravings in the papers leave much to the imagination. But you could get me a picture of her, I mean an actual photograph, couldn't you? Then I'd know for sure.'

Yes, thinks Petit, I might be able to do that.

'Why?' he asks.

'Like I say, Inspector, I'm not sure. But get me that photograph and then we'll see. Can you do it?'


Petit does do it.

It transpires that the concierge had the studio cleaned up, ready for new tenants, and then, the following afternoon, it was broken into, and robbed, though there was nothing left in it to rob.

'So what were they doing?' Petit asks her.

'Who?'

'The burglars. What did they want?'

'I would say that's your job, Inspector. I told the police and they said since nothing was taken there was no point investigating. But the hall door was broken and who's going to fix that?'

'And what of the Després' possessions?'

The concierge explains that all the effects of Marcel and Ondine have been boxed up and are locked away in the cellars underneath the cour, though she takes great pains to wonder aloud to Petit about who will pay for the cleaning and the storage and how long she should store the items for and really, she doesn't think she can be bothered to let Petit into the cellar until he produces five francs, which appear to change her mind.

Grumbling, she unlocks the door to the cellar and shoves a lantern into his hands.

'They're at the back, last alcove,' she says, and wanders off, slipping the money into some unseen place in her dress.

It takes Petit half an hour to go through the crates. It hasn't escaped him that it's more than a little strange that the Després' studio was broken into while none of the other apartments in the block, which did contain items of value, was.

Finally, he finds the photograph of Ondine. The glass has been cracked by someone as clumsy as he is, so he flicks the catches on the back, and slides the photograph itself out of the battered old frame, which he puts back in the crate.

That evening, he meets Buguet again, as arranged, at the Lion Blanc in the Rue Saint-André-des-Arts.

'This is her,' says Petit, sliding the photograph across the desk.

Buguet is barely managing to suppress his satisfaction, and without saying anything Petit knows that he knows something about her. He also knows that it's going to cost him. Buguet already has his palm loosely placed upward on the table top, casually inviting the receipt of funds.

Petit puts ten francs in his hand, at which Buguet frowns, but the inspector isn't as much of a fool as the photographer clearly hopes he is.

'Come on, I don't know what you're going to tell me yet. And this is a dead case. So I think that's enough for now.'

Buguet scowls but without real feeling; as much as anything he wants to show off what he knows.

'Yes, that's her. I met her once.'

'You did?'

Buguet nods, enjoying dropping his facts like stones into a still pool.

'Up in Montmartre.'

'Go on.'

Buguet hesitates. 'You must understand,' he says, 'that I am a respectable photographer. I work for the hospital now, and for a few select clients. Nothing untoward at all, you see?'

'Go on.'

'Yes, well, it does happen that we photographers run into one another from time to time, and my work used to take me to some of the less salubrious quarters of the city.'

Petit is on the verge of losing his patience when Buguet suddenly cannot stop himself any more.

'Well, you see, as soon as I read about that murder and saw her engraving, I said to myself, I know who that is. Well, I didn't know her name, though I do now of course, but I met her in Montmartre, and she was working for some of the photographers up there, who, well, you know. Some of them sell a different kind of service, don't they? I'm sure you know what I mean.'

You mean pornographers, Petit thinks. But he merely nods briefly to show that he understands. Once again he's taken with the notion that Buguet is somewhat seedy; into his mind comes a vision of the photographer thirstily swigging at his chemicals, though, for all Petit knows, that not only might not get you intoxicated, it's probably lethal. He stirs himself.

'Who was she working for? You have a name?'

Buguet closes his hand around the ten francs.

'No,' he says. 'I don't, but I can tell you this. I thought she'd posed for one of them, maybe more than one. Someone pointed her out to me and said that was her line, you see, but—'

'Who pointed her out?'

'Some guy in a bar. I don't know who he was. We just got chatting and he knew I was a photographer. He thought I—'

'Oh, yes, but that's not what you do. Or ever did. Correct?'

'Correct,' says Buguet rapidly. 'Anyway, when I saw her engraving I thought, That's her: a pornographer's girl. And then I see this, and I know for sure.'

'You do? How? You mean you recognise her?'

'Yes, but not only that. Look . . .'

Buguet takes the photo off the table very carefully as if he's handling treasure, and tilts it towards Petit.

'See it?'

Petit stares.

'See what?'

'Hard to see to the untrained eye. Look, top left. You see?'

Petit takes the photograph from Buguet and scours it, trying to see anything out of the ordinary.

There stands Ondine, in a long, formal dress, some dark material, in two alternating vertical stripes. Her head is slightly tilted to one side, her lips are made up, and her eyes too, and there is that unmistakable sultriness about her. Her hair is piled and pinned on her head, a single coiling strand hanging down, brushing her cheek.

'Not her,' says Buguet, so Petit looks elsewhere. The ground cannot be seen; the portrait finishes around knee-height. There is a typical studio background – a backdrop that pretends to show a view through to a balcony, with tropical scenes of a beach beyond. The tropical theme is incongruously picked up by a potted palm behind Ondine's right shoulder; the walls are papered with a narrow stripe, again some dark colours.

'Look!' urges Buguet, and with his fingertip points out a faint white mark on the photograph, a tiny smudge of lighter paper, narrow, as long as a nail clipping.

'So? An imperfection of the print, perhaps.'

Buguet sits back, pleased with himself.

'An imperfection, yes, but not of the print. You would find that mark on any copy of this photograph. You would find that mark on *any* print of *any* photograph made by the camera that made this one. It is an imperfection of the camera lens. To the layman, to the untrained eye, it's as good as invisible. But to a professional, it is obvious. It is a glaring thing, quite awful. And it just so happens that, in the course of the professional photographer's work, he comes to know his enemies, so to speak. This photograph was taken by a highly active pornographer of Montmartre, a man too cheap to buy a new lens for this camera, or even have the defect polished out. He knew that most people wouldn't even spot the imperfection, but those of us in this business came to know the mark.'

'And you have seen it often?'

'Often enough,' says Buguet, holding out his empty palm again.

Petit's smile fades.

'On works of a pornographic nature? An industry you claim to have nothing to do with . . .'

Buguet senses he is on thin ice. He withdraws his empty palm.

'We photographers come across most aspects of the business. Eventually.'

'Pornography is not a business, Buguet. It is an illegal activity, as is the trafficking of obscene materials.'

There is a silence.

'So,' asks Petit, 'who is this pornographer with the damaged lens?'

Buguet sits on his hands, miserably, and Petit knows he's not stalling for further bribes.

'I don't know.'

Petit pockets the photograph.

He maintains a blank face towards Buguet, but finds that he is conflicted again. *So what?* he thinks. So Ondine Després might once have posed nude, perhaps undertaken modelling of an even more explicit nature than that. That alters nothing at all. Marcel shot her and then, within forty-eight hours, someone made the decision to have him removed from police custody and put beyond reach in the asylum of Salpêtrière.

Still, this is no proof of anything, it is merely something that rubs away in his brain, demanding further thought.

Buguet stirs in front of him.

'If the inspector is pleased with . . .'

Against his better judgement, Petit puts five more francs in his outstretched hand, for this is how crimes get solved, he knows that as well as any detective who's been working the city for twenty years. But then, he reminds himself, there is no crime to solve. Nothing to be done. So why is it that when Buguet mutters, 'No, I don't know who he was, but of course you could find out,' Petit is unable to stop himself asking how.

'You should know that as well as anyone. You're the police librarian, aren't you? Pay a visit to the Library of Hell.'

Buguet leaves, and Petit stares through the window at the busy street. He's heard of it, but never been there. Still, there's a first time for everything, he thinks, and there and then determines to pay a visit to the notorious collection of banned writings, obscene images and immoral publications: the Library of Hell.

# AB INITIUM

Dr Morel forgets all about the visit from the young inspector. His memory is, like most people's, good in matters in which he is interested, very poor in areas where he is not. Right now, there is only one subject that interests him, and that is Marcel. In truth, that is not quite the case: Morel is not interested in Marcel, not all of him, anyway. He is interested in Marcel's mind, his memory, in where it resides and what it can do and how it works.

He is delighted that as the days pass, Marcel has a few more lucid periods, though none of them lasts long, and sooner or later he retires into whatever the furthest corner of his mind is, where he lurks while his body rocks out its angst like a metronome of pain.

Almost four weeks have passed since Marcel's arrival at Salpêtrière when one day, as Morel enters his cell, he finds his patient standing, facing the door calmly, as if waiting for him.

'Good morning, Doctor,' Marcel says, and Morel is very briefly surprised by this sudden change. He recovers quickly however; he's seen enough wild changes of behaviour in his time not to be thrown by it, or to think that it might be permanent. They all relapse in the end, he thinks, they all relapse. Nevertheless, this provides him with his best chance yet of probing more deeply into the landscape of Marcel's memory.

'Good morning, Marcel,' he says. 'How are you feeling today?'

'Where am I, Doctor?' Marcel asks.

'You don't know?'

Morel is suddenly concerned that his patient has slipped from the exalted pedestal of hypermnesia to that of the common amnesiac.

'In some sort of hospital. But which one?'

'This is Salpêtrière, Marcel. You have heard of it?'

Marcel nods.

'And you know why you are here?'

Marcel nods again, and Morel's expert eye sees the panic that lurks just behind the façade. He must tread very carefully this morning if he is to get what he wants, something he both craves and fears.

Morel wants to prove that Marcel's memory is limitless, and yet this is something that cannot be proved categorically. It would be easy enough to *disprove* the theory: if he were to find one instance of Marcel failing to recall something accurately, then in an instant the concept of perfection would be blown away. Yes, he would still have a phenomenal ability, but Morel wants to believe, and to prove, that Marcel's memory is absolutely without limit. And that, of course, cannot be done; that is the irritation that dogs Morel. He can only *disprove* the case with one hundred per cent accuracy, to prove it lies beyond his reach. Nevertheless, he hopes that with enough time and enough testing, he will have as good a case as can be made, and then, he has no doubt, he will write the paper that will assure his place in the canon of the great alienists. It must be done.

Morel decides to move Marcel away from thoughts of hospitals and of murder. He has, more in hope than belief, brought with him his chalkboard and chalk.

He motions to Marcel, gets him to sit on the bed once more, and places himself on the low wooden stool. He begins to record a sequence of numbers.

'A little exercise, eh?' he says. 'Something to warm up with, as the athlete warms his muscles before the race . . .'

He finished writing a series of numbers, and displays it to Marcel, who stares at it with a mixture of boredom and contempt. As Morel whips the board around and waits, Marcel begins to rattle off the numbers.

'Nine, four, three, three, six, two, nine . . .'

Morel almost shrieks.

'No!' he says. 'Wait! Stop, stop! You're wrong . . .'

Morel cannot believe it. Marcel is wrong. He is getting the numbers all wrong. Just as the doctor feared, everything is disproved, everything comes tumbling down.

'No, no,' says Morel. 'You're wrong. You—'

Marcel interrupts the interruption. 'Doctor. I am not telling you the numbers on your board today. I am telling you the numbers that were on your board the first time you tried this game.'

Morel is dumbstruck. 'You're . . . ?'

'Aren't you tired of this?' asks Marcel. 'I am. What are you trying to establish? That I can recall these numbers? You know I can do that by now. Are you waiting for me to fail?'

Yes, admits Morel to himself, that is what I am waiting for, and yet, I do not want it to happen.

'To settle the matter, I thought I would recount the numbers from the first test.'

'But that was almost four weeks ago!' declares Morel.

'It would not matter if it were four months ago.'

'Or four years . . . ?' asks Morel tremulously.

Marcel nods. 'Or four years.'

Morel squints at his patient. 'How do I know these are the numbers from that first day?'

'Perhaps you should have made a record of them on paper. That might have been a useful addition to the experiment.'

So, Morel thinks, I have learned that the patient can be impudent.

'Or,' adds Marcel, 'you might take my word for it.'

'How do I know you're not lying?'

'I don't lie,' says Marcel, so simply that Morel cannot find a way past this remark for a moment. When he does, it's an idiotic question.

'You don't lie?'

'That is correct.'

Well, you must be the first one on the planet who doesn't, Morel thinks, but only for a moment. Then he remembers the work that Bleuler, once a pupil of Charcot in this very hospital, is now doing in Switzerland on certain personalities who do not display normal social function. Does he recall that one of the indicators is the inability to lie?

'Doctor . . . ?' prompts Marcel.

Morel shakes himself. He is wasting his best chance yet to explore and he decides to move right into the matter directly.

'Have you always had this ability?' he asks. 'To remember?'

'Yes, I have,' says Marcel.

'And no one ever spoke to you about it before?'

'What do you mean, spoke to me?'

'Have there not been people who understood how remarkable it is, to forget nothing? Didn't your teachers in school mark you out?'

Marcel sits for a moment, remembering.

'I don't think so. I didn't do very well in school, in fact.'

He laughs, a strange kind of laugh. As if copying someone else's laughter, Morel feels.

'Not with your memory as it is?'

'I don't know,' Marcel says. 'My teachers didn't seem to like me. They were often angry with me.'

'Why?'

'They said I wouldn't work.'

'Is that true?'

'I thought I was doing as they wanted me to. I think I often didn't understand them.'

*Or maybe they didn't understand you*, thinks Morel.

'I see. But no one knew about your memory? Your parents? Friends?'

Marcel thinks about friends. It's a word he doesn't associate with childhood very much. There was Ginette, of course, but Marcel wonders if she counts as a friend. He thinks about that, and then he chastises himself. Yes, of course she was a friend, even if he hadn't understood everything about her, or what she wanted, and after all—

'Marcel?'

Morel taps Marcel on the knee, bringing his attention back.

'Your parents?'

Marcel thinks about that too.

'My parents worked hard. And they were good to me. But I don't know if they knew about my memory. Perhaps I can explain it to you like this, Doctor. I don't think I knew myself about my memory for a very long time. I spoke to no one about it, and I assumed that everyone could do what I can do. I know that isn't the case now.'

Morel battles between curiosity and frustration.

'But someone must have noticed something, eventually? No?'

'Well, for example, there was Monsieur LeChat. At the newspaper. He found out about my memory, but he grew cross with me too.'

'And the patron of this club where you have been working? He must have given you the job because of it . . .'

'Yes, but he thinks it's—'

'He thinks it's a trick, am I right?'

'Yes, that's right.'

Morel nods and closes his eyes for a moment. Such is the way with most people when faced with the impossible. Rather than admit that the impossible is possible, that a miracle has occurred, it is easier to pass it off as a mistake, as a fake, as a trick. That way, we do not have to change our understanding of the world.

'Could you tell me more about your childhood, Marcel?'

Marcel appears to be staring at a spot hanging halfway in the air above their heads.

'Marcel? Marcel . . . ?'

Morel taps his patient on the knee once more, and starts to understand why his teachers did not recognise the power of his mind. All too often, it seems that Marcel becomes lost inside it.

Something occurs to him then, and he tries a different approach. Perhaps he has been looking at this the wrong way. He has been trying to prove that Marcel's memory is without limit, is of infinite breadth, but perhaps it would be as instructive to find out how far back it goes.

'Marcel, could you tell me your earliest memory? Can you perhaps remember your early childhood, can you tell me something about that?'

'Yes, of course,' says Marcel. 'But what do you want to know?'

'Can you remember a time with your mother, perhaps, when you were very small?'

Marcel seems puzzled.

'Yes. Of course. But what shall I tell you? Am I to tell you about every day of my life? How my mother would tuck me into bed every night? She would sing, most nights, I suppose if she wasn't too tired, and lift up the bars of the bed, before—'

'Wait,' says Morel. 'The bars on the bed?'

'Well, I suppose bed is not the word. A cot would be the word, wouldn't it, at that age?'

'At what age?'

'I mean, when I was a baby.'

'A baby? You cannot surely expect me to believe that you can remember being a baby?'

'Doctor, I already said that I don't lie.'

'Yes, but . . . Very well. Tell me more. How old are you? Can you speak?'

'I knew how to say a few things. Mama, Papa. Horse.'

'Horse?'

'I had a wooden horse. A toy. It had a red mane for some reason, made of leather and a red tail, also of narrow strips of leather, and it was about so big, and was on wheels so you could roll him along the table, if you wanted, though I didn't like to do that because I had damaged one wheel by dropping it on the—'

'Yes, I see. Very good. Very good. And this is your earliest memory. Your mother, the cot, the horse?'

'Oh no,' says Marcel.

'No?' asks Morel, and he leans in a little closer. His voice drops a note or two. 'Can you tell me what is?'

'That's harder,' says Marcel.

'Why?' whispers Morel.

'Because it is before I had words. I can recall the feelings and the sensations, however. Would you like me to tell you?'

Morel can only bring himself to nod.

'So,' says Marcel, and he looks up and to the left into the shadowy space that hangs by the ceiling in the corner of the cell. 'It's dark. Almost completely dark, though sometimes, very rarely, there is faint light. No, light would not be the word. You see, Doctor, it is hard because there aren't words to go with the things I saw and felt. But perhaps I can say that the darkness decreases slightly. Yes, I feel happy putting it that way: the darkness decreases from time to time, just a little. But it doesn't matter whether it is completely dark or not, it's a good thing. I mean, I am safe; I feel safe where I am, and it's warm, always just right. It's dark, and I'm warm. And from time to time I hear my mother talking. I don't know what she's saying, of course, but I know her voice by now and she sounds happy, well, almost all the time, although there was one occasion when I know that she was upset, and her breathing came out in hard sobs and I think now that she must have been crying. But anyway, aside from her voice, I could sometimes hear other voices, and aside from the voices, there was always the drum. You know, the drum, drum,

drum, the beat, you would say, I suppose the beat of her heart, so close by. And I used to like that, to hear that, I mean, because . . .'

Marcel talks on. He talks on, and on, and on, but Morel is no longer listening. It has dawned on him what Marcel is talking about, and he is so taken with wonder, this doctor who has seen everything in his time, who has seen the strangest things of human nature, of wild monstrances, of extreme apparitions, of energetic emanations from the mind and body of woman and man, he is so taken with wonder that his skin grows cold, and the hairs on the back of his neck arise, and his own heart starts to beat a little more profoundly. Just as Marcel's mother's must have done from time to time, as the unborn boy listened to it, and felt her warm blood coursing around him, as he listened to her heart, from the warm, dark safety of her womb.

# THE LIBRARY OF HELL

A few days after Marcel has returned to his beginning, Inspector Petit finds himself with a little spare time and within walking distance of the National Library, in the Rue de Richelieu. Petit is struck by another imposing façade, and this is one face that does not lie. The exterior, the entrance, with its nobly carved BIBLIOTHEQUE NATIONALE above the portal, all these things lead you to believe that beyond lay the most important repository of books in the world, not just France, and such is the truth of the matter.

Petit has seen enough of libraries recently, and he hurries across the courtyard to a small office to begin his enquiries. Things begin simply enough as he shows his Sûreté identification card, but when he mentions the collection he wishes to consult, the man behind the desk freezes momentarily and, though he gives the inspector the information he needs, makes no further eye contact with him.

Irritated, Petit stomps his way up a flight of stairs, and then another, heading higher and towards the back of the building. Somehow he expected Hell to be downwards, yet it seems the guardians of the national shame have chosen to locate their underworld on the very top floor, out of reach of all but the fittest of perverts. Still nettled, Petit takes the chance to remind himself that he is not the pervert; the perverts are the men (and women, he supposes, my God!) who created this material in the first place, so why the clerk downstairs treated him with contempt is hard to fathom. He is a police inspector, after all, pursuing, what . . . ? This is not his case; it is not anyone's case.

There is no case at all. There is a curious link between two photographers, and a break-in at a studio. That is all. Yet he finds that he is driven to follow matters a little further before he can entirely let the matter of the murderous memory man go. It's worst at night, the voice inside him, her voice. Her voice, telling him not to fail anyone else as he failed her. In the middle of the night it seems so real, though he pushes it away as best he can. In the morning, he knows it's just his fancy, yet the result is the same: he cannot let it drop. He cannot.

At the far end of a low-ceilinged corridor he finds the door he has been looking for – a small brass nameplate states the single word: 'Hell'. He has been told to wait for the keeper of the collection to join him, and yet, like Orpheus and countless others before him, he cannot help testing the waters of this underworld, and so he tries the doorknob.

It turns, but the door is locked.

His timing is, as usual, awful. He still has his hand on the knob when a shrill voice reaches down the corridor to him.

'No admittance to Hell without a librarian!'

The line is delivered absolutely without humour or even irony.

Caught red-handed, Petit waits for the librarian in question to permit him entrance. Down the corridor walks a prim middle-aged man, with pince-nez riding well down his nose, and on his shoulders a few flakes originating from the little remaining hair on his pasty white head. He does not see much sunlight, Petit surmises.

'Aubenas,' says the librarian, without smiling. 'You are the policeman?'

'Inspector Petit,' says the naughty schoolboy, suddenly remembering an especially hot morning in Africa when he impaled a Mandingo warrior with his bayonet. He briefly hates himself for being cowed by this keeper of books.

'This is a police matter?'

Petit nods with as much dignity as he can muster.

Aubenas ferrets in an inside pocket for the key to Hell, and slides it into the lock in a most precise manner, which makes Petit's lip curl for some reason he can't identify. Aubenas then stands aside with obvious displeasure at the etiquette of allowing his visitor to enter the room before him.

Petit decides he would like to punch the pompous prick on the nose. Why does everyone he meets seem to have to lord it over him? What is it about him that invites such gentle but persistent humiliation?

He steps through the doorway, banging his head on the lintel as he does so. He doesn't need to turn to know Aubenas is silently smiling at this, and anyway, he's more than interested in the room before him. He expected a small attic space with a few file cabinets of dirty stuff. In actual fact, the Library of Hell is a long room that stretches away beyond window after window, and then turns a corner out of sight. There are shelves to the ceiling, which again are higher than he imagined from the low corridor outside, with ladders on rails to reach the top levels of filth. There are cabinets, many, many cabinets, and plan chests too, for larger scale perversions, he presumes.

He had also expected there to be some obvious sign of the nature of the material held by the library; he now realises of course that that would be absurd. On the face of it, therefore, the library looks just as mundane, as everyday, as *dull*, as any library has a right to. But what lies inside those cabinets, and in those chests? What lies between the covers (he almost thinks the word sheets) of the thousands, the tens of thousands of books on the shelves?

'How may we assist you?' Aubenas snaps.

'Quite a place you have here,' Petit says, and before the librarian can get on a high horse of any kind, adds, 'Yes, I am looking for a pornographer, a particular pornographer. I gather you're the expert.'

He lets that one hang a moment, before adding, 'I would like you to look at this photograph.'

He pulls out the envelope that contains the photograph of Ondine, and hands the whole thing to Aubenas, who, Petit notices, is clearly expecting something salacious and is also equally clearly disappointed to find Ondine fully clothed.

He hands the photograph back to Petit with a bored air.

'What of it?'

Petit pushes the hand bearing the photograph back towards its owner.

'Look closer. Do you see the small imperfection?'

'The light is not good,' Aubenas says, but he seems more intrigued now and moves under one of the high oval attic windows.

Petit follows him and points out the mark.

'I've been told that this mark can be found on the work of one particular pornographer, that it most likely appears on all his work.'

'Who told you that?'

Petit ignores the question. It's time to take control. Anyway, a thought has occurred to him.

'How do you catalogue photographs of a pornographic nature?'

In answer to his own question, certain different approaches spring into his mind, each of them intriguing in its own way. How to do such a thing? By some scale of obscenity? By deviance? By position?

'By studio,' Aubenas supplies the underwhelming but obvious solution to the problem. 'The recovered works of each studio, more often than not meaning of an individual photographer, are filed together. This is a newer area of the library, of course. Perversion, in all its forms, was around long before photographic records of it could be made.'

He begins walking down the length of Hell towards a section in the corner where locked file cabinets stand in rows.

'Do you know the man with the imperfect lens? Have you seen it before?'

Aubenas gives a quick shake of his head, which sees the end of the life of a few more of his straggling hairs.

'I have not. But I do not study these things closely.'

Petit studies his face and wonders if that's true or not. This whole place seems like an embarrassment to the library, not to say to France, and yet Petit finds himself wondering if Aubenas has the only key, and how often he makes his way up to Hell.

'Nevertheless,' Aubenas adds, 'there are no more than fifty or sixty photographers whose work has been added to our collection. Seventy at most. It shouldn't take you long to find which of them bears the mark of imperfection that you seek.'

He pulls out a smaller bunch of keys and unlocks the cabinets. Petit notes from the small handwritten label on the first cabinet that it ranges from A to C.

Aubenas slides open the top drawer, and invites the inspector to inspect.

'You can work on the top of this plan chest, if you wish.'

Petit pulls out a packet wrapped in card, and slips the first photograph out. A cursory glance shows a man taking another man's erect penis into his mouth, in front of a scene of a tent in a desert.

Petit slides the photograph back in the packet. Aubenas is watching him.

'The light is terrible in here,' Petit mumbles. 'Perhaps you could provide me with a lamp?'

Aubenas's nose twitches. The pince-nez stays in place.

'We have electric light in the library proper.'

Petit holds his gaze, until the librarian backs down, mutters something incoherent, and disappears to find some source of light.

Alone with the greatest deviance that France has managed to create, record and ban, Petit begins to work his way methodically through the packets.

Whoever this first photographer is, or was, he seems to have had a penchant for men engaged in activities with other men. Petit knows that such things occur; indeed, the Paris police has an entire vice squad much of whose time is spent pursuing such individuals. But he has never had such bold, crude physical evidence put before his eyes. He tries to concentrate on looking for the mark; upper left, that's where it will be, upper left, never mind that there's a naked man putting his hand up another—

He stops.

He's looked at fifteen photographs from this pornographer, and found no mark. What he has found has upset him, if he's honest. The culmination, or should that be nadir, is an image of two boys. Young boys. If he is to get through the perhaps seventy files, he won't be able to look at each and every photograph. Thank God.

Thank God and yet, now that he's looking at the work of one Benoit Antoine, he finds he is taking a little longer over each image. Antoine seems to have favoured women, young women, captured in positions of sexual union. The first shows a naked girl kneeling before another, with large lolling breasts, seated in an armchair. Behind them, a mountain scene is laughable. Would they want to be quite so unclothed if they really were on an alp? That thought barely enters Petit's head however; he's much more taken with what the kneeling girl is doing with her tongue, and how far apart the seated girl can get her legs.

He shakes himself, because he's heard the quick click of Aubenas's returning footsteps.

'Anything?' asks Aubenas.

Petit shakes his head.

'On to the Bs,' he says, shoving the Sapphic work of Antoine back into its plain brown card packet.

'Your light,' says Aubenas, putting an oil lamp on top of the chest. Petit now wishes he hadn't asked for it, but perhaps it will make things faster.

'Very good,' says Petit, and bends to his work again. Aubenas stands and watches him, something that grows extremely vexing in no time at all.

'Perhaps you'd like to help?' he suggests, and Aubenas shrugs to show that it's all the same to him.

'I'll start from D,' he says, 'and leave the Bs and Cs to you.'

Why? thinks Petit. Something you want to see in the Ds? Something you *don't* want me to see? Perhaps . . .

Perhaps nothing. Perhaps he's just being methodical. Petit has learned from his time in the police archives that librarians like method.

And, in truth, it doesn't take them long to find the pornographer.

Petit is working his way through the Bs, when he suddenly wonders if he'll find a file marked Buguet among them. He flicks ahead to see, and finds that the sordid photographer was telling the truth, or, at least, if he wasn't, he hasn't been caught yet.

Returning to his sequence, he pulls out a file marked BARA-DUC, and lo and behold, the very first photograph shows the tell-tale imperfection.

'I've got him,' says Petit, and shows the photograph, which is of an orgy of some kind, to Aubenas.

Aubenas nods.

'There are others?'

They scan the next few photographs and there it is, on every one, the faint but identical mark. On any single photo, it wouldn't amount to very much. Placed side by side, the repeating mark is as clear a sign as can be found.

'Baraduc?' asks Aubenas. 'That's interesting.'

'Why? You know him?'

'I do not know anyone in here,' Aubenas says. 'I know the man's work. An interesting case. Somewhere in your archives, at the Quai des Orfèvres, you will most likely find another file on him. Some twenty years ago he was arrested in a case that became rather famous. For a while.'

'Of what nature?'

'Baraduc was a spirit photographer.'

Aubenas annoyingly leaves that hanging, forcing Petit to have to ask.

'A what?'

'A spirit photographer. It was all the rage for a year or so. Baraduc was the foremost culprit. He was tried for a series of cases of fraud. He claimed to be able to photograph the dead, and produced some hundreds of photographic likenesses, each at a high fee, of course, for the bereaved, who in their grieving state were all too easily fooled. He was caught in the end, by one of your more enterprising inspectors, I seem to recall, who had Baraduc produce photographs of a dead uncle, who was not only not dead, but who had never lived in the first place.'

'Aha,' says Petit, 'a spirit photographer . . .'

'Very curious case. In court he tried to claim that not all the instances were false, merely some of them. It mattered little. He was arrested. And then ten years ago he popped up again in this line of work . . .'

Aubenas waves a finger at the series of images before them.

'You have your man, Inspector. Hermés Baraduc took the photograph of your girl, whoever she is. I trust that will be all for now?'

Petit nods.

He hovers.

'I can put this material away,' Aubenas says curtly, and Petit leaves, not looking back until he reaches the doorway, when, again like Orpheus, he cannot help but take a backward glance. He sees Aubenas in silhouette, motionless, staring at a photograph that he is holding close to the light.

Petit feels sickened, not just at the thought of the odious librarian getting pleasure for himself, but at the memory of how his own body had reacted to the sight of those two women on the alp, not more than twenty minutes before. Yet on this subject, the voice in his head, the voice of his dead fiancée, is strangely uninterested.

# INCONSTANCE

The poor doctor is beside himself. Since the session in which Marcel revealed his very earliest memory to the world, he has shut up again, closed like an oyster unwilling to release its treasure.

For days Morel tries everything he can think of to bring Marcel back to life; he tries everything he has tried before and he tries things he has not, but none of it makes the slightest difference. Marcel is dead to the world around him once more, the situation becoming so bad that they are compelled to force-feed him again on two occasions.

One day, unable to suppress his frustration, the doctor's patience runs dry.

'You are a fraud!' he declares to Marcel's unheeding form.

Morel stomps up and down the tiny cell, as best he can, limited by the confined space and by his gait, which is not conducive to stomping at the best of times.

'I don't know how you do it, but it's a trick! No one can do what you claim to do! And your memory of the womb is absurd! Do you take me for a complete imbecile? No one can remember before they were born. No one! For memory to function, language is required. Without language, such a thing is impossible!'

He goes on in this vein for a while but soon runs out of steam. Marcel had spoken about words, after all. He'd spoken about how it was harder to explain his memories before he had words, but not that it was impossible. And if Morel is honest, he supposes some of his own memories were formed with sentences, while others, the majority in fact, only require words to explain them, to communicate them to others. The memories themselves come rushing in without language itself, as feelings: fear, happiness, sadness, pain. And what of animals? It's known that some animals at least have memories, rather sophisticated in some cases, if one considers creatures like the salmon, who can return across oceans to the very river in which they were spawned. Or even the humble bee, who finds nectar, and then flies home to relate that information in some unknown way to his fellows. All that is done without language, apparently.

He thinks of the recent work of Henri and Henri; their paper *Enquiry into the First Memories of Childhood* in which the first memories of one hundred and twenty-three people are noted and analysed. Most of the subjects report their first memory coming from the ages of two to four. A few of the subjects report a memory from before the age of two. None from before the first birthday. And now Marcel declares he remembers moments from before he was born . . .

Morel looks at his subject disgustedly.

He actually says *pah!* and turns to leave the cell, when he remembers the book he brought with him. He pulls it from his pocket, and throws it across the room. It misses Marcel and falls open on the floor.

'I was going to get you to prove yourself with that,' Morel grumps, 'but I can see I am wasting my time. Good day.'

He leaves Marcel behind, a still body.

If his body is still, his mind is not, but Morel cannot see Marcel's mind. This is what frustrates him so greatly: he wishes he could look at the damn man's thoughts directly and not have to poke and tease at them from outside, through the medium of Marcel's body – of his tongue. He wants to be able to see the workings of the clock, not merely wonder that the hands always tell the correct time. But he cannot. The only way he can learn about Marcel's memory is at second hand, remotely, having to rely on the patient's ability to think, to speak, to interpret, to tell the truth. Why, to think he claims not to be able to lie!

Morel moves away. He has other patients, there are reports to write and lectures to give, but all of that will be done with only half his attention, he knows, until he can solve Marcel. That is how he puts it to himself. He must solve Marcel.

In Marcel's mind, all is far from still. He is caught in an endless whirling cycle of memories that fall hard and fast one after the other, tumbling over themselves, as he struggles to regain his composure. All too often, he fails. He tries to remember good things, just one good thing. If he can focus on that, perhaps he can calm himself. He searches hard and finds a happy thought, a time when Ondine had only recently moved in to the studio, a week or so after their little wedding. She was wearing white, as she often did, with the little purple velvet boots she was so proud of.

While he set a pan of milk on the top of the stove, Ondine laughed at the sight of the seamstresses across the passage.

'They're like goldfish in an aquarium. Or perhaps it's like watching them on the screen of the cinematograph,' she said. 'They're there, but not really.'

'At the cinematograph, the people on the screen do not wave back at you if you wave at them,' Marcel pointed out. He came up to join her, resting one hand on her arm briefly, though hanging back, as if he did not want to draw attention.

'And neither do these little fish,' Ondine said, going right up to the glass and waving and mugging at the seamstresses, who, it was true, gave not the slightest sign of seeing her, but kept their heads bowed, concentrating on their work. The lips moved on one of the three, but only a lip-reader would have known what she said.

'See?' said Ondine, laughing. Marcel laughed too but also, as Ondine turned away from the window, noticed that one of the three caught his eye; just faintly, enough to bring back memories of that happy night under the stars.

Marcel pulled Ondine away and asked her to finish heating the milk for the coffee, and all of that was a happy thought, but despite his attempts to prevent it from happening, it is followed in his mind by a connected one. At first, Ondine was proud of her handsome husband's memory, and would take the chance to show him off to anyone she could: to waiters in cafés, to newcomers at the cabaret, to anyone at all. However, he soon found that there were aspects of his memory that displeased her just as much. As the weeks passed, and the first glow of marriage dissipated, they had their first argument; when Ondine let the milk stand too long on the stove, and it burned. That was not what caused the argument, they fought when Marcel pointed out that it was the third time she had done it in a week.

'I didn't,' Ondine protested, but Marcel knew that she had and took the trouble to tell her at what time and on which days it had occurred.

It wasn't a big fight.

'So I'm a little forgetful,' Ondine said, pushing Marcel backwards on to the bed, 'but you forgive me, don't you?'

The burned milk was soon forgotten.

But not by Marcel. Only by Ondine, who let it burn for a fourth time the following day.

When it happened again, she tried to blame Marcel.

'You were cooking. You left the milk to burn, not me!'

'Absolutely not,' said Marcel, quite matter-of-fact. 'You were cooking. You set the milk on the stove.'

'How do you know?' shouted Ondine. 'How can you be so sure? Maybe it was you!'

'It wasn't me. When I put the milk on the stove, I take the can from the shelf and I put it back where it was. There.'

He pointed to an empty spot on the bottom shelf, to the far left.

'When you cook, you take the can and put it back anywhere. In this case, right there, on the floor.'

And he pointed to where the large metal milk can stood on the wooden boards, in front of the cupboards. He then proceeded to tell Ondine where she had left the milk can the previous three times she'd let the milk burn, at which point Ondine looked Marcel straight in the eye, told him he was a piece of shit, and stormed out.

Marcel remembers that scene. He remembers all the times they argued about burned milk. He remembers every word that Ondine called him, every name, every time, and he remembers all the pain he felt at being so clumsy with her, so stupid as to care about burned milk, so cross with himself for not seeing why it was that it made her angry. So angry for not being able to see that.

Of course, Ondine came back.

She came back after that first time, when she'd sworn at him.

When she came back into the studio, he just stared at her.

She hesitated in the doorway, expecting him to apologise, to rush into her arms and beg her forgiveness, for that was how men usually operated with Ondine. Marcel did not do these things, not at first anyway. To start with, he just stared at Ondine, with a stupid look on his face. He glanced across the passage, he looked at the seamstresses, the three seamstresses, and then he looked back to Ondine.

'What?' asked Ondine, angry that she didn't get the reaction she was used to getting. 'What's that look for?'

Marcel seemed to stir.

'I . . . Nothing. I'm sorry. I'm sorry, and I apologise.'

And then he came to her and held her and she told him it was okay, and they made up and they made love, though if Ondine was honest, it was neither the first nor the last time that Marcel seemed a little weird with her. A little cold.

Still the memories whirl around in Marcel, still he is unable to calm the storm. He remembers how they made love that time; it seemed that Ondine made love to him with anger in her, which was a new experience for him. He had thought love was only about love until that time, and then he saw something else in it: that there could be other emotions, not just passion, but something harder, something more . . . He couldn't find the word, not then, but it would come to him later when he walked in to the studio on that first Saturday in July and found Bishop putting himself into his wife from behind.

He replays the scene again, as he has done so many times, and as he will continue to do, over and over again. He sees every detail, recalls every emotion, senses every action and reaction, smells every smell, as he takes the gun from the top of the cabinet and points it at Ondine and pulls the trigger, and she falls on to the floor, where blood starts to seep out from under her, and then he's running, and then he's not running, but kneeling on the cobbles in the passage, staring at the ground, rocking, and rocking.

Marcel spends around four hours on that single scene.

When he is done, he is exhausted. In truth it is only exhaustion that lets the memories recede for a while, allowing him to get some rest, recover some energy, some mental energy, for a short time, until the torture can be resumed anew.

The light in the cell has grown dim, but as he opens his eyes, he sees the cobbles of the Cour du Commerce, just as if he were still there, kneeling, staring down, rocking in confusion.

Then, the cobbles fade, and into his vision swims a book; thrown at him by a frustrated alienist.

He picks it up, blankly, and places it on the small stool by his bed, and he notices that the book is a foreign dictionary, a French–Russian dictionary.

Tired, Marcel lies back on his bed, closes his eyes, and begins to remember killing his wife, all over again. The word he applies to himself is the same one he applies to Ondine and Bishop's sex. Animal.

# THE STUDIO OF HERMÉS BARADUC

Still working in his own time, things move slowly for Petit. It is another week or so before he can find a moment to pay Monsieur Baraduc a visit. There has been a stabbing in the 6th, and as part of the investigation the examining magistrate concerned, a supercilious oaf with the splendid name of Henri Huberman, has dispatched Petit out of the arrondissement and up to Montmartre to interview a sister of the victim. Petit conducts this interview rapidly and without great interest; the sister knows, or claims to know, of no reason why anyone should want to kill her brother. Petit notes in passing that Boissenot's theory of the end of the world seems to be holding good, because there was an unnecessary ferocity about the killing. The man was robbed for a few francs. Why then was his body so broken and beaten? There was a certain terror in the whole thing, Petit admitted, and so the Principal Inspector's theory seems vindicated once again.

What really holds Petit's mind this afternoon is the knowledge that he is no more than three hundred metres from Baraduc's studio, a short walk up from Place Blanche, just off Rue Lepic.

He takes a light lunch in the Brasserie Cyrano on the corner of Rue Lepic. It's not his normal taste to eat somewhere so large, but, being August, many of the smaller family restaurants are closed. He tastes little, and despite his wish to hurry, forces himself to idle away the time. Baraduc will himself be out at lunch no doubt, no point arriving too soon. At this moment, Petit doesn't ask himself why he is bothering with this case that is not a case. He has merely found that things have unfurled themselves before him, and lain down at his feet, so that he has an easy path to tread. Nothing has required much hard work or any great insight, and he has been pushing on open doors simply because they are open.

He watches Pigalle go about its business. It's a hot day, the city is quieter than usual, with many people taking their annual holidays. It is possible that Baraduc is among them, but only a visit to the studio will tell if there is the small white card in the window: CONGÉS ANNUELS.

He leaves the Cyrano at two, and takes a cigar from the tabac next door. He doesn't smoke, but selects a small elegant-looking thing called Maria Mancini, purely for sentimental reasons. Paying for the cigar and a book of matches, he puts Maria between his lips, and puffs her into life. If only it were that easy, he thinks, suddenly bitter. Only the need to seem to be doing something prevents him from hurling the cigar into the gutter there and then.

He strolls on, pretending to saunter like an aficionado of the cigar would if he had such an important business to concentrate on, until he reaches the Rue Constance. After fifty metres, the street takes a ninety-degree turn to the right, and there, Petit notices the name of the narrow *impasse* that goes on straight ahead: Marie Blanche. This second omen, this second reminder of his dead fiancée, is enough to test his character severely. He takes the cigar from his mouth and drops it under his heel on the pavement. His foot twists, and he is forced to admit to himself why he cares so much about the case that is not a case; of Marcel the Memory Man killing his young wife and getting away with it. Of course Petit cares. Of course he does. If he doesn't, when his own fiancée was taken from him and the killer or killers never found, then who will?

There is no one around. This is a quiet backstreet on a quiet day in a quiet month; shutters are closed on many buildings, he is alone in the city. He looks up from the crushed body of the cigar called Maria, and on the first floor of the corner building hangs a sign: Atelier Baraduc. Underneath, smaller writing promises the client ten photographs for the sum of five francs as an introductory offer, and that is all.

He makes his way through the street door, up to the first floor. It's dim on the landing but after a moment his eyes adjust to the darkness and he sees the half-glazed door of the photographer's workshop, with Baraduc's name there once more.

He doesn't knock, but tries the door and finds it locked. As the handle clicks he hears muffled sounds from within, a scurry, and hushed voices.

Petit bangs on the door.

'Baraduc?'

Some more hushed tones from inside trigger something in Petit that he didn't know existed in him: sudden rage. Without reason, he kicks at the frame of the door, by the lock, causing the cheap wood to splinter and the door to swing open.

He is in an outer office of some kind, containing a desk, a couple of chairs, and a very sizeable safe on short but sturdy metal legs. He sees immediately that the source of the noise lies beyond the wooden door leading to the studio itself. As he enters, the sounds suddenly cease, and then he hears a floorboard squeak. He crosses the room in two steps and flings the door wide, to find a fat man pointing a pistol at him, and a young woman sitting, perched on the end of a couch, her hands frozen in the act of pulling on a boot. The room is furnished sparely. Aside from the couch, there are a chair or two, a large camera on a tall wooden tripod, a flash pan on another tripod and, in the corner of the room, rolls of what Petit assumes are backdrops, like the one of a meadow that hangs behind the girl.

Petit looks at the pistol, but doesn't think to worry. He can see immediately that the man is scared, and perhaps a little confused too. The girl looks from Petit to Baraduc, and still does not pull on her boot.

'Baraduc?' Petit asks, and the man gives the faintest of nods, almost without realising he has.

'Who are you?' he asks, and something in his intonation implies he had perhaps been expecting someone else.

'Petit. I'm from the Sûreté.'

The gun lowers slightly.

Then rises again.

'You force your way in. You have no—'

'I'll pay you for the door,' Petit says, surprising himself as he does so. I will? he thinks. Maybe I will. Maybe it's part of the business of being an inspector. For God's sake, if they have to buy their own revolvers and ammunition, if they have to cover the cost of bribes to informants, he may as well pay for a damn doorframe.

Petit pulls out his Sûreté ID and cautiously proffers it to Bara-duc, who squints at it and then lowers his gun completely.

'What do you want? I've had enough of you people.'

'You people? Which people?'

'You're vice squad, right?' says Baraduc, and then, seeing the blank look on Petit's face, adds, 'You're not vice squad. So who are you? You have no right to barge in here like this. I'm done with that stuff now. I'm just making a portrait for this young lady here . . .'

He waves a hand at the young woman. She's clothed, but it's clear to Petit that she was recently unclothed. He wonders how undressed she was before his knock on the outer door, and if the answer is 'considerably' then he's very impressed with the speed at which she can throw her garments back on.

Petit catches him giving her a look that means 'for heaven's sake take your hands off your boot, or put the damn thing on.' It takes the girl a moment or two to get his meaning, and then she does the smart thing and pulls this second boot into place. She stands, straightening her blouse, and from the loose way her breasts move beneath it, Petit guesses that her undergarments are elsewhere in the room. In fact, yes, there they are, hanging over a screen in the corner behind him.

Baraduc sees where Petit's eyes are focusing, and laughs a small and nervous laugh.

'There is nothing amiss here,' he says. 'Merely a standard portrait session for this young actress. She must have some shots, after all. Inspector, shall we perhaps make ourselves comfortable in the office?'

He holds a hand out towards the outer room. Petit is thinking to himself that the man must have a lot to hide for him to relent so easily about the broken door when there is a commotion in the stairway and the sound of voices. A second passes before a man staggers happily into the room with a young woman draped over each shoulder. All three are evidently drunk, and in high spirits, giggling at something only they know, until the drunken man sees Petit.

In an instant, he appears to sober up. At least, he stops giggling, and glares at Baraduc.

'Hey!' he announces. 'You said it would just be me this time. No men. Just me giving it to the girls, right? That's what you said, and—'

Baraduc is on him in a moment. He waves the pistol in his face, not in any threatening way, but enough to shut him up.

'Be quiet! How dare you? The inspector here has come to pay us a visit. So why don't you take the girls, all of them, down to Louis's and have another drink or two and then we'll take all your portraits later, when the inspector and I have finished chatting? Yes?'

The first girl has emerged from the studio now, and takes one look at the drunken man and sighs.

'Come on,' she says, 'I'll explain downstairs.'

When they are gone, and Baraduc has finished experimenting with trying to close his broken door properly, and has slid the gun into a desk drawer, he slumps into a seat behind his desk. He looks very tired and old.

Petit points at the chair across the desk from Baraduc and raises his eyebrows.

'Yes, of course,' says Baraduc. 'My apologies.'

Petit sits and considers where to start, but the pornographer starts for him.

'So, you're not vice squad? Then what do you want?'

There is no point pussying around, Petit thinks. The time for subtlety ended when he put his foot to the door.

'One of your girls. Your models. From a while back. I don't know when. She's dead. Murdered. No, calm yourself. I'm not accusing you, we know who did it. I just want to know who she was.'

Baraduc listens to this and is silent for a few moments, during which he clearly attempts to work out if there is some trick or deception or plan behind the inspector's words, something that could incriminate him. He doesn't know what it could be; but Baraduc is perpetually guilty; he's made a living from the exploitation of people's fears and lusts, and most of that work has been illegal as well as immoral.

'Who are you talking about?' he asks finally, having ascertained that that question at least can do him no harm.

'Ondine Després. She would have been Badiou when you knew her.'

Baraduc's face does not change. 'I don't know her,' he says flatly.

Petit rubs his forehead with thumb and forefinger, takes a deep breath. 'Monsieur Baraduc. I am not the vice squad. But I very easily could be. Their office is just down the hall from mine. On my way back to give my report this afternoon I could spend two minutes telling them that you appear to be continuing in your work, work that you have been imprisoned for twice, I believe?'

He stops, and knows he need say no more.

Baraduc looks down, he holds up a hand. 'Yes. Ondine. What do you want to know?'

Petit shakes his head. 'Well,' he says. 'Everything.'

So Baraduc tells him.

It takes half an hour, during which the first girl appears in the doorway again, and is waved away by Baraduc once more. Mostly, he concentrates on his story, and it is not a pleasant one.

He tells how Ondine came to Paris when she was a young girl. Her mother was dead, her father was a rough drinking man. Nothing remarkable about either of those two things, or in a young person coming to the city to seek a better life. And like so many migrants of this kind, they arrive only to find they are in competition with so many other wastrels and vagabonds. Those are the actual words Baraduc uses, but Petit doesn't smile even to himself, inside. He merely nods and allows Baraduc to go on. The photographer seems to relax a little, as he explains that Ondine had the dream that she would become an actress, become a rich and famous actress, adored throughout Paris, and maybe even beyond. There was only one problem, Baraduc says. 'She couldn't act. I saw her attempts myself once. Terrible.' But what she lacked in dramatic talent was amply compensated for in other ways.

'You saw her?' Baraduc asks.

'I saw one of your photos of her, in fact,' Petit says, and notices that Baraduc colours a little at this. Petit lets him dangle for a moment before pulling out the portrait of Ondine from her room, her respectable portrait.

'This is one of yours, isn't it?' Petit asks.

Baraduc nods.

'I presume there were others in which she was unclothed?'

Baraduc does not move, nor say anything. Time moves, and memories flood into his mind, none of which he chooses to share with the policeman.

'You see for yourself, then?' he says at last. 'Everyone wanted her. Every man, I should say. Most of the girls hated her. Jealous.

Of her looks. The effect she had on men. Yes, Paris is full of girls, and many of them are very lovely. Very lovely.'

Baraduc winks at Petit, who finds that Marie has returned to his thoughts. Just put one foot wrong, he thinks, just say one word too many, and I will climb across this desk and throttle you with my bare hands, just as someone did to my fiancée.

He takes another breath, and points at the photograph. 'Ondine?'

'Yes, Ondine. The fairest of them all. Or perhaps fair is the wrong word, but there was something about her eyes, you know. Something that seemed to promise things to men. Dark things. And those lips. And I need not draw the inspector's attention to her physical figure.'

No, you need not, thinks Petit.

Finally, Baraduc seems to be able to move away from the subject of Ondine's body. He relates how, unable to find work as an actress and finding herself unable to take a decent enough occupation – a waitress, a laundry girl, a flower-seller – she fell in with the kind of people who know what to do with a pretty girl.

'She became a *fille publique*?' Petit asks.

'No!' says Baraduc, almost with a trace of pride. 'Never! Not Ondine. Not as far as I know, anyway. She never worked the streets. They had her in a *maison* from the off. And not just any *maison*. She was at Le Chabanais. The best! Perhaps you are unaware of the clientele there, Inspector?'

Petit can find no way to answer that question that he likes, and so he chooses not to. Anyway, Baraduc is still not finished, and tells him how Ondine rapidly worked her way to a life as a high-class prostitute, a *demi-mondaine* no less, with wealthy lovers and a few, very well-paid assignations, at addresses that the young inspector might fail to believe.

'So what happened?' he asks. 'When she died she was working in a cabaret. And not a good one.'

'The Cabaret of Insults, yes,' says Baraduc. 'What times we live in.'

Petit decides that Baraduc should get together with Boissenot so they could discuss the end of the world together.

'Well?'

'Well, she grew too old. That's all.'

'Too old? She was twenty-eight. She'd been working the cabarets for a few years. She was too old?'

'The circuit, if I may put it that way, in which she operated. They prefer their girls on the younger side. By twenty-five she was done. And unfortunately, in all those years, she never got any smarter, she never learned to be careful with money. She lost it as soon as she earned it. So at twenty-five she was faced with a choice: the streets, or the cabaret. And you know the rest.'

'And how did you come to know her?'

Baraduc hesitates again, and only relents when Petit reminds him of the vice squad.

'I was invited to photograph certain occasions at which she was present.'

'What occasions? With whom?'

Another long pause, a very long silence indeed, ends when Petit bangs his fist on the edge of the desk.

'With whom?'

'Rich men,' Baraduc mutters, 'powerful men, even. There were some . . . gatherings. They wanted matters recorded. Photo-graphically, you understand. I met Ondine, and offered her a series of portraits.'

Petit understands. 'Five with clothes, perhaps, and five . . . for your own commercial purposes?'

Baraduc closes his eyes and nods.

'And these assignations?' Petit asks. 'These gatherings. Who were they with?'

Baraduc does not answer. He suddenly seems to have grown suspicious once again, more so than before, if anything.

'Why do you want to know all this?' he asks instead. 'You know who killed her. I know who killed her. We read about it in the papers. It was the talk of the streets up here for a week or two. That husband of hers did her. Shot her all to bits, right? Then gave himself up. So why are you asking me questions, when she's dead and the murderer is heading for the guillotine?'

Petit does not bother correcting Baraduc on the inaccuracies in his account. And he has no answer for Baraduc as to why he is here. But it's none of his business anyway, and it hasn't escaped his attention that the wily pornographer is trying to change the subject.

'Who were they, Baraduc? Who were they?'

Petit does not get his answer, for despite every threat of the vice squad, of violence on his own part, every coercion and even bribe he can muster, Baraduc refuses to say more. He declares that Petit can set a torch to his workshop, and throw him in jail, it will not change the fact that he never knew the men's names.

And Petit knows that he is lying, and wonders what on earth scares Baraduc so much that he would risk losing everything, even his liberty, so long as it means keeping his mouth shut.

# AWAKE

Still Morel worked with Marcel, when he could. There were good days and less good days, and on one exceptional day Morel learns something stunning about his patient.

As Morel sits on the little stool, and notes that Marcel is 'awake', as he has come to call it, he notices that the French–Russian dictionary that he threw at him one angry day is sitting on the little shelf beside the window.

For days, Morel has even forgotten that he brought it to the cell, but someone must have picked it up and put it on the shelf. Perhaps that someone was Marcel. Perhaps he looked at it.

More in hope than anything stronger, Morel stands and plucks the little book from the shelf.

He holds it towards Marcel. 'Did you look at this?'

The way he asks makes it sound as if Marcel has been a somewhat mischievous urchin.

Marcel looks at the book, and nods. 'I did.'

'Did you . . . read any of it?'

'I read it all.'

The doctor considers this remark. In anyone else . . . But Marcel is not just anyone else.

'So you would . . . you should therefore be able to remember the words you read.'

Marcel nods. 'Perhaps,' he says.

'Only perhaps?' Morel seems affronted. He opens the dictionary and chooses an easy word to start with. 'Apple!'

Marcel closes his eyes. 'яблоко,' he says.

Morel does not speak Russian, but the dictionary has a phonetic transcription next to each word; it was his intention to test Marcel and see if the words he offered sound like the transcription.

Morel thinks he might have been right, but is not sure.

He tries another word. 'Ginger!'

'имбирь,' says Marcel.

That seems right too, but now he wishes he'd chosen an easier language. He wanted only to be sure it was a language that Marcel had no prior knowledge of.

'River!' says Morel.

'река,' says Marcel, and then stands up and delivers a speech to Morel, slowly, but entirely, in Russian.

Morel curses himself, and he curses Marcel, and then he holds up his hands.

'Wait, wait, wait. There's an orderly. Miskov or Metkov or something. Born in Russia. Let me go to fetch him and don't you forget a word of what you just said until I get back. Do you hear me, young man? Not a word!'

About fifteen minutes later, Morel returns with a middle-aged man with a bemused look on his face.

Morel instructs Miskov to wait.

'Now, then, Marcel. Start again. You say what you said in Russian, and this fellow will translate for me. Go ahead.'

So Marcel says what he said before. At first, the orderly frowns, shaking his head.

Morel is hopping from foot to foot, growing worried and angry by turns.

'Make him say it again,' the orderly says to Morel, who snaps his fingers at Marcel in a most indecent manner. Then, with his head tilted to one side, the orderly begins to speak. 'He is saying the words very badly,' he explains to Morel.

'Never mind that!' Morel says. 'What did he say?'

'Doctor,' the orderly begins, falteringly. 'Why do you . . .

practise this method to check for me? You do not . . . convince
you . . . to the memory? Nothing can be considered good for
you?'

Morel stares at Marcel.

'You learned the language?'

But Marcel is speaking in Russian again, and the orderly
rushes to keep up.

'Of course not. I just do not give a word for word and hope
that the result is closer to reality. But reading the book, I remember those words. I suspect that your friend is suffering from the
pronunciation of the natives, and I apologise for that.'

Morel is about to demand a further display, but his patient is
already speaking again, and once more, the orderly translates as
he goes.

'I do not understand you. I do not understand the lack of
faith. Why are you wasting your time? I prefer you to help me.
Are you a doctor, is not it? Why can you not find a way to free
myself from the pain? I ask you to help me and the demons in
my head. I cannot live in vain. Nevertheless frozen. To start help
me find my way.'

Morel stares at Marcel again. He stays that way for such a
long time that eventually the orderly gives a small cough and
enquires quietly if he should return to his duties.

Morel barely nods, but the orderly takes his cue and leaves,
whereupon Morel slumps back down on to the stool by Marcel's
bed.

It has taken a while for the jumbled meaning of Marcel's bad
Russian to assemble itself in Morel's head, but when he does, he
finds that the struggle to understand has done something else: it
has placed him in a position that is unfamiliar to him. In fact, it
has made him feel something he has not felt in years: empathy
for his patient. Empathy, for God's sake. It was there once, in
his work, so very long ago when he started out. It was covered
up, slowly, piece by piece, as patients came and went, and as

he no longer saw them, only the disease they presented. And yet now, in a moment, empathy has risen from its grave, looked him in the face and declared him to be a fool.

Morel takes a sudden involuntary breath, short and sharp, as if sucking life back into himself, and then he is so swept up by the revival of this long dormant emotion that he quite forgets himself, and he does something else he has not done in years.

He puts out his hand, and takes Marcel's in his own, and he shakes it.

'Yes,' he says. 'I will. I will try to help you.'

But for the moment at least, it is too late. Marcel is no longer 'awake'; he has returned to some prisoned corner of his mind, triggered by the recollection of Russian, of a particular Russian, or, rather, someone pretending to be Russian. He starts to replay an evening not so long ago, from the spring just gone and the fabulous ball held by the art students at the Moulin Rouge.

# THE BALL

It had been a long time in the making, this ball. Friday 21 April was the date on the invitations, yet preparations had begun months before. Marcel and Ondine first heard about it from Fraser and Fossard, of course, for the event to be held was the Bal des Quat'z' Arts – the annual celebration by students of the four disciplines practised in the art schools of Paris: painting, sculpture, architecture and engraving. The atelier of each art master would vie to outdo the rest, both with their costumes, and with the giant figures or tableaux in wood and paper that they would create. Fraser and Fossard, who belonged to the atelier of the great Gérome, explained to Marcel and Ondine about the vast female figure they and the other students of the workshop were making: Bellona, an imperiously naked Roman war goddess, fifteen feet high, brandishing a sword and shield.

All sorts of materials were going into her construction: yards of cloth, broken and splintered wood from broken easels, old stools and picture frames, along with much wire and rope. As the weeks passed, they spent less and less time on their art studies and devoted their energies to the completion of the centrepiece of the Atelier Gérome, the final stages of which saw the armature covered in a thick layer of papier mâché to create the skin of the goddess, artfully painted so the final result appeared as solid as any sculpture in the Louvre.

As for their own costumes, the mismatched pair of Fraser and Fossard kept their mouths shut.

'It's a big moment,' Fraser explained, 'when everyone arrives in costume at the Place Blanche. No one wants to reveal his secret ahead of time! But rest assured, my friend and I will not disappoint. You can find out on the day, when we leave the cour and take the bus to Pigalle!'

Marcel said he would like to come to the ball, if it was to be so wonderful, but Fraser explained that the ball was strictly for art students only, with admission limited to those on the individually named invitations.

'Never mind,' Fraser said with a straight face. 'You won't miss so very much.'

Then he punched Fossard on the shoulder and burst out laughing at some private joke that left Marcel mystified. It was Fraser who had told Ondine that there would be work for dancers, most likely unpaid but with the chance of large tips, for this was the one night in the year when art students forgot how penniless most of them were.

So Ondine made a couple of trips to the Moulin Rouge in the weeks before the ball, and presented herself at the small office on the Boulevard de Clichy that dealt with the hiring of staff.

As the days ticked away, and the ball approached, Marcel asked Ondine what her part was to be, but she, like Fraser and Fossard, refused to tell. At first Marcel just laughed at all the secrecy, but as the event drew nearer, and still she refused to say, he began to grow jealous.

'What is your costume like, at least?' he asked. 'Is it very fine?'

'The finest!' said Ondine, laughing again at some private joke, which only provoked more jealousy in Marcel. 'Perfect. It's completely me.'

'Tell me!' he begged. 'Or I'll have to get a job there too.'

'They only want dancers,' Ondine said, pouting. 'And girls at that. So stay at home and count your pennies like a good miser.'

Marcel ignored the jibe. 'I haven't seen you making the costume,' he said.

'It's not here,' Ondine replied. 'It's being made there.'

'But what is it?'

'It's magnificent!' Ondine declared. 'And if you're good I'll show it to you when I get home.'

Marcel's curiosity grew worse, and the more he pressed, the more affronted Ondine became. As a result, she did in fact begin to drop small hints, but nothing concrete, just little snippets that only made Marcel more and more envious that he was not going. Ondine began to tease him then, and called him Cinderella for the rest of the week, until finally the night arrived.

By this point, Marcel had determined to have nothing to do with the matter. For something to do, he had tried to see if he could get an extra night's work at the Cabaret of Insults, but Chardon didn't see the need. At six o'clock, he took himself off to get something to eat in the Rue Saint-André-des-Arts, and after that, he went to find himself a drink. He tried to put it all out of his mind, but he could not. After another beer, he suddenly rushed back home to demand that Ondine let him in on the secret, or not go at all.

He was too late. He arrived to find the studio empty, no sign of Ondine, who must have left to go and make ready. In the hallway, he bumped into Fraser and Fossard. At least, he assumed it was them. Coming out of their studio were two men: one a Roman senator dressed in toga and sandals, a coronet of laurel leaves atop his head, the other an Apache Indian, half naked, covered only in burned red paint and a blanket to which a number of chicken feathers had been sewn.

'Marcel!' cried the Indian, and Marcel peered at him closely. 'Fraser?'

Fraser laughed loudly and slapped the senator on the back.

'See?' he said. 'He does know who we are after all!'

Fossard made a very grumpy-looking senator, which caused Fraser to laugh every time he looked at him.

'Cinderella, are you looking for your prince? She's already left, I'm afraid. Look, don't be like that. Why don't you come with us to Pigalle? You can see all the ateliers arriving in cavalcade. It's a grand procession, and almost as much fun as the ball itself. Almost!'

Marcel hesitated.

'Come on!' Fraser said. 'Got anything better to be doing? No. So come along.'

So Marcel went. All along the Boulevard Saint-Germain were small crowds of art students in costumes of all kinds. Within five minutes they passed Adams and Eves in pale body suits and fig leaves, a cross-dressing Queen Victoria, a gaggle of Norman knights, a Byzantine emperor, a posse of Tartar bandits, count-less cavemen, gladiators and African warriors.

As they passed each group a great cry went up as they made challenges to each rival atelier. They passed on to the Boulevard Saint-Michel to the Luxembourg Palace and the Théâtre de l'Odéon, to scramble on to the tops of the buses of the Mont-martre line, which were quickly overloaded beyond legal nicety.

Marcel remembered something. 'Where's your goddess?' he shouted to Fraser as they clung to the top of the bus.

'We brought her up this morning. She's hidden in the Moulin Rouge, ready for her big moment.'

They swung up towards the Place Blanche, where they found a near riot in full swing. Marcel had never seen the place so crowded, and it was a wonder. The front of the Moulin itself was a blaze of electric lights and coloured paper lanterns. The illuminated arms of the mill revolved, and sent a glow across the place, picking out the fantastic costumes of the students and the bemused faces of the locals, who were, after all, used to a thing or two.

They climbed down from the bus and for a while it seemed as though they would be content to stay on the pavement, but grad-ually the numbers dwindled as the revellers headed inside.

'Well, this is where we leave you,' said Fraser, patting Marcel on the back.

'Surely you can get me in somehow?'

He felt more than ever that he wanted, that he needed, to join the fun, not only to see what Ondine would be wearing, but just to enjoy himself, let himself go.

'You don't have one of these,' said Fraser, and pulled out his invitation, a thick printed card with his name and the name of the atelier to which he belonged carefully added by hand. 'And even if you did, all the masters' assistants from each atelier are waiting inside the door to check us off a list. You just can't get in. Sorry! You don't even have a costume.'

And they went, Fraser and Fossard, leaving Marcel to watch the whirling mass of colour and potential debauchery in the place dwindle even further. He was about to leave when he saw that luck was on his side. Across the place, wandering down the Rue Lepic in a very unsteady manner, came a medieval knight in what appeared to be full plate armour. No one was with the knight, he appeared to be extremely drunk and, furthermore, his face was covered by a helmet and visor. The only question was how to get the student to part with his costume and invitation, and there was only one answer. Marcel did have money, after all, and Ondine was always telling him to spend it, so he did. And he was clever.

First, he merely offered to buy the knight a drink to carry him forward into the evening, then, as they downed their drinks, it took very little to convince the young student that he would really be better off selling his costume and invitation. Of course, the knight refused at first, but then Marcel put a pile of francs on the table top large enough to change his mind.

'You can even have my clothes into the bargain,' Marcel added, and they went out to an alleyway along the Boulevard de Clichy to change.

From the invitation, Marcel discovered his new name was Grasset. He pulled the helmet firmly on to his head and set off to join the back of the crowd trying to force their way inside. The student whose costume he'd borrowed was slightly shorter than him, so that the armour made him look a little foolish, with his ankles and wrists showing, but other than that, there was no reason for him not to gain admittance. Inside the door was a long line of the masters' assistants, or *massiers*, and on the wall behind them, a card pinned with the name of each atelier.

With great difficulty, Marcel peered out of the visor at his invitation as he edged forward and saw that he belonged to the atelier Cormon, and made his way to the *massier* of the Cormon studio, holding his card out in front of him.

'Who's this?'

Marcel waved the card, and the *massier* snatched it from him.

'Grasset? I might have known. Late as usual and drunk too I suppose.'

Marcel pointed a gloved finger at the side of his helmet, to show that he couldn't hear well. Then he pointed at the front to show he couldn't see much, for that matter.

The *massier* stared at him for a long second, and then cursed.

'Idiot,' he said. 'Get inside. The procession's about to begin.'

Then Marcel was inside. Though he knew it was a risk, he dared to take his helmet off. With it on, his vision was abysmal. Besides, there must have been upward of a thousand people in the great hall of the famous cabaret, and they couldn't possibly all know each other. On top of that, it was dim, apart from the gleaming lights from decorations and displays and the Chinese lanterns hanging from the ceiling. There was so much to see, and he wanted to see everything, so he set his helmet down behind a fake column at the side of the hall.

Music played and yet over the top of it quite different songs were being sung, a great tumult of noise and colour. Marcel looked for Ondine, but she was nowhere in sight. He moved through the crowd, laughing as people jostled him good-naturedly and challenged him to duels more than once. Around him he saw splendid things: noble kings and elegant queens, courtiers following behind in silk robes. There were more gladiators, some of whom were naked, and a family of Egyptian mummies carrying a sarcophagus. A tombstone walked past with an inscription down his back of a suitably sombre nature.

All around were women, too. Not students, of course, but girls brought in, some paid, some unpaid, to dress up in their finery and to entertain and to dance, yet still he could not see Ondine. He passed a group of three nymphs who wore nothing but swirls of green paint for clothes, and his attention was only taken away by a girl dressed in the Turkish style performing an impromptu belly dance for a crowd of cheering legionnaires. Marcel watched for a while spellbound, until a voice spoke at his shoulder.

'Such clothing is worn as least obscures the view, eh?'

He turned to find an Apache warrior grinning at him. Then the Apache swore.

'Marcel! What the devil? How did you get in here? Are you mad?'

Marcel stared at the Apache.

'Where on earth did you find that get-up?' said the Apache, and now Marcel shook himself.

'Fraser?' he said. 'I—'

'No need to explain yourself, but if they catch you . . . Be careful!'

Marcel nodded, wishing he'd kept his helmet with him.

'The procession's about to start! We're fifth. I have to join the others. See you. And be careful.'

Fraser rushed away to find the rest of the atelier Gérome, and as he did, a gong sounded, the band changed their tune to a magnificent ceremonial march, and the procession of figures began.

It was as if he entered a fairy-tale world. There was no other explanation for the extravagance, the richness, the strangeness of what passed before his eyes.

The first atelier to come by had created a tableau of hefty men clothed in furs and skins, carrying a bier made of tree branches bound with leather thongs, upon which sat naked cavewomen and even a few prehistoric children. It was wonderful, the cheers were immense. Behind it came the mummies, now carrying an open sarcophagus, with a sinuous model dancing inside. She was draped merely in a few carefully placed shreds of bandages, nothing more.

After that, a horde of Apaches staged a mock battle with gunslingers of the American west, and then came a scene of a Greek bacchanalia, with many young men wearing no more than a bunch of grapes in their hair and a vine leaf for modesty.

Then, towering above the others, Marcel saw Bellona, the goddess, fifteen feet high and just as Fraser had described, apart from the fact that a weird green light shone from her hollow eyes. The onlookers were in an ecstasy of delight and a great shout went up, not at Bellona but at something hidden behind her, in the procession. Marcel could not see; he tried to move but was pushed back into place by a Russian, in fact, a Cossack, and then the procession moved on and he saw.

Behind Bellona, eight Roman soldiers carried an immense shield, flat. Upon that, four of the finest artists' models of all Paris lay on their backs, head to head, their legs upraised to meet and support another slightly smaller tablet, seemingly of gold, upon which stood a woman. She was naked, save for a sparkling crown of jewels in her auburn hair, and a belt of electric lights that encircled her waist, illuminating the whiteness of her skin, and the darkness of her hair and the crevices of her sensuous body.

Marcel gazed in wonder at the woman, and felt desire.

She looked like a goddess, and she knew it, and then someone learned her name, and a great roar and chant was thrown up.

'Ondine!' they shouted. 'Ondine! Ondine!'

Marcel heard the name in horror. Ondine? Ondine!

His wife, naked for all to see, smiled down at the crowd as they admired her. Marcel saw that she was holding one gaze in particular, the gaze of one of the men carrying the vast shield, who looked back up at her with eyes that displayed his lust.

Suddenly, Ondine broke that locked gaze, and turned, to see Marcel. She looked at him standing there pathetically, dressed stupidly as a cardboard knight.

Marcel stared, and stared, but no one knew who he was, or cared.

'Ondine!' they chanted. 'Ondine, Ondine!'

She smiled, and looked away.

# COMMONPLACE

The Monday morning after his visit to Baraduc, Petit arrives a little late for work. He is sleeping badly, and he knows why, though it is something he has tried to repress or ignore for a long time. The episode with the photographer has brought things back to mind, even though there is no direct correlation between his activities and the inspector's own wounds. Maybe it was just seeing her name twice like that. On the cigar, Maria; on the street name, Marie. Maybe it was that and nothing more. Whatever it was, she is back even more strongly than before, back in his waking thoughts and in his dreams, and at least now he knows why he wants that bastard Després to get what he deserves. He had a beautiful wife, and killed her, just out of anger. And there was Marie, his fiancée, waiting for him to return from Africa and leave the army for good. And he did leave, although the causality was somewhat different: he left the service after she died, and he knew now, *because* she'd died. If only he'd left when she first begged him to, he might have been in Paris when someone broke into her mother's home and took the lives of them both.

After Marie passed away, something had changed in Laurent Petit, and he knew that he was done with killing for France on foreign soil. The police had seemed an easy option and, until he joined, he had no idea that he would see almost as much death as an inspector with the judicial police as he had as a soldier. At times, he had to agree with Boissenot: there was something about the city, some kind of disease or mania, some anger with mere existence that drove people to insanity, drove them to kill.

The key difference for Petit was that he wasn't the one doing the killing. Not unless he can get Després out of his cell in the Salpêtrière and somehow dispatched to the guillotine. Then he'll be very glad to be responsible for one more death; he, Petit, who had had no control over whether his wife-to-be lived or died, would see that Marcel, who had played God, had no control over his fate.

Or so Petit is thinking as he makes his way to the Quai des Orfèvres this Monday morning. But the events of the next hour will start to change all that certainty in his mind, certainty that he has been feeding off, like an opiate, for these last few weeks, keeping him numb, keeping him from feeling too much other than a gently brooding hate.

'You're for it,' says Drouot as he comes into the office.

Petit scowls at him, and Drouot holds up his hands.

'You obviously had a rough weekend. Sorry. But you've been summoned.'

Petit cringes slightly. He knows he's been late once too often. 'Boissenot,' he says, and hangs his head.

'Oh, come now,' says Drouot, 'you should have higher aspirations than that. Cavard wants to see you.'

'The chef wants to see me?' asks Petit. 'Are you sure?'

Drouot spreads his arms wide. 'Would I joke about a thing like this?' he says, and as Petit starts to head towards the chef's offices, Drouot stops him. 'He's not in his office. You need to head to the other building.'

He points aimlessly through the wall. 'He's in the Prefect's office. He said he would wait for you there. As soon as you got in.'

Petit sprints out of the Sûreté offices, and is still running, across the Boulevard du Palais, when he wonders why on earth the chef wants to see him there.

By the time he gets to the tiny antechamber outside the Prefect's office, he is panting and flustered. He takes a moment before knocking gingerly on the door, remembering how he put a boot to Baraduc's door with really no call to do so.

A voice beyond calls to him to enter, and he does. Before he can even begin to explain about his late arrivals at work, he senses that this has nothing to do with them.

Paul Delorme, the Prefect of the Paris Police, the man in charge of all of them, sits behind a large, though not expensive, desk. The desk is full, but well organised, all the piles of papers neatly stacked and at perfect right angles to each other, with only a clear space for a blotting pad in front of him, and in one corner the obligatory photograph of himself in ceremonial dress, and another of his family. Petit has never met him before, and there is a lot to take in. Delorme is a tall man with a neatly cropped beard. He has the air of a businessman about him, or a politician, very different from Cavard, Petit's boss, sitting in one of two chairs on Petit's side of the desk. Cavard is a powerful man too, but he's a cop, nonetheless, hands-on and practical. Cavard is of the streets, while Delorme . . .

Petit does not know what to make of Delorme, not exactly, not yet. He senses ill-will and authority and that's a combination that unsettles him.

From rumours he has heard around the building in his short time as an inspector, he knows there is no love lost between the two men, and yet they are obliged to have a daily briefing.

No one says anything immediately. Cavard stares at the carpet, Delorme reads some papers, and Petit sweats, wondering whether he should wipe his handkerchief across his brow or whether that would make him look guiltier than he already feels.

'Petit?' asks Delorme.

Petit takes a step forward, wondering whether he will be invited to take the chair next to Cavard. A tiny glance in his direction and Petit stops where he is and stays standing. Delorme returns to the papers he was reading.

It's Cavard who speaks next.

'Petit, how long have you been with the Sûreté? Eighteen months, I think?'

Petit nods. 'Yes, Chef.'

'I would not expect to have anything to do with someone of your rank quite so often, yet here we are again.'

'Sir?'

'You remember that I consigned you to Devil's Island, as it were? The archives? I trust you didn't find that particularly enjoyable, Petit, and it was not supposed to be. It was supposed to teach you a lesson. I fear it did not. Do you know what the lesson was, Petit?'

'Not to question the decisions of superior officers, sir.'

'Exactly. And you an ex-military man. I would have thought that you would understand such things, would have understood them long before you came here. And yet you left the military. Why was that?'

Petit hesitates a fraction of a second. 'I wanted to return to civilian life to marry, Chef.'

'And you are now married?'

A longer pause. 'No, sir.'

Something in Petit's tone allows that this remark is left hanging, and no one speaks. An angel passes. Her name is probably Marie.

'Petit,' Cavard says, breaking the moment. 'You will recall, I'm sure, the reason that I asked you to drop the investigation into the Després case. You will recall that I told you that the Préfecture had declared Després to be insane and that he should be incarcerated in a hospital best suited to take care of matters. I find myself this morning in the position of asking you to recall this once more, here in the office of the Prefect, since he has invited me to do it here, in his presence, so that there may be no further question or doubt about the matter.'

'Sir, I didn't think—'

'No, you didn't think that anyone knew that you were still working on the case. But you have been heard talking to people, asking questions, and we have a complaint from a Monsieur Baraduc that has come in. Something about a door . . . ? In addition, the Després apartment was ransacked a few days ago. You wouldn't happen to know anything about that, would you, Inspector?'

Petit shakes his head firmly.

'So that is an end to the matter; I would like you to assure the Prefect here and now that you have, this time, understood. Otherwise you can find yourself a new profession, Petit, all right?'

Cavard is clearly furious, not only with Petit, at the way he has been made to upbraid one of his men in front of the Prefect, but also with Delorme himself, for making it happen in this way. Yet he suppresses his displeasure as best he can. He and this idiot of an inspector are, after all, from the same team, and by and large the Préfecture only means one thing to the Sûreté, and that's interference. There is no one with more power over police matters in the whole of Paris than Prefect Delorme, save the Minister of the Interior, and after him, the President of the great republic. For that reason alone, Cavard does what Delorme wants him to, and the magnitude of Delorme's power is manifest. In the setting of the office, of the view it commands over the Rue de Lutèce outside, of the size of the desk if not its quality, of the way in which he has said only one word since Petit entered, and yet has got precisely what he wanted.

'Sir,' says Petit, with all the solemnity and honesty he can muster. If they wanted to scare him, it's worked. And he knows he's going to have to let Marcel get away with murder. But he wants to know one more thing before he is dismissed.

'Sir?' he asks.

Cavard glares at him. 'What is it?'

'Who. I mean, may I ask, who, within the Préfecture, made the decision about Després? Sir?'

There is the longest silence of all since he entered the Prefect's cave, during which Cavard seems too angry to speak. Slowly, Delorme tilts his head up, and takes a moment to focus on Petit's form in front of him. Petit, who has fought hand to hand with naked African natives brandishing wickedly sharp spears, and seen his fellows drop next to him and thought nothing much of it until long after the fight was over, finds that he has to suppress the urge to pass water on the carpet there and then.

Delorme opens his mouth. 'I did,' he says. Then he looks back down at his papers.

Cavard is still staring at the carpet, but gives a tiny wave of the hand to show that Petit had better get out while he still has a job. As he does so, Petit is left with one final moment to take in the room.

It lasts a second, maybe two, before he turns, but by the time his hand reaches the doorknob, his heart is pounding, and for a very different reason than his fear of Delorme. In that brief space of time, Petit scans the men in front of him one more time. He finds he is looking at the tops of both of their heads, both of thinning hair. His gaze falls on the photographs on the desk, turned face out, so that the visitor can see who the Prefect is. And who he is, the photographs declare, is a true Frenchman. A family man, with a sturdy and dependable wife, and two children, an upright boy and a pretty girl. So says the first photograph of his family. And what of the other, of Delorme in his ceremonial dress? It cannot have been taken so very long ago. Like Petit, Delorme has only been in post for a year and a half, since the legendary Lépine went off to Algeria, and yet Petit has time to notice that already the Prefect has lost a little more hair since the picture was made. This photograph speaks of power; it speaks of tradition, and the authority that Delorme has just wielded at Cavard and the young inspector.

Yet that's not the thing Petit notices about the photograph. What he notices, in that short space of time, is that there is a mark on it. A slight imperfection, one that only an expert eye, or someone who has perhaps only recently become an expert on the matter, might see. A tell-tale blemish in the upper left corner of the picture, caused by an imperfection of the lens that captured it, and one that tells Laurent Petit that the Prefect of Paris Police had his portrait taken by the very same ex-spirit photographer and erstwhile pornographer who took indecent photographs of Ondine Badiou.

The chance of a coincidence seems far too unlikely to Petit. Besides which, there is the simple question of what the Prefect is doing associating with such riff-raff as Baraduc. He can surely afford much better photographers, with much more salubrious addresses. It doesn't prove, of course, that Delorme had anything to do with Ondine, or even that he knew her. And yet why in hell should he have concerned himself with what was otherwise a relatively commonplace and, for want of a better word, uninteresting murder? In two days he had had the thing shut down, closed up and forgotten, even before Petit had really started work.

Petit leaves the office, trying to repress a sudden urge within him to run, an urge created from the belief that he is about to start shouting things at the top of his voice. Things that might get him in a lot of trouble.

He decides he needs time to calm down, to think matters through. He might be jumping to conclusions; he needs to work calmly and rationally through everything he knows so far. He walks back to the Quai des Orfèvres the long way, taking an anticlockwise tour around the perimeter of the Île de la Cité, giving him time to think. During which time he comes to the conclusion that he is not mistaken. There is something very odd about this matter. There has *always* been something very odd about this matter, right from the start. That's his conviction, and though there is nothing more he can say, nothing he can prove, he knows that he is going to continue to work on the affair, even at the risk of his job. He owes that much to his own poor Marie, and to Marcel's dead wife, Ondine. But if Petit is right, that there is something very strange about the entire business, he has no idea just how strange it will turn out to be, and he is wrong about one thing, one very important thing indeed. Namely this: Ondine Després is not dead.

# TRAUMA

# ONDINE

In order to understand how it came about that the entire world, apart from two people (one of them the 'victim' herself), believed that Ondine was both dead and buried it is necessary to unravel the twisting together of several remarkable occurrences.

Where better to start than with the resurrected lady herself, Ondine Després? As we have seen, Ondine came to the city with dreams that outreached her. She was sixteen at the time. Her mother being dead, her father working very hard at trying to drink himself into his wife's grave, Ondine believed that her life would certainly be better if she left the suburbs of Lille where she had grown up and sought greater opportunities in Paris, which like all capital cities exerts a great magnetic pull upon its nation's ambitious young people, perhaps greater than it ought to. Certainly she knew that things could not be worse than at home, where a house that had always been poor was declining even further.

On arrival in the city, she was already more streetwise than many of her contemporaries. She was sure of herself and who she was, and believed that she had two gifts: that she could act, and that she was attractive to men. Sadly she was only right about one of them. It was something she had been well aware of for some time. As a girl as young as seven she'd learned that rich old men in the park on Sunday could be made to part with a few centimes if she appeared in front of them in tears, claiming to have lost her father. A wipe with a handkerchief took the tears away and a couple of coins would put a smile on her damp face. Indeed, these centimes would mount up in her father's pockets, it being a ruse he had developed to supplement the amount of money he had for beer. By the age of twelve she had grown too old for tricks like that, but by then she had already learned that she didn't have to do very much in order for things to go better for her. A smile here, a fluttering glance there, and men would offer all sorts of treats: an extra ball of ice cream, a free ride on the carousel when the fair came to town.

By the time she arrived in Paris, she had these arts perfected, she felt, to such a degree that she could get men to do things without them even knowing they wanted to. The right kind of lingering touch on a forearm could work miracles, she'd found, nearly as good as looking up at someone from under her eyelashes and biting her lip almost imperceptibly. It would be hard to judge Ondine at sixteen for being manipulating and calculating, because God had given her just two gifts (well, one), and she was going to make the best of what she had. It would be hard to say she was conniving when she could not for one moment have stepped back and asked herself if what she was doing was wrong in any way at all.

And no one had ever given her to understand that she was anything other than startlingly attractive. As she moved from a girl to a young woman and her body developed, she found that even more doors seemed to open for her, though as the acting dream died, the doors all led to a certain kind of house. It was in one such house, at the age of twenty-two, that one of her clients decided that, although she was undeniably striking, she was also somewhat arrogant, cocksure of herself. The gentleman decided to formulate a question to test this theory.

'When,' he asked, 'that is, how old were you when you knew you were beautiful?'

The question was not really a question. It was a trap. It could, he thought, be answered in a few ways. There could be genuine modesty (perhaps rare) in which the girl could actually not feel herself to be beautiful, and would stammer out some reply to that effect. There might be an answer suggesting false modesty, implying the girl knew well enough that she was good-looking but also knew it was perhaps a little gauche to admit it boldly. And then, there was the answer that Ondine actually gave.

'I was eight,' she stated with pride, and without hesitation. There was no irony, no self-awareness or sham of modesty, and the customer of the house felt his suspicions were confirmed. Once again though, we might defend Ondine by pointing out that this was at least honest, and that circumstances had made her this way.

Her mother had worked until she'd died but earned very little. Her father worked until his wife died, and then began drinking with renewed energy. Ondine had grown up very poor, and as a young child had been unable to understand why her parents did not simply just 'get' more money. Hunger was frequent, clothes were few and far between and never fine, heating was limited in the winter and all in all it was miserable to have no money. As she grew a little older and learned that money comes from the process of exchange, it was her father who taught her, in the park with the old rich men, that the asset she had of value was her beauty. No wonder then, that she came to treat it as a commodity, one that she did not value in and for herself very much, but which was of immense value in what it could get her. As she made her way into the working houses of Paris, and was very soon ensconced in the finest of them, she realised that there was something else about her gift, about her commodity of exchange. It was inexhaustible. When she gave her beauty away, men gave her money for it, and yet, in actual fact, she gave *nothing* away. Her beauty was still hers. It did not leave, piece by piece with each transaction. When she slept with a man, she saw the hunger in their eyes as they tendered money to the madame of the house. They barely noticed the currency leaving their hands, all they wanted was to be enfolded in her beauty, and ravish it in return. And when it was over, and she began to dress again, she saw that her long, slim legs were still long and slim;

her breasts were still firm and her lips still sensual; her eyes still smouldered if she made them do so and her hair hung in tresses just as fine as half an hour before. And yet, the customer's money was still sitting in madame's drawer, and a respectable portion of it would be in Ondine's purse later that night. Her beauty remained hers, her beauty was infinite.

So she earned a lot of money, and lived a wild life. She was many men's favourite, and knew it. She was invited to the most extravagant parties, to the most lavish orgiastic soirées, and she met a lot of very powerful men. It was during this time that Monsieur Baraduc took her photograph, the one that Inspector Petit has been dragging around Paris, as well as other photographs for her rich clients' personal consumption. Ondine believed she was happy. It would be arrogant in turn to say that perhaps she was not, for who are we to judge? Happy or not, one thing she was for sure: hungry.

Is it simplistic to say that her desperately poor upbringing, and the teachings of her father, left her with a lifelong and insatiable hunger for security through money? Just because it is a simple explanation doesn't make it untrue. What might be harder to work out is why, having found herself with money, it was *never* enough, although she spent it like water. Was she fulfilling some inbuilt process as she strove to get rid of what she'd deservedly earned so quickly? Centimes in the park, centimes in the park.

There might also be other reasons why enough was never enough; some people just seem to be made that way, after all. But Ondine was wrong about something in all this: that her beauty was infinite. It is one of the potential curses of the young that they can never conceive of being old, and although her customers did not manage to steal one ounce of her beauty, as the years went by, time did.

At twenty-five any sane man would have found her to be barely approaching the height of her sexual attraction, but the world in which she lived was not composed of entirely sane men. They were rich men, powerful men, and those men who have the urge and the fortune to become rich and powerful have very often also the seed of other motivations. Those who are simply born rich and powerful, perhaps even more so. And the house in which Ondine had come to work was full of both, men of all backgrounds and creeds with one characteristic in common aside from their money: they liked their women young.

And thus, at this still tender age, Ondine found herself with stark choices: move to a brothel of a lower nature where she would take a smaller cut of much less money, take to the streets where she would almost certainly become diseased, or use her body in the cabarets. There remained in her a tiny memory of that desire to act. And so she chose the cabarets.

# MARIE

As Inspector Petit drops yet another coffee cup on the floor of his rooms, and it smashes into small pieces, it suddenly occurs to him that he was not always clumsy. Far from it, in fact: at school, where he fenced, and in the army, he was elegant with the rapier. At some point since, however, he has developed an unerring knack for breaking something every week, bumping into people every day, banging his head on lintels frequently and usually rounding everything off by spilling ink across his paperwork just when his reports are most behind-hand. He knows when it started. It started when Marie was killed.

Marie and her ageing mother. They don't know which of them died first. The house was broken into, doors were opened. Hands closed around the throats of mother and then daughter, or daughter and then mother, until they stopped breathing. Items of value were taken, and the killer, or perhaps killers, left. As if it weren't bad enough, as if it doesn't kill Petit that he was in Africa when it happened, as if he hasn't cried for how Marie must have felt as she died, desperate, alone, in the dark, painfully, horrifyingly, there's something else about the death that skewers at his mind. He hates himself for even feeling it, let alone putting it into words; it makes him ashamed to have loved Marie, it makes him writhe with guilt, but it's this: he cannot bear that the killer, a man without doubt, lay on top of her as he strangled her. He touched Marie's beautiful throat, pushed himself down on her as she lay in her nightgown, must have felt her breasts under him, felt her legs moving between his. It's this, more than anything, that still haunts him about the murder, and this, and the guilt of feeling this way, is slowly killing him.

Something else has been occupying his mind, and it is this: memory.

Until he met Marcel Mémoire and Dr Morel he had never given memory a first thought, never mind a second one. Memory was as invisible to him as the air he breathed. He merely used it without awareness, without contemplation or any consideration, but now, things have changed. He has been thinking about memory a lot; he's been thinking about the patricidal shoemaker in Morel's care, the one with the memory span of less than five minutes. Something about that man, about his predicament, truly terrifies Petit; he is constantly haunted by the vision of the man making and remaking that simple wooden puzzle again, and again, and again. Like Sisyphus and his stone, he thinks, except it's not like that, because it wasn't Sisyphus's punishment just to roll a rock to the top of a hill in Hell for all eternity; it was also his punishment to *know* that he would have to do it for ever. Whereas poor Henri is perhaps not so poor; maybe it's a blessing, to be able to forget. Is it possible, Petit wonders, that Henri's own mind in some way *decided* to become amnesiac, to prevent him from further harm, further pain? The good Dr Morel will have a theory about that, no doubt. He will have to ask Morel about that the next—

He stops himself. There will be no next time. He will not contact Morel again, and he will put this whole affair from his mind, just as he wishes he could put Marie's murder from his mind. Yet he cannot. She will not let him.

Of course, it would not do to become like Henri, with a memory measured in seconds, but perhaps it would help if he could just forget a little bit more. The incident occurred, he thinks. There is no changing that. Marie is dead, and how she died was not good at all. But if he could be spared the remembering of it, if he could be freed from reliving the trauma every day, maybe then he could begin to feel easier.

Knocking on the threshold of Petit's thinking is a fleeting connection to Marcel himself, but he does not open the door to allow it in. Not yet. For now, he can only see his own torture as he endlessly replays his imagined creation of how his wife-to-be died, her lovely soft breasts spilling loose from her nightdress as the monster took her.

And now, as if it were not enough to grieve for the wife he never had, he has been cursed with this laughable affliction, this cack-handedness. Not something you can wear as a badge of honour, a noble scar on his heart from the death of his fiancée, a twisted form of mourning wear, a black armband on his soul. No. It is ridiculous and he is frequently ridiculed for it, most often by his friend Drouot whenever he hears of Laurent's latest exploit in incompetence.

He doesn't bother picking up the pieces of the cup, not yet. At least it was empty this time.

August has become September. He has a fine view of the city from the window at the back of his rooms on the top floor of a house in the Rue Laplace. Already, leaves are starting to turn, and though there remain plenty of hot days in which the city seems to stand still in a furnace of its own expired breath, there have been some chilly mornings too, where the cold of the night before lingers in the pavements, sucking heat from Petit as he makes his way down to the river.

From here, in the Rue Laplace, a street below the Panthéon, he can see clear across the river, though the water itself is hidden from sight by the tall buildings of Haussmann's Paris. The city rises up again beyond, and there is the hill of Montmartre, with that ridiculous-looking basilica slowly appearing on top of it, still as much scaffold as stone. Under the hill lurks Pigalle.

It is September; Petit has not acted. He has done nothing about his suspicions, not one thing. To begin with, he had to fight to keep his mouth shut, especially that first morning. He'd calmed a little by the time he got back to the Sûreté offices, but still had to bite his tongue, so much so that he said almost nothing all morning, which only made Drouot wonder if he was angry, or ill. As the days passed and he managed not to tell anyone what he knew, or, as he often corrected himself, what he suspected, and as he successfully repressed his ideas, there came no point when he decided to speak. Having begun this process of repression, there was never any reason to stop it.

And yet. And yet, every day as he fixes his coffee, he can almost see into the heart of Pigalle, where he is absolutely sure lie the secrets at the heart of the matter. Every day is a reminder that he has done nothing, and every time he is reminded of the murderous memory man is another time that he finds himself feeling angry at the world for allowing Maria's killer to remain unknown. The guilty should be punished, the guilty should be punished. He doesn't even have to tell himself that, it just runs through him, deep inside, rotting away, like an abscess forming. Of course, such things don't just form; one day, when enough time has elapsed, they erupt. But today is not yet that day.

The pieces of the broken cup remain on the floor.

# FACES

It remains to be explained how Ondine still lived, and one particular matter can shed light not only on how that is the case, but why it is the case too. This concerns Lucie, Ondine's friend at the cabaret.

In truth, they were not such good friends, but they themselves had not yet realised that. They clung to each other, having known and worked with each other at three previous clubs before pitching up at the Cabaret of Insults. Familiarity in the face of the unknown is a powerful force. Their first job together ended when Lucie was sacked, but ever since the time they were reunited at the theatre known as the Grand-Guignol, they had stuck together. A small and seedy venue that had recently opened, the theatre specialised in shows of a gruesome or sexual nature. It was the declared aim of the patron to have as many people faint in every show as possible, from exposure to one, or both, of these two things. Ondine and Lucie had stuck it out at the Grand-Guignol for a few months, and then worked in another dive before they reached the nadir as far as either of them was concerned: the Cabaret of Insults.

Still they found no one they liked more than each other, and they did know a lot about each other by this time. They were open about their hopes and dreams, and Lucie knew (almost) all of Ondine's past adventures. When men came through their lives, they discussed them and shared titbits of information, but all the while the seed of the destruction of their friendship waited in the wings. That seed was the business of envy. Lucie had just as spectacular a body as Ondine, as all the girls in the club did, but no one else had Ondine's face, that remarkable face, which stopped men in their tracks. Lucie was envious when Ondine found another man willing to buy her drinks and dine her until she grew bored of him. And while men would spend idle time with Lucie, she knew she had never come close to finding a man to marry. Ondine let such men slip through her fingers every week, or so it seemed. For example, there was the American, Bishop. Ondine and he had been pretty tight for a good long while, until something unprecedented happened. He'd been the one to get bored of *her*. Ondine was not too distraught about this. More confused. Bishop had started going with a girl at the Moulin Rouge, which only added insult to the injury. Then that weirdo Marcel had come along, and Lucie had been able to do nothing to prevent Ondine rebounding from Bishop into his arms, so fast, so hard in fact, that they got married.

Lucie did everything she could to put Ondine off, doing her best to convince her friend that she wasn't really in love, that it wouldn't last, that it was a mistake, and so on and so on and, as it happens, she was right. It didn't last. Lucie had a hand in that, too.

She had begun to suspect something about Marcel, something no one else had suspected. Everyone knew by now about his remarkable memory, that amazing brain, and if he was a little weird sometimes, well, what of it? That was bound to be the case with someone like him, and, after all, there was no one else like him, so who knew how he should behave?

One day, more envious than ever now that Marcel and Ondine were married and apparently very happy, she decided to tell Ondine what she had come to realise.

Ondine, of course, did not believe what she heard. At first she barely understood what Lucie was saying, and when she did, she simply knew it could not be true – Marcel remembered everything.

Their conversation grew heated, until Lucie finally snapped.

'I'll bet I could take him to bed and make him think I was you!'

Ondine slapped her, then stared at her, then decided to make a fool of her.

'Very well. Try! I'll give you a key, you can put on my clothes! And then you can try!'

The bet was made in anger, and concluded in rage.

Lucie knew a lot about how Ondine and Marcel lived. In her happiness, Ondine had been willing enough to share all sorts of details about her marriage, even her sex life. And it was this that Lucie used, gleefully.

Lucie had thought it through. She had taken great care with her dress, for example, wearing the same white blouse and white skirt that Ondine had been wearing that day. We use the word 'same'. Such an artless word. It makes no distinction between *same* meaning the exact one, the article itself and no other, and *same* meaning from the same mould, or manufacturer, or two things that simply look alike. Lucie didn't know that to Marcel no two things are *the same*, that to him each pebble was each pebble and that he could remember the difference between them all. She also didn't know that this was what lay behind what she had begun to suspect. It was in the things Marcel did, little things he said, and sometimes things he didn't say, when meeting someone for the first time each day. It was something she'd wondered about. It was also, in fact, something Fraser and Fossard had wondered about, though they had taken their initial musings no further.

Lucie had. And though she didn't know that Marcel, who could remember each expression of every face at every moment of contact, *could not connect all these different faces up* and allow that they all belonged to the same person, she had rightly guessed the result: Marcel was blind to faces.

The one lacuna in his memory. He could not remember faces.

This is what Lucie had guessed, and was now about to prove with relish. Marcel, after all, was very handsome, and when he walked into the studio, she wasted no time taking him to bed. Once again, she saw that moment's hesitation in him as they greeted each other. But she was in their house, and before Marcel had time even to think to inspect her clothes, something that had got him out of trouble in the past, she was out of them, standing naked and pulling him backwards on to the bed, as Ondine had told her she often did.

So Marcel relaxed, and they made love. They were still making love when Ondine, who had in the intervening time suddenly started to doubt whether this plan was such a good idea, let herself in and found her husband having sex with her best friend.

The confusion that arose was inevitable, and yet it was the confusion on Marcel's face more than anything else that convinced Ondine that he genuinely hadn't known that he was not making love to his wife. Of course, that took much, much longer than it takes to say, and the fight was brutal and vicious. Lucie had not meant to be still in the act when Ondine returned, naturally, but caught she had been. That was the end of their friendship, but not before Lucie had told Ondine exactly what she thought of her, and also planted a thought in Ondine's mind that would be the end of everything else, in time.

As Ondine struggled to throw Lucie out of the door, and as she started to believe what Lucie had just explained, which Marcel was now confirming in tears, that he could not tell her face from one time to the very next time he saw her, Lucie screamed, 'He doesn't know who you are! How can he love you when he doesn't know who you are from one day to the next?'

That was it. That was all it took to get something lodged in Ondine's mind. Time and again over the next few days she came back to it. She now believed that Marcel had genuinely thought he was making love to her. She didn't know how it was possible, but she also knew that other odd thing about him: that he could never lie. And since he believed that Lucie was *her*, she couldn't very well blame him for doing what she often delighted in doing with him, on that bed under the stars.

Ondine did, certainly, blame Lucie, who could have chosen any number of other ways to prove the point, but instead did it by taking her husband to bed, while she, Ondine, in her stupid confidence, had agreed to the scheme. It mattered little, it mattered not who had done it, or why, all that mattered was that Ondine dwelt upon what Lucie had said.

She brooded.

How *could* he love her? How could he be *in love* with her, when he didn't recognise her from day to day? How could he even know who she *was*?

After a week of such thoughts, the damage was done.

# THE LACUNA

It did not take Morel that long to make the same discovery about Marcel that Lucie had. It was something that Marcel had managed to manage, for a very long time; after all, he only could be sure who his own parents were because they were the man and woman who appeared in his room every morning when he was young, and who waited for him at the breakfast table when he was older. Ginette, perhaps the other most important person in his life until he came to Paris, was someone he learned to recognise by context and by dress, but even then he was in danger of having his secret uncovered. One day, a cousin of Ginette's was visiting, and it was she who answered the door when Marcel went to ask the doctor about paying a bill. There was some uncertainty in his mind, but he gambled that he was speaking to Ginette, and called the cousin by that name. She laughed and looked confused and told the real Ginette what had happened, not knowing how well Marcel knew the doctor's daughter, that it was not just a case of unfamiliarity. But since the cousin did look a little like Ginette, and since Marcel explained he was not feeling himself that morning, he got away with it.

It's one thing to avoid detection when no one is actually looking for you, but still another to keep all your secrets when you are being studied on a daily basis, at close quarters, by one of France's leading alienists. Thus, as Morel made his visits to Marcel, he too noted the brief reticence his patient displayed on every meeting, either with himself or with other doctors, warders or staff of any kind. This had aroused his suspicion. At first, he didn't know what was amiss, he could merely tell that

153

something was. Eventually he guessed that Marcel needed to wait until he was given information to confirm he knew who he was speaking to, and Morel, like Lucie, decided to test his theory, though thankfully for all parties concerned, not in the same way.

One day, Morel dresses the Russian warder up in his doctor's outfit. The long black morning coat, the cravat, the shining shoes. He puts the two pens in his top pocket that he always keeps there, poking up. And then he dispatches the Russian into Marcel's chamber, while he stands unseen outside the door. Morel has primed the warder with an opening line, which the Russian delivers like a piece of ham on a stage.

'Here I am, here I am, Marcel. Your doctor bids you good morning.'

The line could not have been delivered more clumsily or with greater fraudulence, and yet without any hesitation or doubt he hears Marcel answering.

'Good morning, Doctor.'

Morel notes that even the warder's thick accent was not enough to signal that anything was amiss, and he bowls in straight away to confound his prisoner with his discovery.

'Aha!' he says, 'I have you!'

What can Marcel do but confess? He tells the doctor that yes, this is how it's always been. For the rest of their time together the doctor falls into deeper and deeper despondency. The genius has been unmasked at last. He is fallible, there is a flaw, and what an enormous flaw it is, in Marcel's memory.

The doctor listens glumly as Marcel tries to explain about faces, how they all are different, because they move all the time, because from day to day they are not the same colour, or temperament, that hair has changed, and so on. Morel barely listens. He was chasing the idea of perfection, and that noble goal has just been removed. Yes, Marcel is still remarkable, but Morel was after a bigger prize than the merely remarkable. He was chasing the unbelievable. How is he to create his great reputation on anything less? He considers that thought for a moment, because something is bothering him. It takes him a long while to work out what it is: that the desire to achieve immortality in the scientific world is no longer quite as strong as it was before. It's been replaced, in part, by an irritating notion that he actually wants to help Marcel get better.

Overnight, however, something occurs to him. He wakes in his solitary rooms at the far side of the hospital in the middle of the night, and sits up in bed.

'He remembers each face!' he declares, by which he means that Marcel remembers each individual face as an *individual* face.

Next morning, he puts this theory to Marcel, with great excitement.

Marcel looks at him and says rather bluntly, 'Yes, that's what I told you yesterday.'

'Yes, yes, my boy, but listen: is it the case that since you can remember each individual face, you are in some way unable to connect them all together? That you cannot conceive they all come from the same person?'

Marcel sighs. And nods, yes, that is the case.

'But why,' asks Morel, more to himself than to Marcel, 'should you be unaware that one group of facial memories, mine for example, are closer in similarity than those of another group, those of Dr Martin, for example? Or that photographer, Buguet?'

Marcel doesn't really know, and says so.

'Perhaps they are more similar to you,' he offers, 'but not to me.'

He shrugs, but Morel isn't listening too closely now. He is elated.

'There is no lacuna!' he announces happily. 'I thought we had found a gap in your talents, my boy. But we have not. This problem you have with recognising faces is not a gap in the strength of your memory; it is *created* by it. It is because you remember *too well* that you cannot know whose face is whose.'

Marcel says nothing. He doesn't particularly care about any of this; it's something he's lived with his whole life. And he is not especially enjoying the daily attention of being Morel's star pupil.

'How are you getting along, anyway?' Morel enquires eventually.

Marcel gazes at the floor. 'When will I be released?' he asks.

It is the first time he has asked such a question, and Morel takes that in itself to be a good sign.

'You wish to leave?'

Marcel shrugs.

If he does want to leave, it does not seem to be a burning desire.

Morel rolls his head from side to side, something he does when he's unsure.

'You are a menace to society. You murdered your wife, did you not? In a fit of rage. The Préfecture has decided to incarcerate you here, and since it has, it would be a question of our finding you safe to release back into the world. I notice you have been reading? Newspapers are not really allowed in here, you know, but I gather you have been reading through old ones. Are you looking for something? No? Just something to pass the time, perhaps. Well, I see no harm in it, you have to keep that mind of yours exercised, do you not?'

Marcel stares at the floor. He is not listening. In his mind he is replaying the moment he killed his wife, for perhaps the ten thousandth time. It haunts him badly, what he did, and as Morel has noted before, Marcel's prison is not one made with walls and bars.

The doctor has not been idle; he did not make a vow lightly to Marcel that he would help him, and he has been studying the rarest of sources for any clue upon the subject of the hypermnesiac. That is what he tells himself: that he is trying to help Marcel, and it is partially true, although he also realises that if he does still want to make his reputation with the case (he had already sounded the words Morel's syndrome often enough in his head to have begun to expect to find it in the literature he is now reading) then he will need to verify that no one in living memory has written the subject up already.

He doubts it. From the reading he has done so far, he has found plenty on the subject of amnesia, and next to nothing on its other extremity. The most promising, and simultaneously heart-stopping work was that written some twenty-five years previously by Ribot. In the Sorbonne library, Morel worked his way through Ribot's stolid and yet utterly limp prose, finding a chapter at last entitled 'EXALTATIONS OF MEMORY, or HYPERMNESIA'.

Damn it, thought Morel, so the word has been coined already. Hypermnesia. Never mind, it was an obvious enough thought. Let's see what the fool has to say.

He did so. For the most part, the chapter covered what Ribot terms 'partial hypermnesia', and cited cases such as the boy who fractured his skull at the age of four, about which he remembered nothing until, at the age of fifteen, he was struck with a fever, as a result of which the full and complete circumstances of his childhood fracture returned to him. Or, another case: an old forester from Poland, who had lived in France almost all his life, and who for thirty or forty years had heard not a word of Polish to the point where he could not speak his native tongue, suddenly had the gift of Polish language restored during an attack of anaesthesia brought about by a fall.

Morel found himself wanting to dig Ribot up so he can insult him to his face, for nonsense such as this: *Hypermnesia of this kind is the necessary correlative of partial amnesia, it proves once more and in another way that the memory is made up of memories.*

The memory is made of memories?

Oh genius, thought Morel. And there was more: *the mechanism of this metamorphosis being inscrutable, there is no reason why we should dwell upon it here.*

In the library that afternoon, Morel started to sense that Ribot dwelt on nothing because, in fact, he *knew* nothing. Of cases of what he called General Excitation of Memory, he listed only more pale and ridiculous examples: the railway worker who, being nearly hit by a train, reported that his entire life passed before his eyes; or a near-drowned person with the same experience to relate.

The doctor found himself growing ever more happily indignant with his predecessor's flaccid work. He started muttering and pointing at sections of the text and snorting, so much that he drew the attention of other occupants of the library. But if he seemed angry, he was far from it. He was delighted that the only thing he'd found so far with anything to say on the subject of hypermnesia had, in truth, nothing to say at all.

Morel's syndrome, Morel's syndrome. It sounded very, very good to the doctor as he made his way back to the Salpêtrière.

In the cell, Marcel's tiny prison, the two men sit in their reveries. The old doctor suddenly snaps out of his and something inaudible escapes his lips; he turns to look at Marcel, who is sitting exactly where he left him, minutes ago, before the doctor began his own small reminiscence.

It gives him the tiniest insight into what Marcel's whole life must be like. At any moment, any thought can trigger a thousand memories and each one of those memories a thousand more. Morel envisages a labyrinth, a maze of infinity, and finally understands what he is up against. If he is to help Marcel, he has to help him stop going into the maze. It is that which disables him, so often, so intensely, so deeply: these wanderings in the lost pathways of his mind.

A square of light starts to slide along the floor, and, after a while, up the wall; a late burst of sun on a cold autumn day. Twenty minutes later, by Morel's watch, it shines on to Marcel's face, into his eyes. He doesn't move. He hasn't moved in all that time. Morel puts his watch away, standing.

The only real way to help Marcel, the doctor suddenly realises with a start, would be to do the unthinkable, the extraordinary. The impossible, perhaps. To Morel, it would also be undesirable, and so he keeps the idea to himself – that the only true way to help Marcel would be to help him learn how to forget.

# MEMENTO MORI

Since its invention, and rapid development, photography has been put to every conceivable use. In Paris, as elsewhere in the world, this means it has been employed in some of the less-spoken-of areas of human life, two in particular. The two subjects of which we speak here, sex and death, are said by many to be the two greatest mysteries of existence. Strange, then, that for the most part we talk about them as little as possible in polite company. But times come and go and, like fashions, what may not be spoken about a little less one day is spoken about a little more openly the next.

As Petit makes his way up to Pigalle again, crossing the Place Blanche, the city around him has seen a slight waning in its appetite for a relationship with death. The height of the expression of mourning and the Victorian death cult have started to ease, yet this is still a time in which affairs connected to death are somewhat more elaborated upon. Photography knows this, and quickly attached itself to death.

Baraduc was one of the men who made it that way. He began his career at a tender age, learning the ropes of his craft from his father. They ran a small but reasonably healthy trade by offering photographic services to the bereaved. Originally, this meant only the making of death mask photographs; a subtle business that required more than just skill with the photographic arts. In order to make the subject suitable, the mortician's skill in make-up and dressing were invaluable; the correct choice of flowers, a new pillow perhaps: these were all details that Baraduc and his father were happy to supply, and if they did not come cheaply, so much the better. No one was going to quibble about cost at a time like that. So they took their photographs of the recently deceased, looking for all the world as if they slept. Sometimes, in fact, it was even possible to take the portraits with the subjects' eyes open, and if luck was on their side, they could produce a photograph of the loved one as if in life.

As a few years passed, the younger Baraduc told his father about a new fashion for deathbed photography. In America, he said, and elsewhere, they take the photos of the dead *before* they actually die. That, his father said, was a smart idea. They could beat their competitors to the job. So they branched out into pre-mortem photography: reproductions of the terminally ill, making one last effort to sit upright in bed, and produce a smile if possible. And then, very soon, rest. The younger Baraduc was gifted at this work; his special touch was the placement of red flowers in the portrait. These he would paint in by hand, pains-takingly, on the black and white print, something that his customers would marvel at. The finest he ever achieved: a string of red rosebuds across the chest of a tiny girl who had died before her first birthday; her eyes open, her little fist clenched by her cheek as if in thought, the rosebuds, bright red, symbolising both death and unfulfilled promise.

So business was good, but still Baraduc the younger was not satisfied. He wondered aloud to his father one day about all the clients they were missing. When his father asked who he meant, Baraduc explained that far too many potential customers were being buried before anyone thought to have their likeness recorded. Supposing, he said, they could photograph people from beyond the grave?

That, his father said, was a terrible idea, and sounded blasphe-mous too. He scowled, and Baraduc didn't mention it again, although he knew there were charlatans who claimed to be able to contact the deceased and made good money doing so, very good money, in séances in the drawing rooms of polite Parisian society.

If these mediums, who he knew were fraudulent, could make such claims, why should he not go one better and produce photographs of deceased spirits? In secret, he experimented with a variety of techniques: methods such as the double exposure, such as the retouching of the negative plate. He worked and perfected his art, and was about to have a second attempt at convincing his father that this was a powerful money-making idea, when his father upped and died. So much the better, Baraduc decided, as he took his own father's death mask one afternoon. I can go it alone, now, and we will see what we will see.

What he saw was that there was, as he suspected, a very good line to be had in spirit photography, but he needed an accomplice to make it work. There, in his studio in Pigalle, he had the perfect set-up, and he brought his wife in on the secret. She had been working long and poorly paid hours as a *blanchisseuse* and was only too happy to try her hand at something new. And she was very good at it indeed; sitting in the antechamber of Baraduc's studio with the deceased, listening and sympathising, prompting and eliciting, until Baraduc himself, ear-wigging from next door, could pull out the most suitable of his stock portraits. Young or old, thin or corpulent, dark hair or light, and so on. After a while he even developed a system of composite facial features; this nose on this shape face, those eyes and these ears. Once they'd been put through his system of processing, it would all be very much the same. And then, as Madame Baraduc explained in mystical tones the delicate nature of their work, her husband would set to in the darkroom, preparing a plate to be reinserted into the camera when it was time to take the portrait itself. The bereaved would be brought into the studio and placed in a large wing chair, suitably formal and sombre. Instructed to focus his or her mind upon the relative, Baraduc would open his lens to the plate for a second time, thus superimposing the living person on an admittedly blurry image of the deceased lurking in the shadows behind the chair. And if the likeness of the dead was not that clear, or that accurate, no one said anything. Anyway, who can say how death will change us? All their clients went away in tearful wonder at what had occurred, clutching the print to their chest in fond recollection, all of them until that cunning little devil who turned out to work for the Chief of Police, the one with the uncle who wasn't only not dead, but hadn't ever existed.

It was while Baraduc was serving his shortish term in prison that he decided what to do upon his release. In the meantime, his wife left him for the proprietor of a café down by the opera house. But so much the better, Baraduc thought, for what he had in mind, because she would never have approved of his next scheme. This was to transfer the art of photography from one of the main pillars of human interest and fear to the other: namely, sex.

Times being what they were, and Paris being what it is, the licentious was only ever just beneath the surface anyway. Especially in Pigalle, where he found he could pay a prostitute a remarkably small sum of money to take her clothes off and have her photograph taken. An image that he could then reproduce and sell as many times as he liked. The girls he worked with didn't seem to understand this at first, and business had never been better. At first he worked within the law as much as he could; there was decent money to be made in photographs that were merely risqué. But it was a fine line between the risqué and the illegal, a line that, after a while, Baraduc decided to stampede right across, once he saw how much more money he could make with the genuinely obscene.

It was funny, he found, underneath the hood of his camera, peering at the image before him, upside down, of two people having sex. A man and a woman, two women, two men, three women and one man. It made little difference to him. At first, he was moved by some of the acts that occurred on his couch, and frequently felt a strong desire to participate. In those days, he found it best to take the edge off his desire by participating in some quick and frantic activity of his own, with one of his previous prints to aid him, before the models arrived. Later, the whole business became so banal that he could contemplate the most extreme sexual acts without wondering about anything other than whether he had his focal length correct, and if there were perhaps a better way of arranging the pot plants in the foreground.

And once again business was good, until the *brigade des moeurs*, the vice squad, came to call and he found himself in prison once more.

# WHAT THE CAMERA SAW

That is Baraduc's history. Petit knows a little of it. He has been doing some reading, down there in the police archives, though it still gives him the shudders to descend the staircase into the basement, remembering his month of 'hard labour' re-cataloguing ancient crimes: the deeds of long-dead Communards and executed anarchists. He's been doing his reading on Baraduc for the simple purpose of knowing his enemy: what it might be useful to know, what could be used against him, if need be. What he, Petit, wants, is more information. Although he can't prove it, he is sure that Baraduc knows the names of the men Ondine used to entertain. Petit can guess who one of them was, but he'd like to hear it from someone else's mouth, because then, well, then, perhaps there is more to Ondine's murder than at first appears.

Petit is working on a number of matters as September drifts along, and in time, vanishes from the calendar. October arrives, and still Petit has nothing to show for his efforts. By now, the cool mornings have even been superseded by ones of frost, frost on the parapets of the bridges across the Seine, on the iron railings of the Tuileries, on the lawns of the Jardin du Luxembourg. It is cold everywhere, and he shudders at the thought that winter might have already come before autumn has had a chance to say anything. The journey up to his apartment on the top floor of the Rue Laplace requires climbing twelve flights of stairs, two per floor. The balustrade is of heavy wood, covered with peeling layers of light blue paint, and even that is cold, and seems to suck the heat from his hand as he makes his way up.

He has not spoken to anyone about what he told Cavard, and he has not spoken to Cavard himself again either, on any matter. They have passed in the corridors of the Sûreté from time to time, and it may have been Petit's imagining, or it may have been true, that Cavard gave him a glance intended to make him keep his silence. Maybe it's just his weak, squinting eyesight.

Cavard's words of warning finally wrought a change in Petit's mind, and he has dropped the non-case of Marcel and Ondine Després. Not only that, but he is glad of it; he's found that since he managed to put it from his mind, his torment over Marie has lessened slightly. He has applied himself with great diligence to his duties, and made two arrests in the past week alone. Any more of that success, he knows, and he will start to upset people; other detectives for one. So he has been playing it quiet, doing his work, and not thinking about anything other than his current assignments.

He works on various cases, all of which would give Boissenot apoplectic joy if he knew about them, for all of them do indeed contain elements of unnecessary violence that seems to him to herald the end of days. Petit doesn't see it quite that way; he just thinks that people seem to be particularly desperate as the year (and the century!) winds towards its conclusion. Desperation can make all sorts of people do all sorts of notably unusual things, of that he is sure.

Somehow he has got dragged into the investigation of a spate of murders around Montmartre. The deaths are connected to the Apaches – the various gangs of wild villains who live continually on the edge of the law. Most often, the gangs operate a live and let live policy, and prey on 'civilians', particularly tourists come to see the sights of Pigalle. But now there appears to be a vendetta of sorts between two of the gangs, sparked by an argument over a prostitute's turf. One of the Apaches' most lucrative sidelines is pimping their girls on the streets; one of them wandered on to some other girl's turf. This second girl had a knife, and slashed the interloper across her face. She was in turn shot, and that murder generated a series of reciprocal killings, culminating the week before in a shootout between the police and the gangs in Rue d'Orsel.

Cornered in a dilapidated apartment, the Apaches put aside their differences for an hour or so and combined forces to plug away at a group of twenty armed officers and five inspectors, Petit among them. Law and order eventually won the day, but not without the loss of men on both sides. Petit distinguished himself again with some fine shooting, which only caused Drouot later to wonder if it's the fact that they have to buy their own ammunition that makes Petit such a good shot.

After these excitements, Petit is looking forward to a week where he barely leaves his office, and writes up innumerable reports. He has a vision of these reports: as he looks around him at his fellows, all scribbling away, into his mind's eye comes an image of the paperwork making its way down to the basement archives, where he very much doubts that anyone will ever look at it again, unless in the future some poor dummy like him gets into trouble and is sent to do 'hard labour'.

What's the point? he asks himself, though he knows what the point is: to catch criminals and to record the process of doing so in the hope that these recordings will aid that very process.

So life has started anew for Petit, although Marie is never far from his mind. He still finds he cannot look at a woman with anything other than disinterest. In the past, he might have felt desire, now he feels emptiness. And if he sees an especially pretty girl, Marie floats into his mind and everything closes down again. Despite this, life is as good for Petit as it has been for some time, and that is why it's deeply annoying when, one day and out of the blue, his mind is opened up once more, and turmoil injected into it.

Following up on some interviews over the Apache shootout, he finds his colleague Drouot sighing over another case in Pigalle.

'I just don't have the time for this!' he complains, and when Petit asks what is so vexing, Drouot whines about having to visit the burglary of some tin-pot photographer off the Rue Lepic.

Petit's heart pauses momentarily, just to be sure that Petit understands what a big event has occurred.

As calmly as he can, he makes an offer to Drouot. 'I could take that on for you, if you like. I'm nearly done with my reports on the Apaches.'

'You are?' says Drouot. 'I thought you—'

'No. No, I'm done. Here. Give me that file, won't you?'

So Petit finds his way back to Baraduc's lair once more, and his heart is full of things to say, as well as skipping every third beat with some good reason.

When Petit arrives at Baraduc's studio, he finds the place in chaos. There are two workmen in the doorway; the door is hanging loose. Beyond it, Petit can already see that the whole place has been turned upside down: burgled, perhaps, ransacked, certainly.

There is a *gardien* standing a little further down the hallway, whom Petit questions after showing him his Sûreté card, keeping his thumb half over his name in an attempt to avoid further questions at the station.

Yesterday, the *gardien* explains, Baraduc's landlord came to call and found the place almost as Petit sees it now. Chairs overturned, drawers rifled through. A burglary, the landlord assumed, but then, the expensive photographic equipment was left behind. There is, however, a massive safe, far too large to move without heavy winching gear. From fresh-looking scrapes around the lock, a failed attempt to open it has been made.

Petit raises his eyebrows at that news. Whoever it was, they were looking for something, and he suspects that they were looking for the very same thing he is: information, in the form of photographs.

And Baraduc? The photographer is missing, says the *gardien*, hasn't been seen since before the discovery.

'Who's been here since? Apart from you?' asks Petit.

'No one,' says the *gardien*. 'Just taken shifts with the other boys.'

'Good,' says Petit.

Petit sends the *gardien* to call for the locksmith. While he waits, he drifts around the studio, looking for places in which a photograph or two might be concealed. He tries a few things, but none of them produces any results, and eventually he feels a little silly.

As he waits for the locksmith, he wonders why Baraduc has gone missing. If he was found in the studio by the thieves, they would presumably have forced him to open the safe. So it is reasonable to assume that Baraduc found the mess later, and then decided to clear out. Maybe get out of Paris for good. That would seem like a smart plan. If that is the case, Petit reasons, whatever the burglars were after will presumably have been removed by Baraduc before he fled.

Eventually, grumbling about his interrupted lunch, the locksmith appears. It's frightening how little time it takes him to open the safe, and when he does, he clears off immediately, leaving Petit alone with the contents, which are nothing.

Nothing of importance. Nothing worth having such a beast of a safe for. He concludes that Baraduc did indeed clear out, though in a hurry, or he would have taken his camera equipment with him too.

It is as he is hanging his head in frustration that Petit sees what he missed before: the corner of a thick piece of paper lying in the shadows under the safe.

He picks it up.

A single photograph.

For the very first, and almost certainly the last time in his career as a detective, Petit marvels that he has actually found a clue. A clue, something to help him solve this case. Not something he has paid for, or bribed someone for, or coerced someone for, but an actual, genuine clue.

It is a scene of debauchery: a darkened space, with illumination from candles placed at the tips of large eight-pointed stars hanging from the ceiling. By this light, Petit sees an altar of sorts, though the cross hanging above it is upside down. On the altar, lying backward with her face hanging upside down towards the camera, is a totally naked girl, her legs spread to allow access to a naked man, who it must be presumed has his penis inside her, though that cannot actually be seen.

Around them stand numbers of men and young women. Some of the men are clothed in odd robes bearing weird symbols, others are naked. One or two are aroused. All the women are naked, some with symbols painted on their skin, others wearing horned headdresses. All these figures are watching the activity of the man and girl at the altar.

The girl, well, it's hard to be sure, but she might just possibly be Ondine Badiou. The man, it's easy to be certain, is Prefect Paul Delorme.

Petit leaves the studio, wishing to leave as little impression of himself on the *gardien* as he can, and slips away down the Rue Lepic. He is lost in thought, but even if he were not, it's doubtful he would have noticed the two men who come out of the Impasse Marie Blanche and who begin to follow him. At the corner of Place Blanche, they are joined by a third man. No words are exchanged between them, but as the first two men turn and make their way back to the studio, the third man starts to follow Inspector Petit along the boulevard.

# EROS IN SECRET

This damn photograph. There is a meeting that very afternoon, immediately after its discovery. He risks arriving late in order to stop in a café at the bottom of the Rue Montmartre, where he installs himself in the quietest corner. He has slipped the photograph into an envelope he found on Baraduc's desk, and now he resists the burning urge to open it once more until the waiter has been and gone, and returned again with his coffee.

In the meantime he stares across the café trying to pretend that the photograph is not screaming at him, demanding him to witness its depravity and vice. As the waiter returns, he nods with a smile that is calculated to invite no lingering or friendly banter. It succeeds, and so with due care Petit slides out the photograph again, leaving its edge still nestling in the thick card envelope, ready to be slid back in at a moment's need. Indeed, as an unknown customer suddenly bowls out of the toilets, banging a swing door as he does so, Petit manages to slip the photograph back inside with impressive haste, but also then somehow sends the whole thing skidding across the wooden floor, where it lands almost under the feet of the customer.

The customer stops and picks it up and with a polite nod hands it back to Petit, who cannot even force a smile of thanks in return. His heart heaves. The man leaves and Petit breathes out a long sigh, after which he steels himself and stares at the picture. Now he can clearly see that it's Ondine and the Prefect. Petit does not know whether to laugh or be sick. That fake! What a façade of deception he has created, Petit thinks. How he likes to promote himself: the straight, upstanding pillar of law and order. The family man! Banging away at this courtesan, which is merely to say a well-paid prostitute, and worse, what is all this symbolism around them? The altar, the inverted cross, the animal horns? It clearly signifies blasphemous acts, worship of unholy beasts, evil deities, but this is an area Petit knows nothing about. Still, it is enough to know that Delorme's career would be over in a moment should the right people hear of it. But there, thinks Petit, is an issue. Who are the right people? This question occurs to him because as he looks more closely, he sees that there are onlookers in the photograph. Lurking in the background, shadowy faces. With a crawling sensation, he has the feeling that he knows some of the other men present, that he has seen their faces, either around the Palais de Justice, or as engravings in the newspapers. He has a feeling that one man, with a neat white beard and somewhat overweight, is a politician, and he curses himself that he isn't better at remembering faces and hasn't been more interested in politics in his life to date. But then, the photograph is so unclear, really these other people might be anyone.

He slides the photograph away from him, quickly. Why does he feel guilty? Why the shame? He is merely doing his duty as a policeman, and if that means looking—

He stops. He will think no more about that. For now, he drains the coffee in a gulp, leaves a coin on the counter as he makes his way out, and rushes down to the river, to meetings, pointless interviews and, always, paperwork. Though it is a dull and thankless day, he is glad of a mountain of work to climb, because he does not want to think about the photograph, about what it has shown him, about what it means.

Despite his best efforts, he cannot help thinking about it, and once he even takes the envelope out of his bottom drawer to a toilet stall, trying to identify the men's faces. Still, he doesn't recognise anyone other than Ondine and Delorme, but he has the strongest feeling that these are important men, powerful men.

By the end of the day, he is so tired that he finds he doesn't want to do anything but go and drink some wine somewhere where nobody knows him, and then crawl home.

He feels the photograph burning its way through the envelope. He has felt its presence continually, even when he dared to leave it unattended in his desk drawer. Now, it feels like an urgent demand or a nagging tooth; saying, *For God's sake do something.*

He tries to ignore this voice, but he does not succeed.

# AT THE QUAI DES ORFÈVRES

Petit now has a theory. It's simple and he likes it. His problem is that he has no one to tell it to.

He considers, for a long time, telling Drouot, the closest thing he has to a friend in the force. One day, as another weekend approaches, he invites Drouot to join him for lunch in a brasserie on the Place du Châtelet. He spends the whole meal trying to work around to telling his friend what he knows, or what he suspects, and only succeeds in sending a salt cellar spilling across the table. Drouot can tell something is even more amiss with his clumsy colleague than usual, but since he's getting a free lunch out of it, he decides not to care too much. By the time he gets up to leave, announcing he has a busy afternoon ahead of him, Petit is no closer to a confession.

He doesn't go straight back to the office.

Crossing the Pont au Change, and then the Île de la Cité, he slips down the stone ramp from the Quai des Orfèvres to the quayside itself, and wanders along, watching the drab olive water pushing by. In the little park at the tip of the island he finds an unoccupied bench beyond the trees, and stares down the length of the Seine, waiting for the water to bring him answers. The water, however, is flowing away from him, taking all possible answers with it.

He cannot tell Drouot, he decides. Tell *anyone* what he thinks, anyone in his department, and it will be the talk of the building before the day is done. It will be the subject of gossip and rumour and, whatever happens, he will come off worse for it. If he is going to tell anyone at all, he decides, he has to be bold. There is

only one man he can share his thoughts with. The only problem
is that not only is Petit scared of him, he has a very strong suspicion that he, Petit, deeply irritates his intended target. Cavard.

René Cavard, Chef de la Sûreté. Chief Inspector of the Judicial Police.

At the end of the day, Petit ambushes Cavard as he leaves his
office.

'May I walk you out of the building, sir?' he asks.

Cavard breaks stride for a moment.

'Very well,' he says, then, after a pause. 'Very well, Petit. What
is it this time?'

Cavard sets off again at a brisk pace and Petit hurries after him.

'I have something,' he begins. He stops.

'You do?'

Petit nods. They pass through a doorway and Petit keeps his
mouth shut as they pass other people making their way home.

'Listen, Petit. You and I got off on the wrong foot. Or, rather,
you did. Twice. I am not as bad as you think. Why don't you just
tell me what's on your mind?'

Petit looks at Cavard and wonders if it's true that he's not so
bad. He knows that he is well liked by the majority of his men,
that he has the familiar touch of the common man, despite his
elevated position. It's just that his eyes never waver, never give
anything away. He seems permanently to scowl at Petit, but
maybe that's just his face, maybe it's because he has weak eyes.

'Could I talk to you outside the building, sir?' asks Petit, and
Cavard grunts.

'It's Friday evening and my wife is most unhappy if I'm not
home on time on Friday evening. Such of course is the lot of the
policeman, but Friday is the worst day on which to offend.
According to my wife.'

Petit nods energetically. He wonders again whether he has
made the right decision. One thing above all else tells him he

has: the enmity that he witnessed between Cavard and Prefect Delorme. No love lost. Nothing for Petit to lose, either, except his job. But he doubts it will come to that.

So he tells him.

He tells Cavard his theory: that something lay behind the decision from the Prefect's office, from the Prefect himself, in fact, to move Després from police care into the asylum at Salpêtrière. A decision that was taken very, very quickly, by the one man able to make it, and by a man, moreover, who had something to hide. Possibly.

He tells Cavard these suspicions, and places his final card on top of those he has played already: his one concrete piece of evidence: that Delorme and Ondine Badiou shared the same photographer, a noted pornographer, who incidentally, he adds, has gone missing. Whose studio was ransacked, just as the Després apartment was also ransacked. Too much for coincidence.

'Someone is looking for something, sir. Something they want hidden. Such as this.'

He puts his hand in his pocket and pulls out the envelope with the photograph. It would be a rational fear for Delorme: that there may have been copies of photographs such as this one in the apartment. That would be enough reason to have the place searched.

There is nothing else to be done. He hands the envelope to Cavard.

Cavard has listened in deepening silence throughout this exposition, and now stares at Petit in silence. Then, without even a glance at the envelope or its contents, he lifts his head to the world around them. They have left the Palais de Justice and all its unreality behind them and the thronging everyday Paris busies itself around them.

'That's my bus,' Cavard says, nodding down the street.

'Sir—'

'Have you told anyone else these notions?'

'No, sir.'

'Listen to me, Petit. You think the Prefect of Police was indulging in orgies with this demi-mondaine, and that upon hearing of her murder he had the culprit moved to where no one in the police can touch him, or would care to, in order that he might prevent word of his association coming out?'

'You have to admit that it is at least possible.'

'It is. But then again, it is at least possible that we will fly to the moon. One day. But not today. Not on my watch, so to speak. Petit, my bus approaches. I want you to drop this business. It seems to have become an obsession with you, and obsession can be a good thing for an inspector. But not in this case. I advise you, no, I order you, to drop it. Furthermore, if you know what's good for you, you will say nothing of this to anyone else. Whatever this envelope contains I strongly suggest that you forget it ever existed.'

With that, he slides the photograph into his jacket, steps up on to the omnibus and is gone, off to the Friday evening world of domesticity. He leaves Petit staring into thin air, with Cavard's final words repeating themselves in his head.

# BEAUTY AND TRAUMA

It will easily be understood how Marcel's inability to recognise a face had a significant role to play in the false murder of Ondine, but it had just as big a part to play in why that fictitious event occurred at all.

It was sad to see what was once an intense love between Marcel and Ondine, each broken in their own special way, turn inside out and around on itself, change and vanish. On the surface, at least to begin with, matters between them were not so bad. Ondine didn't mind so very much that Marcel had slept with Lucie, because, as we've seen, she knew he could not be blamed for it, it being an expression of his desire for Ondine herself. She was at daggers drawn with Lucie, of course, but that is only to be expected. They tolerated each other's presence in the dressing room and on stage as best they could, and Ondine began to think about moving to a new club for a time, though part of her was determined not to be the one to be moved to a new 'turf'. That being said, it was hard, when Lucie had clearly disseminated word of her accomplishment with Marcel through the other girls of the club. Stifled laughter and quick changes of conversation were frequent, Ondine found, and she began to construct yet another layer of protection around herself, one on top of so very many others. And there, of course, is the sadness. If Ondine had been someone else, had been born someone else, in better circumstances, how she might have blossomed and flourished and what a better way she might have made in the world. The same can be said of anyone, perhaps, and if, if, if can take you anywhere. Ondine was born who she was, and her young life and her experience and her adolescence and her womanhood had repeatedly taught her only bad things about the world. She never even thought about it, but the way she dealt with such matters was to wrap her emotions underneath layers of protection; a hardness to counteract the hardness she encountered. Then came Marcel, and in his naïve love she had sensed something she'd never had in her life before: tenderness. But that very naivety was what destroyed them, for Ondine simply could not bear the fact that her husband *could not possibly* know who she was, just as Lucie had said.

They talked and fought about it for days after the event. Marcel would protest that it wasn't true, that he could and *did* know who she was, in fact, he had a better idea of who she was than anyone, for who else can say they remember every single aspect of their lover? Who else can say they remember every word and deed and moment between themselves and their lover, the bad along with the good, and still love them, despite the unpleasant memories? That, said Marcel, showed just how much he loved her. That only caused Ondine to demand just how *unpleasant* he found her, and it must be admitted, though Marcel had a point, he did not make it in the most flattering way. And Ondine, who had been shown since she was very young that she was best appreciated for her looks, could not bear the fact that Marcel did not appreciate that beauty.

'But I do!' Marcel exclaimed.

'So you can tell I'm beautiful?' Ondine asked.

'Yes, of course.'

'But if you cannot recognise my face then you do not know that this beauty belongs to me.'

'Surely that should make you happy,' Marcel wondered. 'For it means I love you for who you are, not for how you look.'

But Ondine *wanted* to be loved for how she looked. It was how she had been made, and from that trap escape is precious and correspondingly rare. So she began to find ways to hurt

Marcel. Small things at first, which she told herself were just to test whether it was really true that he could not tell who she was. When he arrived for work, she would be sure to be seen flirting with a waiter in the club, or one of the men in the other acts. She'd stroke their cheeks and plant blatant kisses on their lips when she knew Marcel could see, and when Marcel took her to task, she'd exclaim that he had been lying, that he *could* recognise her. The truth of the matter was that Marcel had a lifetime's worth of techniques to help him guess who someone was so he wouldn't be shown up, and almost all the time he was right. But the damage was done, the process of decline had begun, and all these incidents only served to prove to Ondine that Marcel had been lying about his blindness for faces, and only served to develop a rapidly growing jealousy in Marcel.

At home, in the studio, he would shout and scream at her in a way he never had before as she continued to push him with ever growing indiscretions. She had walked stark naked into the men's dressing room at the cabaret, which had led Monsieur Juron, that expert of insults, to make some especially obscene comments, even for him. It was the talk of the club. And she began to fall for the American again, and it seemed Bishop was taking an interest in her once more. His latest little fling with an English dancer had concluded and he and Ondine started to spend more and more time together, something that Marcel was only too aware of.

They no longer walked to the club or home together when they were both working, and this was how, on her way home one day, Ondine was set upon. She'd cut through the Place Ventimille, she told Marcel later, weeping, all their arguments forgotten for a time. She explained how from nowhere three men grabbed her and pushed her to the ground. She'd tried to struggle, and get up again, when one of them hit her across her jaw. She saw a knife. Then there were the shouts of a *gardien*, and the men panicked and ran. She didn't get a decent look at them, because it was dark, and she was so shocked that she'd barely taken anything in. It all happened too fast, she told Marcel. She held a wet handkerchief to her face, where her lip had stopped bleeding but was swelling quickly.

'Did they take much?' Marcel asked.

'Of course not,' said Ondine. 'I don't have any money, do I? If I did I wouldn't be walking home.'

This relatively minor incident was to have a significant effect on their fates, however, because as a result of the attack, Ondine persuaded Marcel to buy a gun on the black market. She wanted to be able to protect herself. They'd argued about it. Ondine pressed Marcel to give her more money, so she could take the tram or a bus home when she was working and he wasn't. He told her what he always told her, that he didn't have more money, but Ondine knew that wasn't entirely true. Once upon a time, after all, he'd sold a small house in Champagne. He couldn't have spent it all yet, she knew, because he had no idea how to spend money, not like she did. That was his trouble, she said, and then they'd fought again, until finally, relenting, Marcel set about finding out how to spend some of his money on a gun. It would be this gun that he used to shoot his wife.

The days were running by, bitterness and anger were growing, and it would not be long before Ondine organised her own death, yet her anger with Marcel was far from the major force behind that plan. There was something else, something even more pressing, that brought her to that point.

# DOCTOR MOREL

Events continue to conspire against Petit. As he leaves work one day, he checks his pigeonhole. He finds an envelope bearing his name, written in a fine hand.

Something tells him this is a significant moment. He is developing a nasty little sense of impending connections, and so he waits until he has left the offices to open it. He doesn't even realise that its brief contents have interrupted his walking. All the note says is this: 'Come and visit me. I have something to show you. Morel.'

That is enough.

Five minutes later he is aboard an omnibus, which rattles along by the river till it turns and deposits him at the corner of the Rue de Buffon, a short walk from where lies the entrance to the hospital.

Morel is expecting him, almost nervously it seems. There is none of the pomposity of the old doctor that Petit felt upon their first meeting. Morel even goes so far as to thank the young inspector for coming.

'And so quickly too,' he adds. 'Most efficient.'

Petit takes no notice of these potentially patronising remarks.

'How can I help you, Doctor?'

'Our mutual friend, Inspector,' Morel says. 'He interests me greatly. We have made some progress since you saw him last. Would you walk with me? I would like you to see him again.'

Petit does as he is invited to without further question. The doctor is acting strangely, that's apparent. They walk through the grounds of the hospital. Across the lawns, gardeners are raking brown leaves into neat piles in the twilight. Otherwise it is quiet, and the hospital has an air of settling down for the evening. As they walk, Morel starts to explain what he has learned about Marcel.

There is the business, first of all, that he cannot lie. It is something that Morel has tried to test, he explains. He has tried to catch him in the act of lying; has set complicated traps for him to fall into, but so far, he has not done so.

'It really appears that he is unable to lie. Of course, this is another thing, like his memory itself, that it is only impossible to disprove. If he *did* indeed lie, we would know for sure that he is able to. Like the rest of us, eh? That's obvious. But since I have not been able to get him to lie, we don't know for sure that that means he is *unable* to. Do you follow my logic?'

Petit nods. That makes sense, just about.

'In truth, though, he seems unable to lie, even for the sake of it, even to make a joke. I asked him yesterday to tell me that he was a gorilla in the zoological gardens. He was unable to; it seemed to cause him great trouble even to think about it. So I let him be. Of course, he may be a very great actor, and as for the traps I set him, well, he does have that memory to help him with his lies, if lying he is. But I suspect that he is indeed unable to lie.'

Morel speaks about the various doctors who have catalogued such an inability in other forms of insanity and illness.

'Curious, isn't it? That lying seems to be such an essential part of being human.'

Like forgetting, Morel thinks, but he keeps that part to himself.

'Very well,' says Petit. 'So he cannot lie. What else? Why have you brought me here?'

'Aha!' says Morel. For a moment there is a flash of his former pomposity, but it vanishes rapidly as he comes to what he wants to relate next. 'Well, I have also discovered something even more remarkable.'

And now, Morel explains how Marcel is unable to recognise a face from one moment almost to the next. This concept Petit finds much harder to understand, and even when he has, he finds it even harder to accept. Morel repeats himself and elucidates and elaborates. He gives Petit the benefit of his theory on why this phenomenon might very well be caused by the perfect memory, far from being a flaw in it. But still Petit is doubtful, so Morel plays the game he played before, and has Petit don the white smock of the Russian warder, before entering Marcel's chamber.

Marcel takes Petit to be who he is told he is: a new warder. Marcel greets him expressionlessly, and only then does Petit, who knows that Marcel's memory is foolproof, see for his own eyes that he is blind to faces.

They stand for a long while in the cell, the three of them, blinking at each other in the half-light, until Morel explains to Marcel that Petit is in fact the inspector who came to see him before.

Marcel looks up at Petit, and there is deep sorrow in his face. He turns to Morel and asks him, 'Should I say what you asked me to say?'

Morel nods.

Petit turns to question the doctor, who merely holds his hand up, inviting patience.

'Inspector,' Marcel says. 'I have been speaking with the doctor about what I did. How I shot Ondine. We have been discussing it in some detail. I spoke about the moments before and after. And the moment itself. And he has some knowledge of what occurred from the reports in the newspapers. But Inspector, you should know, I only shot Ondine once.'

There is a silence. Petit is thinking. Morel is stifling a smile, and Marcel speaks again.

'I only fired the gun once, Inspector.'

Petit feels the touch of destiny creeping on to his shoulder again. It gives him a little shake, as he understands what Marcel, what Morel, is getting at.

'They said you fired four times. Or five. Almost all the witnesses said you fired the gun five times.'

Marcel nods. He closes his eyes.

'Yes,' he says. 'But I didn't.'

Petit believes him.

# BOUNDLESSNESS

Thus it is that Petit comes to the truth of the matter, or begins to approach it at least. The question of Ondine's apparent death, the motives and mechanisms behind it, all this starts to unwind, but only after a *miserably* long time spent with Marcel in his tiny chamber.

Of course, there is also the fact that Petit cannot be seen to be spending any time on the case that is not a case. Before, this meant merely the threat of a rebuke from his superiors. Now, Petit is fairly sure that he might be dealing with people who consider that the stakes are somewhat higher, and that those stakes could include his life. Prefect Delorme, he has already learned, is a dissembler and an impostor, of sorts. He pretends to be a fine upstanding citizen when he is nothing of the kind. From the destruction in Baraduc's atelier, Petit has seen first hand that he plays the game hard, and in the photograph he has seen things the Prefect would potentially kill to keep secret. Then Petit made the decision to tell Cavard, and although he didn't see the chef in the picture, something tells him that he made the wrong decision to share his suspicions with his boss's boss. Perhaps, Petit thinks, perhaps I should leave it alone after all, but this is only an idle idea that crosses his mind from time to time. He knows it is not real. He knows he cannot let this matter rest now, not if he ever wants to find any peace over his Marie. Not if she is ever to let him go.

It is clear to him that there is something amiss about the murder itself. Up to now, he has only been interested in its aftermath and its possible causes. Yet this small detail about the number of bullets fired has opened up a whole new world of wondering to him; and he is convinced that something does not add up.

In his own time, therefore, when he should be sipping coffee in his favourite café, when he should be knocking back a beer with Drouot, he makes his way to the Salpêtrière. Very soon, the guards know him by sight, and merely nod as he makes his way into the hospital to find Morel, who insists on being present at every session.

It is slow work. All Petit wants is for Marcel to tell him, in his own words, what happened that evening in the Cour du Commerce. But even that seems to be an impossible task for Marcel to manage.

He stares at Petit as if *he* is the one who's mad, as if *he's* the one who murdered his own wife. That's a thought that derails Petit for a moment as he wonders whether Marie would still be alive if he'd come back from Africa the first time she'd asked him to.

Just tell me! Petit thinks. Why is it so hard just to tell me? My God!

'Listen,' he says, leaning closer to Marcel. 'You came home. You saw your wife with another man. You shot her. You ran away. Correct?'

Marcel stares.

'Is that correct?'

Marcel stares some more until Petit cracks, and shouts.

'Is that correct?!'

Morel puts his hand on to Petit's sleeve as if restraining him.

Infuriatingly, Marcel blinks and stares and then blinks some more, and then turns his head to say, 'In a way.'

'In a way?'

Marcel nods. 'Those things are true. But so are a million other things.'

'Yes,' says Petit eagerly. 'And I want you to tell me those things.'

'I could, for example, tell you that I saw mouse droppings on the stairs, and that there is paper peeling in the corner above our bed or that Bishop has a strange-shaped mole on his thigh.'

'So why don't you?' snaps Petit.

'Because . . .' begins Marcel, then stops. 'Because it would take too long to say it all. It would take for ever.'

'So let it take for ever!' cries Petit. 'I'm here. I'm waiting.'

'I know you want to know things,' adds Marcel, who never seems entirely to respond to the question in hand, 'but I don't know which ones you think are important.'

'Exactly!' says Petit. 'I don't want you even to try, I just want you to tell me everything, really everything, that happened that night. Let me be the one to decide what is important and what is not.'

Morel speaks for the first time. He speaks softly to Marcel, who still seems unsure.

'Marcel, when in your life was anyone prepared to sit and listen to you say everything you needed to say? Everything that is in that head of yours? This is your chance. It may be the only chance in your life to let everything out, the only time when someone will listen to everything you want to say. It may make things easier for you, make things clearer. Perhaps it would help you, perhaps not. But why don't you see?'

So Marcel begins to speak. 'Where should I start?'

Petit pulls a notebook from his pocket. 'Why not start the last time you saw Ondine, before the evening, I mean? When was that?'

'At the cabaret. Around seven o'clock.'

'Very well then,' Morel says. 'Begin.'

Marcel speaks. Within moments, Petit realises the scale of what is about to happen. Even Morel is surprised at the level of detail that Marcel not only remembers but which he finds it necessary, in some way vital, to relate. After half an hour has passed, Marcel has only managed to explain what happened in the first five minutes of being at work that day. For the purposes of brevity, all Petit notes down is that Marcel had been out in the city, and met Ondine backstage as usual around 6 p.m., when everyone was getting ready for the show, just as they always did. Petit could have written so much more. Marcel also told them about the rough marks on the wooden floorboards just behind the stage door where a new piano had been dragged into the theatre. These marks were new, Marcel noted, and later he saw the new piano, well, it wasn't shop new, it was second hand but new to the cabaret. Marcel saw that it was German and had seen better days, that the cover to the sounding board was shiny with the scuff of toes on the pedals, and that some of the felt was missing from the back. Marcel spent ten minutes describing a strange smell coming from the small kitchen, something rather like artichoke but somewhat earthier than that, and it reminded him a little of a tart his mother used to make. As he came in through the stage door of the cabaret, he told them, he was by coincidence already remembering something else from his childhood: a moment when his father had been angry. Marcel didn't know why then, he still doesn't know why, he never found out and yet he remembers that his father was very angry, so angry that he threw a plate and it smashed on the wall of the kitchen, and the funny thing was that his mother didn't even react. She hung her head in her hands and then she shooed Marcel out of the room and up into bed, where he lay listening to his parents fighting about something in voices just low enough not to be overheard.

Petit realises that Marcel is now lost in a memory *within* a memory. As he did all those weeks ago when he first met Morel, he has the most awful feeling of standing at the edge of some abyss. The feeling is so strong that in his mind he turns away from the horrible void, leaving him with a nagging sensation in the backs of his legs, as if he were about to step uncontrollably into that yawning chasm behind him. A memory of a memory.

An infinite memory from inside another infinite memory. The potential endlessness of it all makes him reel with panic. He suppresses the desire to whimper, or even scream, and is about to urge Marcel to stick to the point when Morel taps his shoulder with his bony forefinger. The old doctor gives Petit a slight shake of the head and Petit knows what he means. If we're going to do this, we're going to do this. We're going to let Marcel say everything that is in his mind, no matter now how long it takes. And Petit knows better than to argue.

But time is against them. That first evening, Marcel has, with many subsidiary discursions and irrelevant distractions into his past, only managed to explain what happened in the first ten minutes after six o'clock that fatal night.

Petit returns home and after climbing up to his rooms, collapses on the bed, his head full of someone else's memory, of someone else's distress.

He closes his eyes and is asleep in moments.

# IN THE CHAMBERS

It is two days before Petit gets the chance to return to Morel, and when he does, they use the next three hours allowing Marcel to explain what happened up to the point where he and Ondine parted. All Petit notes is that Ondine reported that she was feeling unwell and had decided to tell Chardon that she was going home sick, and that Marcel stayed in order to do his act as normal. Put like that it seems so simple, and yet it takes Marcel hours to explain everything he saw, said, heard, smelled, felt and thought during this time.

Petit leaves, and returns the following day, wondering why he is bothering, where it will all lead, what he is trying to prove anyway. He also finds that he is becoming paranoid: all this sneaking around in his free time has given him a bad case of nerves. He compares himself with the man he once was, the young man in the army in Africa, and he envies that former self. Not a moment's doubt or fear or duplicitous thought ever entered his head in those days, largely because, he now realises, very little actual thought ever passed through his mind, and of self-awareness there was nothing at all.

He tries to rid himself of the notion that he is being followed to and from the hospital, but it is hard to shift. One day, for example, he doubles back on himself and so catches two men furtively turning away. Panicking, he hurries straight into the nearest café and orders coffee. He lurks in the back of the salon, sipping his drink slowly, keeping an eye on the window, convinced that there is a shadow just beyond his view. Eventually, he tells himself he was imagining the whole thing, and forces himself to leave. As he walks briskly out of the café, he stumbles straight into the two men. It's all he can do not to run, and, this time, they don't follow. Yet Petit is disturbed, even as he leaves them behind at the corner of the street, to find himself wondering why the men were speaking a foreign language. Russian, if his guess is right.

Such little things trouble him, and he longs to immerse himself in his work at the hospital. Yet it is so achingly slow. He wants to punch Marcel on the nose, tell him to hurry up, to get to the point, but he always manages to prevent himself. After all, there is Morel, staring with those piercing yet watery eyes in that drooping face.

Marcel's story continues as the evenings pass. He relates how he decided not to stay at work when his act was over, but to go home before the end of the show and see Ondine, despite the fact that they were not on the best of terms at the time. Normally, although Marcel was finished at some point in the first half of the evening, depending on where Chardon had put him in the bill, he would stay on for the whole night to come home with Ondine, whose duties of course ran to the very last dance number.

Petit is desperate to interject, but Morel has insisted that they allow Marcel to talk through the whole event once at least without interruption before returning to ask any questions the inspector might have. So be it. The trouble is that it's taking not hours, but days.

In fact, as things fall out, actual weeks begin to pass, partly because Petit is unable to get to the hospital every evening, being frequently wanted on police matters, but more because of the horrendous circularity of Marcel's thinking. Increasingly Petit finds himself washing his hands when he gets home. He has developed a peculiar notion that he might catch this disease from Marcel, this disease of too much memory. He has enough memories of his own, he thinks. He wants no more, he certainly doesn't want to become a prisoner in his own mind, and he fully sees that Morel was right about that.

And in his appallingly circular way, Marcel does mention everything, in the end. Eventually, Petit has a better picture of his relationship with Ondine. They had been arguing, frequently, then making up and declaring love for each other once more. From everything Marcel says, Petit doesn't like the sound of Ondine. He knows very well that he is no expert in what he terms *the question of women*, and he only has Marcel's side of things to go on, but he senses a manipulative and controlling individual in Ondine. If anything, he almost gets the feeling that Marcel is too kind to his dead wife, given the things he is saying about her. It seems that she had been continuing to provoke jealousy in him, and as he hears, in bits and pieces that he has to assemble himself like a jigsaw puzzle without a picture to follow, the whole story about Marcel sleeping with Lucie, Petit's eyes widen. Over the next few nights, Marcel tells how the situation with Lucie was only really resolved when Lucie left the cabaret and went to work elsewhere. He's heard she went to find work in Lyon, which is a place he has always wanted to visit, because when he was a boy there were Bibles in the church in Étoges that had been printed there, and there was a tiny engraving of the Rhône meeting the Saône in the centre of the city and it looked rather wonderful, because—

Petit bites his lip. He has vowed, if it kills him, never to interrupt, never to impose a question, not until Marcel has told the story at least once, in his own strange way. But it's hard. It's three whole days before Marcel returns to the matter of Ondine going home sick and Marcel heading home to find out how she was. Morel and Petit have learned that even that night they had had a row, because Ondine had been flirting with the American right in front of her husband. As he relates these matters, Marcel grows silent again. The evening's séance ends, and Petit walks through the ever colder, ever darker streets to his apartment.

Séances, thinks Petit as the nights go by, that's the word. They have the feeling of such supernatural nonsense; these nights cramped in a darkened chamber, the old doctor looking on like a desperate widow, and Marcel, his eyes often looking into places far from the room, places and times far away, unseeing eyes yet ones that, at any moment, might make contact with the voice that Petit wants to hear, the voice that will finally relate exactly what happened in the studio of Marcel and Ondine Després and shed light on what took place there back in July. As if supernaturally.

For Petit knows, when Marcel gets to these matters, that he will not lie. What he hears from Marcel will be no mere perpetrator's alibi, nor witness's unintended falsehoods, no matter how well meant. As the days pass, Petit is ever more sure that Marcel cannot lie, that it would not be possible to lie, given all these details and facts that are already overwhelming his mind. Where, in any such mind, would be the extra mental capacity required for untruths?

Finally, Marcel reaches the stairwell of their apartment in the Cour du Commerce.

'It was almost ten o'clock and I came in through the entrance in the Rue Saint-André-des-Arts. The cobbles were damp, which wasn't from rain, because you remember how dry it was in July? Such a hot month. When it's hot in the city it's never like how it was hot when I was a boy, because the vineyards always made it cooler. All those leaves and the shade of the vines. I would lie there on hot days and if the workers came too close I would roll under the canopy to the next row and hide myself. My father told me about *veraison*. You know about *veraison*? It's when the grapes ripen and change colour. He spoke to me about it as if it were something you could see happen. Well, I was a child, I thought I would be able to see it happen, so I used to lie under the bunches of grapes and watch, waiting for them to change colour before my eyes. They never did! But I used to love lying there and listening to the sound of the harvest. By then, of course, the grapes had changed colour; I used to think they must wait until I was asleep and then all change at once, because I never saw it happen. But I did see lots of other things in the vineyards. I saw two people once, with only some of their clothes on, rolling around. Of course I know what they were doing now, but I didn't at the time, so I asked my mother and she didn't say anything but I saw her look at my father and they smiled a little smile at each other and I knew they knew something I didn't. And I saw mice. If you lay still you could see mice and other little creatures, worms and beetles. There were beetles just the same as those in the woodwork of the windows of the barber at the end of the cour. I was thinking about that too when I came into the alley that night. It was late but Jean, that's the barber, was still sweeping up in his little shop and I nodded at him but I didn't smile in case it wasn't him but someone else working for him and he didn't nod back so maybe he didn't see me or maybe he was angry with me. I don't know.

'Le Procope was noisy but then Le Procope is always noisy, especially on a Saturday night. It was unusual for me to be home so early on a Saturday night but then again, there was no reason I had to stay at the cabaret, because I've seen the acts a thousand times before and most of them don't bear watching once. Although I do think Monsieur Juron is funny, but he does repeat himself a lot. I mean he uses many of the same swearwords and although he changes his insults he is often just rearranging things he has said before. But anyway, he's funny and I love the faces people pull when he's being rude to them. Sometimes I think they are only pretending to be upset but sometimes they really must be because they storm out. And often when they do they seem to have forgotten that they haven't paid their bill and then old Chardon will chase after them and start arguing with them, which some people find funny, but I don't.

'So I was thinking about all these things when I started to climb up the stairs to the sixth floor and there were sounds from all around. I heard someone arguing on the fourth floor and of course the noise from the café and the restaurant. And horses on the Boulevard Saint-Germain and just the general noise of the city and that's when I saw the mouse droppings I told you about, on the stairs. I knew that the concierge would have something to say about that, though she hadn't been in her little room when I'd come in which was good for me because she hates us all for coming back so late and even though I wasn't as late as we usually are after work, it was still past the time that she considers respectable people return home. Anyway, she wasn't there, so that was good.

'And then I was opening the door to the studio and I heard another sound, and it's a sound I know well but what troubled me was that I wasn't the one making the sound happen, I mean the noise that Ondine made when we made love and she would cry out. I heard her crying out in that way and then I moved a little into the room and I saw her with Bishop, who has a mole on his right thigh about the size of a fingernail. I saw it once in the changing rooms at the club and some of the other men teased him for it because they said it looks like a penis.

'And then I remembered that Bishop had left after his act that evening and that was no surprise because his act finishes before mine but I was still angry with them both because of what had happened in the cabaret earlier and I was so angry then that I came forward into the room and then I didn't know what to do so I was about to leave when Ondine laughed at me and she called me all sorts of things that I don't want to tell you and then I saw that the gun, our gun, was sitting on the countertop right in front of me and she told me that if I was a real man I would do some-thing about it and she laughed again and I picked up the gun and then Bishop ducked out of the window on to the ledge but I didn't care about him and then Ondine opened her legs and showed it to me and rubbed herself with four fingers and told me how good

Bishop's penis was and then I pulled the trigger five times and Ondine fell down and blood ran out across the floorboards and then Bishop was back in the window and came into the room again and I pointed the gun at him too but he shouted at me, "Run!" so I dropped the gun and ran out on to the landing and down into the street but by the time I got there I didn't know what to do next and my head was full of so many things that I could barely walk and I remember them now because I remember everything and Ondine had told me lots of things about herself in the time we were together and I was thinking about those things and then I remembered the time I found a dead fox at the edge of the woods beyond the vineyards and there was lots of blood but it was black and sticky but the blood that Ondine let out was bright and thin and it ran and I ran but I stopped and my mind was just too full so it stopped too.'

Marcel finishes so abruptly that Petit is startled. Morel gives a little jump and sits more upright in his chair. They both lean in towards Marcel and inspect him.

'It was too much,' whispers Morel. 'It was too much to recall the moment. He has returned to his catatonia. There will be no more tonight, or for a while, I fear.'

Petit rubs his head. 'So, we got to the end at last. Now, Doctor, when I return I would like to ask him questions.'

Morel nods solemnly. 'You may. But don't come tomorrow. I will need some time to coax him out of this state, I think. Give me a week and then return.'

'A week?' protests Petit, but then he relents. He has waited long enough to get to the end of the story, he can wait a little longer. He slopes off into the night, thinking about chambers, something he will think about frequently until he is allowed to return to the hospital.

Chambers. The little chamber he shares with Morel and Marcel. The chamber where Marcel shot Ondine. But most of all he is wondering about the chambers in the cylinder of the revolver. He knows, because he has taken notes of everything he considers to be important, that Marcel claimed he only shot Ondine once. And yet then he told them that he pulled the trigger five times. If Marcel does not lie then how can this be? There are only two explanations: first, that Marcel does indeed tell falsehoods or, second, that his memory is not infallible after all. He wonders if Morel wants to discuss this possibility, because he knows how set the old boy is on showing that Marcel's memory is perfect. Leaving that aside, there is only one other possibility, one way in which those two apparently contradictory statements of Marcel's can in fact not be a contradiction.

Supposing most of the chambers of the gun were empty? Suppose there was only one live round in the cylinder? That way, Marcel could have indeed pulled the trigger five times, but the gun only fired once.

When he returns a week later the matter of the gun is the first line of questioning he puts to Marcel. He wishes he could have seen the murder weapon, but he cannot risk asking questions at the police stores. He knows the gun was a St Etienne 8mm, something he remembers easily, that being the gun he wore on his hip in Africa. The St Etienne is a six-chambered weapon.

Marcel seems composed again. He greets Petit with his usual wary nod until he infers who has come to see him, and then he relaxes a little. Morel has worked wonders on him in the week, and Marcel is as normal as he ever seems, so normal in fact that you would never guess the corridors of madness that lie just behind his eyes.

'The gun,' begins Petit. 'Where did you get it?'

'Fossard told me about a *zonier* who trades in ex-army weapons.'

'Fossard?'

'Our neighbour. He's an art student. He's from Marseille and—'

'Thanks, yes, Fossard. I remember now. Shares rooms with the Scottish man.'

Petit is determined to keep Marcel on the right track now. He's let him have his head, and maybe it did do him some good after all, because now that the catatonia has gone, he is as lucid as he has ever been in Petit's presence.

'So where does this *zonier* work?'

'He's in the slums by the fortifications. By the Porte de Sèvres.'

Petit knows this place. South, out towards the old Champs des Manoeuvres, the army drill fields, where they're knocking down the ancient city walls, is one of the most notorious of *zonier* slums. He had no idea arms dealing was going on out there however; the *zoniers'* usual business was rag-and-bone stuff and maybe a little prostitution for the girls.

'You bought the gun with how much ammunition?'

'I didn't want to buy the gun at all. It was Ondine. She was attacked one night and—'

'You bought the gun. How much ammunition did you buy with it? How many rounds?'

'Just the six in the chambers.'

'Just six?'

'Just six. No more. I—'

'Yes, you didn't want it. I know. Now, Marcel, I have a very important question for you. Did you ever use the gun? Before that night, I mean, did you ever use the gun?'

'No. Never.'

'Did you keep it loaded?'

'We did. Ondine said we had to in case we needed it in a hurry.'

'And did anyone else know about it?'

'No, no one. Although I suppose Bishop must have because it was out on the table, right there, when I came in.'

'Yes, I meant to ask you about that. Where did you keep the gun? Did you always keep it in the same place?'

'Yes,' Marcel says. 'We kept it in a drawer in the kitchen, under a towel. A drawer we didn't use for anything else. But Ondine always took it when she went out. Because of those men who attacked—'

'So why do you think the gun was out on the table?'

'I have no idea,' Marcel says. He thinks about it for a while. 'Ondine was showing it to Bishop?'

'I think we can assume that since you didn't take it out and that no one else knew about it, your wife had taken it out and had showed it to Bishop.'

'Why did she do that?' asks Marcel, but Petit ignores him.

'You state that you only shot Ondine once?'

'I did.'

'And yet you also state that you pulled the trigger five times.'

'That's true.'

'How can those two statements be true? You mean you missed her with four of the shots?'

'No,' says Marcel. 'I mean the gun didn't fire after the first shot. I pulled the trigger and I hit Ondine in the stomach and then I fired four more times but the gun didn't fire and then Bishop shouted at me and said if I knew what was good for me I would run. So I ran, and—'

'Yes. You told us that part. Marcel. Please think as hard as you can. You have this amazing skill, this incredible memory. I want you to use it now. Please take yourself back there again, and look. Look around the room. Is there anything else strange? Is there anything that isn't right, or that strikes you as odd?'

Morel makes to intercede. He worries that Petit will send Marcel back into the semi-conscious state that he's just spent several days freeing him from. But Petit is feeling in charge for this brief time, and relishes it. He gives a gentle but powerful nod to the doctor.

Sit, it means. Say nothing. Let me do my job now.

'Well,' says Marcel. 'There are a few things that are confusing.'

'How so?'

'Well, for one thing, there were the clothes that Ondine was wearing.'

'She had changed since you saw her at the club?'

'Yes, and no. To most people, well, most people would say she was wearing the same clothes. To me, she was wearing different clothes. She was wearing a black skirt and a white blouse, just as she had at the club, but they weren't the same ones. I suppose to most people they would look the same, but there was a small rip in the hem of the skirt that she wore at the club, and when I got home she was wearing another one like it. She has three just the same.'

'Just the same apart from the rip in the hem?'

'Exactly. Do you know that—'

Petit holds up his hand again. 'Marcel, what else was odd?'

'They had made coffee.'

'What? Why is that odd?'

'It isn't. But Ondine had made coffee and not put the pot back where it goes on the shelf and also she had changed the sheets on the bed.'

Petit resists the urge to scream. He is struck by the idea that this is all a total waste of time. Coffee pots, changed sheets. What does any of it matter? How will any of it come to be useful? He takes a deep breath and is about to ask a further question, when Marcel adds something else.

'Bishop,' he says. His face darkens as he speaks of something he clearly finds painful to remember, but then so much of what Marcel remembers causes him pain.

'What about him?'

'I don't think they were actually having sex.'

'Why not?'

'When Bishop pulled away, his . . . He was soft. It can't have been doing it. They were pretending.'

Petit thinks about that, and has absolutely nothing to say.

'And there's something else,' says Marcel, his voice low and trembling. 'I don't understand this at all. I shot Ondine and she fell on the floor by the bed, and her blood ran out from under her.'

'Yes?'

'Yes, but at the same time as I saw her blood, well, I can see it still now: there was blood coming from under the bed.'

'From Ondine?'

'No, it couldn't have been. There was blood already there before she fell. What does that mean?'

Petit thinks he has a pretty good idea what it means, but he's not about to say.

'I think that's enough for tonight,' he says instead, and bids Marcel good night. 'Doctor, perhaps you would walk me to the gate?'

Morel keeps any sign of surprise to himself, and does as the young inspector has asked him to.

'Well?' he says, as soon as they are sure they are alone.

Petit doesn't answer at once. He wonders how much he should tell Morel. Does he need to know about Delorme and his grubby secret? No, Petit thinks, he doesn't, and yet it would be so very nice, he would feel so very relieved, if he could tell someone about it, just for the sake of doing so. But he forces himself to be professional.

'Doctor, I have a theory about what happened that night. It is extraordinary and in order to prove it I will have to make one or two enquiries. I don't want to make these enquiries, because, as you know, I am not supposed to be coming here, and I am not supposed to be speaking to Marcel. But I have to know.'

'What is it you need to know?'

'I have to see the post-mortem report on Ondine Després.'

'So why don't you?'

'Because I am very truly worried that if the wrong people know I have asked for that report I will wind up in the Seine with a knife in my back.'

The doctor stops walking.

'Why?' is all he can say.

'I can't tell you why.'

There is a long silence. They are close to the walls of the hospital; the giant gates loom out of the darkness of the November night, and they both shiver.

'And if I were to take a look at it for you?'

'You?'

'As a senior physician at one of Paris's most important institutions I can make a direct request to see the reports of police surgeons. I could say it is for the well-being of my patient. That he wishes to confront what he has done and I have concluded that he should read the report.'

'I don't like it. It sounds too suspicious to me. They'll guess someone is still looking into the matter.'

'Who, exactly, are they?'

'I don't want to tell you that,' says Petit, and then, he thinks, I don't actually know. 'But Doctor, I can't drag you into this. I'll find another way to get the report.'

'Well, if you're sure. But let me know. And Inspector, it might do you good to tell me what you know, or what you think you know, at least.'

They part.

Petit goes home and broods on how to get hold of the post-mortem report.

Two days pass.

On the third day, he leaves for work, and finds a large envelope crammed into his postbox in the ground-floor hallway.

There is a note that can only be from Morel.

'*I decided to take the risk. M*'

The note is pinned to a thick card folder, containing two sheets of paper: the post-mortem report of Ondine Després.

# BERTILLONAGE

Petit makes a snap decision. Part of him thinks it would be best to run straight back upstairs and hide the report somewhere better than under a towel in a drawer. Another part of him thinks it would be best to keep it next to him at all times, and when he says *next to him*, he means under his shirt, by his skin. It's this latter course of action that he takes.

There and then, he opens his shirt, folds the sheets of paper in half, and tucks them next to his hip, above his waistband. The envelope he tears steadily into four pieces, then eight, holding them in his hand, tucked into his pocket, until halfway down the Rue des Carmes he takes a quick look around and quickly drops the pieces into a hole in the gutter that leads to the underworld. Let the sewers have them.

For some reason he has a sudden vision of returning home that evening to find his apartment burgled and wrecked, much like . . . much like Baraduc's studio. That's when he knows he's right. There are greater powers at play than his own, than the police force of Paris. Who those forces are is unclear. Delorme, yes, of course. But who else?

Out of nowhere his mind makes the connection he failed to make a few days before. Those men following him at the café. If they were speaking Russian, if they were following him, that would probably mean they were Tsarist agents. It's an open secret, at least to those who work in the police department, that the Okhrana have a station house in Paris, that their presence is tolerated in certain quarters, even welcomed by some. There are forces among the police who share

the same sentiments as the Okhrana: anti-communist sentiments.

When Petit makes this connection, his heart starts to pound
so hard that he's amazed that Drouot can't hear it across the
desk they share. He can't think for one moment what the
Okhrana might have to do with the case of Marcel Després, but
that doesn't make him any less worried.

He knows he has to act normally, as if nothing is wrong, but
he fails. All week he has been dropping even more things than
usual, and now when he tries to stand, he sends his chair spinning backwards, causing Drouot and half the room to look up
at him.

'Anything wrong, old man?' Drouot asks, for once not immediately taking the chance to tease Petit. That in itself worries
him. If Drouot, who is about as insensitive as it gets, has realised
that something is genuinely amiss with his colleague, then he
must be showing it pretty obviously.

Petit does something he finds unforgivable.

'Marie,' he says, and pulls a face. 'The anniversary.'

It isn't, in fact, but it's close enough for no one to question
Petit's connection to that time, and therefore his emotional
response.

This mention of his dead fiancée is enough to make Drouot nod
and apply his gaze firmly and immediately to his paperwork once
more. Petit hates himself for using his beautiful Marie as the cover
for his discomfort, but it works. Everyone knows what happened to
him, to Marie. Everyone in fact wonders how it was that Petit still
decided to become a police inspector even though the very Sûreté
for which he works had absolutely zero success in finding the
murderer. Petit knows why. It was because, in those days, he didn't
think very deeply about things. Such a short time ago, and how
much has changed. Why? he thinks. Why have I changed? When did
I start thinking? And would I rather *not* have done; would I rather
*not* be able to remember all this suffering, this trauma?

Petit sits in the stall in the bathroom as he did once before, shaking. He checks that the report is still folded up by his skin, but he refuses to allow himself to read it until he is far away from police headquarters. He is already drawing far too much attention to himself; he doesn't need anything else to make matters worse.

The rest of the day crawls by. Drouot looks up at him across the desk from time to time and pulls a half-grimace, half-smile, a look that Petit finds utterly disconcerting. He waves a hand airily back, meaning I'm fine, it's nothing, but knows he isn't doing a very good job of convincing anyone of anything. His eyes glaze over at the papers on his desk. Every time he catches himself, he tries to concentrate and get working again, but every time he does it is at most five minutes before he is visualising Baraduc's studio, and wondering whereabouts the photographer has got to. Maybe he's in the bottom of the Seine, put there by . . . who knows?

Finally the time comes when he can leave and still make it look respectable. Drouot leaves him be, lets him go with barely a goodbye. He heads for home through the dark evening in the most circular route he can devise. He takes a bus in completely the wrong direction, gets off on a whim just as it is about to move on, checking carefully that no one gets off after him. He ducks into the Metro and doubles back, once again stepping out of the carriage just at the last moment. He finds a quiet café in an unfamiliar neighbourhood and forces himself to wait for half an hour, all the time watching the streets outside, then slips the waiter five francs to allow him to leave through the kitchens. In the street, he hails a cab and has it take him nearly all the way home, the jolting of the horse snapping into his head like hammer blows, every one. Finally, in a deserted street, he steps from the cab and briskly walks the final few hundred metres back to the Rue Laplace, knowing all the while that this entire charade of his will have been pointless if someone is waiting for him outside his apartment.

He nods to the concierge and wonders about asking him to keep an eye out, but decides against it; the old boy is unreliable at the best of times; any fuss might only make anyone else more suspicious.

Heart in mouth, he climbs to his rooms, half expecting to be jumped on at each turn. But there is no one there.

He fumbles his key from his pocket, drops it on the landing, just as the middle-aged lady who lives opposite him emerges from her rooms.

'Monsieur Petit?'

'Good evening, Madame Faralicq,' he mutters. He manages to get the key into the hole, enters, locks himself in, and places a chair against the door, resting its back under the door handle, and its two back feet in a gap between the floorboards. He kneels down and peers through the keyhole. He sees Madame Faralicq standing looking towards his door for more time than she has a right to, then she totters away down the stairs.

No, he tells himself. She's just an old lady and she lived here long before I started getting mixed up in this business. It's just the fear.

He rushes to the table and pulls the papers from inside his shirt.

And reads.

The body of Ondine Després, he learns, was penetrated five times by bullets that matched those of an Etienne 8mm. One of these bullets entered her stomach, just above the navel, rupturing several organs and lodging in her spine. The other four bullets entered her face, completely disfiguring her. However, positive identification of the victim was made by several witnesses to the event: the American, Bishop; the concierge; Monsieur Jean Bertand, the barber; as well as a general crowd of onlookers who knew Ondine well.

Petit pauses to consider this. Her face was unrecognisable, yet everyone knew it was her. He reads on.

It is fortunate, in this case, he is told, that the exacting system of Monsieur Alphonse Bertillon has once again proved invaluable in identifying a person connected to a crime. The attached sheet of paper is a copy of that earlier report. It is very helpful, the report notes, that Ondine, when she was still Badiou, committed a minor indiscretion some dark evening a few years before. She was involved in a squabble with a girl who she worked with, resulting in a breach of the peace for which each girl was imprisoned for the night. It being the new practice then to apply Monsieur Bertillon's system of measurements to everyone who passed through police custody, the record of Ondine's visit was readily found in Bertillon's filing system, proving beyond all doubt that the corpse before the police surgeon was indeed Madame Badiou or Després.

The report ends.

Petit is cold. And suddenly he notices how hungry he is. He rummages in his cupboards and finds a piece of cheese that he wolfs down without pausing, walking all the while around his room, thinking. He pours himself a glass of wine, and he doesn't taste that either. There are other things to think about.

He does not trust this system of Bertillonage. He knows it has been proved effective in the ten or so years it has been used by the Sûreté, but still Petit finds it somewhat medieval. It cannot be that simple to take a series of bodily measurements and prove that there is a unique combination for each individual. Height, arm length, leg length; finger ratios, facial proportions . . . Surely, thinks Petit, these would be the same for a great number of people. He's heard that in Argentina or somewhere equally unlikely they have developed a system based on the pattern of lines found on the pads of everyone's fingers. Apparently, being unique to each person, they can identify anyone with one hundred per cent accuracy, and can be detected from the prints left behind on the most unlikely of surfaces. This system came before the powers that be here in Paris, Petit knows, and was rejected. A powerful lobby from Monsieur Bertillon himself, combined with the argument that it's one thing to know that fingerprints are different, but quite another to catalogue them so that they can be searched. Monsieur Bertillon had just made a name for himself again, staking his reputation on the retrial in the Dreyfus business, the treason trial of that Jewish officer. He's not someone to be easily overruled. So for the time being, these measurements and their results are what Petit has to work with.

In truth, Petit doesn't know to what level of detail the measurements are made, but in Ondine's case the proportions of her facial features would have been useless.

He reads the report again.

Something in it does not ring true, and he soon realises what it is: hair colour. The Bertillon report mentions that Ondine has auburn hair. Ondine had auburn hair at the time of her arrest for the little fracas. The police report from this July, on the corpse found by the two *gardiens* in the studio of Marcel Després, states that the victim had auburn hair, but that brown roots were just starting to show. Ondine has auburn hair, yes, but she did not have dyed hair, at least as far as he knows. Could that have been missed in the Bertillon report? There is only one way to find out: he will have to ask around at the cabarets where she worked. Someone will know, but in a sense, he tells himself, it doesn't matter. He knows what happened now. He just needs to prove it. It's time to stop moping around the city like a lovelorn boy.

He takes a bottle of brandy from the top shelf of the kitchen area in his rooms, and pours a large measure into his now empty wine glass.

He rummages behind the books on his bookshelf, and pulls out a large amount of cash, and places half on the table. The rest he puts in his wallet. He takes out his gun, unloads it, checks it, loads it again, and finds the bulk of his ammunition: sixteen rounds in addition to the six in the gun. These extra he stands in their little cardboard packet on the table top, and then places his Sûreté identification next to it.

He looks at everything he has. With these few things, he thinks dramatically, I have to change the world, or one small corner of it, anyway. I have to overturn something that everyone else believes to be true, even Marcel himself: that Marcel shot Ondine. And I have to uncover the involvement of one of the most powerful men in Paris and, therefore, in France.

He takes a clean handkerchief and makes a small bundle of his tools. He undresses, till he is in his shorts, then tucks the bundle into the top of his sock and ties it around his calf, tightly, using the long laces from his old army boots that he has kept all this time. He always knew they would come in useful.

He dresses again, in clean clothes.

He stands briefly in front of the small mirror he uses to shave, the only one in his apartment. He barely recognises his face.

It is not the one he has become used to seeing recently, one that is cowed and timid. The face before him now is the face he used to own, when he thought less, and did more. It's the face he wore as a soldier on the eve of battle. A face that does not question every single thought and every single deed.

Marie's voice is gone now, something he doesn't even notice. But it's true: she has left his thoughts, for he is no longer remembering. The time to brood and remember is over. That is a gift he has, that everyone in the world has: the ability, when necessary, to forget. Almost everyone, that is.

Petit heads out into the Parisian night.

# THE ART OF FORGETTING

On Morel's desk is an ever-growing pile of papers; they are the notes he has taken during and after every session with Marcel. As the months have gone by, this pile of papers has risen towards the ceiling of his little office at the back of the hospital. He has often worked far into the night to collect all his thoughts after a spell in Marcel's tiny room.

This evening, he stands looking at the work he has done so far. Once or twice, Raymond, the Chief Physician of the hospital, has asked him about his special case. It is an open secret that Morel is obsessing about something. The word is that Morel has found a man with perfect memory, and the word is also that Morel will not let it go until he has proved it for sure. Raymond is a younger man than Morel. He regards the old boy with a mixture of indifference and superiority. By and large, he allows the older doctor to do what he wants, because he will retire soon anyway, and in the meantime, he does little harm. Morel is smarter than Raymond believes, however, because Morel knows what the upstart Chief Physician thinks about him, but he does not care. All he cares about is his work and, as he stands looking at the pile of notes about Marcel, he lets out a faint sigh.

In front of him is a sheet of paper on which he has been trying to organise his thoughts, because he has come to the conclusion that it will not suffice to write a paper about Després, it will have to be a short book. At least. Possibly a long one.

Now, he stares at the papers, gives another sigh, and rubs his eyes with his forefinger and thumb. He has not touched the notes tonight. He has not touched them in three weeks, in fact. Maybe he won't ever touch them again, not unless he can include one final chapter. The chapter in which he, the noble physician, seeks and finds a cure for what ails Marcel Després. The chapter in which he discovers the art of forgetting, and teaches it to the man with the indelible memory, thus freeing him to live a normal life once more. Morel has come to the unalterable conclusion that in order to function as a normal human being, a balance is required, a balance of remembering and forgetting. Look at the murderous shoemaker, after all: without the ability to form new memories he lives trapped in some perpetual present, devoid of meaning. And look at Marcel: he is perhaps a little better off than the shoemaker, but really, all his problems stem from the fact that he lives permanently in the past, lost in labyrinths. And as he ponders these matters, the doctor realises something else, something about himself. Somewhere along the line, sitting in that cell, day after day, something has emerged from within Morel that has long lain dormant in him: the desire to care for a patient, even just one.

This is what Morel has been working on these past three weeks, and it is to this that he now returns, to what should be the crowning achievement of the book, of his life's work as an alienist. The art of forgetting.

Together, they have been working on various avenues of thought, various ways in which forgetting might be accomplished. Marcel has applied himself fully and enthusiastically to the work. He can see how much it would benefit him to be freed, even a little, from the curse of perfection.

At first, Morel wondered if what underlay the perfect memory was some deeply set *need*. Perhaps, from some childhood incident, Marcel had become programmed to be terrified of forgetting, and this in turn caused his mind to develop the unbelievable skill that it has. He dismisses this thought when he recalls that Marcel claims to have always had this memory, even in utero. But perhaps the theory itself is sound: that the mind's desire to memorise everything is driven by the need not to forget.

On this principle, the doctor provided Marcel one day with paper and pencils, and they spent several mornings having him write down every aspect of the murder that he possibly could. If these are written down, he reasons, maybe his brain will accept that they do not need to be remembered. To test this idea, Morel forced Marcel to restrict himself to the moments immediately before and during the event, but even then, it took four mornings to record everything. Morel was struck with the nagging fear that Marcel could go on writing for ever, and after four days he took the papers away. The next day, he returned and engaged Marcel in conversation about the murder, hoping for signs that his memory might be incomplete on some tiny aspect or other.

It was not.

Undeterred, Morel concluded that perhaps he should not have chosen this most dramatic event as the first for Marcel to attempt to forget. Anyone, any normal person, would have all these things etched on their remembrances for the rest of their days. What prevented Marcel from functioning normally was the day-to-day minutiae of life in which he was constantly trapped in memories within memories within memories. So they spent the next two afternoons having Marcel report everything he could about his first days in the asylum; including recording the number squares that Morel first set him as a challenge. That done, the doctor returned the next day and Marcel sadly rattled off a hundred numbers, a hundred numbers even Morel was starting to memorise.

The doctor has come to the conclusion that the writing method is yielding no positive results whatsoever, and today he has decided to move matters on. There is, after all, a very powerful tool at his disposal, one he has used many times in the past. It's just not a method he likes very much.

Hypnotism is widely used in the chambers of the Salpêtrière. It was another of Charcot's specialities when he was Chief

Physician, and it was the one area in which Morel never quite saw eye to eye with the great man. He never voiced his concerns out loud, and Charcot himself seemed to be so far wrapped into the process and so enthused by its apparent successes that he never appeared to step back and look at what was going on. Morel did. He learned how to hypnotise patients too, of course. There were a hundred ways in which it could be done: passes with the hand; caresses with fingertips on the face or arms; the intent gaze of the alienist stabbing deep into the eyes of the patient and so on and so on. The patient's eyes would become vague, or moisten, and eventually they would close as they entered the hypnotic state. With a well-practised patient, Charcot could merely tap the top of her head (and it was almost always a she in those days) and she would fall into the trance, as if struck by lightning.

It was the willingness with which the patients submitted to the procedure that first unsettled Morel, though he thought little of it at the time and did nothing about it at all. Perhaps unsettled is putting it too strongly, perhaps it's enough to say that a seed was placed deep in his mind which one day would start to emerge. And the results were spectacular: Charcot could have the women enter all sorts of hysterical states through hypnosis, holding out the prospect that hypnotism could be used to control these states when they emerged unwillingly.

Unwillingly, willingly, Morel began to think, which is which? Is there any difference? And then again, the fact that hypnotism appeared to be possible with birds such as cockerels and doves seemed to rule out any possibility of collusion between the patient and doctor, that the patient could be acting out what the doctor hoped to see, even on an unconscious level. And unconsciousness could apply to either doctor or patient. Or both.

Morel had watched time and again as Charcot stood behind a lady seated on a chair, placed his fingertips on the tops of her eyelids, and began to speak to her so intently and softly that within moments she was under the spell. And what was the alternative? What other ways were they developing to cure these women of their hysterical attacks? There was the Holtz-Carré machine; but it soon grew tiresome watching the warders strap a struggling woman, naked, to the arms of the chair so that the discharge from the great spinning wheel could be applied to her body in various places. Yes, they left the room docile and meek, but perhaps that was nothing more than exhaustion. Electrostatic baths were little better.

Hypnotism seemed to offer clean painless solutions. Yes, it had been twice refuted by the Académie des Sciences, but that was when it still reeked of Mesmerism, the mystical connotations of the pre-scientific ramblings of its creator Anton Mesmer still clinging to it. Attraction fluids, animal magnetism, remote metalloscopy. Such things were surely best left outside the gates of the hospital and confined to the salons of rich ladies with idle speculations to indulge. Charcot's paper of 1882 began to rewrite the map, and then came the epic battle of Charcot, in Paris, versus Bernheim, in Nancy. The questions of two great themes, sex and crime, were investigated. Could a woman be forced to submit to a sexual liaison under hypnosis, and if she did so, was this rape? Did it not in fact mean that she was willing all along? And could a man be forced to commit a murder while in a hypnotic trance? In Nancy, Bernheim had his patients commit all sorts of heinous acts in an effort to find the limit of behaviour under hypnosis. They would eat offal, they would eat refuse, even human excreta. He could have them striptease, unknowingly. And then came the 'laboratory crimes', in which a series of 'murders' were committed using unloaded pistols, fake arsenic and more. And still the hypnotised patients did everything that was bid of them. All the while, dissenting voices started to ask not only about the morality of such experiments, but also about the matter of complicity. Were these people, no matter how depraved the act they committed, actually *willing* to do these things, and the supposed state of hypnotism merely gave them licence to do so?

These dissenting voices entered Morel's head, though he said nothing till after Charcot had retired, and even then, very little, for the new man, Raymond, seemed not to hold great store by the practice.

For all this, Morel is able to hypnotise patients. He has done it many times, and he still believes, when you strip away all the over-the-top and extravagant nonsense that Charcot and particularly Bernheim got up to, there is a quiet, subtle useful avenue of experimentation that only hypnotism can offer. Thus he has decided to see if Marcel can be hypnotised into forgetting.

He places himself in front of his patient late one winter's afternoon and explains what he is going to do. He will put Marcel into a hypnotic state; this will take some time, he explains, but once there, he will begin to talk to Marcel's mind, to the deepest part of his mind, and he will suggest that one particular memory is forgotten, erased, removed for good. They discuss what this should be.

'You have something in mind, Marcel?'

Marcel thinks for a bit.

'Shall we start with something small?'

Morel nods. That seems sensible.

'Then make me forget the name of that policeman. The inspector.'

Morel considers this. Very well, he thinks. He can see no harm in that, he can see no way in which that might cause anything detrimental to happen. And if it does, he can always remind Marcel of the name. A good and simple test, straightforward.

Marcel seems strangely excited. Morel conceals his own feelings as he sets to work with the passes in front of his patient's eyes, causing them, after a period of time, to close. After a while longer of gentle speech, Morel satisfies himself that Marcel is 'asleep'. He makes the suggestion to Marcel that the name Petit will leave his mind for ever, at once, and he does all this with such self-confidence and such conviction, while Marcel seems totally enraptured, that it is all the more distressing, that despite their best efforts and the small scale of the task they have selected, that the method of hypnotic forgetting appears to have failed utterly.

# A NIGHT IN PIGALLE

There are days, Petit has come to realise, when you merely exist. These are not necessarily bad days, merely days when your senses are closed. You see little, you smell little, you taste almost nothing. Sounds impact upon you but cause no effect and leave no trace. You move through your world, doing what must be done, without awareness. You work, you walk. You talk to people who ask something of you, you say a couple of words to the man who sells you your newspaper, but when the end of the day arrives, you might suddenly sit down on the edge of your bed, and wonderingly say to yourself 'hah!' as you realise that you missed the entire day. Or perhaps you might go to sleep, still without realising anything at all.

Many days have been like that for Petit. He watches as his mind does something it has been doing a lot of lately: that is to say, it makes a connection. Without his bidding or intention, new ideas and thoughts keep rising to the surface of his consciousness. This time he makes a comparison between himself and Marcel. Marcel is trapped because he thinks too much, he cannot free himself from a cyclical whirl of memory, whereas he, Petit, is trapped because he doesn't think at all.

Or it would be closer to say he *didn't*. Now he is like a sleeper of some fabulous story, emerging from his cave and rubbing his eyes as if for the first time. If he thought little before, he now sees that when Marie died he forced himself to think even less. But the water in a spring cannot be dammed up for ever, and now he is paying the price for it; his new thoughts gush from the darkness and burst across the meadow of his mind.

If there are days when your life passes without you taking any active part in it, then Petit has come to see that there are also days when every whisper of sound has meaning, when every glance from a stranger has import, when every tiny detail of life suddenly seems vital, and not only that, seems connected to every other detail, so that you perceive the world as a web winding around you and off in all directions, with you as its protagonist.

Today, this evening, is such a time. That is why, without any logical reason for it, Petit has prepared himself for flight, if need be. Before the night is out he will learn that he was right to do so.

It is late already: seven o'clock. Early for an evening in the city of Paris, but late, given how much he has to accomplish.

He makes his way first from his apartment, down to the Boulevard Saint-Germain, and crosses over into the Cour du Commerce. Everything is usual, everything is normal; life goes on in the cour just as if Marcel had never blasted five rounds into his wife, which Petit thinks is as it should be, because it never happened. These diners in Le Procope, the coal boy on the corner, the rag-and-bone man picking through the gutters, they should all act just as they are, as if a murder never happened up there on the sixth floor. But, Petit tells himself, a murder *did* happen, just not the one that people think. That's what he has come to prove. To start with, he is going to use a piece of mental evidence, something that Marcel himself offered up, from the detail of his memory.

He marches through the porch of the house, not even glancing at the concierge who is whining away at some poor unfortunate tenant about boot marks on the floorboards.

'Hey!' she cries out, as Petit passes. 'What do you think— You there!'

Petit takes no notice. The miserable concierge starts to hobble after him, but by then he is already two flights of stairs ahead of her.

When he reaches the door to the apartment that was Marcel and Ondine's he does not knock. He tries the handle and finds it locked. He can hear the concierge making progress up the stairwell and that is enough to cause him to act. As before at Baraduc's studio, he shoves the sole of his boot against the lock with a short stabbing motion. The door flies open and he marches in to find a middle-aged couple jumping out of their skins. After a moment's pause, they immediately begin shouting at him and make threats of violence, which they are unlikely to carry out.

Petit ignores them both, striding into the area where the bed sits. Without pausing, he drags it away from the wall, and as he sees what he knew he would find, his heart starts pounding. There, on the floor, are the obvious stains of blood, murky brown on the wooden boards.

The concierge bustles into the room.

'I will call the police!' she announces as the tenants begin to yell at her for not stopping this madman.

'I am the police,' Petit says, but not loud enough for the shouting trio to take any notice. He turns to the concierge, pointing backwards at the bloodstain as he does so.

'Did you know about this?' he demands.

Her face pales.

'I . . . No. I . . .' she stammers. 'No, I have no idea. I had no idea at all. What is it? What?'

Petit doesn't wait to hear more.

He is out of the door and away, just as the concierge remembers who he is, and begins to hurl abuse at him down the stairwell.

He leaves by the Rue Saint-André-des-Arts, and storms up the Rue Dauphine, looking for a horse and driver. He hails one by the river and asks for the Place de Clichy. Best not to go too close to start with, he wants to make his way on foot, not draw attention to himself by cruising through Pigalle in a cab. There are gentlemen who do such things of course, and they attract bees as to a honey jar.

On the way, he has time to stop and piece everything together again. He has guessed what has happened, but he has little proof. Marcel, from his prison, gave him one piece of evidence hitherto unknown: there was a bleeding body underneath the bed. He knows that if Marcel says it happened, then it did; he does not forget, he does not lie. There was blood coming from under the bed before he pulled the trigger for the first time.

Yes, Petit has only been making guesses, but each guess seems to have been accurate so far. The inevitability of each correct assumption feels like a wall of water, that spring water maybe, pushing at his back, pushing him on to the next guess, yet threatening him somehow too. His next guess is the identity of the body under the bed, and he has come to Pigalle to find that out.

He steps down from the cab and immediately wishes that he had taken the Metro, for even here in the Place de Clichy, with its relative lack of degeneracy, he is immediately assailed by three prostitutes at once, all eager for his business. He manages to get rid of them only when he asserts that he has not come looking for women, and at that they bridle and misconstrue, and one remarks that in that case, he should be down at the Hôtel Marigny.

He thanks the lady for her concern and pushes himself along the Boulevard de Clichy, towards Pigalle itself. Pigalle, home of the lowest strata of Parisian society, barring the *zoniers*, who could barely be called part of society at all. And yet also here are the haunts of free-thinkers and radicals, of the avant-garde of both art and politics. Petit walks steadily, not too fast, not too slow, trying to look as if he has somewhere to go and someone to be with. He tries to present an air of a complicated nature; that he *would* accept one of the many offers he receives as he makes his way, indeed, that he often *does* accept such invitations, but not tonight, tonight he has something special in mind that these half-dressed beauties are not able to fulfil. If he manages to pull off that image, it's because there is some truth to it. He finds that he is stirred by the voluptuousness around him, in all its seedy horror, and despite the fact that these *filles publiques* are almost certainly riddled with disease. Maybe that's part of why he finds himself titillated: the frisson of danger they exude. But that is not a way to die, with the syphilitic pox. That is a way to torture yourself.

A girl steps right in front of him, a young girl, forcing him to break stride for a second. Before he can sidestep her, she pulls up her long skirts and shows herself to him, naked underneath her dress.

'Want it?' she coos and then laughs, causing a gaggle of her friends to cackle from the street door to their rooms.

Petit tries to keep his cool, tipping his hat and winking at her as if he's also amused. But he isn't. The reality of where he is and who these women are strikes him hard, and at the next corner he turns down the Rue Blanche, walking a little faster. There seems, he discovers, to be an optimum speed to this. Too slow or, weirdly, too fast, and it appears to make the street girls and the pimps call out. Somewhere in the middle is the speed that the locals walk at, those who everyone knows aren't interested, and he soon learns that's all he needs to do to avoid attention. This in turn allows him to look a little bit more at the life around him. It is not his first time here, not by a long way, but now that he has woken from his sleep, now that his mind has decided to start thinking, he sees everything with new eyes. He sees the palls of smoke that drift up from every knot of people, on every corner, huddling into their little groups despite the cold winter air. Candles flicker and gas lamps glow through every window, catching faces in the act of laughter, or passion or rage, whatever it might be. Petit sees whole lives, whole worlds frozen in a momentary glance at someone through glass.

The brothels, the bars, the roughnecks. A gang of Apaches bowls down the street on the other side, knocking a couple of young adventure-seekers into the gutter as they go. One of the young men squares up as if to fight, but his friend pulls him away. In his mind, Petit finishes the story the other way, and sees both men bleeding in the gutter with their throats slit and their money in the Apaches' pockets.

Things are a little quieter in the Rue Chaptal, but there is a greater air of menace. Darkness, only a couple of widely spaced street lamps, and silence – this is a sad, dying street in some ways, just a few steps from the hubbub of the Places Blanche and Pigalle.

The sound of his footsteps rings down the street, and then he arrives at the impasse he has been looking for. He must have passed it a dozen times in his career as a policeman, and never before noticed it.

Running north back up from the Rue Chaptal, a short, dead-end street, with the light from two gas lamps making the cobbles shine and, at the far end, the place he has come to visit. It is not the Cabaret des Insultes, because Petit doesn't want to draw attention to himself by asking questions there. Once again, he is working from details supplied by Marcel's memory: that Ondine used to work in other places before she came to Chardon's. He recalled, and Petit recorded, that she worked in this place, at the end of the alley, the small, new but undeniably notorious Théâtre du Grand-Guignol, the theatre of horror, the theatre of fear.

Everyone has heard of it, everyone knows the stories of the shows they perform, yet very few Parisians have actually witnessed matters for themselves. The theatre is tiny, but in its short lifetime has developed such a reputation for horror, for unbridled violence, for sexual daring, that it is talked about across the capital, discussed in the boardrooms of businesses and commented upon in the gazettes and papers. Its themes are of the lowest of the lowlife of Paris: of working girls, of bordellos. Corruption and decay. Murder. Incest. Drugs and drink. Sadism and torture. Such things are its nightly fare and a whole new genre of play has had to be created to fulfil the urges generated within the building, a new play every few weeks, each more depraved than the last.

Petit decides to act as a punter, and pauses for a moment outside to peruse the playbill, a gaudy depiction of a woman with one breast exposed and a man looming over her with a long sharp metal spike of some kind in his hand, held at such a height and in such a way as to suggest that it is his phallus. The play is called *Elle!* and, just inside the door, Petit pays for a ticket at a small kiosk.

There is not long to wait until the curtain rises on the drama. Petit takes the little time he has to hang around in the foyer, trying to take stock of the staff of the place, which seems minimal. There is the girl who sold him a ticket, and a man, for some reason in an antique soldier's uniform, standing by the door into the theatre. He sees a man who might or might not be the director; he comes and goes from a small office, smiling and greeting some of the playgoers, then retreating to his lair.

The play is about to start. Petit heads into the auditorium itself, having his ticket torn in half by the soldier. He finds a spot as near to the back as he can, on the end of a row.

It is half full, with the air of a small chapel, seating perhaps only a hundred. People drift in, milling about, laughing uproariously, and sometimes perhaps nervously, for the theatre's reputation is that its mission is to shock, and does not consider a night to be a success unless at least one paying customer has fainted or been sick.

Then a trumpet sounds from somewhere behind the curtain, the lights are dimmed, and the curtain lifts.

Almost as soon as it begins, Petit regrets his decision. The play concerns the fortunes of a young woman of rich society, orphaned as she has barely reached womanhood. Desperate, innocent, she eagerly accepts the help of her mysterious uncle, who has designs upon the pretty young thing. He rapes her.

The whole thing is as sick as can be devised, and yet the mood is strange: overly theatrical, deliberately pantomime in places. The rape scene depicts the uncle in a melodramatic long black cape, which swirls around him as he pushes the girl back on to an ornate table, thus obscuring whatever it is he is doing to her, though all in the room know full well. Not wishing to disappoint those who have heard that nudity is frequent at the Grand-Guignol, the evil uncle rips the girl's blouse open to display her ample right breast to the crowd. Petit can almost hear them drool, moving towards the edge of their seats. There is a tremendous eager silence in the room as the girl screams, her breast wobbling lasciviously with every thrust from the caped villain.

It is inevitable that Petit's thoughts turn to his beautiful Marie. He shuts his eyes but the damage is done. The scene is soon over, culminating in an all-too-real stage effect in which the uncle throws vitriol at the girl's face, disfiguring her. Her skin, her actual skin appears to blister and peel and bleed, right before the eyes of the crowd, who gasp in horror and delight combined. Despite himself, Petit opens his eyes for a second, unable to ignore the cries of the crowd; in the row in front of him a woman does indeed retch, and staggers out of the theatre, her husband at her side.

Petit shuts his eyes again, but it really is too late. All his suppressed imaginings of Marie's final moments erupt in him at once, so powerfully and with such terrible images, that it is all he can do to prevent himself from screaming out, there and then. So many times these images have haunted him, things he does not even know for sure occurred, but which he can imagine, and has done so a thousand times. The murderer sitting on her stomach, or spreading her legs. His hands on her throat with such strength that he can take one hand off and rub her wherever he wishes. Poor Marie. Poor, poor Marie. In the darkness of the Théâtre du Grand-Guignol, tears run down the inspector's face, and he makes the final decision to see this whole strange affair to the end, no matter what, or who, that takes down in the process.

The interval arrives, during which Petit stares into nothingness, suppressing his anger, his grief and, most of all, the disgust he feels. He detests the crowd around him, he detests the people who put this thing on the stage. But above that, he detests himself, because he too felt something watching the girl being exposed and taken, something he does not like to believe exists.

The second half commences, which follows the decline of the young girl, tricked out of her fortune, her face an ugly mess on one side, as she falls into the life of a girl on the streets. The end concerns her revenge on her uncle, but by the time that scene arrives, and she pierces his eyes with a red-hot poker, Petit has left the theatre.

He's noted that the man who he takes to be the director of the theatre is watching from a small gallery to one side, with glee, too, Petit sees. Feigning the need to be sick, the inspector staggers from the auditorium and out into the foyer, which attracts no attention at all since he is far from the first to leave. The foyer is dark, the door to the street is closed, the girl is missing from her kiosk.

Petit tries the handle of the little office, and expecting to find it locked almost falls through it when it opens easily under his hands.

He steps inside, closing the door behind him gently, and by the half-light from the window finds a lamp on the desk, and matches. Once he has the lamp going he sees some drawers and cabinets, and he sets to work immediately. He very soon finds what he is looking for: a pay book, with lists of all the staff of the theatre, the details of payments made to them, and their addresses.

He flicks back through the months and there, in 1897, he sees Ondine's name, and right underneath it, that of Lucie Rey. It is for Lucie that he came here, for her address.

He tears the page from the book, and is gone.

Back out in Pigalle, little has changed. But once again Petit is very strongly aware of how every move and every action that he makes feels as if it has been laid down for him, with utter inevitability. He knew who he was looking for, where he would find what he needed. That it would all work out, that the door to the office would be unlocked thanks to the carelessness of the director of the gruesome theatre. Lucie's address is also in Montmartre, not far, but a steep climb up the hill, that leaves him panting as he makes the Rue Gabrielle.

It is there that he learns from Lucie's old landlady that she did indeed leave for Lyon.

The old lady is kind and immediately trusting, and Petit wonders how she survives in Montmartre as he asks if she can tell him when exactly it was that Lucie left.

'Yes, why, yes, I can,' she says, 'but you'll have to wait a moment. It's in my book. I'll have to check. Why don't you come inside?'

Petit does, again asking himself how the old lady has not been murdered in her bed for being so naïve as to let a total stranger into her house. He hasn't even told her he is a policeman. He stands for a moment in a small hallway and then she returns with a ledger open in her hands.

She shows it to Petit.

'There; the last week was the 26th June. She left on the Saturday, I remember.'

'You're sure?'

'I'm sure. She'd paid for the whole week and I offered to refund her a day's rent, but she refused.'

Petit's eyebrows rise. A second angel in Montmartre! What is the world coming to?

'There is one thing, though,' the lady says.

Petit knows this is the next moment of his journey.

'Yes?'

'Yes. She left some things. Lots of things, in fact. In a trunk. She said she wanted to get along to Lyon and settle herself and would have the trunk sent for when she was ready and able.'

'And?'

'Well, she still hasn't sent for it. That was five months ago, wasn't it? I haven't heard a thing. It's still in my basement, the trunk, I mean.'

This news does not surprise Petit one bit.

'Did she say anything else? Did she mention anyone that day? Please try to remember, it's very important.'

'It is?' asks the old lady, who is so sweet that Petit finds he is suppressing the urge to weep. 'Well, yes. She said she was heading down on the night train, but was going to see an old friend first. Though, you know, I thought there was something funny about the way she said that. I couldn't work out why, but it stuck with me because there was something else to it. If you know what I mean.'

'Yes,' says Petit. 'I know what you mean.'

Petit thanks the woman and heads out into the night again, back downhill, as fast as his legs will go. Every cab in Paris seems to have vanished, and so he walks as briskly as he can back towards the river. He has one more call to make on this most active of nights, but as he reaches the bottom of the Rue des Martyrs, he is taken with the sensation that he is being followed again, as so often over the last weeks. He tries to shake the feeling: it would not be the first time that a group of Apaches have spotted a solo gentleman on the streets of Montmartre and decided to make easy pickings. But as Petit turns at the sound of footsteps behind him, there is nothing.

Apaches would not be so subtle. Perhaps it was just the echo of his own boots in the deserted street.

He presses on, and finally finds a cab on the Boulevard des Italiens to take him to the hospital, passing police headquarters as he does so – but who in that building, he thinks, can he trust?

It takes him a while to convince the night porter at the Salpêtrière that he must speak to Morel, that it is an urgent matter, but after some wrangling and the intimation of the crime of obstructing a policeman in the course of his investigation, the porter calls directly to Morel's rooms.

The two men confer, briefly, for two or three minutes, and then Petit sees the time. If he is not careful he will miss the last train at the Gare de Lyon, and that's back across the river from the hospital.

He bids the doctor good evening and sets out, but has only gone a short way along the avenue when he finally knows he was right. He feels a hand on his shoulder before he even hears anyone. The hand tries to pull him round and instinctively he turns rapidly with it, sinking his fist into the man's throat with a hard jab. Even as the first man collapses, choking, he realises another assailant has stepped out of the shadows under the lime trees and he feels two arms grab him. The man says nothing. Petit feels his breath on his neck and the heat of his body against his in the cold night, he feels bristles against his cheek and then jerks his whole body forward, lifting the man off his feet.

Petit takes a half turn and then straightens, stepping back as hard as he can, hoping he has judged where the tree is. He does it perfectly, and winds the man so badly that he too falls to the ground, gasping horrid short little breaths that will not fill up his lungs.

Petit runs, turning back once. By the light of the street lamps, he sees the first man getting to his feet. There and then, Petit changes his mind: the Gare de Lyon is across the river but he is right outside the Gare d'Orléans. He will have to make a connection, but maybe that's for the best. He does not know who attacked him, but he can guess. And he can guess why. Perhaps it would be better to throw anyone else off the trail a little.

He sprints through the entrance and buys a ticket on the next train south, the night train to Clermont-Ferrand.

He finds his berth and throws himself into his seat, breathing heavily from the running, from the fear, from the fight. The evening is done, and now, more than ever, the feeling that he is finally aware of his life overtakes him. He knows he has lived hours that will prove to be among the most significant of his life; that ten years' worth of importance was played out between seven and eleven o'clock.

Anxiously, he peers through the curtain of the carriage, expecting at any moment to see the two thugs appear again, but they do not. He must have given them the slip before they had the chance to see him duck into the station. With an enormous sense of relief he hears the engine let out a shriek of a whistle, and he feels the first jerks as the wheels slip and then grip on the iron rails. The train moves; he can sense its weight as it gradually picks up a little speed, and he knows now what that momentum must feel like, for he feels it himself.

Within minutes, Paris is behind him.

# HISTORY

# NIGHT TRAIN TO
# CLERMONT–FERRAND

The facts of the matter were these:

At a little before seven o'clock on the evening of the first Saturday in July 1899, Lucie Rey passed under the fine arch from the Rue Saint-André-des-Arts that leads into the Cour du Commerce. It was a typically busy evening in the alley, and the quarter in general was humming and banging; the life of the city rushing along, people in the streets like blood in the veins of an anxious person. Deep in conversation with one of the locals, the concierge at Ondine and Marcel's building noticed Lucie, and shrugged. She used to come around a lot, that girl. Not so much recently. If at all. But so what? Who really cares about anyone else's story until it collides with your own?

Lucie made her way up the stairs, her small suitcase in her hand, her ticket to Lyon safely tucked in her purse, ready to take her away from Paris. It had surprised her when Ondine invited her to supper, and of course intrigued her a little too.

'Marcel is working,' Ondine had said. 'I'm going to pull a night off. I want to make it up to you, Lucie, before you go. Just us girls, like old times. Please say yes.'

And Lucie, after a great deal of thought, had indeed said yes. She had wondered whether it was too much to do on the night she was taking the train south, but then again, why not? She was packed and ready to go. She had been packed for almost a week, in fact. She had no other friends with whom she wanted to spend time, her trunk was already stowed in the cellar at her landlady's house. Why not?

Nonetheless, she was nervous as she climbed to the final landing and as she knocked on the door she suddenly had second thoughts. And did she hear Marcel's voice, after all, from behind the door? A moment later, she knew she'd been wrong, because Ondine opened the door and was quite alone.

It was a warm evening, that Saturday in July. One of the big windows that overlooked the cour was open, as well as the smaller one that looked east across the rooftops of the Latin Quarter. The noise of the streets below contrasted with the silence of life on the rooftops. Across the way, the seamstresses' studio was dark and empty. Saturday evening had come and they were out in the world, trying to find someone to love, and to love them back.

'We get a nice breeze up here,' Ondine said, taking Lucie's bag and coat from her and setting them on a chair at the table. 'Makes the climb up the stairs worthwhile . . . Lucie! How are you? I . . . I am so sorry.'

And Ondine *was* sorry. She came forward and before Lucie had time to think she found her old friend with her arms around her and even a tear coming down her cheek.

Lucie stepped back.

'Ondine . . .' She didn't know what to say, so she said what she thought might be expected. 'Forgive me?'

Ondine waved her worry away. 'There's nothing to forgive. It was Marcel I should have been angry with. For not telling me. How could he keep something like that to himself? Have a drink, won't you?'

'I will,' said Lucie, and took the hefty tumbler of red that Ondine poured for her, followed by one for herself.

'Santé!' Ondine said, lifting her glass.

They drank, catching each other's eyes for a brief moment. For that moment, Lucie suddenly doubted what was going on, but she pushed that thought away. It was too late now, she was here. It would be a story to tell, at least. To her new friends in Lyon, when she made them, friends who would be better than this one ever was. So Lucie smiled.

'What are we having?' she asked. 'I'm famished!'

Ondine faltered slightly. 'Well, not much,' she said. 'Times being what they are. Some cold things. But there's plenty of wine.'

Ondine realised then that it would have been a good idea to have put a pot on the stove, to make it look right. But she didn't have to worry.

'Come and look,' she said to Lucie, and pulled her over to the big windows, where she did a strange thing. She shut them.

'It's still so hot, won't you leave them open?' Lucie asked.

But Ondine didn't answer. She pointed across the roofs at nothing, and Lucie, wondering, followed Ondine's gaze, so she didn't see Bishop climbing back in from the smaller window on the other side of the apartment, in stocking feet. He came up behind them both and for a moment felt a delicious thrill, that actually he could kill either of them. But then again, Ondine was proving, as before, to be most energetic in bed and there was also the fat packet of cash that had recently come into her possession. So he stuck to their plan and grabbed Lucie from behind, one hand over her mouth, the other arm around her arms and chest, and dragged her to the bed so fast that the poor girl never knew what was happening.

Ondine skipped quickly to the drawer where the gun was kept, and wasted no time putting it to Lucie's face. As Bishop pulled his hand away, she fired just once. Just before she did, she saw Lucie's eyes open wide from fear, so wide, that she almost hesitated. But she did not. She pulled the trigger.

The St Etienne was not a powerful gun, but at point-blank range it ruined Lucie's face. After a little while, her body stopped moving. Bishop and Ondine sat back, breath heaving in and out of them, waiting for the sound of rushing feet or cries of alarm. None came: the cour was noisy and full of life and one shot, muffled by the face of the victim and the mattress underneath, made no impression at all.

'Quick!' said Ondine, though in reality they had all the time in the world to carry out the rest of their plan.

They stripped Lucie of her clothes, and left her naked on the floor, winding the bed sheet around her head to try to contain the worst of the bleeding. Then Ondine changed the rest of the bedclothes, wrapping the mess up into a bundle, which Bishop took out across the rooftops and threw into an inaccessible valley between two mansards, along with Lucie's suitcase and coat.

Ondine undressed, and so as not to get blood on her, before she dressed again they wrestled Lucie into the clothes that Ondine had been wearing. Satisfied, they pushed her body under the bed, and then they began to drink.

They had not intended to drink too much, but their nerves and the horror of what they'd done cried out to be silenced, and they took perhaps a glass or two too much. It didn't matter: they had achieved the first part of their plan; the second act was yet to come. Bishop congratulated Ondine on her acting; the tear! How had she done that? And Ondine told him that she could have been a fine actress, if only she'd had the chance. Hadn't her whole life been spent making men believe that she desired them? Wasn't that acting, real acting?

Bishop nodded, sombrely. He took the remaining five cartridges out of the gun and put four of them under a cloth on the side, ready, for later. The fifth he threw across the hidden rooftops. Then he loaded the gun with the single blank round that Ondine had managed to filch on a visit to see her old friends at the Grand-Guignol, where such stage trickery was commonplace.

The hours crawled by. Neither of them looked towards the bedroom; they did their best not to think about what was there.

They had both nearly been sick when half of Lucie's face vanished and so they forced their attention elsewhere, which was why they failed to see the blood edging out across the floor-boards until it was too late to do anything about it.

They drank, then they began to discuss Marcel's money; the stash that Ondine once thought he had.

'I still don't believe it,' she said. 'He says he has nothing, but I don't think he understands what he's talking about.'

So they hunted round the apartment.

They didn't find it. But they did see the blood seeping across the floor, which made them afraid. They rubbed at the blood and Bishop threw a bundle of bloodied towels across the roofs, after the suitcase and bedsheet. Then he grew angry, and they quarrelled, until they realised that they had to keep their voices low.

'Maybe he keeps it in a bank,' Bishop hissed. 'Ever think of that?'

Ondine sneered at him. 'He doesn't believe in banks. He's from the countryside, you know the sort. Only he never told me where it is, so shut up and keep looking.'

Still, Marcel's money remained undiscovered. Bishop even tried lifting a floorboard or two, but they were all firmly nailed down. It was the right idea, and had there not been a dead body bleeding underneath the bed, he might have looked there, and found a loose board, hiding an oilcloth package containing thousands of francs. He did not.

After a while, Bishop swore, straightening his back and waving a hand around the room.

'So maybe he really doesn't have any money. At least we have what you got from your fat cat.'

The thought of that made them both feel a little better. Though she was pretty sure Prefect Paul Delorme had set those men on her all those weeks ago, the fact was he had responded twice to her blackmail threats, responded with almost as much cash as she'd demanded. Better yet, she had a packet of photographs to keep as insurance, despite the two she'd sent to Delorme. That must have put the wind up him, she thought. He'd claimed not to remember her when she first got in touch. So she'd sent him something to remember her by: an image that left nothing to the imagination, crude and blasphemous in equal parts. And still better than all of that was the fact that, now they had Delorme's cash, she was about to disappear, she was about to die. If she could not have Marcel's money, she would have Delorme's, who, believing her to be dead, would send no more thugs to try to kill her. It was all so neat, Ondine thought. So perfect, it made her smile.

They took to drinking again, and the hours wore on, and they even started to doze, and so were nearly caught out. Ondine woke with a start as they sat slumped across the table from each other.

'What's the time?'

Bishop checked his pocket watch. 'Nearly ten!'

They scrambled, for they knew Marcel would be home at any moment, and began to get ready.

Bishop, still in his stocking feet, dropped his trousers and waited for Ondine, who had crept to the door to the studio and out into the hall, to peer down the stairwell. Only seconds passed before she scampered back inside, closing the door silently behind her, and took her position. She pulled her skirts up and began to give out load moans of pleasure as Bishop started shoving his soft penis against her backside.

'What's the matter?' Ondine hissed between moans. 'Don't feel like it?'

'Shut up,' Bishop muttered, and slapped her hard across her buttocks.

She squealed, a real squeal, and Bishop felt the fear inside him. The first part had been easy; this part was much harder. He suddenly doubted Ondine. She had told him, convinced him, that she could make Marcel so mad that he would use the gun. There it was, on the side, just as they'd left it, with one round in the cylinder so he wouldn't make too much noise, just enough. There was the big window on to the cour that they'd opened again, hoping now that sounds would be heard. Ondine had told Bishop that she had been working on Marcel, making him madder and madder every time, that he only needed a nudge to tip him over the edge, but Bishop had never been convinced.

'What if he doesn't buy it?' he asked. 'Why do this anyway? Why not just force him to tell us where the money is? Kill him and get out of here?'

And so Ondine had explained, yet again, that she didn't want Marcel to die. The money would be nice but it was not really what she wanted. She wanted him to suffer. She wanted him to believe he had killed the woman he loved, his own wife, and then she wanted him to be tortured by that knowledge for the rest of his life.

'Which will only be until he goes to the guillotine.'

But Ondine knew the law. That under French law the murder of a wife caught in the act of adultery in the marital home was an *excusable* crime. He would receive hard labour at worst, and all the while, that ridiculous mind of his would torture him with the memory of what he'd done.

Bishop still protested, but Ondine wouldn't give in.

'I can make him do it,' she said, again and again, and even, 'I need to do it.' Finally, she came up with a fall-back plan, something that convinced Bishop they may as well try. 'If he doesn't use the gun, well, we'll just set him up, won't we? When he comes in and finds us, there'll be a scene. If he doesn't use the gun, you take it, fire it at him. You miss, of course, but make him run. Then, when he's out in the street, we carry out the rest of the plan, and you tell everyone he killed me.'

Bishop nodded at that, because it was easy, that plan. It could not go wrong. And either way, Ondine would vanish from the world, safely out of reach of Delorme's roughnecks.

As things fell out, however, Ondine was right. She did manage to make Marcel so mad with jealousy and rage that he took up the gun, and pulled the trigger, not just once, firing the blank round at her, but four more times, each met only with a click.

Ondine threw herself down, landing on her front on the carpet, bursting the thin rubber packet of pig's blood hidden under her blouse, another trick from her days at the Grand-Guignol.

It was a moment that struck her powerfully. For the briefest possible length of time, she hesitated. She had seen the anger and the desire in Marcel's eyes. In that moment, she had made him hate her, hate her so much that he fired the gun. He fired it five times. Ondine almost got up from her death throes on the floor. She almost confessed, yes, Marcel, it was all a game, all a joke on you. But then she remembered what Lucie had done, and how her stupid husband didn't even know who she was from day to day, and she lay still, and died.

Bishop ran to Marcel, ripping the gun from his hands, and screamed into his face to flee, for God's sake. Run! You idiot, you madman! Run! And run Marcel did.

In the time it took Marcel to get halfway down the stairs, Bishop and Ondine were in action again, no hesitation now. Bishop loaded the gun with the four live rounds left, while Ondine pulled Lucie's body out from under the bed, and then Bishop put one bullet in her torso, the rest in her face, obliterating it totally, shot by shot. Then he dropped the gun where Marcel had stood, while Ondine climbed out of the smaller window and went to hide herself in a spot hidden from sight, where she would remain until the small hours of the night, until she could come down and disappear for ever.

Bishop, meanwhile, began his part of the act, all this before Marcel burst into the street with a roar of horror and fell on his knees. People gathered round as Bishop came to the window and shouted out for the whole cour to hear: 'Murder! Murder! He's killed Ondine!'

And this time, the shots had been heard. With the window open, and the quieter air of ten o'clock, many people had heard.

This was how it was done, Petit thought to himself as the night train rumbled south towards the hills of the Auvergne. More or less. He had pieced it all together now, every detail, even down to why Ondine had changed the sheets on the bed.

Unable to sleep, Petit stared out of the window at the unseen landscape hurrying past outside. On to this black screen he projected his new history, a different history from the one that everyone believed, even Marcel, the supposed murderer. He didn't get it right first time, of course. There was much back-tracking and rewriting, but finally he found a version that made sense of everything, which he could barely fault, as elaborate and extraordinary as it seemed. It made sense of everything: of Delorme's involvement, a powerful man who had been black-mailed, and feared there was worse to come. A man who wanted the whole thing closed down without an investigation. There was only one thing that puzzled Petit on that speeding night train: the presence of the Russians, and what connection they had to the affair.

There was one way to find out, and one way to prove his whole theory, come to that: he must find Ondine. He was convinced she was alive, that Lucie's faceless body was the one that had been measured and flung into a pauper's grave outside the city walls. Lucie Rey, as far as his enquiries had shown, was the perfect victim: no family, few friends, no money, no one of consequence at all. The news of her intended departure to Lyon must have precipitated her death; triggered Ondine and the American into action, for this was too good a chance to waste.

So it had been done, the truth disguised by lies, and history rewritten.

# THE DOG

The dog knows how to be a dog.

This piece of information was what Dr Morel told Inspector Petit during their short interview the evening before.

'The dog knows how to be a dog,' Morel said, apparently uninterested in Petit's urgent whisperings about switched identities and absconding murderers. 'The dog knows how to be a dog, whereas man, he does not know how to be a man.'

This had brought Petit up short for a moment, a big mistake, allowing the doctor to resume his musings. Irrelevant musings that appeared to come out of nowhere as far as Petit was concerned but which had been prompted by the old doctor's thoughts about Marcel. About how complicated the life of the average person is, never mind that of someone as extraordinary as Mister Memory.

Now, in the dark early hours of the morning at the station in Clermont-Ferrand, Petit sits on a crate and watches a mangy hound sniffing around for scents, for traces of food perhaps. The conversation returns to him.

'The dog knows how to be a dog,' Morel said. 'When he is hungry, he scavenges. When he is thirsty, he finds a puddle. When tired, he sleeps, when attacked, he fights back. He does not reason or worry or debate or doubt himself; he knows how to be a dog. But! Ah! Men and women! They do not know how to be. If I have learned one thing in my days as a doctor of the unwell mind, it is this. And it does not just apply to the sick; take a look at the so-called healthy man or woman, and you will see it there too. This thing called consciousness with which we are blessed is also our curse, for how should we be in the world? Should we be honest, or should we lie? Should we act as if we felt differently from the way we do, or should we allow all our fears and feelings to run riot and rule us? We question and doubt and fear and hesitate. This is the curse of humankind – that we do not know how to be any more. Perhaps we never did.'

Then Petit managed to get the old doctor to be quiet and told him to listen very hard. He hurriedly explained his theory, and now Morel paid very close attention, for he asked a couple of pertinent and perceptive questions, rapid fire, before allowing Petit to vanish into the night once more.

Who can Petit trust now? Who is he working for? Why? These questions chase each other around his tired mind. He makes it a fifty-fifty call whether he can trust Cavard, or not. He wants to believe that he can, and that worries him. Maybe he is letting that affect his judgement. But if he cannot trust his boss, then he believes he can trust the doctor, and, in a strange way, he knows he can trust Marcel too. He can trust Marcel to be Marcel, and not to lie. And if he cannot trust Cavard, then these two curious men are his only allies in the world. He thinks about them both: the doctor and the patient. Each is curious in his own way. It is not particularly easy to like either of them, not directly. Talking to Marcel is like swimming in fog, talking to Morel can be like trying to converse with an uninterested stone. Yet Petit has sympathy with both of them; he can empathise with the lonely man, the isolated man, and that is what all three of them have in common, albeit for very different reasons. Marcel, trapped by his unerring, tireless memory. Morel, who has dawdled his way down a cul-de-sac of uncaring medicine so far that perhaps there is no coming back. Petit, whose happiness was taken away in a few moments by a hand he will never even know. He thinks about Marie for a time, allowing himself to feel miserable, since there is nothing else to be done right now. Her face appears before him, but with anguish he realises that he is finding it harder to recall her image to mind, harder to remember his gentle fiancée as she actually was. Instinctively he reaches into his pocket for the portrait of her, and realises he did not bring it with him, a realisation that makes him feel sick. His head hangs.

He finds himself remembering (now aware enough to realise that he is remembering, that he is watching himself remember) that conversation he had when he first met Morel. Morel had begun to open his mind to the ways of the memory, of its meaning, of its central importance. That without memory, we would have no identity. He finds that he understands it much more now. Memories, he sees, are what make our personality; through a self-narrated linking of moments from our past, we create ourselves, define ourselves. And each memory is itself only a construction of infinitely small moments of time, each of which has no meaning in itself. A bee lands on your arm. A watch stops. A leaf falls. You feel afraid. None of these things has any meaning in itself. It is only the story we make by linking such moments together, and the narrative that creates, that gives us any meaning, that gives us a personality.

And if he can no longer remember Marie's face without the aid of a photograph, then does that mean it is as if she never existed?

Instead of Marie, Petit finds that he is holding that photograph of Ondine, her arrogantly beautiful head tilted on one side. He stares at her. She stares back, and it is she who wins.

Petit watches the stray, its nose hunting through the air for something elusive but clearly desirable, and he understands what the doctor meant. He is tired, hungry and cold. He has no plan but to wait for a train to Lyon and then see what might unfold there. He has probably thrown his job away and, since the attack last night, he knows his life is under threat, as he suspected it might be.

He wonders, *Who were those men, anyway?* Some henchmen of Delorme's no doubt, but how they knew what he was up to is worrying. It crosses his mind that there is a chance they followed him into the Gare de Lyon and were on the night train too, but he has kept a close lookout, and he doubts it. If they had, he would surely not have survived the journey, for he fell asleep at last towards the end, which would have given them ample opportunity to strike. If they traced him as far as the hospital however, then that would leave Morel and Marcel open to danger as well. As soon as the telegraph office opens, he will send a telegram, warning Morel to take precautions, to strictly forbid access to the hospital. If Delorme wanted to have Marcel shut away, so he could not reveal Delorme's blasphemous activities, then the Prefect must have believed Marcel was privy to what Ondine knew. That is a reasonable fear, Petit thinks, but by no means certain. Would Ondine have shared the full sordid details of her previous life with her husband? It seems both possible and impossible. But that must be what Delorme fears: that an investigation of Ondine's case would lead to him, too. Maybe now, now that matters have escalated, Delorme sees a simpler option: kill Marcel, kill Morel maybe. Kill *him*, Petit.

He is struck by an overwhelming wish not to be himself any more, but to be the dog. It sniffs around the station platform, scampering away when a porter swings a boot at it, trotting towards an early morning passenger now and again, hoping for handouts. Simplicity itself, it knows its place in the world, and doesn't think twice about how to do it.

Petit lifts himself from the crate and as the station clock chimes six o'clock a small and grimy café opens its doors for business. He enters and orders a string of coffees, which he nurses for the next hour, waiting for the telegraph office to open at seven, and for the train to Lyon half an hour later.

# MOMENTS

Two evenings later, Petit proves that his wild idea is correct. After a couple of days of hunting around the city, he has never once doubted that his hunch is right, that Ondine and Bishop will be found in Lyon. It was why Lucie intended to move there too – Lyon being home to the biggest theatre and cabaret world outside Paris. He reasons that if you're a cabaret performer and Paris is out of the question, it's short odds that Lyon will be your next best bet. Since most of the musical cafés, theatres and cabarets in the city are to be found in the old town, to the west of the rivers, that is where he devotes his attention.

The old town crouches, squashed between the Saône and the hill of Fourvière, at the top of which sits the basilica. Unlike the Sacré-Coeur this church is completed, but it has been put there for much the same reason, apparently to venerate God but, as everyone knows, in reality to celebrate the suppression of the socialist commune, just as in Paris. And just as in Paris it looms over the city, speaking of the power of the Church and its ever-watchful, ever-vindictive eye.

Petit has scurried through the narrow medieval streets of the district, making a list of the theatres and cabarets, and visiting them each in turn. Not once does he falter. He keeps his enquiries casual and vague. He plays the tourist, the young man of money come for some fun, and there are enough of those in Lyon for him not to attract anyone's attention. He doesn't know what he is looking for exactly, but he believes he will know it when he sees it. On the second evening, he finds himself perusing a playbill for the La Grande Rouge, a theatre-cum-cabaret tucked just off the Place Saint-Jean. Something about it catches his eye. It is somewhat newer than other posters he has seen, which have presumably been advertising the same bill of acts for months, if not years. This one is newly printed, and among a wide variety of acts it contains a listing for a hypnotist: the 'Séance de Magnétisme', presumably some kind of pastiche throwback to the days not so long ago when the craze swept through the parlours of rich ladies. On stage, no doubt there would be some lurid little twist to the affair.

Didn't Marcel mention that the American, Bishop, had worked such a routine in the States before coming to Paris? As Petit thinks harder, wishing for a moment that he had Marcel's gift, he becomes more certain of it. Yes, he's sure. He remembers that Bishop never did the act in the Cabaret of Insults because Chardon thought it dull and unimaginative.

It is a great moment. One by one, things that were no more than feelings, guesses, wishes almost, are becoming real before his eyes.

That evening, as he buys a ticket and sits towards the back of the small theatre, drinking wine by the glass as his thirst takes him, he feels an enormous sense of vindication. He knows that neither Ondine nor Bishop knows what he looks like. They do not even know he exists. They might worry that one day someone would come looking for them, but as far as they know their plan worked extremely well. This sense of anonymity gives him a sense of power, and he relaxes, actually enjoying the first few acts: some dance numbers and a comedian. From nowhere he becomes aware of something else, something remarkable. It has only been two days, but he realises that he has not done one clumsy thing in that time. Since every day usually brings at least a handful of slightly gauche actions, this in itself is something to be noted. But more than that, though he does not know how he knows, he is certain that the clumsiness has left him for good. He sits a little further back in his chair and takes a sip of Beaujolais, and says 'so' to himself, as if he is a clockmaker who has just figured out how to put a temperamental mechanism back together. Why should that be, he wonders, why should that be? He thinks about the fight with the two men outside the hospital, the way he moved without thinking about what he was doing, for there was no time for that. Skilful and strong. Not a trace of clumsiness.

Then the hypnotist comes on. Petit has never seen Bishop, only had a description of him. Bishop has never been in trouble with the law and Petit was never able to find a photograph of him. But the man on stage is clearly not French. His accent is obvious, though the language itself is not bad. What clinches it is when he calls for a volunteer from the crowd, a woman just a few seats from him puts her hand in the air and is invited on stage. It is Ondine.

Such an obvious trick! Do they get away with it every night? He can see why Chardon was against using it at the cabaret. What if someone returns another evening? Does Ondine change her appearance from time to time? Yet there is no mistaking it is her. He has gazed at her photograph enough times to be able to spot her at once, Ondine Després, back from the dead.

Inspector Petit sits back in his seat, and smiles to himself.

In another moment of time, far away in Paris, René Cavard is pondering a matter brought to his attention by Principal Inspector Boissenot: the matter of the missing inspector, Petit. Petit, Cavard thinks, what have you done now? Already their paths have crossed twice, and now it is his absence that is causing Cavard concern. Boissenot did not seem overly worried that one of his men has just upped and vanished. He threw his hands in the air and declared that the young man is probably at the bottom of the Seine. He probably put himself there because he never could get over that fiancée of his getting herself murdered, and anyway, didn't it all just go to show what he was always saying, that the end of the world is in sight?

Cavard is taking things more seriously. There was that conversation, after all, that evening, after work. That business about the murdered ex-courtesan and, oh God, Prefect Delorme. Cavard decides that he does not like the way this is falling out, one little bit.

Chef Cavard is liked well enough by the policemen of the Sûreté. He has been in charge of the judicial force for five years, and in a quiet way he has fought little battles, the right battles, to protect the budget, to argue for an increased number of detectives, to weed out corruption, which is rife both in his judicial investigative force and the *gardiens* of the municipal force.

His problems are twofold. First, it is true that his weight is not declining, especially not since he became deskbound. Second, he is not liked by those he refers to in his own mind simply as 'them'. By this he means the establishment; the press, or the sections of it on the right; the Ministry of Justice, whose foremost representative is Prefect Delorme. Matters were not helped by a misprint (and can he ever shake the feeling that it was deliberate?) in one newspaper, which, on the announcement of his appointment, called him not Cavard but 'Canard'. The duck. Unfortunately, the mistake turned into a nickname that he has not been able to rid himself of. And with every passing year, as he gets a little rounder and waddles a little more, the name seems ever more appropriate. Among his own men, the name is used affectionately, for the most part, and he does not mind that. It helps them to feel he is still one of them, and that helps them to be honest with him. But outside his men, it is a different matter. More than once the right-wing press have employed the headline 'Confit de Cavard', a reference to that most French of fat-laden foods, the *confit de canard*, salted duck leg cooked in its own fat, to describe a foul-up by his department.

He is staring from his window one morning, looking across the Place Dauphine. It is a cold November morning, the little triangular place providing inadequate shelter from gusts of wind that blow in from the river, over the Pont Neuf, to swirl the last leaves of the year into small eddies. He shivers, but barely notices how cold it is; his mind is wondering whether to follow things up with this young Petit, or whether to have him dismissed in his absence and sweep anything that comes along under the carpet. So Delorme had something to do with the dead girl. He paid for her services, possibly on many occasions. So what? That doesn't necessarily alter the obvious assumption that it was Marcel who killed Ondine. Yet Cavard knows that Petit is right about one thing. It is very odd that the Prefect's office should have weighed in to have the accused man declared insane, and incarcerated in Salpêtrière. That rings alarm bells in his head that he wants to ignore, but cannot.

What makes matters worse is the question of the examining magistrate, his greatest frustration as a police officer, and part of the mystifyingly stupid chains of command that make his life much harder than it needs to be. At the top of everything, on top of everyone, sits the Prefect, Delorme. He presides over the two arms of the police: the municipal police, the men on the street, controlled by twenty Commissaires, one for each arrondisse-ment of the city, who all report directly back to him; and the judicial police, of which Cavard is director. Chef Cavard has five principal inspectors reporting into him, and under them are around three hundred inspectors or, he wryly notes to himself, two hundred and ninety-nine since Petit went absent without leave. It would be simple enough were it not for the existence of the examining magistrate. These men were hand-picked by the Prefect. They reported to him, and only to him; in rank they were superior to everyone, even the Chef of the Sûreté. And yet fully *one quarter* of the chef's inspectors worked for the examin-ing magistrates, appointed on a case-by-case basis at their whim, not the chef's. It never made sense that someone else controlled his men, and in practice it could be as irritating as hell. Cavard got on well with some of the examining magistrates, many of them less so. Some seemed entirely in the pocket of the Prefect, others did their job as they were supposed to, with only the best interests of the law at heart. Either way they were powerful men: the examining magistrates appointed detectives to cases; they carried out initial questioning of arrested parties, often extracting confessions in the most unofficial ways. They were behind the practice of 'cooking' suspects in 'kitchens', the back rooms of station houses, not with their own hands of course, but through the roughest *gardiens*, the patrolmen.

With a nagging feeling, for he has forgotten who the examining magistrate is in Marcel's case, Cavard turns back to his desk and drags the file closer to him. He flips it open and reminds himself. His heart sinks. Peletier. Rarely has he come across a more unpleasant and conniving man. A careerist, still quite young but with his sights set high, Peletier was the sort to inform on his own mother if it brought him greater advancement. Cavard knew he was one of Delorme's cronies, and there and then he decides that he is too overworked and too afraid to take on this fight of Petit's. Whatever the young inspector has done, wherever he has gone, whatever he has found out, Cavard decides to opt for a quiet life, and turn a blind eye to anything that comes across his desk.

No sooner has he made that decision, however, than the day's dispatches are brought in by one of his two clerks. He has developed the habit over the years, not a good habit it must be said, of flicking through the whole pile of missives before tackling any of them. He knows he ought just to work his way through from top to bottom, because all of them are important or they wouldn't have ended up on his desk. However, he can never resist the urge to find out if one dispatch might be more important than the others. The result of this weakness is that within a few seconds he finds he is reading a communiqué from the Chief of Police in Lyon, who informs Cavard that he has one of his inspectors, a man called Petit, in his presence, who has insisted on the arrest of two performers from a cabaret in the city. Even now the two, an American man and a French woman, are in custody. Petit wants to arrange for their transport back to Paris. He looks at the date on the communiqué. It is marked URGENT. It is three days old.

Cavard manages to resist the urge to screw the paper up into a ball and toss it out into the winds of the Place Dauphine, but only just. He holds it in his hands, for a long, long time, reading it again, and over again, praying to God that Petit knows what he's doing.

Not so far away, but two days before Cavard receives this news, Dr Morel gets the second of two telegrams from Inspector Petit. In his whole life before, Morel has only ever received two telegrams; now he has had the same number again in as many days.

The first telegram was curious, alarming. It spoke of someone trying to convey too much information without the time or space to do so. It read: TAKE EXTREME CARE WITH PATIENT. AND SELF. DANGER.

At first, Morel had not paid it much attention. He was as busy as ever with Marcel. He had been working on the idea that in order to forget, Marcel needed to change the way his memories were laid down in the first place. If successful, it meant that Marcel would still remember everything that he already knew, everything that had already happened to him, but it might mean that he could be freed from the ever-increasing additional memories he was storing from day to day. In order to work on these matters, Marcel needed new memories to try to forget, and Morel knew that there should be a lot of them. Marcel's daily routine in the cell and the little time he was permitted outside would have been child's play for anyone to remember, so Morel had brought in reading material: vast amounts of reading material in the form of newspapers. One or two new papers a day was not nearly enough to trouble Marcel, and Morel had the additional conceit that he might be able to overwhelm Marcel's memory by sheer weight of information. So Morel had the archives of the hospital reading room emptied, and vast towers of old newspapers teetered against the wall in Marcel's chamber, while Mister Memory worked his way steadily through the diet of information, page by page. From time to time, though it was not his prime intent, Morel could not resist picking up a paper that Marcel had discarded and quizzing him on some trivial fact of news or gossip or even an advertisement from three, five, even eight years before. Each time he felt a return of that childish glee he used to feel when they had first met, that he was about to catch Marcel out, and each time he was disappointed. Each time *so far*, he told himself, and bided his time for the next chance to try to trip up his patient.

Once or twice, Marcel seemed to spend an extra long time reading this article or that; and there was even a moment when he stopped reading and held the paper out for Morel to see.

'Look,' he'd said, and showed the doctor a report about that café bombing, the one back in '94.

Morel blinked. 'What of it?'

Marcel almost seemed to smile. 'I wrote that! Or rather, Monsieur LeChat did. But he wrote it from what I told him. Almost word for word.'

Morel reads the article through, from time to time glancing up at Marcel, but Marcel seems lost again, afloat in an endless sea of remembering.

Engaged in these activities, Dr Morel paid very little attention to Petit's telegram until the porter on duty came to him one day and said that two rather suspicious men had been asking questions about Marcel, claiming to be relatives. What had puzzled the porter was that the men seemed to speak French with a foreign accent of some kind, and wasn't Marcel as French as could be?

Morel nodded at all this, saying nothing, and dismissed the porter, who seemed reluctant to leave until he had imparted one further piece of news. It happened, said the porter, that one of the orderlies, Miskov, was standing by the window of the gate-house when the men came. Miskov kept his mouth shut, just listened to everything they had to say, but when they went, he told the porter that the men's accent was Russian.

'I see,' said Morel, though he did not see at all. But he did speak to the director of the hospital and they agreed that they would put the younger, fitter members of their staff on gate-house duty for the time being, and that all visitors would have to show proof of who they were before admittance to the grounds.

That being done, Morel returned to his work with Marcel, and continued to try to overwork his brain with news that had passed into history, all the while trying different methods to block the formation of the memories in the first place. The form these methods took varied widely. He was indiscriminate in his approach; some tricks involved Marcel's cooperation.

'Try thinking about something else as you read,' Morel suggested one day. Another: 'Put one hand in your pocket as you read and focus on it. When you take it out again, you will not be able to recall what you have read.'

Marcel did recall what he had read, but he kept working hard on all Morel's ideas, some of which were enacted by the doctor. Morel tried making all sorts of noises as Marcel pored over the papers, or he would produce smells that filled the room with obnoxious or delightful scents. He tried administering certain herbs to Marcel, as poultices on the back of his neck or as teas to be drunk the night before. Still nothing worked, yet Marcel seemed happy, occupied with activities that surely pushed his mind harder than anything or anyone had before. A certain still-ness seemed to creep into his being; the doctor wrote in his notes that Marcel seemed calmer, more logical, more able to hold what he deemed to be a normal conversation, as if this gargantuan task of reading was finally occupying enough of his mind to create some inner tranquillity.

So Morel was happy, and his patient was as well as he had been in all the months at the hospital, when the doctor received his second telegram from Petit. This one was composed of only three words, reading: WE WERE RIGHT.

Morel took the telegram straight to Marcel that very moment. He waved it in the air as if it were news of a peace treaty or a royal birth.

'Marcel, my boy,' Morel said, his eyes flitting across his patient's face, not knowing how to explain, what to say, how to deliver the news. 'Marcel. You will be exonerated. You will be set free. You are not guilty.'

Marcel let the paper he was holding slide to the floor. He stood up silently. He did not understand. He could not understand. So Morel tried to explain it to him, told him about Petit's idea, showed him the telegram.

'What?' asked Marcel. 'What does that mean? We were right? Who is right?'

Morel shrugged. 'The policeman is generous. It was his idea. His theory. You didn't do it, Marcel. You didn't do it. You were tricked. It was elaborate, but it was a trick.'

Marcel sat down again, rubbed his hands across the back of his head, then stared at the wall. An infinite amount of memories began interconnecting with a second infinite amount of memories, and before his eyes, Morel saw all the hard-won progress they had made start to vanish. Marcel's face, his body, his very spirit seemed to diminish, there and then.

Before he disappeared entirely, Marcel had one last thought for Morel, one question.

'But why?'

Morel spread his arms out wide, and shook his head, for that was a question it might take a lifetime to find an answer to.

# AN EXCHANGE

November had become December. That Friday, the first of the month, Chef Cavard enters the citadel of justice that dominates the Quai des Orfèvres with renewed determination, having spent the night working through possibilities. For the thousandth time he wishes ardently that he had a telephone on his desk and could phone the Chief of Police in Lyon. No doubt he could arrange for access to a telephone, but there would be little point: the Lyon police are no doubt as stuck in the past as they are in Paris. Nevertheless, he will telegram to Lyon and arrange the details of Petit's return with the couple, who are accused of multiple crimes, foremost of which is murder. Though Cavard is not yet sure who has been killed, only that Ondine Després has not been, after all.

He stumps up the stairs to his office, calling to his clerk to come straight in for a briefing. The clerk, a somewhat ageing and nervous yet scrupulously efficient man, follows Cavard into his room, pad and pencil in hand.

'Telegram, to the Lyon headquarters, attention Chef Guérin,' he begins, but no sooner are the words out of his mouth than the clerk coughs, and holds up a hand as if to beg forgiveness.

'I'm sorry, sir,' the clerk begins, but then seems too tense to continue.

'What is it? Are you ill?'

Cavard looks at his clerk but sees that he is no paler than usual.

'No, sir. I am afraid that I was told to ask you to report to the Prefect this morning, first thing.'

Cavard says nothing. Inside he fights the urge to swear, but instead he merely tells the clerk to take the telegram first and get it sent off, and then he will go to see the Prefect.

'I'm sorry, sir, but I was told that you ought to see the Prefect straight away. Especially if you asked anything about Lyon.'

Now Cavard cannot hold his anger. 'Who the devil told you this?' he snaps.

'A clerk from the Prefect's office came over half an hour ago. He . . . well, he gave me to understand that it was rather important. Sir.'

Cavard waves the clerk away, and he scurries back out to his antechamber.

Cavard does not like being summoned to the Prefect's office at the best of times, and yet again it has something to do with that boy, Petit. When he gets hold of that young upstart, in private, he will tear him to pieces, he decides, even as he plops his hat back on his head, stomps down the stairs, and out into the bitter December morning. He puts his head down against the wind, crosses the Boulevard du Palais and slams through the door into the Préfecture. He allows himself some ire and some impatience with the staff on the desk, announcing his wish to see the Prefect.

The man behind the desk is not falling for it. He makes it plain he knows that Cavard has been summoned, and sends the chef on up to the first floor, by which time the walk and the climb up the stairs have somewhat dissipated his anger.

Just before knocking on the door, he squares himself. Then he gives two sharp raps on the wood, and tries not to be irritated that the Prefect allows five seconds to pass before calling him in.

Cavard is immediately aware that the air between them is laden with unspoken threat. Delorme barely makes eye contact as he nods at him, and points across the desk at the chair he wishes Cavard to sit in.

Cavard is tempted to take the other of the two, just to show he is not a dumb animal, but he prevents himself from doing so.

There is no point in winning trivial battles when a greater struggle is clearly about to emerge.

What happens next throws Cavard entirely.

'It seems,' Delorme begins, 'that congratulations are in order.'

'Prefect?'

Delorme is practising his usual nasty habit of spending more time looking at the papers on the desk in front of him than at the man he is speaking to.

'Yes,' he says, shuffling some pages for the sake of it. 'Your man, Petit, made quite a find down in Lyon.'

'Would you care to enlighten me?' Cavard says, and then tells himself off. Keep it civil, he thinks. Pretend the man is not the obnoxious little upstart that he so clearly is. He has risen so fast, he can barely contain his smugness at being better than everyone else. To Cavard's way of thinking, Delorme owes his meteoric rise to his ability to engineer popularity in the right places. It was not that long ago that Delorme was just a Commissaire of an arrondissement, now he is Prefect of Police, the youngest ever to hold the office.

Delorme's gaze lifts and fixes Cavard, but only for a moment. He smiles, and Cavard knows he's being got at, and successfully.

'Yes,' Delorme says, 'I will. It seems that this Ondine Després was not dead, after all. She had left the city, with an American. They were party to the murder of another girl, a mutual acquaintance, one, let me see, Lucie Rey. Your man worked this out and found them in Lyon.'

Cavard's mind is being made to work faster than it has done in a good while, and after a moment he is forced to concede that he can make neither head nor tail of this news.

'So the memory man, Després, is innocent?'

'That is not yet clear,' Delorme states, a little too fast, perhaps, something that Cavard notices even in his baffled state. 'We are trying to establish the full facts at the moment,' the Prefect continues.

Cavard has the sense of the ground shifting from under him. 'We?' he says.

'The examining magistrate. Peletier. You know him? A good man. He is working on certain new aspects to the case now. He has been reporting to me.'

Cavard takes a deep breath.

'You, sir? Isn't this all a little . . . beneath you?'

Delorme's head whips up, and he stares hard at Cavard without saying anything for a long, long time. Cavard does his best to hold his gaze, then smiles and lets his eyes slip to the side. He finds he is looking at a photographic portrait of the Prefect, and he remembers what Petit said about it. In that moment, Cavard realises he needs to play a much smarter game than the one he has been playing. He feels the Prefect's attention on him soften, fractionally, and he tries to take control of the interview.

'What can I do for you, sir?' he asks, smiling as genuine a smile as he can produce.

'Do?' asks Delorme, his voice full of condescension. 'I don't need you to do anything. The case is back in the hands of the examining magistrate. If we need further assistance from your department, I will let you know.'

'Very good,' says Cavard, yet he knows there is something else. There has been something underneath all this, something in the choice of language that Delorme has been using. Cavard knows he has maybe one chance left to learn something that is useful. He stalls for the chance to get it. 'Then why did you want to see me?'

Delorme does not look at Cavard. He picks up a piece of paper by the corner with his fingertips as if it is poisonous. It takes Cavard a moment to realise that the Prefect is lazily holding it out towards him, for him to take it. He does so, and starts to read, even as Delorme relates what it has to say.

'I asked you here because an incident occurred that concerns you and your department. Yesterday morning, your man, Petit, left Lyon with the Després woman and her lover, an American named Bishop. Along with Petit were two men from the Lyon station. It had been arranged for them to meet officers of the Paris police in Dijon to effect a handover from one force to the other.'

Cavard thinks, *Arranged?* Who arranged it? Which officers? None of his men have been requisitioned, that he knows of. Delorme must have sent some of his own men . . .

Delorme is not finished, however.

'It seems that an unfortunate incident occurred just after the changeover in Dijon. The party were travelling in the mail carriage at the back of the train, the arrested parties in handcuffs. Just after the exchange, it appears that the American, Bishop, managed to free himself and attacked his custodians. The details are not clear, but the police officers involved were forced to employ their weapons. In the struggle, the girl and the American were shot dead.'

Cavard stares at Delorme, speechless. Two captives, one of them a woman, attempted to overpower three armed policemen?

Yet still Delorme is not finished.

'Yes, an unfortunate turn of events,' he says, only now looking at Cavard again, 'especially as the inspector from your department was also killed.'

Cavard does not breathe, he does not move. He looks back at Delorme, very carefully choosing his next words.

'Killed?' he says eventually. His voice trembles and he tries to control it. 'How so?'

'I am waiting for the details. I understand that the American was strangling the inspector. That my men fired upon the assailant and your man was, unfortunately, also hit.'

Cavard says nothing, but he openly stares at Delorme with hostility. He says nothing, but his eyes say it all. You're lying. You're lying and you know you are. You think you can lie and scare me into letting this all slide away. But I won't.

With his mouth, Cavard says, 'Most unfortunate. Anything else, sir? I have a busy desk.'

Before Delorme has another chance to lie, Cavard rises to his feet.

'I'll take a copy of this report?' he says, waving the lies about Petit's death at the Prefect, before leaving as calmly as he can manage.

Outside, in the street, Cavard heads away from the Palais de Justice and goes north over the river, where, without knowing it, he sits in exactly the same seat, in the same café in the Place du Châtelet, where Petit once sat, confessing nothing to his friend Drouot.

He reads the lies of the report Delorme gave him once more, and knows it cannot be the case that a man and a woman in handcuffs managed to overpower three armed policemen. He would very much like to know who the two Parisian men were, but he knows they came from Delorme's inner circle. Cavard feels a spasm of guilt over Petit. He misjudged him. He had put him down as a young fool with loose ideas. Now he is dead. He finds himself picturing Petit's final moments, as the Prefect described them.

It is true that Bishop was a cabaret worker, and had picked up some escapology skills. In truth, he did not free himself from his handcuffs, which had been secured competently by the Lyon police. They were unlocked by Delorme's men, who met the train at Dijon. The handover was made, and the Lyon men left the carriage. Before the train had even fully left the station, Petit suspected something was wrong. He asked the two men who they reported to and what their names were, and when they refused to answer, the young inspector grew suspicious. One of the two men told Ondine to stand against the wall, and Petit immediately saw what was about to happen. Both the men from Paris had their guns pulled.

Ondine guessed it too. And Bishop, who tried to charge the nearest man, and was taken down with a bullet at close range. He lay on the floor, groaning. Ondine screamed, briefly, once, looking from her lover to Petit.

'I was dead,' she said, and there was a world of unspoken meaning behind it. For a moment, the man who'd shot Bishop hesitated. Petit took his chance, leaping towards the other policeman, even as he shot Ondine.

Petit's former clumsiness did not return to trouble him; he knocked his man down swiftly, with a clean blow to his throat. But there were two of them, and the other stepped back and in the same instant fired into Petit's chest, throwing him on to the floor. This same man turned his gun back on Bishop, firing once into his forehead, and it all happened so fast that there was not even time for anyone to make a sound.

Petit lay on the floor of the truck, his life running out of him. To outward appearances, he was already dead, but he could still hear, he could still think.

The man he'd knocked to the ground stood up, rubbing his throat.

'Quick,' he said, because the shots had been heard, the brakes of the train were grinding. He knelt down and unlocked Bishop's cuffs, then put his gun, which had fired only once, into Bishop's dead hand. His friend fumbled in Petit's jacket pocket and found a bundle of cash, money extorted by the dead couple from Delorme, to be returned to him. He searched the rest of Petit's pockets, hunting for something else perhaps, but found nothing.

By the time the train came to a halt at the far end of the station yard, and the platform guards arrived, the scene was set: the attempted escape, the inspector taken in the struggle, the American dispatched, and the girl caught by a wild shot.

Petit knew he was dying, and yet he did not die unhappily. The actions of the men from Paris proved he was right about everything: that they were involved in covering up Delorme's deeds, and that the Prefect was behind it. But more than that, as Petit lay with his eyes closed on the floor of the mail carriage, and his life left him, he had only one thought in his head, the memory of one person. Into his mind's eye came Marie, clearer than ever, as clear as the last time they had been together in life. And Petit was happy, because he knew he could give up struggling and fighting, that he could let go of all the questions about what to do, and how to be and how to live on without her, for he would be reunited with her, very, very soon.

In Paris, in his café, Cavard wonders about Petit's final moments. He orders a small jug of wine, and pours himself a large glass. Wordlessly he raises this generous measure to Petit's memory and drains it. Then he vows to bring Paul Delorme down, and yet he is afraid, he is more afraid than he has been in a long while.

Cavard guesses that Petit would have only kept in touch with him. Having taken the decision to trust him with the telegram, Petit wouldn't have been stupid enough to risk bringing anyone else into the business. So Petit must have requested that Guérin, the Chief of Police in Lyon, ask Cavard himself to arrange the dispatch of officers from Paris. Since Cavard never got that request, he now knows that Delorme's corruption reaches across the Boulevard de Justice and into the ranks of his own men.

# A FEW WORDS ABOUT MAGIC

Is Paris a fairy tale? If so, then all the world is too. The magical is all around us, though hidden and disguised so as to make it very hard to notice. It becomes un-commonplace. Yet still it's there if you look hard enough, and in the right way.

Morel has been working closer than ever with Marcel. With a flash of insight, he has been testing out other aspects of his personality, though at first Marcel is uncommunicative. The news that Ondine is not dead, that she merely pretended to die, that she tricked him into thinking he had killed her, is too much for him. Days pass. More days, and still Marcel cannot fathom how and why it can have occurred. How much did she have to hate him, he wonders, in order for her to do such a thing? What does that say about him? Is he truly so bad? He believes he must be, and days pass as he broods on that. All the time, something else bothers him too, something he has to accept: namely, that he didn't know the gun was loaded with blanks. When he pulled the trigger, he believed the gun to be loaded with live ammunition. So what does *that* say about him?

Marcel continues to torture himself with such thoughts, but Morel persists. One day, as the doctor walks across the gardens of the Salpêtrière, it occurs to him that by focusing exclusively on Marcel's memory he has treated him more like a slide under the microscope than a person. It is clear that there are other unusual things about Marcel, not just his memory. There is, of course, this inability to lie, something that still has not been disproven. And maybe there are other things too, which perhaps hold the answer, the key to his outrageous memory. Morel's theory is that rather than trying to walk through the front gates of the castle, there is some small sally port to the side or rear that will allow easier access, undefended. Thus he has switched his efforts to testing other aspects of Marcel, the man.

There is, for example, the question of his problem-solving abilities, for, at times, Marcel shows prodigious skill with puzzles in logic or mathematics.

'A man and his wife,' Morel said to Marcel one day, 'are picking mushrooms in the forest. The husband says to the wife, "Give me seven of your mushrooms and I'll have twice as many as you!" To which the wife replies, "No, give me seven of yours and we'll have the same amount." Now,' Morel finishes, 'how many mushrooms does each of them have?'

Marcel stared at Morel for a moment, and Morel was wondering whether he should have told him he was setting him a puzzle, or what all this business about forests was, for that was the kind of thing that could very easily fox him, when Marcel replied.

'She has thirty-five and he has forty-nine.'

Morel was impressed. 'Very good, Marcel. Very good. Most impressive.'

Morel was indeed impressed. He had tried that puzzle out on Chief Physician Raymond the day before and he had needed pencil and paper and ten minutes to figure it out. But when Morel asked Marcel to explain how he solved it, it took him fifteen minutes of a long and rambling story about the husband and wife and the forest and how tired they were and what their baskets were like and that it was a sunny day but shady under the trees and how when the husband bent over from tiredness and sat down next to the basket and then said 'aha!' that at the same moment he, that is to say Marcel, suddenly saw the answer, saw them handing mushrooms to each other, along with many more details of the forest around them.

All in all it takes Marcel about a thousand times longer to explain his method than it actually took him to think it.

Nevertheless, the answer is correct and his speed impressive. Morel tries him with other puzzles, with similar results, although occasionally he would get derailed by the images he saw as he worked through a problem.

On another occasion, Morel read a poem to Marcel, a simple poem, one learned by children in school. His patient was absolutely unable to grasp its meaning. Morel explained that the poem was about a man treading grapes, a man whose greed is aroused by the sight of the river of what will become wine, and no longer finds himself satisfied with his humble life. Marcel seemed stupefied by this explanation, and read the poem over to himself again and again, and was soon lost in a reverie from which he did not recover for some hours. Perhaps Morel's choice of subject matter was a foolish one, because after all this world of grapes and wine was the one in which Marcel had grown up.

Morel continues to broaden his investigations, all the while learning more and more, and begins to glimpse a fuller picture of Marcel in the process.

There is, after all, the question of Marcel's beliefs. He once claimed, for example, to be able to raise or lower his temperature at will, he even claimed to be able to lower the heat in one hand while raising it in his other. Morel tried to verify such claims with a thermometer, and though he saw some changes, he did not satisfy himself that the results were undeniable. Marcel also claimed to be able to cure himself. If he was able to concentrate properly upon some developing illness, he could imagine that it would pass, he said, and it would indeed pass. Of this, Morel could make no test, and he was more struck by what Marcel had to say about it in general.

'For me, there's no great difference between the things I imagine and what exists in reality. Often, if I imagine a thing is going to happen, it does. Of course, I realise it could just be coincidence, just chance, but deep down I think it's because I pictured it that way.'

How many moments were there in his life, Morel wondered, when his imagination succeeded in convincing him of something, even though his reason ought to have thrust it aside? Some grain of magic would remain, tucked away in some remote part of his awareness, some naively magical thought. And how many nooks and crannies were there to the man's mind where imagination would become reality, as in a fairy tale?

Such were Morel's musings upon Marcel, and this was the new direction that his work was about to take, when it all came abruptly to an end.

They come for Marcel one cold and dark afternoon in the first week of December. A fuss at the gatehouse escalates, so that Morel hears their approach even as he works with Marcel in the chamber. Moments later, the door opens and Miskov stands looking flustered and angry behind three men: two *gardiens*, and someone who clearly is in charge of them, a man in plain clothes, the type, Morel can see immediately, who knows he need listen to no one but himself.

Miskov begs Morel's understanding, that these are policemen and would not take no for answer when told they need an appointment to see anyone, that they cannot just come in to the hospital.

Morel draws himself up. With his sense of propriety aroused, and his anger set, he rails against these intruders, but they are not overawed by a shortish and elderly doctor with a white beard and watery eyes. The man in plain clothes announces himself to be the Commissaire of the 6th, and that he has an order signed by no lesser person than Prefect Delorme; they are to remove Marcel Després to the station house, where he is to be held indefinitely.

'You cannot do this!' Morel declares. 'You have no jurisdiction here! You have no right to take a patient of mine!'

It all does no good. Within minutes, Marcel is being escorted to the gates of the hospital, where he's bundled into a waiting Black Maria, which speeds away into the dark streets.

At the commissariat, the station house of the 6th arrondissement, Marcel is shut up in the same cell he was placed in nearly
six months before, upon his arrest. He sits on the low, hard
bench fixed to the wall and disappears into his mind, while
outside two guards keep watch.

A few hours later, there is a visit from a man who calls himself
Peletier. He explains to Marcel something about who he is,
which Marcel doesn't understand. He only understands that he
is no longer under arrest for the murder of his wife, but instead
for the rape and murder of Lucie, a crime he concocted and
enacted with two parties, now deceased.

So, for the second time, Marcel learns that Ondine is dead.
He thought he had killed her, in a jealous fit of rage. Months
passed before he learned from the doctor that he had not, something he was still struggling to comprehend, and now, he learns
in a moment, unexplained, that she is dead again.

It is too much. Unable to bear it, Marcel vanishes into himself
once more. Questions pile in, question after question, yet above
them all is one more prevalent than the others, which colours
everything else he is thinking. He is now on trial for a murder he
knows he did not commit. He did not kill anyone, it seems, and
definitely not Lucie. Yet he *had* killed Ondine. He had *thought*
he had, and even though he has now been shown to be innocent,
it does not remove the fact, the very obvious and appalling fact,
that at the time he pulled the trigger of the gun, he wanted to kill
her. And if he wanted to, what does it matter whether he actually did it or not? The logic of that puzzle seems undeniable.

If he is to be tried for the death of Lucie, which he fully
believes he did not do, then so be it. In his mind, he is still guilty
of murdering Ondine, for he pulled that trigger, he pulled it five
times, and at that moment, he wanted her dead.

Such thoughts torture Marcel as he sits in the cell, and his
mind works so feverishly that it blots out everything else. He is,
for example, completely unaware of a conversation that takes

place outside in the office of the commissariat, even though it is plain for all to hear through the walls. At the conclusion of this discussion, the door to the cells opens, and a third policeman joins the other two.

He nods at them, silently; they nod back, a little bemused.

Marcel sees nothing.

# A LETTER FROM THE DEAD

Cavard has not been idle. Far from it; he has been very busy indeed, yet he has been extremely careful not to let his activities be seen. He knows that there are men in his department, in the Sûreté itself, who are in Delorme's pocket. This does not surprise him: the Prefect must have made some allies in his time as Commissaire, and no doubt he found it expedient to maintain these allegiances when he moved across the Boulevard de Justice into the Préfecture. The real question for Cavard is who these people are, but he recognises that this is a longer struggle than he has the time and energy for, so, instead, he turns the problem on its head, and asks himself whom he knows he can trust.

There are three inspectors he knows of. He believes he can trust them for they all quietly share a sympathy with the same branch of politics that he does, the extremes of which were repressed so brutally less than thirty years ago during the time of the Commune – the politics of the left. No one now declares themselves to be a Communard, and Cavard is no exception. Yet he knows from his time before he was made chef that there are a few men, like him, who still believe in the principles behind that movement, that the people should rule the state, not the other way around. Of course, to the outside world, all policemen are politically neutral. In practice, there are leanings and there are factions, the very same divisions that Delorme has made good use of in rising so far, so fast.

Cavard has briefed these three inspectors, privately, outside the walls of the Quai des Orfèvres, and has charged them with bringing him information about Peletier. It is from these three inspectors that Cavard learns that Delorme has had Després moved out of the hospital and placed back into a cell in the 6th.

This in itself is a stroke of fortune. Delorme would really be pushing things to have Després taken to a station house in an arrondissement other than the one where his crime was committed, and this is lucky indeed for Cavard, because though Delorme has Peletier in his control, and many others besides, the Commissaire of the 6th is an old friend of Cavard's. Yes, he will do what he's ordered to by the Prefect, but it does at least allow Cavard to send a man or two of his own to keep watch on Després as he sits in the cell. For Delorme is not the only one with contacts in another man's department; Cavard himself has cultivated a few contacts in the municipal police force, and it is time to make use of them. There is, after all, no need to allow a repeat of the incident on the train at Dijon, Cavard reasons, no need at all.

As it is, Cavard is left to ponder this move of Delorme's. First, he had Marcel plucked from the station house and placed in a hospital, declaring him to be criminally insane. Now, nearly six months later, he overturns his own decision and has the prisoner removed from the Salpêtrière and re-arrested, this time for the rape and murder of the other cabaret worker, Lucie Rey. This makes no sense to Cavard, and it troubles him greatly.

He knows that Petit was right: that Delorme has something to hide: his connection to the dead Ondine Després. All Cavard can conclude is that matters have developed. That things, unknown to him, have been changing. That it must have been enough to have Després locked up and isolated from the criminal justice system all those months ago. Yet now, something has forced Delorme's hand, something powerful enough for him to have three people murdered – for Cavard is in no doubt that Delorme is behind the deaths of Petit, Ondine and Bishop – and to bring Després himself back into the realm of the law. But why?

That is what is nagging at Cavard, but even as it does, there is another suspicion eating away at him: he is certain that Delorme will be having him watched. It is not possible that Delorme would *not* take this step – both men know that they dislike each other, and that some bigger battle than the murder of a nude dancer is at hand. Cavard was an inspector himself once; he is now the Chef of the Sûreté. He knows how things are done, he knows the fundamentals of policing. The press and the lurid detective novels that people buy in cheap editions have one view of the work of the police inspector. To their way of thinking, crimes are solved by the application of the mind; the quick-witted policeman and the wealth of modern techniques at his disposal are all that is required to unravel even the most complex of cases and catch the criminal. Clues are found, theories followed, evidence is measured and studied, and the guilty are caught and brought to justice.

In practice, Cavard knows, things are rather different. All this fuss about Bertillon and his system of bodily measurement, for example. Cavard's nose wrinkles as he thinks of it. Bertillon is a bit of an idiot, whose system was only trialled because his father pulled some strings. As far as Cavard can tell it has done almost nothing to aid and abet the methods of the Parisian policeman to date. Thank God they have not yet succumbed to this business with fingerprints, he thinks. What nonsense is that? Do criminals generally walk around the scenes of their crimes with paint on their hands? And so what if everyone's prints are different; how to keep track of them all? Cavard knows that there are other, younger minds in the department who are pushing for all such new scientific developments, and yes, maybe he is stuck in the past, but for now he would rather rely on the only two proven methods at his disposal: namely surveillance and bribery. Of bribery, there is little to be said; if only the press, if only the public knew that ninety per cent of crimes solved are solved by one criminal informing on another, and that the wheels of that process are oiled by money, they would have a very different view of the police inspector. Cavard knows full well that were the truth known, it would be divisive, explosive. Even within the police, different factions hold opposing views about the morals of using criminals to solve crimes. Cavard does not make such judgements, he only knows that without bribery, and sometimes more physical coercion, criminals would not inform on each other. And once a tip-off has been extracted, then the only other really useful tool the policeman has comes into effect – surveillance. So much can be gained by careful, covert watching, but it is a slow business sometimes, and an expensive one in terms of manpower.

Yet Cavard knows it is his best bet. So he has not only briefed his three inspectors, he has briefed them to take the utmost care that they in turn are not being watched. Only to make contact when they know they can safely do so. Further, Cavard himself is practising the same care; he believes he will catch Delorme out, sooner or later. He already has the photograph that Petit gave him that day by the bridge, and he could take it to the Minister of the Interior right now or, better yet, he could take it to the press. But something tells him that there is more to play for, and that he should not show his hand too soon. And in the meantime, Cavard must keep Després alive in that cell, and do anything he can to stall his trial.

So yes, placing a *gardien* of his own choosing in the commissariat to 'help' watch Després was a risk, but one he knows he can defer slightly – he has let it be known that it was the Commissaire's decision. Nothing to do with the Chef of the Sûreté.

So a kind of stalemate endures for a week or so.

Cavard hears that a date has been set for Marcel's initial hearing, in three days' time, otherwise all is quiet. A thought occurs to him. Before, when Marcel was accused of the murder of his wife for adultery in their own home, his punishment would have been much less severe. The most he would have received would have been a short prison term, possibly with labour, but in either case, one that could have been commuted for good behaviour in a few years. Now that he is charged with the rape and murder of someone other than his wife, and without the 'excusing' factor of adultery, the sentence will be very different: it could mean the guillotine, though more likely transportation to the penal colony of Devil's Island, the 'dry' guillotine. For death there is almost as inevitable as with the falling blade, if without the same quantity of flowing blood.

And so the stalemate would have continued when, one day, Cavard receives a communication from beyond the grave.

# DR MOREL

Sunday, 10 December. The city freezes. Ice has encased the river with a tight grip, and here and there skaters take their chances, as they do also on the lakes of the Bois de Boulogne. Along the boulevards, wooden stalls have been set up and brought Christmas with them; from the outlying quarters families have come to gaze at colourful presents and toys for sale, drink hot wine and eat chestnuts, hot from the brazier.

At every street corner, itinerant musicians play their music and sing songs, and are joined by the rough crowds that gather round; these are not songs for the drawing room but they are popular and bring cheer to everyone.

Down the Rue de Rivoli, Chef René Cavard spends some rare time with his family. His wife has her hand tucked behind his arm; their three children skip on ahead and hurry back when they get too far away, then start again, for they are eager to see what is for sale, and Christmas is not so very far off.

Madame Cavard leans her head against her husband's shoulder and smiles, watching her two girls and their little boy all in a good mood for once, and René seeming as calm and happy as he has in a long while.

Cavard is far from quiet inside, however. Yes, if he stopped to notice, he would see that on the outside he seems less irritable than has been usual the last few years, but that is only because he has found something that is giving him purpose and direction. Only now does he realise what he has been missing. So he is happy to play the contented husband, and at this moment, it is more than play. He *is* content. But he is not unwatchful, and

276

even as they stroll along the street, Cavard keeps an eye out for
Delorme's men. Just because it is Sunday does not mean they
will take the day off, but Cavard has seen no one who he really
suspects of being a policeman, and no one seems to be following
them, except that for the last fifteen minutes he has noticed an
old man shuffling along not far away. He has stopped when they
stop and moved on again when they have. He could be a beggar,
waiting for the right moment to stretch out his palm, but he is
well dressed. He moves with a strange, shuffling walk, with his
feet turned out, and on three occasions he has made eye contact
with Cavard, with pale, watery eyes.

Cavard stops looking at him.

'Justine,' he says to his wife, 'will you see to the children for a
moment?'

Madame Cavard frowns. 'Is something wrong?'

'Far from it, but Christmas is coming. For everyone, not just
for the children.'

Justine Cavard laughs, and smiles, and walks on ahead to the
children, telling René as she goes not to spend too much on her.

Cavard stops walking, and turns. As he expected, he finds the
old man at his side immediately.

'Can I help you, sir?'

'Cavard?' says Dr Morel, and when Cavard nods, the old man
holds out his hand.

'I need to speak to you,' he says.

'How did you find me?'

'I have been following you. I was told where you lived; I
followed you here by cab.'

Cavard looks up and down the street. Justine is looking at
toys with the children, but really, this place is too public. He
nods at a café in the arches that line the north side of the Rue de
Rivoli.

'Meet me there in ten minutes,' he says, without looking again
at the old man.

Dr Morel does as he is told. Even he has now understood the need for caution. He was very careful to check that he was not followed out to Cavard's house, and he told the cab driver to keep his distance as they made their way back into the city this morning.

He finds a table for two in the café, which since it is so cold outside is very busy, and sits facing the door, waiting for the policeman to return.

When Cavard does, he is in a very different mood.

They are interrupted briefly as a waiter comes with Morel's coffee and takes Cavard's order.

The waiter gone, Cavard takes control, speaking quietly, but in as relaxed a fashion as he can muster.

'Who are you?'

'My name is Dr Lucien Morel. I am—'

'I know who you are,' Cavard says. 'Forgive my interruption, but I don't have long. I do not wish to keep any more secrets from my wife than I have to. I presume this has to do with the case of Marcel Després?'

Morel nods. 'I have something for you,' he says, and from inside the depths of his large woollen overcoat he pulls out a large envelope. 'I received this almost a week ago. I confess I was afraid to know what to do, when you read it you will see why, but then I decided . . .'

Cavard is no longer listening. As casually as he can, he opens the lip of the envelope and peers inside. He slides out a letter, folded in half, and sees that there is a collection of photographs as well. Even the most cursory glance shows him that the pictures are better left alone for now.

He reads the letter instead.

*My dear Dr Morel,*

*You will have to forgive me, but I do not know who to turn to. You and I have each concerned ourselves with the case of Marcel Després, and though we started from different*

*positions, I think we have moved closer to each other in our
appreciation of the man in your care. I am sending this to you
because I do not know whom I can trust within the police,
even within the Sûreté. I ask that you hold on to these
photographs, and this letter, until I return to collect them from
your care, but if I do not, if you have not heard from me in
any way by the 5th of December, then we will have to take
our chances. I am not certain whom to trust because I know
there are enemies within the Sûreté offices, but if you take this
envelope to the top, it will prove one of two things. If nothing
happens, we will know that Cavard belongs to the enemy
camp. Or perhaps he is a good man, in which case you will
soon know . . .*

At this point, Cavard looks up sharply at the old doctor, who
stares back at him expectantly, with a mixture of confusion and
hope on his face. His eyes water, and he dabs at them with a
handkerchief. He says nothing, and Cavard keeps on reading.

*I am about to escort the two persons of whom I spoke to you
from Lyon back to Paris. This has been arranged by the chef
here, Guérin, with Cavard directly; he is sending men to meet
me in Dijon. This in itself has given me hope that we can trust
Cavard, and gives me the courage to urge you, if I do not
return to Paris, to go to him yourself and show him the
enclosed photographs. The girl is the supposedly dead wife of
Marcel Després. Cavard will know who the man is, even if
you do not recognise him yourself from likenesses in the press.*

*You must give these to Cavard, the photographs and this
letter, for they are proof that I have stumbled across some
hideous business that the man in the pictures will do anything
to conceal. He has had Marcel declared insane in an effort to
prevent his case coming to court, for that might well lead to
an investigation that would prove more than awkward. I do*

*not know exactly what these facts are, as yet, but I suspect
they are something more than the lurid scene in the pictures,
though that alone is probably enough to have him removed
from office. Tell Cavard these photographs were in the
possession of the 'dead' woman. They are dangerous. Now
that Ondine is found, it is my task to make sure she, and I,
reach Paris alive.*

*I've written Cavard's home address on the back of this
letter. Do not go and find him at the Quai des Orfèvres – you
must find him at home. And if I do not return, and you are
forced to act on this letter, then you will know that you must
take extreme care, at all times.*

*Yours in good faith,*
*Laurent Petit, Inspector de la Sûreté*

Cavard reads the last lines over again, and then, carefully, slides
the top photograph a short way out of the envelope. What he
sees makes him nearly gasp out loud, and he slides the picture
back hurriedly. There is Delorme, once again, clearer in this
photograph.

'Well,' says the old doctor, but not as a question. It is a state-
ment of the fact that Petit played his last cards, and now, so has
Morel. Everything therefore depends on Cavard now.

'Well,' says Cavard. 'So you knew my inspector?'

Morel nods. 'An impetuous young man, but I liked him well
enough. Does this really mean . . . ?'

'Inspector Petit was killed in an incident on the train returning from Lyon. So was the woman of whom he spoke. This
now only leaves Marcel Després for the man concerned to take
care of.'

'Who is this man? I didn't recognise him. I do not read the
newspapers so very much.'

'Maybe it's better that you don't know,' says Cavard, but
Morel shrugs.

'I suspect innocence is not going to help me now, should danger come.'

Cavard sighs, and hangs his head. 'Delorme,' he whispers.

The doctor blinks, twice, forcing water from his eyes, which he dabs away.

'What are you going to do?'

'There are the dossiers,' Cavard says, more to himself than to Morel. He is thinking things through. 'The *dossiers blancs* – we hold a file on everyone in the Sûreté archives, and when I say everyone, I mean everyone. Every public figure, every politician, every Chef of the Sûreté itself. Even the Prefect. If there are any rumours about him at all, that's the place to start. I have to go. My wife . . .'

Cavard makes to stand up, then, before he is even halfway out of his seat, sits down again, acting unconcerned.

'Maybe I will finish my coffee first,' he says, looking over Morel's shoulder.

The old doctor is not a trained policeman. He sees Cavard's gaze and cannot help but turn to see a table on the other side of the room, where three men catch his eye, then look away. They are all in their thirties, and all three look as if they were built for action and movement.

'How long have they been there?' Cavard whispers into his cup.

'They came in when you were reading the letter,' Morel says.

'And you didn't think to warn me?'

'I am not a policeman, sir, I do not know the rules.'

There is a silence for a long while, during which Cavard sneaks another look across the room.

'Delorme's men, no doubt,' says Cavard.

'No, I don't think so,' Morel says, making Cavard look up at him, despite his best sense.

'Why not?'

'They were speaking Russian. There was a lull in the conversation in the room. I heard them speaking Russian, just for a moment. I presume the Prefect doesn't employ Russians in the Paris police?'

'You're sure?'

Morel thinks of Miskov, and of the experiment with Marcel and the dictionary. For a moment he almost mentions that there were Russians calling at the hospital, claiming to be relatives of Marcel's, but he is not a policeman, and he does not think that it is relevant.

'Quite sure,' he says. 'Who are they?'

Cavard doesn't reply at first. He cannot help but take one more look across the room before he answers.

'Okhrana, I suspect. Tsarist secret service.'

Morel's eyebrows rise. 'Here? In Paris?'

'There are many things of which the people of this city are unaware,' Cavard says, smiling. 'The presence of the Tsar's agents is just one of those things.'

'But why are they tolerated? Why are they not stopped? Removed?'

'Stopped from what?' Cavard says. 'Their presence here is tolerated for very good reasons. They can be useful. At times.'

And at other times, Cavard thinks, they can be difficult customers. He himself has had little to do with them, but there are some stories that make his hair stand on end.

'And their presence here today only proves what we have been discussing. There is something bigger going on here than the private perversions of powerful men, which I do not believe are enough to bring Delorme to kill. Not because he's above that sort of thing, but because it's messy, can lead to all sorts of other problems. No, I think Petit was right. There's something bigger in his past, something he fears Ondine knew, and who knows what she told Marcel . . . ?'

'So?'

'So now I must go or it will be my wife who I am afraid of.'

He stands, and places his hat on his head.

'But . . .' begins Morel, with a wild look of panic in his eyes.

'You will be fine. It is broad daylight. Wait fifteen minutes. If they are still here, pay and leave as normal. Take a cab straight back home. You live at the hospital? Very good. See your guard is doubled on every gate. Good day.'

Cavard leaves, realising he should have added one more thing. *Thank you, Doctor*, he thinks. *Thank you.*

There is one more matter for him to think about now. The Russians. Were they really Okhrana men? Or just tourists, who by chance happened to find the conversation of an old man and an overweight policeman very interesting?

Cavard knows the truth. It's time to move a little faster. It's Sunday, but he can send Justine home in a cab, and he can get into the archives with no one seeing him apart from the weekend watchmen, who will defer to his rank. He is convinced the answer lies in Delorme's *dossier blanc*. Cavard knows he must hurry, for Monday morning will bring Després's initial hearing, and after that, time will be very short indeed.

He dispatches his wife and children back to safety, and then finds a quiet street corner to look through all the photographs. As he does, he is horrified to see well-known faces in the pictures. Among them, quite undeniably, is the Minister of the Interior.

# MAY AMONG THE VINES

It is May 1884. Marcel walks down from the road, cutting through the vineyards to take a more direct route to the village. He has been to Montmort-Lucy to speak to the ironmonger about some work for his father. He left early, when a frost was still biting the ground. Now it's midday, and though it's early in the spring, the sun is strong and the vines are dripping with dew, their leaves steaming as the sun moves overhead and catches them. There is nothing more fresh on the whole of the earth, thinks Marcel. The vines show the very first sign of their fruit: tiny green dots the size of pinheads that will become heavy clusters of grapes by the early autumn. He has seen it many times, but still it delights him. How things grow. He is seventeen years old.

As he walks, he thinks. He counts every time he has walked down between the rows of vines like this, and is over a hundred before he loses interest and remembers that he is supposed to stop at the *boulangerie* and collect bread before coming home. His mother is unwell, a rare occurrence, and has not gone to work, though it is a Saturday. Somewhere out in the endless vineyards, sounds of people working drift over to him.

Something white flutters at the corner of his vision and he turns his head as he keeps walking. There is someone in the row next to him, though he cannot see who it is; just a pair of bare feet and the bottom of a white skirt. He can guess from the way she moves and from the design of her dress that it is Ginette, and he guesses that she knows he is there, for he realises that she has been keeping pace with him.

The row of vines end, and they step out, on the edge of the vineyard, at the edge of the village, on the border between the two, and meet.

'Hello, Marcel,' says Ginette. 'I thought that was you walking there.'

Marcel nods. 'Hello, Ginette,' he says. He looks down at her feet. 'You don't have any shoes on.'

'The soil is so cool and wet. And the vine leaves are wet, too. You know?'

She shifts on her feet, and her cheeks are tinged with pink.

Marcel says nothing, because he doesn't know what to say. He remembers the *boulanger* will be closing soon. He looks at Ginette again.

'My mother is ill.'

'Oh,' says Ginette, 'I'm sorry. Shall I ask Father to come and see her?'

Marcel remembers that his father told them they couldn't afford a doctor and that it was nothing too serious, so he knows what to say.

'No.'

Ginette blinks, and now she does not know what to say either.

'I'm going to get some bread,' Marcel says.

He leaves.

'Goodbye, Marcel,' Ginette calls as he goes, and he turns and waves, smiling.

'Goodbye, Ginette.'

Marcel remembers it all from the cell at the back of the commissariat in the 6th. He plays it over and over again in his mind, this tiny exchange. He could have chosen any of the moments between them, but today this is what comes to his mind: he was buying bread when his mother was ill, and Ginette had no shoes on. Her feet were muddy; the hem of her skirts too. This was all before the incident with the bee sting, where there was no bee.

He is trying to understand something about this exchange; something that a more normal man would have realised long before, but although he knows that there is something to be understood, it remains just beyond his grasp, elusive, tantalising and mysterious.

Marcel starts again at the beginning.

He walks down the hill from the road, cutting through the gently sloping vines to the village, and there are Ginette's muddy feet in the row next to him.

# THE DOSSIER OF PAUL DELORME

Chef Cavard greets the two watchmen at the Quai des Orfèvres as if it's common practice to come to work on a Sunday. He does not carry it off, and the two men peer curiously back at him through the little hatch in the wall. They are so confused by his presence that they even seem unaware that he is asking them to let him in. They know who he is. Cavard, the head of the Sûreté. But that he is asking to be let into the building on a Sunday is almost too much for them. One is old, the other older still. Mostly these men are former soldiers who earn a pittance watching for intruders, fires and other incidents when the offices are closed. He wonders if he should have tried one of the smaller doors to the side of the building, but no doubt he would have faced the same mystification anywhere; he must be the first Chief of Police ever to show his face on a Sunday. He hesitates between telling them that he has urgent and important business (which is, after all, true) or that he has left something behind. An umbrella, or such, which is also probably true. In the end he decides on a simple course.

'Open the damn door or I will have you both sacked,' he barks, and before another minute has passed he is striding down the deserted and darkened corridors, heading for the archives in the basement.

As he waddles down the steps to the archives, he only now realises the problem: he does not have a key. The head archivist and his assistant have a key, but they are not here. The watchmen will have a key, but Cavard does not want to ask them; the whole point of coming on a Sunday is to conduct an enquiry off the record.

He tries the handle of the door, and rattles it gently, looking behind him and up the steps as he does so, furtively. He forgot to check if he was being followed as he came in off the street, the business with the watchmen having distracted him for a moment. Yet he knows that there can be no Okhrana agents in the building, nor any of Delorme's men; it is merely reflexive guilt that makes him glance over his shoulder.

He considers his options. The double doors are half glass. Beyond he can see where he needs to be, murky in the faint light that seeps down from fanlights that lead to the pavement level. A sharp tap with the elbow and he can climb through. Probably. At least, he might have been able to ten years ago . . . But also, ten years ago, he knew how to do other things. He pats his pockets and finds his fountain pen, lifts it up in the gloom and pings the clip on the cap.

It was a present from his wife, but he sees no other option, and he prises the clip out and bends it sideways, leaving the cap itself as a useful handle. He kneels slowly down beside the lock, and starts to work.

The lock is not complicated. Though the building itself is well fortified, internal doors are not seen as a threat, for only policemen will be inside the building. On this occasion, however, the policeman in question happens to be the Chef of the Sûreté, who will be disgraced, lose his job and his pension if he is caught breaking into the archives. So be it, he thinks. He let that young inspector down, badly, and the only way he can think of making amends is to prove whatever it was that Petit suspected. In addition, he genuinely believes that the city of Paris will be a better place if Delorme is removed from office.

A minute more and Cavard feels the little metal tooth that he is pushing finally flick over inside the barrel of the lock, and the door pops open.

A minute later, in the half-light, he discovers that he will be defeated. Most of the archives are low-level security, but the *dossiers blancs* are quite the opposite. They contain highly secret information about the most powerful men, and women, in France. Having checked in a file card system on the archivist's desk, Cavard reads that the dossiers are kept in the strongroom. A room beyond a door that stands behind the desk. He curses himself for acting without thinking; he would have known this if he'd given himself a minute to think first.

To be sure, Cavard steals round the desk up on to the little platform, and tries the handle of the strongroom. It is locked, firmly, and the lock is a much finer precision piece, consisting of a Swedish-made four-pin cylinder, in combination with a permutation lock. He has neither the skills nor the tools to pick the cylinder lock, and even if he had, he would still need the code for the wheels of the permutation lock.

It can't be done. He thumps a hand against the metal door of the strongroom, once, and then leaves, having the sense to make a detour to his office, where he indeed finds an umbrella he can convincingly display to the watchmen on his way out.

As he sets off for home, darkness is falling across the city. He broods. The only means of getting that dossier is by making a request for it from the archivist himself, and in order to obtain permission the archivist needs the written approval of the very man Cavard wishes to investigate: the Prefect, Paul Delorme.

It is as he broods on this puzzle that he realises that in his dismay at being defeated and in his hurry to leave before being discovered, he left the outer door to the archives unlocked.

# MOREL MAKES A DISCOVERY

When we stop loving, it becomes impossible to go on. Whatever the object of our love was, a person, an idea, a career, when the love for it vanishes, so does the desire to continue. To do so from that point is to move like a mindless machine, because it is what we are made to do, not because it is what we want to be.

These are the thoughts that crowd into Dr Morel's mind one morning as he crunches through an early snowfall that has covered the courtyards of the Salpêtrière. He walks, but with no particular energy. His strange gait, however, at last has a purpose, now no longer clearing imaginary snow but the real thing. Though he is unaware of it, he clears a neat little pathway as he goes.

What has died? His desire for the truth. It has finally dawned on him that although he has spent his whole life seeking the truth, about mental *illness*, about what caused his patients to be the way they are, he has been seeking an illusion. There is no such thing as the truth, that is what he has now learned, and he has learned it because of Marcel.

The only question he now asks himself is why studying this strangest of strange men with his perfect memory has finally brought him to this realisation. He is close to understanding, but for now, this morning, in the cold, in the snow, the connection eludes him.

With this love of the pursuit of truth suddenly dead inside him, he finds it takes an almost unbearable effort of will just to go through the motions of the morning's rounds, and bitterly but with some comfort he tells himself that at least he is an old man. He will not have to be troubled long by this emptiness.

In its place, Morel sees just one tiny spark of desire: he would like to make Marcel's life easier. He wishes he could have 'cured' his memory, but there is no hope of that; his patient has been taken away from him and if what the police-man, Cavard, said is true, he will be tried and possibly executed. That at least will bring an end to Marcel's maze-wandering mind, and the suffering that has gone with it. But Morel finds that he would at least like to speak to Marcel once more, and perhaps see if there is any way of making what may be the final days of his life a little easier. He determines that if he is allowed, he will visit Marcel in his imprisonment, before the end, what-ever that might be, comes.

That same Monday morning, Cavard faces no choice but to summon the chief archivist to his office, a man he barely knows. He could not risk returning to the archives to re-lock the door on Sunday. Instead he tried to arrive early and make good his error, but even at six he found the building crawling with too many people to take the chance.

He has spent two hours bitterly chewing over the possibilities, and decides he has to gamble. It still takes half an hour for the archivist to arrive in Cavard's office, and when he does, he is clearly resentful at being summoned.

Gilbert, the archivist, gives off the air of a man permanently lost in the stacks, while at the same time clearly believing that everyone else is lost, not him. He mutters something about doors and Cavard, as innocently as possible, asks what the matter is.

'The doors to the archive,' Gilbert says, 'were found unlocked this morning.'

'Who found them so?' asks Cavard.

'I did,' says Gilbert, and Cavard wonders why he didn't say that in the first place. 'I left ahead of Monsieur Tissot on Friday, and he was to lock up. He obviously did no such thing but now denies the possibility, even the *possibility*, that he was remiss in his responsibilities and failed to do his job. I have to consider how to take this matter to a disciplinary level and meanwhile Tissot himself is creating all—'

'I unlocked the door,' says Cavard, so abruptly that Gilbert clearly cannot understand what has been said at first. Cavard repeats himself. 'I unlocked the door. Over the weekend. I did not lock it again. It was an error, for which I apologise.'

Gilbert stares at the chef for a good amount of time. Then he half gets out of his chair and looks behind him, at the door, as if checking for an escape route, or possibly to be sure that no one else has entered, before sitting back down again.

'Chef?'

Gilbert may be pompous, Cavard sees, but he clearly respects rank. That's a good start.

'I apologise again, for the lack of security on your archives for a period of ten or so hours. It was unforgivable. I also apologise for letting myself in in the first place.'

Cavard cannot bring himself to say 'breaking in' and Gilbert does not correct him. Anyway, he *broke* nothing, the most gentle of thieves.

'Can I trust you, Gilbert?'

Gilbert panics visibly. He runs his hand over the top of his thinning hair and checks the exits once again. Cavard senses he needs to help him, that the librarian is out of his depth. But what to say?

'How can I put this? I, your chef, am a firm believer in this country of ours, in its declarations and laws. I believe what the state believes, and I believe in the three words that are carved over the entrance to this building. Those three words are the basis on which our society is founded. Do you know which of the three I find to be the most . . . vital? The one that I find myself feeling the most . . . passionate about? Of course I believe

in liberty and equality. Who can say they do not? But brother-
hood is the thing above all else, is it not? That we are one family,
seeking to work together, rather than enemies, seeking to do
each other down. Do you understand me?'

Gilbert shakes his head, and Cavard tells himself to keep
calm and be patient. Probably nothing like this has ever happened
in the archivist's whole career.

'To put it simply,' Cavard adds, 'I am a man of the people.'

Now Gilbert understands. Chef Cavard has just as good as
admitted that, were he ten years older, he would have been
manning the barricades of the Commune eighteen years ago.
Such an admission is a dreadful risk for a man in his position,
and as Gilbert checks the door for the third time, that is all the
signal Cavard needs to know that the old archivist perhaps shares
his political sympathies.

Cavard presses on.

'I would never do anything to endanger the well-being of the
nation. I would never do anything to undermine our security,
and, furthermore, Monsieur Gilbert, I would never ask you to
do the same. I will tell you why I broke into the archives over the
weekend, and then you can decide how to answer me.'

Gilbert nods.

'I need access to a *dossier blanc*. I have received information
that leads me to conclude that the subject of this particular
dossier is guilty of crimes against the state, and that the explanation for them can be found in the dossier.'

Cavard, of course, knows no such thing, but if he has gambled
correctly that Gilbert is a man of principle, this is the sort of
suspicion that will make the quashing of his conscience easier.

'My problem,' Cavard concludes, 'is this. The ultimate authority to whom you and I need to apply to access that dossier is the
very man who is its subject.'

He lets that hang, for as long as is needed, but Gilbert is not
stupid. His eyes widen so far that Cavard is almost convinced he

intends to make a bolt for the door there and then. But he does not. He wipes his hand over his head once more, and then, in the lowest whisper he can manage, mouths a single word.

'Delorme?'

Cavard nods. 'Can you get it for me? Unofficially.'

Cavard believes he has Gilbert in the palm of his hand, so he is taken aback when the archivist shakes his head.

'I cannot get it for you, officially or otherwise.'

'Why not?'

Gilbert speaks louder now. Although what he says is extremely potent, even dangerous, for some reason he feels the need to say it loudly. It is as if he has been affronted, as if this is the only chance he will ever have to set something right.

'Because it is missing.'

Now it is Cavard's turn to be unsettled. He has to force himself not to show any lack of equilibrium.

'It is . . . ?'

'Missing,' says Gilbert, and again he speaks a little louder than Cavard would like. He almost takes pride, as if he is getting some evil matter off his hands, when he adds, 'And as to who took it, and why, well, you're the policeman. It was removed from the archives immediately after the Prefect's appointment. I don't feel I need say more.'

Cavard sits, screwed into place in his chair, while the world revolves around him.

'But only Delorme could have authorised that.'

'Indeed. It was Delorme himself who came. Said he would borrow it. That was over two years ago. He has not seen fit to return it. And I have not seen fit to ask for it back. I presume it would do little good.'

'No,' Cavard stammers at last. 'I agree with that presumption. Who else knows about this?'

'No one. How stupid must you think me, Chef? Delorme is a powerful man. And I do not trust him one bit.'

'You kept this to yourself?'

Gilbert hangs his head, just a touch.

'Never mind,' says Cavard, waving a hand. 'Perhaps that's for the best, now . . . Listen. I have one more question. Did you ever read it?'

'I did not.'

'So you don't know what was so explosive that he had the file removed?'

Gilbert shakes his head, then looks directly at Cavard. He seems more nervous than ever. Eventually, he lowers his eyes.

'Like I say, you're the policeman.'

As Gilbert goes, they agree, without the use of words, but by their eyes alone, that all this will remain secret between them. Gilbert merely mentions that perhaps he forgot to lock the door on Friday after all, not his assistant, Tissot. The matter can be allowed to rest. Cavard nods, and watches the departing archivist before slumping back into his chair.

Yes, he is the policeman. And if this conversation tells him one thing, it's that the secret that Delorme is hiding is something very large indeed.

# THE END OF THE WORLD

Two of the inspectors on whom Cavard has been relying have been watching the movements of Delorme himself, outside work hours. The third has been testing the waters of the world of the Okhrana. None of them has found anything of use and Cavard is getting impatient.

'I cannot press too hard,' says the man who's been trying to make contact with the Russian secret service, and Cavard knows he is right. He himself told him to exercise extreme subtlety, for if Delorme catches wind of their investigations, matters will be escalated very rapidly.

Yet time is running out.

On Tuesday morning, as Cavard sits in his office, one hand on an envelope that contains the lurid photographs of their Prefect and of the minister, the exact amount of time he has is announced.

He is sitting with Boissenot, toying with the idea of showing him the photographs. In desperation, he wondered whether Boissenot, being Petit's boss, had any inkling of what his young inspector was up to. It appears that he did not, and now it is too late to do anything but take the risk and trust Boissenot.

Cavard goes for the direct approach.

Still with one hand on the envelope, he says, 'Boissenot, what do you think of our Prefect?'

Boissenot's eyes still for a second as he takes in the question. Cavard can see he is trying to work out the meaning of this enquiry, as well as a hundred other things, such as whose side he is on. Cavard knows it's a gamble, but he has to make something happen now.

'What . . .' says Boissenot. 'What do I think of our Prefect?'

'That is the question I asked.'

'He is the best man for the job, I would say. Wouldn't you?'

No, I wouldn't, thinks Cavard. And neither would you.

'I'm sure you're right,' says Cavard neutrally. He is trying to weigh something up. If Boissenot is one of Delorme's men and he shows him the photographs, then bad things will happen. That would prove which side Boissenot is on, but otherwise it would not help very much. On the other hand, Cavard thinks, if I show Boissenot the pictures and nothing bad happens, I will know I can trust him. But what else will I gain?

Without trying, he thinks, I will not know, and so he slides the envelope across the desk and invites Boissenot to look at it.

When he does, he shakes his head.

'Well?' asks Cavard.

Boissenot puts the pictures back in the envelope, and slides it back to Cavard.

The silence is killing Cavard.

'Well?' he repeats, and now Boissenot sighs.

'Chef, I . . .'

'Yes?'

Boissenot hangs his head. Points at the envelope. 'That was the Minister of the Interior, was it not?'

'It was,' says Cavard, and Boissenot rolls his eyes, slumps in his chair.

'So? What next? What do we do with this?'

'Unholy ceremonies, but all just an excuse for a wild orgy, no doubt.'

A silence develops, then, since Boissenot has not said it, Cavard says it for him.

'The end of the world?'

'The end of somebody's world,' Boissenot says.

They are disturbed by a knock on the door and one of his

three inspectors makes to come in. When he sees Boissenot, he hesitates, but Cavard waves him in.

'Close the door, Longchamp. The Principal Inspector knows our business.'

Longchamp comes into the room, closing the door behind him, glancing at Boissenot.

'Sir, it's all over. The trial.'

'No, the trial is set for tomorrow. There's still a little time.'

But Longchamp is already shaking his head. 'It *was* set for tomorrow, but Peletier had it moved from the Cour d'Assizes to a Cour Correctionnelle, on technical grounds. It was held this morning. Després was found guilty and is to be transported. He will be dispatched to Toulon by train on Thursday morning. A ship leaves for Cayenne on Friday evening.'

Longchamp waits for his news to be digested, but Cavard is too shocked to speak.

Boissenot says what they are all thinking. 'Cour Correction- nelle. No jury. Just three magistrates, all, we can have no doubt, in Delorme's pocket. And Després will be transported.'

'No,' says Cavard. 'He'll never make it as far as Toulon, never mind Devil's Island. Delorme wants him on that train, no doubt with men of his own as guards. Then he'll pull the same trick that did for Petit in Dijon. Fake an escape, a couple of bullets, and it's all over. That's why he wanted the case moved, that's why he wanted the charge altered to murder of the other girl. He needs to get Marcel out of Paris so he can do away with him with no fuss.'

Boissenot nods. It seems likely.

'But why? What's so important?'

'That remains to be found. What is clear is that Delorme thinks that Marcel Després has some powerful information about him. More than this trash in the photographs. That might be an embarrassment, but despite your theories on the modern world, Boissenot, surely not worth killing over. Let's assume

Ondine blackmailed him; that still doesn't explain why the Okhrana are interested. No, I think Delorme fears Marcel knows something else about him. Something big. And maybe he does.'

'So we need to interview him.'

'I cannot go near that station, and neither can either of you. The Commissaire's a good man but Delorme will have men all over the place. If we go there, we will all swing one way or another, you can be sure of it.'

'So what do we do?'

Cavard grimaces. Thinks of the old doctor at the asylum.

'I have a way. I don't like it but I have a man who can get in to speak to him.'

Yet the day is still not done with Cavard. Just as Longchamp and Boissenot leave, there is another knock at the door. He looks up sharply, now fearing the worst at every turn.

'Come in,' he barks, and into the room comes his clerk, holding a card folder, bound with a ribbon.

'Yes?' asks Cavard.

'The file you ordered. From the archives.'

The clerk nods at the two visitors and places the file on Cavard's desk. He is about to go when he turns and speaks to the chef.

'It's nearly lunchtime, Chef. Do you need anything else?'

Cavard shakes his head, just managing to restrain himself from telling the clerk that he has ordered no files from the archives.

'Then I'll take my lunch now,' says the clerk, and leaves.

Cavard pulls the file towards him, and opens it. The first thing he sees is that it is the internal record of a policeman, whose name means nothing to him. The second thing he sees is a note pinned to the inside of the folder, and so he understands that the folder is just cover to get a message to him unobtrusively.

*I'm working late tonight. Perhaps you would care to join me?*
*G.*

Cavard stares at the note for a long while.

'Chef?' asks Boissenot, and Cavard lifts his head.

'We have much to do,' he says, 'and little time to do it. Boissenot, do you have a safe at home?'

Boissenot nods.

'I do not want these left on police premises any longer,' says Cavard, sliding the packet of photographs across the desk towards him. 'Take it home and lock it up. Keep it there. Do you have a last will and testament?'

Boissenot swallows hard, nodding, as Cavard continues.

'I want you to write a note concerning the provenance and contents of the collection and add it to your private papers. Tonight. If we go down we will take them with us, do you understand? We have a day or so in which to conclude this matter before Després will be transported for a crime of which he is innocent.'

'And so?' asks Longchamp. 'Do we use this to expose Delorme before that happens?'

'No,' says Cavard, 'we do not. We keep working to find what he is really guilty of, and Després will go to Devil's Island.'

Longchamp rubs a hand on the back of his neck. 'That's –'

Boissenot nods, interrupting.

'That's the way it has to be. Després is a bystander, but we cannot move to save him. Unless he holds the key to this, we have no use for him.'

'But supposing there is nothing else,' says Longchamp. 'Just these photographs and whatever sordid club Delorme belongs to. What if you're looking for nothing? Després will rot in a penal colony. For nothing.'

Cavard looks at the inspector, not with any condescension, or criticism, but with admiration. He admires him for something that he himself lost long ago. For while Cavard is indeed a man of the people, he also believes that sometimes the individual person has to suffer for the good of everyone else.

'Longchamp,' Cavard says, 'I hope very much that Després is indeed the key to this puzzle. We will make one attempt to find out. I want you to call upon Dr Morel at the Salpêtrière. Ask him to meet me in the Café Zigomar, Rue Racine, tonight. Get him to take extreme care that he is not followed. Eight o'clock.'

'Very good.'

Thank you, gentlemen,' says Cavard, 'Thank you.'

Outside, it is not the kind of weather to dawdle in. A thin cold sleet presses down across the river, with a wind from the east that only makes it more unpleasant. Despite these conditions, Cavard's clerk, having delivered the file to the chef's desk, and then, having listened outside the door, makes his way out into the cold and down the Quai des Oeuvres. Here he takes the ramp leading down to the waterside itself. He looks behind him as he goes, checking not once, or twice, but three times that he has not been seen. There, by the water, he speaks to a man who appears to have been waiting for him. They converse for no more than two or three minutes, and then the clerk hurries away, off to find his lunch.

# A FINAL INTERVIEW

At the end of the day, Cavard kills time in his office, hating that he is trapped behind a desk when there are things to be done in the world, action to take. But it is for the best. He cannot be seen to be acting. He will have to operate through others, for the time being. They have sufficient evidence of sexual activities to disgrace many big men, but not to bring them to justice. For that, he needs to know what else Delorme is so keen to conceal, for he is convinced, like Petit, that there is more to know. The answer is not long in coming.

When he judges that the offices are quiet enough, he gathers his belongings and makes his way out. Both of the clerks have gone home, and thanks to Longchamp he has a meeting arranged with the doctor.

As soon as he thinks it suitable, and as casually as he can, Cavard makes his way down to the basement once more, and finds the archives still open.

There, behind his throne, sits Gilbert, as promised, scratching away with a pen at some paperwork. As the door clicks behind Cavard, Gilbert looks up.

'You got my note,' he states.

Cavard waves a hand. 'I know of no such thing. I merely thought I would pay a courtesy call.'

Gilbert does not seem to have a sense of humour. He comes around from his desk and pulls out two chairs, out of sight of the door.

'And you read the file?'

Cavard sits, easing himself into the insufficient chair.

'Why are you helping me?' Cavard asks, trusting no one any more. Though the answer is obvious: Gilbert is a good man. However he is also obviously not one for idle conversation.

'Did you read the file?' he repeats.

'The file? No, I assumed that—'

'You didn't see the name?'

'Should I have?'

'Paul Pontalis. The file was of a young policeman named Paul Pontalis.'

'So?'

'Paul Pontalis was an inspector in his late thirties when he left the force. Or rather, I should say, when he ceased to be.'

'He was killed.'

'No, far from it. He changed his name. His mother, being a widow for some years, remarried and her son decided to change his name to that of his new stepfather. For appearances' sake, was the reason he gave. A most traditional family. Still, a very unusual step to take. Unless there were another reason it suited him to take a new name. As I say, he left the police around the same time. You will by now have guessed the surname of his new stepfather?'

Cavard nods. 'Delorme. How did you find all this out?'

Gilbert seems affronted. 'I am an archivist, sir,' he states, as if that is explanation enough. 'Paul Delorme rejoins the Paris police five years later, appointed quite miraculously as Commissaire of the 18th at the express wishes of the then Prefect. He went on to rise rapidly to the position he now holds, always first in line for promotion to a better arrondissement, and then to the positions that really matter. In five years he becomes Prefect. From nowhere. Of course, there may be some who knew him from his days in the Sûreté as Pontalis, but such facts are soon forgotten; it was years ago, and in the other branch of the police. And you know how much, or should I say how little, we correspond with the other lot.'

'Very interesting. But the question is what did Paul Pontalis do?'

'That is the exact question. And when Delorme took his file away, he either forgot or did not know about the existence of a folder on his former life; the one I sent to you this afternoon.'

'It's upstairs. On my desk. Your note is in pieces in my waste-paper basket.'

'I suggest you return that file here or lock it away. In case it too goes missing.'

'Agreed. I will fetch it the moment I leave here. But you can tell me the contents?'

Gilbert nods. 'Paul Pontalis was the Sûreté's liaison officer with the Okhrana.'

There it is, thinks Cavard. That's the key. That's why Russians keep popping into this story. The Sûreté has always had unofficial contact with the Tsar's men in Paris. Delorme did something with the Okhrana. But what?

Gilbert is ahead of him. 'Alas, that is the final piece of the puzzle, I suspect. Once you know that, you will know everything. But you should be asking about Paul Pontalis, not Paul Delorme.'

These are the very words that Cavard puts to Dr Morel over a glass in the Café Zigomar, later that evening.

'You must get him to speak. See if he knows anything about Delorme, but the name you really need to push him on is Pontalis. See if Ondine ever spoke to him about a Paul Pontalis.'

Morel's face is almost without expression. Not for the first time Cavard doubts that he is doing the right thing, but the doctor has already explained that he has been to see Marcel on two occasions. The Commissaire at the station house accepted his story that he still feels responsible for his patient and that he wishes to assess his state of mind at face value, because, after all, it is the truth.

This tells Cavard that fate is on his side, and he urges Morel to make one last trip.

'Do you speak to him on your own?'

'No, there's always been a guard present.'

'You need to find a way to get to speak to him privately. Can you do it?'

The old doctor's face is a blank sheet. He merely blinks from time to time, expressing a little water from his eyes, which he wipes away with a fingertip when it becomes too much.

'I can but try,' says Morel.

'And remember, you must warn him about the train journey. That is the most dangerous time. At this end and in Toulon there will be too many other parties: policemen, station officials. It will happen on the train.'

Morel stands, and without saying anything further, leaves.

Cavard settles down for an interminable wait. He orders an omelette and some more wine, and tries to find something else to think about. He cannot. He thinks about Marcel. He has never met the man, but he wonders if it can really be true that his memory is perfect. What a gift to a policeman! he thinks. What a boon that would be. But Cavard cannot believe it is really true, though the doctor seems to be convinced that it is, and the doctor, like the archivist, does not seem to be a man who jokes about anything at all.

Morel manages to get to see Marcel, one last time. More than that, he demands to be allowed ten minutes of private conversation with his former patient. He is given five, and he knows that he will have to get Marcel to stick to the point if those five minutes are to prove of any use.

He is in luck, for Marcel seems to be as clear and rational as he has ever been.

'I see things so much more clearly now,' he says. 'I don't know why. It just seems to me that I understand a little bit more. You helped me do that, Doctor.'

'I'm glad,' he says hurriedly, 'but we must speak of other things.'

'Of course,' says Marcel, but he won't leave the subject at once. 'I would just like you to know, before they send me away, that you helped me to understand myself. I see what I am dealing with now. My memory, I mean. Before, I only knew I had it; I never saw how it got in the way of my seeing who other people are, how other people act. What they know. But now I do, because of you.'

Marcel tells him more. He tells him how he has begun to understand himself, and how other people see him. He believes this knowledge will prove useful to him. Should he have a future.

Though flattered, and though once Morel would have puffed himself up and delighted in the praise, he finds that now all he wants is to get Marcel on to the subject of Pontalis. Eventually, as the minutes tick away, he does, and when he does, Morel leaves the police station with what he believes is the missing piece that Cavard has been hunting. That Petit was hunting. Over which, and in order to keep quiet, Delorme has resorted to murder.

# A HISTORY LESSON

'You didn't see him?' Cavard asks, but as soon as Morel sits he can see that he is a different man from the one who left no more than half an hour before.

'I saw him,' he says, and, taking a glass from the next table, pours himself a large glass of wine, half of which disappears in one go. He tops up his glass and looks at Cavard.

'I saw him,' he says. 'I have never seen him this way before. He was the most lucid I have ever known him. As if he is finally here in the world. Only now do I see what has been missing in him; it's as if he is detached from the rest of us, from life, from everything that goes on. But he's different tonight. He is all too well aware that he is to be transported to Cayenne. He protests his innocence, as a normal man would, when up to now it has appeared to be a matter of extreme indifference whether he is guilty or not, whether he will be executed, or imprisoned, or not.'

Cavard cannot deny that this is interesting but there are matters that are more interesting still. He lowers his voice.

'And Delorme?'

'Yes,' says the doctor. 'I am coming to that. I told the guards that I wanted some time alone with my patient, for private reflection. There was a fuss, but a man who appeared to be in charge overruled the guards and I was allowed five minutes. I asked him if he knew who Paul Delorme was, and he said, of course, because he reads the papers and everyone knows who the Prefect of Paris is. So I asked him if Ondine had ever mentioned that she had had anything to do with him, and though that was a thought that troubled him, I can assure you he was not lying when he told me that she had never spoken of him. So I tried my final question, and by this time my five minutes were all but up. Chef, you do not know how hard it is to keep Marcel on a subject without wandering off. I asked him if his wife had ever spoken of a Paul Pontalis and again, he said no. But then he said that he had heard of him. In fact, he said, and he was remembering something from a long time ago, he said he had *met* him.'

This is almost too much for Cavard to take.

'He met him? He met Pontalis? I mean, Delorme when he was still—'

'Yes. Quite so. Cavard, do you recall that Marcel Després was once, briefly, a journalist? Well, maybe not exactly a journalist, but he worked for a paper for a time. And you recall that bombing, the one in the station café, that happened in '94?'

Cavard nods slowly, his skin itching with impatience for the connection.

'Marcel covered that incident for his newspaper. He took the names of every one of the witnesses, the survivors, the staff. The policemen present. Pontalis was there that night. That is where Marcel once met our Prefect of Police. Furthermore, Marcel recalls something that was mentioned in passing in the newspaper reports, but which he himself witnessed. There was an altercation between Pontalis and a Russian man shortly after the bombing, a Russian who was later found with a knife in his back in an alley around the corner from the station. Given the uproar over the bombing, an unsolved murder slipped away into obscurity, was soon forgotten. But not, of course, by Marcel. Now what do you make of that?'

Cavard makes a lot of that. The trouble is knowing what is madness and what is truth. He stares at Morel for very long while, saying nothing. He pours more wine for both of them, finds that the pitcher is empty, and orders another one from the waiter. Only when the waiter has returned and departed again does he speak.

'The first thing I think is this. We have been hoping that Ondine Després was privy to some secret about Delorme, and that she had passed this information on to her husband, that he was involved in blackmailing him too. Uncomfortable with a trial involving Ondine's murderous husband, during which who knows what might be revealed, Delorme moves to close everything down. And yet I see the actions of a man who is panicking – he is fighting fires as they break out, and he escalates things to the point where he has people killed to protect knowledge that Marcel never even had. And yet here is a touch of the universe playing its jokes: Marcel *does* know something about Delorme. He just doesn't *know* that he knows. What a memory! As you said, Doctor. Extraordinary. What I could have done with my career if I had had a memory like that.'

Morel shakes his head. 'Trust me, Cavard. You have no idea what you're saying.'

'Maybe. But Després can pull from his head the name of Paul Pontalis. And he was present at that bombing. That was a bad one. You remember . . . That young anarchist, Henry. Went to the guillotine.'

Morel nods. 'Yes, but I don't see the connection.'

'I do,' says Cavard. 'Or at least, I think I do. Delorme, or Pontalis as he was then, was a covert officer for the Sûreté. He was responsible for liaising with the Okhrana. As I told you, they have had their uses, their presence in Paris is tolerated within certain limits. We and they have had one mutual enemy over the last few years. The anarchist. They have the same issues in Russia, with the same perpetrators seeking the same goal: overthrowing the state. In our case, our centrist politicians. In their case, the Tsar.'

'What does this have to do with Delorme?'

'There were rumours about certain operations a few years ago. There were one or two remarkable arrests made, of whole groups of anarchists and sympathisers; potential bombers and actual ones. The story going about the station was that these arrests were not what they seemed; not just good detective work and smart policing. In all my days I have never before or since seen such clean and successful operations. The rumour was that the Okhrana and certain officers in the Sûreté had set up covert groups in the enemy camp. I found out earlier today that Pontalis, that is, Delorme, was one of the officers liaising with the Russians. The story was that they organised the meetings between them, put the word out on the streets in the right parts of town, attracting leftists and the like, that they even supplied the bombs that were to have been used by the anarchists. The plan was that they let these people incriminate themselves so far, and then, arranging one last meeting, had had the whole damn lot arrested.'

'So? But the explosion at the café?'

'Yes. The explosion at the café. From here, we are in the realm of speculation. But that Paul Delorme was present there that evening seems to me to be too much of a coincidence. Perhaps one of the bombers, Émile Henry, never showed up at that final meeting. Perhaps he decided to act on his own. Or there is perhaps a more sinister explanation.'

Even as he says this, and his skin crawls as though beetles are hatching from inside him, he believes he has stumbled across the truth. Petit guessed that there was more to the case than a murder. Then he guessed that there was more to Delorme's involvement than some embarrassment over courtesans. What Cavard now thinks is something so terrible he can barely give it credit, struggles to believe that someone, a Frenchman, an important and powerful man, could do something so despicable. Then, in the next moment, he realises how preposterous that sentiment is. Of course that's what powerful men can do. That's one of the ways in which powerful men become powerful: they do despicable things, and if they get away with it, then stories are rewritten, facts are ignored. History, as we know, is written by the victor.

Morel can see that Cavard has found something, and he waits for a long time for the right moment to whisper, as gently as he can, 'Well?'

Cavard shakes his head. 'Do you remember the wave of revulsion after that bombing? In the press? On every one's lips? That was a watershed. If there had been any lingering sympathy for the days of the Commune, for the left, for the people, all of Paris was finally united in the face of such a horrific act of terror. The blood of twenty thousand Communards may have turned the waters of the Seine red but, well, that was twenty years ago, wasn't it? And here was the most appalling and unmotivated attack against innocent bystanders in a railway station café. No one said anything, no one *felt* anything other than anger and fear in the days that followed. '

Morel nods. He begins to understand himself, but Cavard says it aloud anyway.

'Supposing there was a very clever man who knew that a terrible bombing was just what was needed to make all that happen? To bring everyone together on the same side. On *his* side . . . ? So he orchestrated it all, even using the Okhrana without them realising at first that they *were* being used. He supplies the bomb that the young anarchist delivers to the café . . . The bomb explodes, all Paris is outraged and the political spectrum lurches firmly to the right. For good.'

Morel stares at Cavard. Are such things even possible? Do such minds even exist?

'But what can you do?' he asks eventually, though even the old doctor, who understands little about politics or policing, seems already to know the answer.

'Nothing,' says Cavard. 'It is just a story. And the end of the story is guesswork. I have an idea what happened, but I am unable to be sure. We have no proof of anything. Just a witness who knows that Delorme happened to be at the scene of the bombing.'

'And what happens to that witness?'

Cavard finishes his drink and puts the glass back on the table gently, as if he fears it will break if it makes the slightest sound. He knows that without Marcel he would not have this final piece of the puzzle. A strange man, a captive for many months, held in cells of one kind or another, a funny kind of hero, doing nothing, saying little. Passive and impenetrable, he sat in darkness as the days became weeks and then months while the doctor and others pored over him, probing him and pondering him. And yet, all that time, the secret lay inside Marcel. And now he has provided the one piece of information that could not only save him, but which could end Delorme's career and possibly his life.

Cavard speaks softly, staring at the table top as he does.

'I'm sorry. I can do nothing. We have no proof of any of these events in '94. We can only prove that Delorme belongs to a powerful club of men who like to indulge in outrageous activities after dark. Després will have to take his chances on the train. And if he survives to Toulon, he might even survive the five years he's been given on Devil's Island.'

'You don't think either of those things are likely, do you?' says Morel, and it is not a question, but an accusation.

'No,' whispers Cavard. 'I do not.'

# THE ALLEY

Cavard's mind changes a dozen times before he has even made it as far as a cab. It is late and his wife will be wondering what has become of him. It is so close to Christmas now, and it's even more important to her that he is home once in a while, maybe even to see the children before they go to bed.

He looks at his watch. It is half past nine; those children of his should be sleeping. His wife will be worrying but that is something she is more than used to; as he often tells her, you shouldn't have married a policeman if you wanted to live without worry.

He finds a cab and gives the driver his home address, then, before they are even at the end of the street, he flicks through his pocket book, and calls out another address, Principal Inspector Boissenot's.

Boissenot lives in the new developments in Clichy, just inside the old walls. He is married and Cavard hopes that Boissenot's wife is just as forgiving as his own. It will be even later by the time Cavard gets there, but that cannot be helped. He cannot also help checking that he is not being followed. Every corner he leans from the window and checks backwards, looking for other vehicles that might contain thugs of Delorme's. He seems to be safe, but he does not give up checking. Twenty minutes later, the cab pulls into Boissenot's street. The Rue de Printemps is narrow, with tall Haussmann buildings of six storeys on both sides, apart from a lower stretch of houses halfway along on the right.

Cavard has never visited Boissenot at home before, but he can already tell which house is the inspector's. It will be the one with the five *gardiens de la paix* standing outside, and a gaggle of neighbours hanging around, craning their necks to see. There is a police wagon there too, presumably from the 17th.

'Here?' calls the driver, and Cavard steps down, almost forgetting to pay. He walks slowly towards the scene. Two of the *gardiens* see him coming, and try to block his way, until he displays his identity card to them. He passes through the crowd of people, over the threshold and up the steps to the first floor, where he shows his card to another *gardien* blocking the entry to Boissenot's home.

The policeman nods at him.

'They've sent for an examining magistrate,' he tells Cavard, but Cavard is not really listening. He moves inside, and finds that he is alone with the victims.

It has obviously not been long since the crime was committed. As Cavard enters, he sees through into the kitchen, where a pair of feet clad in women's stockings protrudes from underneath an overturned chair. There is the smell of blood in the air, and burning. Something acrid that makes him want to gag. Hair maybe.

He moves on into the sitting room, and there is Boissenot. He is tied to a chair, and it is clear that he has been tortured. His eyes are open, and blood is still pooling on the floor beneath his hands, which hang to each side of the arms of the chair, mutilated.

Cavard hears voices outside the apartment, down in the street, dimly. He cannot make out what is being said, nor does he focus on it. Instead, he turns, and moves into a small room that Boissenot must have used as his study. A cupboard door stands open, and inside, Cavard sees a mess. The shelves have been pulled out, and there, on the floor, the wooden boards have been up, ripped apart. The voices are coming up the stairs. Cavard kneels and finds the ruins of a board with two holes in it, now in two pieces, split through these holes. He knows the design; he has the same arrangement at home himself: a small steel safe bolted to the floor inside a cupboard. The safe would have been heavy; they would have made a terrible noise wrenching it from the boards, boards that were unsuitable to the task of fixing the thing in place, and which were then perhaps pried away with a chisel.

It was what he came for, this safe, or, rather, its contents. He had finally made up his mind that with or without the proof of Delorme's greater crime, it was the right thing to do to bring him down from office with the scandal. That might then enable Cavard to engineer an investigation to prove the bigger guilt. He would get the packet of photographs back from Boissenot, and by tomorrow morning they would be placed on every important desk in the Palais des Justices, as well as the desk of every newspaper editor in the city. Not knowing who he can trust, and who might be part of Delorme's club, he would scatter the information so widely that not even God himself could suppress it. But the photographs have gone, and that route is now closed to him. Or almost. He now remembers that one picture, the first one that Petit gave him. He barely looked at it at the time, and he left it . . . My God, he thinks. He remembers now where he left it, lying loose in his top desk drawer at home. That's all he has left to play with now.

As he returns to look at Boissenot and pay his respects, he can see just how far the corruption extends into his own department.

'The end of the world, Boissenot,' Cavard whispers, his eyes closed. He wants to bring himself to close the dead man's eyes too, but when he steps forward to do it, he finds he cannot. His hand wavers in the air above Boissenot's face for a while, then he pulls away. He closes his own eyes again.

Rapidly, connections form in his mind. Someone knew about the photographs, and they told Delorme. Delorme has taken the most brutal action possible, and if he knows about all this, then Cavard himself is in danger now. He hears the voice in the corridor, speaking to the *gardien* on the door. He knows the voice. It is Peletier.

He curses, quietly, and decides he has no desire to be found here.

Opposite the kitchen, where Madame Boissenot lies murdered, is another room, its door open. Cavard slips quietly inside, cursing his bad shape and lack of speed, but something still and quiet has arrived inside him, some reaction to the incomprehensible horror of what he has just seen, and he moves easily into the darkened room, where he stands motionless as Peletier enters the apartment, making straight for the kitchen. He spends no more than a few moments appraising the dead woman, and heads out again.

Cavard holds his breath as Peletier moves further into the apartment. The examining magistrate enters the living room, and the next thing he hears is the sound of Peletier being sick on the floor. Cavard takes his chance, moving out of the apartment.

As he passes the *gardien*, he quietly asks, 'What's my name?'

The *gardien* looks back at him blankly. 'I'm sorry, sir, I've forgotten.'

No matter, thinks Cavard, and moves quickly down the stairs and out into the night. That will buy him some time; Peletier won't know it was him inside the apartment. Unless one of the *gardiens* in the street told him, and he can do nothing about that. He puts his head down and moves away down the street, but no one is paying him any attention.

It is at the Rue Saussure that he realises there are footsteps behind him. He hurries and turns left, annoyed with himself; Peletier might have thrown up at the sight of what Delorme's men had done to Boissenot, but Cavard himself, though made of sterner stuff, has dropped his guard long enough to be caught out.

He turns backward as he turns the corner and sees three men following him. They are big men, and there is no one else about. Once around the corner, he uses the moment of grace to put on the best turn of speed he can manage, and seeing an opening on the left, runs into it, hoping to be out of sight before the men make the corner.

He moves as quietly as he can, trying to find a dark doorway to hide himself in. But even by the weak light from the feeble gas lamps that glow from the occasional window, he can see he has made a mistake.

The alley is a dead-end.

He runs forward a step or two, panting hard already, more from the fear than the effort, ridiculously thinking to himself that his last thoughts will be of how he really does move like a duck, how much he deserved his cruel nickname.

He reaches the end of the alley, but there is indeed no way out.

He turns towards the men.

# THE END OF MARCEL DESPRÉS

Marcel is still dressed in his hospital garments when they come to take him to the train. He tries to ask to wear his own clothes again, but they take no notice of him. Even the Commissaire, who has been more than fair to Marcel, sadly shakes his head, telling him that by tomorrow he will be dressed in prison clothes, and in prison clothes he will remain for the next five years.

Or until he is dead, Marcel knows, but that goes unspoken by both sides. Marcel knows about the transportations. In Toulon, in the harbour, a prison hulk will be waiting for him. He has never been to Toulon, and he has never seen a prison ship, but he has read about them. Even before those days of reading newspaper after newspaper, he read about them, and he remembers every detail. One article he read carefully explained every aspect of their construction, of their size, of the number of men who would be held captive inside in darkness and squalor for the duration of the journey to Cayenne. In Cayenne, those who had not succumbed to illness or violence in the darkness of the hold would be transferred to smaller boats to make the short trip out to Devil's Island, the dry guillotine. There, death by disease, starvation, or brutality was the normal turn of events. He would be more than lucky to survive his five years. It would be a miracle.

In chains and under escort he is locked in the back of a Black Maria whose horses make a fair clip of the short journey from the 6th to the Gare de Lyon. At the station, he is removed from the carriage, again under close guard. Marcel is filled with the strange sense that he is in some way very precious. They appear to be taking very great care of him. He is placed in a special carriage at the rear of the train, one half of which contains mailbags, and the other half is a cage, in which he is imprisoned. His ankles are put into shackles which are chained though a ring in the floor of the carriage; his guards climb into the small area between the cage where Marcel is held and the cage containing the mail. There are two of them, and they do not even look at him. They are dressed in plain clothes, but he sees the flash of a gun under the coat of one of them, and he has no reason to suppose the other man is not armed as well.

It is an icy morning, and Marcel freezes. The year is almost up, and it is going out in the grip of a frost that has chilled the whole city. Marcel, dressed in his hospital rags and felt slippers for shoes, shakes with the cold. He is grateful when the heavy doors to the carriage are slid shut and the train begins to make its way.

Marcel knows the timetable. He has read it, long ago, and assuming it has not changed, then this train leaves Paris, Gare de Lyon at 7.43 and will pull into Dijon around lunchtime. There will be a change of engine and personnel and then the train will make its way to Lyon, Avignon and Marseille, where in all likelihood they will change trains again for the short journey to Toulon, arriving late in the evening. At least it will be warmer in the south, Marcel thinks, wondering if what the doctor said is really true, that they mean to kill him before the journey is done. He blinks in the darkness of the carriage, looking at his guards. He does not like the way they do not look at him, do not even acknowledge his existence. Are they truly going to kill him?

The train lurches and rolls as it makes its way forward and the whistle blows from time to time. After half an hour of this, there is a noticeable change, and the engine picks up speed.

They have reached the edge of the city.

There are only two stops on the journey, Marcel knows: Montereau and Auxerre. Two hours pass, though Marcel cannot keep accurate track of the time, before the first stop is made. He eyes the guards. Still they do not look at him.

He calls out to them; he feels suddenly frantic that if he can only make them speak to him, they cannot possibly kill him.

They ignore him, and now Marcel feels truly afraid. The men have their backs half turned to him, they huddle against the walls of the carriage, in silence, rocking with the motion of the train as it lurches into life again.

At Auxerre, an hour later, the pattern is repeated, and though Marcel calls out again, they still ignore him, letting his shouts disturb anyone on the platform outside the windowless carriage.

The train halts for only a few minutes, and then haltingly staggers into motion once more. Marcel peers through the darkness at the men who are going to kill him and is about to cry out when one of them turns and looks at him.

The man says nothing, and Marcel cannot read his face, no more than he can read any face. What does it mean, this look? What does it signify? Marcel has absolutely no idea.

The man stands, and Marcel scrabbles away as far as the chain around his feet will let him, but before another moment has passed Marcel sees that the man is merely stretching his legs, walking round in the small area that is even more confined than the space in which he is held.

As the train picks up speed again, the man sits down and mutters something to his companion, who does not answer. During the whole journey, Marcel realises, this second man has said not one word.

So they move on, and Marcel stares and stares. As another indeterminate space of time passes, he begins to notice that one of the men, the one who has occasionally muttered some comment or other, keeps checking his watch. He does it once, he does it again, very soon after, and then he checks it almost continually, or so it seems to Marcel, as if he is judging a moment. Marcel realises that that moment is the arrival of the train in Dijon.

It is then that Marcel's fate is determined.

He cannot understand why, as the man who has been checking his watch slowly stands up, and as he pulls out his revolver, and as he lifts it to shoot Marcel dead, the second guard, standing behind him, brings the butt of his gun down on his head.

The first man falls to the floor, clutching his bleeding head, and his attacker kneels and lets three more blows fall on him with the revolver, until the body is at last motionless.

It makes no sense to Marcel, no sense at all.

The man now fishes in the dead guard's pocket, and pulls out a bunch of keys, opening first the door to the cage, and then the shackles around Marcel's feet.

He speaks. 'You must help. There is little time.'

His voice is thick with Russian tones, and still none of it makes sense to Marcel, but he remembers the words from the dictionary that Morel gave him, months ago now. The attacker speaks French, clearly, but Marcel decides to speak to him in his own language.

'You are Russian?' he says.

The man is surprised, but he does not stop moving.

In Russian, he replies, 'We do not have long. The train will be in the station soon. Help me.'

'Help you?' asks Marcel, but then he sees that the Russian is taking off the other guard's clothes.

'Get undressed,' says the Russian. 'Help me swap clothes.'

Marcel does as he is told. He strips naked and dresses in the other man's clothes. As they begin to pull the hospital garments on to the dead man, Marcel realises he is not actually dead.

'He's alive,' he whispers in Russian.

'You want me to kill him?' asks the Russian.

'No. No!' says Marcel. 'I thought you had killed him.'

The train's whistle blows.

'Station,' says the Russian, and then, hurriedly, he explains what they will say when the doors are opened and the next set of guards replace them. They lock the man's ankles in the shackles, and he lolls against the floor as the train glides to a stop.

As the doors are opened from the outside, Marcel does as he is told. He speaks because the Russian has a noticeable accent when he says any more than a word. Marcel tells the new guards what he was told to say: that the prisoner tricked them, feigning illness, that he tried to escape, but they overpowered him again. He reminds the guards that Després is a convicted murderer, but that he has spent months in the asylum for lunatics in Paris. He may be delusional; he will try to claim that he is someone else, and that he has been tricked. They are to ignore this, and not to speak to him at all, or interact with him in any way, save to get him to Toulon and on to the prison ship.

Marcel and the Russian leave the station. Marcel still does not understand what has just happened, but the Russian seems reluctant to say much. He himself knows little about what he was asked to do. Working with the Police Municipale, he replaced an officer at the last moment, and though he had no idea why, did what he was told to do by his superiors. Of the deal that occurred the night before in an alleyway in Clichy, he knows nothing, and thus Marcel will never know how Cavard found he was facing up to three Okhrana men, not agents of Delorme's.

There, in that alley, the deal was struck. Though Cavard knows that it may have been these same Okhrana men who helped Delorme, as Pontalis, to carry out his sting operation, they never intended for anyone actually to be killed. And one of their own was killed too. So, having eventually learned who Paul Pontalis became, they want Delorme taken down.

They were willing to help protect Cavard and his family. In return he offers to take that one single photo of his and distribute it throughout the police and to the press.

He does so. Within the week a scandal has erupted that sees Delorme resign from office before Christmas even arrives.

In the alley that night, for his help and silence, Cavard asks for

something in return: to make one thing right. He cannot inter-
vene in the legal process surrounding Marcel, not without too
many awkward questions being asked, but the Okhrana are as
ruthless and resourceful as any of Delorme's cronies. Perhaps
they can find a way out for Marcel . . . ?

The Russian tells Marcel to leave town on foot immediately,
and become someone else. Marcel Després is on a train bound
for the prison hulk in Toulon harbour, and it will be a long while
before that mistake is uncovered and corrected, if at all. As it
turns out, 'Marcel' dies upon the journey to the south from loss
of blood due to his untended head wound.

Marcel himself, the real Marcel, has begun to change. On the
surface, he remains the aimless wanderer through life, unable to
recognise the same face twice, unable to lie, unable to forget a
single thing that ever enters his head. But there are perhaps two
things that have been added to him.

The first is a sense of guilt. He alone knows that he truly
wanted to kill Ondine that night, and that it matters little how
much she provoked him and how much she tricked him into the
act. He could have walked out of that room; instead, he picked
up the gun and fired it five times into her. This guilt cannot be
ignored; the horror of it eats at Marcel continually, even as he
traipses across France without purpose or direction. Yet he starts
to face it.

The second is more subtle, and yet ultimately more powerful.
As the new world dawns, the one that Boissenot was so scared
of, it's apparent that the world has not ended. It simply goes on
as it did before, with some people gone and others surviving.
Marcel is a man with a remarkable mind. He survives. He soon
spends the tidy sum of cash he found in the policeman's wallet,
but by then he has managed to get a job waiting tables in a café
in an obscure little village. He makes the patron happy for a
while, because Marcel makes a good waiter. He never forgets an

order, and though sometimes he is a little cold to the regulars, as if he's never seen them before, he gets the right thing to the right table every time, and he does it with humility.

From time to time he thinks about an oilskin packet underneath the floorboards of his old studio, and wonders if it is still there, and how he could get it back if so, and in his mind he counts the notes. Then he leaves it be. In his mind he closes the door to the apartment, and in his mind he walks down the stairs and heads into the Cour du Commerce. From time to time too he revisits Dr Morel, and the many conversations they had together. Being able to recall the exact content of any dialogue he's ever engaged in, Marcel replays various discussions that the two of them had in the nearly six months they spent in each other's lives.

There is, however, one conversation in particular that comes back to him often. The conversation took place on one of the visits the doctor made while Marcel was back in the station house of the 6th, waiting to be dispatched to Toulon or the afterlife. It is this conversation that starts the evolution of the second way in which Marcel is changing. On this particular occasion, Morel had not bothered asking how Marcel was, for that was plain to see, and the future was very bleak. Morel was in thoughtful mood, and he only said a little, but it's something that Marcel has been pondering a lot as he waits on tables.

It's this.

'Do you know, Marcel . . .' the doctor said. 'You have taught me something. Through you, I have come to see that there is no such thing as truth. That all we ever really know is *perception*. I have been scared by that thought, but now I am not. It frees us from having to struggle towards this notion of truth, as if it were some god to be worshipped. I am grateful for that; it is something you have given me, and now I wish to give you something in return.

'Do you know what memory is for? Have you, with your exceptional abilities, ever stopped to wonder what memory is for? Perhaps not. Most people, if you ask them, will tell you that memory is about the past – it is, after all, about remembering things that have happened. But that is not what memory is *for*. The ability to recall past events is a mere by-product of what memory does for us. It was given to us, by God, or nature, in order that we might be able to negotiate the future. It was given to us in order that we may learn, understand and build upon our previous achievements. That we might create language and civilisations. These are the things that animals cannot do, because their memory is not developed, as ours is, to be able to project the future. That is what memory is about: the future, not the past. The future. Think about that.'

Marcel does. The winter starts to pass, and as it does, Marcel dimly thinks about the future, and as he does so he becomes aware of this second way he has changed. One day, as the sun rises, he wakes up, and believes he knows what it is for sure. There is only one way to find out.

He takes a train ride, using the small savings he has managed to make waiting tables. Then he walks. He walks through the night. When he arrives at the road at the top of the village, the sun is starting to beat down upon the vines, which are wet with dew. Frost clings to the ground in patches though he knows it will be a hot day very soon.

He walks down to the village, taking a short cut through the sloping rows, marvelling at the tiny green pinheads that will be worth wine and gold by the time the summer is done, and as he walks, he is suddenly aware of someone walking in the row next to him.

He looks down and sees a pair of feet, bare and muddy, and the hem of white skirts flicking as she walks. At the end of the row, they step out and meet.

325

They stand at the edge of the vineyards, at the edge of the village, and neither of them speaks, she because she is so stunned that she has no idea what to say, and he because, although he thinks it is her, he wants to be sure before he speaks.

Eventually, he smiles.

'Hello, Marcel,' she says. 'I thought it was you.'

It must be her. 'Hello, Ginette.'

He looks at her feet, but he knows he has already commented on that, years ago, when they were both seventeen. Instead he says something else.

'I went to the city for a while.'

Ginette laughs. 'I know,' she says, and smiles. 'I know you did. And what was it like?'

Marcel thinks about it. 'I didn't like it.'

'Have you come home then?'

Marcel looks at Ginette's hands. What he felt has been added to him suddenly rushes up out of nowhere, almost making him gasp. It has taken him for ever to understand, but here, as they relive a scene from their young lives, Marcel finally understands what was trying to swim to him during his time in the cell in the 6th station house. That Ginette wanted to love him, yes, but more than that: that she was ready and willing to love him for who he is, the way he is, with all his strangenesses. Yet it is too late now. Marcel looks at her hands, and sees a wedding band on her finger.

She sees him looking and shifts on her feet awkwardly.

'You got married?' says Marcel, and he makes himself smile.

Ginette nods.

'So did I,' says Marcel, then quickly adds, 'but I'm alone again. She . . . died.'

Ginette puts a hand on Marcel's arm. 'I'm so sorry,' she says, and then he sees she is smiling. He knows that is strange, that it is not something that people smile about.

'I'm sorry,' says Ginette. 'It's not that . . . It's just that life is so strange. Don't you think? Marcel, I got married, but my husband died too. Two years ago now. Two years . . .'

She stops. She's still touching Marcel's arm.

He puts his hand on hers as she says, 'Don't you think life is strange, Marcel? Don't you think so?'

And he tells her that yes, he agrees, life is strange.

# You've turned the last page.

# But it doesn't have to end there . . .

If you're looking for more first-class, action-packed, nail-biting suspense, join us at **Facebook.com/MulhollandUncovered** for news, competitions, and behind-the-scenes access to Mulholland Books.

For regular updates about our books and authors as well as what's going on in the world of crime and thrillers, follow us on **Twitter@MulhollandUK**.

# There are many more twists to come.

MULHOLLAND:
You never know what's coming around the curve.